CAPTIVATED...

Addie recognized the expression in his gaze, the power in his stride, even if the first time she had seen him, he'd worn a full suit of medieval armor. Sir Robert, the man who'd coldheartedly slain another, who had forcibly carried her away, had come for her before she'd grasped the opportunity to escape.

As she gazed into darkest brown eyes, Addie found herself unable—unwilling—to look away. Half of her feared for her safety, the other half stared in fascination at the most attractive, intriguing man she had ever seen.

What did he want with her? What was to become of her now? Surely she wasn't about to meet the same fate as the fallen knight on the field . . . was she?

Titles by Ginny Reyes

A FAERIE TALE
ADDIE'S KNIGHT

ADDIE'S KNIGHT

Ginny Reyes

JOVE BOOKS, NEW YORK

For Judy Palais,
my wonderful, wise, and witty editor,
whose suggestions made this book so much better
and such a joy to write.

TIME PASSAGES is a registered trademark of Berkley Publishing Corporation.

ADDIE'S KNIGHT

A Jove Book / published by arrangement with the author

PRINTING HISTORY
Jove edition / May 1999

The Penguin Putnam Inc. World Wide Web site address is
http://www.penguinputnam.com

ISBN: 0-515-12506-7

A JOVE BOOK®
Jove Books are published by the Berkley Publishing Group,
a division of Penguin Putnam Inc.,
375 Hudson Street, New York, New York 10014.
JOVE and the "J" design
are trademarks belonging to Penguin Putnam Inc.

PRINTED IN THE UNITED STATES OF AMERICA

10 9 8 7 6 5 4 3 2 1

Chapter 1

YORK, PENNSYLVANIA—SPRING 1885

"NO, NO, NO, Heidi!" Addie cried in dismay and exasperation. "You're not to kill Liam Flaherty. You're under his command. Carl Fieldhouse and Frederick Meyer are your Lancastrian enemies. Joust them."

Meddling with history was dangerous business. Not that Adelaide Shaw had ever intended any such thing, but when one dealt with committed, opposing foes, the outcome didn't rest in the hands of the instigator. Pray tell, when *had* she lost control of her warriors?

Addie studied the scene before her. Pure pandemonium. Her students lunged at and charged each other indiscriminately, mindless of the point of the exercise.

"There, you lousy varlet!" cried Richie Staubaugh.

"My ma checked my hair, an' I don't got no lice," retorted Billy Miller. "*You're* the rotten varmint."

"Boys!" called Addie, running to separate the two, suddenly fearing for the well-being of her stalwart young knights. What had gone wrong with her brilliant plan?

Last night Addie's purpose had seemed crystal clear—inspired, even. Now, however, she realized that giving physical form to inspiration could sometimes be far more perilous than she imagined. Her rival branches of the ruling house of Plantagenet, the White Rose Yorkists and the Red Rose Lancastrians, would determine their destiny all on their own, regardless of historical accuracy.

Her efforts to bring the past to life had succeeded too well—and failed just as miserably.

Addie had always believed in learning by doing. As was often the case, she had decided to lead her students into the woods behind the schoolhouse. There, she had divided them into opposing factions. After presenting the children with a brief summary of the Battle of Bosworth and arming them with twig swords and butcher's-paper armor, she had given the order to engage in combat.

True, her class had never enacted an actual battle, but she hadn't expected the children to take such glee in swatting each other for the sake of a history lesson.

Frowning, she accepted her mistake. Children were, after all, just that: children. As she stared in dismay, her gallant knights continued to charge whomever they found in their path, ignoring the English familial loyalties she had explained in such detail.

Addie tried to catch the children's attention again, to no avail. In her version of the decisive encounter in the Wars of the Roses, her motley Plantagenets would enjoy the freedom from schoolwork, the sunny spring morning, the splendid weapons she had provided, and the opportunity to exact retribution for the most petty school yard offenses rather than resolve political differences.

To her right another skirmish threatened to get out of hand. "Carl!" she called. "You're supposed to be fighting the Yorkists, not your own Lancastrians. Leave Frederick alone. Better yet, join forces and ambush Liam. *He's* with

King Richard, and you don't want Richard as king. Remember the lesson?"

Carl and Frederick gave Addie matching glares, then resumed thwacking each other with their swords, ignoring Liam and his group, who then surrounded the Lancastrians. Addie's school was rewriting the history of England in very short order.

To rethink her teaching tactics, since they had so obviously failed her this morning, Addie sat at the foot of a venerable oak and leaned against an area of darkened bark. Closing her eyes, she called to mind her original vision for the lesson. The images in her head bore no resemblance to the free-for-all she had just blocked out.

But wait. Ah, yes . . . that was better. With her eyes closed, the children's noise seemed louder, more combative, as if they had finally decided to take the exercise seriously. She smiled. Perhaps she hadn't given them enough time to burn off their normal, childish exuberance.

Then her oak creaked and cracked, startling her. Before she could investigate, the support at her back vanished. Addie fell.

And fell.

Eyes wide with fright, she saw only impenetrable darkness—thick, velvety, horrifying in its richness.

A scream formed in her throat, but no sound crossed her lips. The vertiginous impression of hurtling through space continued, and despite her best efforts, she saw, touched, felt nothing. Nothing at all.

The speed of her descent—through what, dear God?—merely increased, its hot rushing sensation abrading her cheeks, her hands, the legs her flapping skirts left bare.

She tried to hold the muslin down but failed.

Panic gripped her. Another scream clogged her throat. The never-ending plunge stole her breath and her ability to reason. She knew nothing but fear.

Was this the end?

What would become of her sister, Emmie?

Anguish melded with fright. Addie had never borne helplessness well, and she fought it fiercely. But despite her concern for her younger sister, the inevitable forced her to surrender. Sweet oblivion set in, and she knew nothing more.

A lifetime later, or so it seemed within Addie's grogginess, the children's cries penetrated the darkness that had set in when she'd begun to swoon. She tried prying open her eyes and found the lids heavy, leaden.

With determination, she lifted her head and willed her eyes to work. When they finally focused, she was surprised to find herself right where she'd been before her fall, at the foot of the oak. Its bright green canopy allowed only a dappling of sweet spring sunlight to touch her face, just enough to realize she'd survived the fall.

Thank heaven. In His infinite wisdom, God hadn't allowed Addie to die, leaving Emmie to fend for herself. As the eldest of the two, Addie had shouldered the care of her sister since the death of their parents six years ago. Now sixteen-year-old Emmie depended on Addie for everything. They were the only two Shaws left, and Emmie was . . .

Well, one could only describe Emma Louise Shaw as . . . different. She was certainly fey and might even be a tad dangerous. Since childhood, Emmie had been fascinated by fire.

Goodness only knew what trouble Emmie might get into without Addie to look out for her.

Mustering all her strength, which at the moment felt puny indeed, Addie fought the queasiness in her middle. Her head throbbed, and she felt strange, unlike her usual sensible self. Overhead, the leaves fluttered in the wind, blurring then growing clear again as her eyes strove to maintain a sharp focus. How odd this swooning business was.

Then Addie remembered her responsibility to the children. How long had she been unconscious? What had they been up to during those unsupervised moments? She shuddered to think what havoc Carl and Frederick and Liam might have wrought.

"Boys and girls," she called, hoping they would come to her, since she felt too shaky to go after them. Had they noticed her absence?

The sounds of her students' contest, which rang out more intensely and realistically than ever, calmed her concern somewhat. At least they hadn't run off in search of mischief.

But when none of the students responded to her summons, Addie sighed and rose ever so slowly. Why did she feel so drained? Exhausted? She had only swooned momentarily.

And she hadn't liked the experience one bit. "It's not one I'll be repeating again," she muttered, her determination as strong as ever. From now on she would carry a phial of spirits of ammonia with her everywhere she went. At the first sign of weakness, she would take a bracing whiff and fight off the unbearable sensation.

With a nod, she set off toward her vociferous Yorkists and Lancastrians, amazed by how real their battle had come to sound.

But violence was unmistakable. Especially when it proved all too real, as she discovered when she faced the source of the clamor.

"Dear God," she whispered at the horrifying sight before her. Instead of a ragtag band of school-age Plantagenets, huge horses thundered across a clearing, the earth shaking under the power of their hooves. Armor-clad knights directed the beasts toward each other, their intent unquestionable as their weapons met in metallic cacophony. Guttural growls accompanied each charge, followed by shrieks of agony when a quarry was struck.

Sunlight glinted wickedly off swords, lances, and shields, causing responding sparks to burst inside Addie's head. The throbbing grew to a pounding, and she felt herself grow faint.

"No!" she cried, refusing to swoon again.

Drawing herself to her full height, Addie took a deep, shuddering breath. She cast panicked looks everywhere, seeking her charges. A hand-to-hand contest twenty-five feet away caught her attention. Two armor-clad men on foot, intent on doing each other mortal harm, fought, daggers drawn and clashing, ripping at the vulnerable spots in their steel protection.

One suddenly yelled, “Willis! Beware behind you!”

The coppery-sweet stench of blood assailed her, as did the cries of the wounded—the dying—beast and man alike.

Bile rose in her throat, its sour burn adding to her lingering malaise. “Carl . . . Sheila . . . Liam . . . Frederick . . .”

When she received no response, her nausea grew.

Reality struck her as hard as the lance that knocked yet another knight off his dun destrier scant yards to her left. There were no children on *this* battlefield.

YORKSHIRE, ENGLAND—SPRING 1485

As he wiped the bloodied blade of his sword on a patch of grass, a movement by the thicket of trees to his right caught Sir Robert Swynton’s eye. *Damnation!*

What female fool would approach a skirmish?

He had just unseated Edwin Morland, his dead wife’s treacherous second cousin, and to prevent his own slaying, Robert had been forced to kill the man. Now, as his men chased away the remaining members of the Morland ambush, he had to divert his attention from the matter at hand to see to the woman who had stumbled out of the woods.

Hampered by his armor, he nonetheless skirted the bodies on the ground and approached with caution. As he came closer, he failed to recognize her. After living his entire life at Swynton Manor, there weren’t many folks around these parts he knew not.

Mayhap she played into his enemies’ plan. A distraction.

He rammed his sword into its scabbard, but for caution’s sake withdrew his dagger. To his surprise, the woman didn’t react to his actions. Instead, after another look toward the field of battle, she leaned against an elm and retched.

As he came closer, she pressed her forehead against the tree trunk and shuddered visibly. Then, with what seemed the very last ounce of her strength, she stiffened her spine, squared her shoulders, and took a step toward the melee. A wealth of brown hair cascaded over her slender shoulders, forming a cape around her, making her appear more feminine, yet more vulnerable.

"Damnation!" What did she think she was doing? Robert hastened his pace.

When he reached her side, the first thing he noticed was the beauty of her velvety gray eyes. But although they shone clear and were graced by long, curling lashes, they stared dazedly ahead, unseeing. "My lady," he said in a firm voice.

She didn't respond but stumbled forward, horror in her expression. With a moan she extended her hand toward the warring men. She whispered, "No . . ."

Her lovely eyes remained unfocused, as if to see beyond the carnage before her. It struck Robert then that the reality of battle had apparently caused her disorientation. To keep her out of harm's way, he gripped her shoulders and held her back.

The contact broke through her abstraction. Waves of tremors shook her. Horror filled her face when she took a good look at him. "No!" she cried, fear in her voice and on her face. "Stay away from me, you . . . you—"

She fought like a woman, scratching and kicking, yet doing him no harm. Had Robert not worn armor, however, her nails would have raked runnels down his cheeks. Frustration glowed in her features, and terror burned in her gaze. Her odd clothing allowed her more freedom than any woman of his acquaintance would have, but he managed to control her.

"You had best be still," he said, again in a stern voice, "or you will likely hurt yourself."

"Let me go! I need to find the children."

Children? "What mean you? You brought children to witness a skirmish? Have you no conscience?"

"I didn't bring children to a skirmish. I'm a schoolteacher, and I have no idea what has happened to my students."

Robert chuckled. Clearly watching a battle had affected her feminine sensibilities. A teacher indeed. He softened his tone. "My lady, I know not who you are, but you have wandered onto Swynton lands. I cannot leave you to your own devices, or you might come to harm. If you will not tell me who you are or where you belong, I shall be forced to take you to Swynton Manor with me. I cannot risk your safety while you remain on my property."

Panic burned in the silver eyes. "Unhand me, you brute. I don't know what museum you ransacked for your costume or what you've done with my students, but you'll not get away with it. Adelaide Shaw never backs away from a challenge."

"I can presume you're Adelaide Shaw, then," he said, mild amusement lingering. She had courage, even if 'twas reckless, for few would speak to a fully armored and armed man in such a way. "Come along now. I cannot leave you here and I must get my wounded home. They need attention."

Daggers of rage shot from her eyes. "I said unhand me, sir, and I insist you do so. I have no intention of going anywhere in your company. I'm responsible for a dozen youngsters, and unless you release them into my care, I will search the woods for them."

"I've no time to spare for children, my lady. Matters more serious than child's play concern me. I have seen no youngsters this day. Aside from my men and those of Morland, *you* are the only one here. And I've no time for arguing. Come along."

He removed his gauntlet, clapped a hand around her wrist, and turned toward Midnight, his stallion. As he had expected, she resisted. And fought him. But although she was tall for a woman, years of training had hardened him, and Robert easily overpowered her.

She let out a cry of frustration when she failed to break away. Cuthbert came running from their left. "Who is she, milord?"

"Adelaide Shaw, or so she says," he answered his squire, casting a sideways glance her way.

"I *am* Adelaide Shaw. And I demand this monster release me posthaste."

Cuthbert snickered. "Shall I bind her?"

Adelaide Shaw resumed her wriggling. Robert hung on easily, letting her wear herself out. It took her but minutes, since she still seemed affected by the shock of what she had witnessed. Finally, panting with exertion, she raised agitated silver eyes to his.

"Please don't hurt me," she whispered, her voice devoid of her earlier defiance. "I need to find the children. They . . . they must be so frightened by all this." She waved at the corpses littering the meadow.

Robert swore under his breath. "You cannot seriously believe there are children roaming the woods back there."

"I'm afraid I do," she said, her voice sad.

"Cuthbert, find Harold and search the thicket. I will send the rest of the men ahead of us. I'll see to Mistress Shaw myself."

With a deferent nod, Cuthbert ran off, calling for the other man.

A scant moment later, Robert became aware of the trembling fingers he held. Mistress Shaw's lips were tightly compressed, her cheeks colorless, her eyes open wide.

He sought to reassure her. "If the children are here, the men will find them. They will ensure their safety and take them home. Or bring them to the manor if home is too far away. Should the youngsters fail to be found . . . well, then I know not what to do."

"That's not good enough," she said, a hint of her earlier strength returning to her voice. "I'm responsible for my students. I can't just turn my back on them."

"What can you do? You can barely stand, you're shaking so. What good will you be to them if you collapse?"

A tear slid down her cheek. "I'm responsible—"

She stopped abruptly, and as Robert watched, every drop of color leached from her smooth cheeks.

"Dear God," she murmured. "Emmie! I must go. She'll be home any minute now."

Again she fought to escape his hold, but he held tight. Who knew what had really happened to her? He didn't, but he knew he could not leave her to wander the woods alone. He had no way of knowing whether Morland had left behind spies. Mistress Shaw would surely become their victim should they come upon her—if she was not one of them.

As to the children she spoke of, Robert doubted any of them existed. He had not seen them as yet.

Once again he entreated her to accompany him. Again she refused.

Sighing in frustration, he brought the difficult woman around to face him and curved an arm around her knees. With his other arm, he encircled her shoulders, then swung her up against his chest. "You'll be coming with me, like it or not."

Again her blows glanced off his armor, but her screams reverberated inside his helm, making his head spin and his ears ring with pain. With one hand, he took the protective piece from his aching head, while with the other he held tight to his captive. "Quiet!"

"I'll be quiet as soon as you put me down," she bit off, fighting for advantage.

Robert merely tightened his hold. "I will put you down once we reach Swynton Manor."

"Now!"

He ignored her demand. Approaching Midnight, he called his master-at-arms, Mortimer Swift. The short, burly man hurried over as the last of Robert's men rode toward home. "Ye called, lad?"

"Aye. Hold her and hand her to me once I've mounted."

"You'll do no such thing!" Adelaide cried, still striving uselessly. "Let me down."

Mortimer's blue eyes widened, and a smile tipped a corner of his mouth. "Not a hardship, Sir Robert."

Taking his bundle firmly in hand, Mortimer's eyebrows rose, and his smile faded as she turned her claws on him. "Mayhap I spoke too soon."

Her oddly shod feet kicked out, causing her skirts to froth

over Mortimer's arm. "How dare you treat me like a sack of potatoes!" she yelled, affronted. "You are no gentleman, but I am a lady. I insist you treat me like one."

Mortimer swayed under her attack, grunting with the effort to hold on. "She'll be denting . . . my finest armor with those . . . those pointy-tipped shoes!"

As he spoke, the woman's foot connected, making a thick, clunking sound. Mortimer howled in outrage. "Not even the Morlands succeeded there," he groused.

Robert laughed. "Mistress Shaw poses more of a hardship than one would first imagine, my man."

"You handle her," said the offended man. "You found her, and so she's yours."

With a chuckle Robert swung up onto his mount, then reached down for the woman. He watched her eyes widen as she noted the height of his horse. Her voice faded, and her mouth opened into a perfect *O* as he set her before him.

A shudder racked the slender body he held close to his chest. "A . . . a . . . a horse . . ." she said in a squeak, then fainted dead away.

"Well." So Adelaide Shaw wasn't fond of horseflesh. Robert smiled and patted Midnight's neck. "Good job, lad. At least the ride home will be somewhat silent."

These days, Robert willingly took comfort wherever he could. After all, he had murderous Morlands to worry about, wounded men to attend to, two demesnes to run, and now a lapful of odd-speaking, strangely garbed and shod, clearly crazed woman to deal with.

It seemed that life, as he had recently come to know it, continued on its merry, mad, miserable way. What would it bring him next?

Chapter 2

HIS ARMS FULL of unconscious woman, Robert paused in the bailey at Swynton Manor. He felt the urge to run to his men's aid, but until he dealt with Adelaide Shaw, he could not fully concentrate on them.

"Mortimer!" he bellowed.

"Aye, lad," the man responded at his elbow.

Startled, Robert stumbled, then regained his balance, hampered by his burden. "I hadn't realized you were so close. Here, I need help with the woman. Find Nell and have her see to our guest's needs. I imagine she will want ale, a meal, rest."

With a wink Mortimer extended his arms. "Now that she's lost her fire, she'll be naught to manage. Go on, lad. See to the men. At this hour Nell is likely in the kitchen. I'll find her, and we'll see to Mistress Shaw."

As his master-at-arms strode away, Robert cast a parting glance toward his newest responsibility. What if she was right? What if there were children roaming the woods a mile away from Swynton? Would Cuthbert and Harold find them? Or would Morland's men get to them first?

Uttering a growl of frustration, Robert hurried into the

great hall. He had standing orders for any injured to be brought here for the treatment of wounds. He wondered how many loyal men had been felled by Morland treachery.

Thomasine, the finest midwife and healer in the area, hastened to his side. "The Good Lord was with you, Sir Robert. Only two dead and a half dozen serious wounds. I've seen to the minor cuts and scrapes, but these others . . . well, I cannot promise much."

Frowning, Robert patted the too-thin hand on his forearm. "I understand, and I know you'll do your best for them. I'll send Father Anselm to join his prayers to your efforts. Their lives are in God's hands, after all."

With a reverent nod, Thomasine scolded a maid for inattention, then hurried to a man thrashing on a pallet. His groans of pain bit at Robert's conscience, and he again regretted the day he agreed to marry Catherine Morland.

His father had longed to unite the two families, and by wedding the young heiress, Robert had finally brought about the elder Swynton's fondest wish. But that move had only brought him misery and strife. Catherine had never accepted him, much less the intimacies of marriage. In his need to produce an heir, Robert had tried to be gentle, but her fear had always made the act one filled with guilt and pain and hate. Yes, his wife had come to hate him, often stating she longed to return to the convent where she had been reared.

When she finally learned she was with child, Catherine forbade Robert entry into her bedchamber, relieving them both of the need for the undesired intimate relationship. Catherine had continued to run the household, but by the time she increased to a certain point, she took to bed, and the orderly running of Swynton Manor had faltered.

Robert had tried to shoulder those duties as well, but he was only one man, and the extensive Swynton and Morland properties required all his attention. The manor had suffered.

Finally, when her time came upon her, Catherine went to her childbed in a panic, the pain attendant to childbirth scaring her unduly.

It didn't go well for her, and she bled profusely. After two days of difficult travail, his son was stillborn. Hours later, Catherine took her last breath and joined the infant.

In a way, her death had provided relief for Robert, even if he had never wished her ill. His relief was short-lived, however, ending the moment the Morlands accused him of murdering his wife. They wanted Morland Castle and its lands back, even if by virtue of Catherine's death Robert now rightfully owned what had once been hers.

After enduring the Morlands' unfounded accusations, Robert was forced to fend off two attempts on his life. The Morlands didn't give up easily, and they wanted what they believed was theirs. Robert was their only obstacle.

Today's ambush had cost the lives of two innocent, stalwart men. Robert felt their loss keenly. Stephen and Matthew had been loyal to him, had fought to protect him from his dead wife's treacherous family. Now two women and five children would go defenseless. Yet more responsibility for Robert to bear.

He didn't need additional worries at this time. He needed his mind sharp and alert to prevent further loss of life, to stay alive himself. He didn't need the preoccupation brought on by the presence of a stranger in his home.

Adelaide Shaw.

What was he going to do about her? Was she truly as mad as she seemed, or merely part of the Morlands' plan?

An hour or so later, after speaking with each of the conscious wounded, Robert headed toward the kitchens. Hungry, thirsty, he sought to satisfy his needs.

At the hearth Nell Bolton stirred something redolent of onions and garlic. His stomach growled. "What have you there for a hungry man, Nell?"

Turning her wimpled head, his one-time wet nurse smiled, her eyes wreathed in crinkles of humor. "For you, Rob, my son, anything you want."

"Your heart, then."

"Nay. That belongs to Mortimer, you know. Even if *he's* too blind to see. But ask away for anything else."

Robert sighed, humor vanishing. "I would welcome peace and quiet if only for one night."

Nell clucked, then ladled a serving of rich brown stew into a trencher. "Aye, son, 'twould be a blessing indeed. Here. Eat up, then see to the lady you brought home. She didn't awaken when I removed her odd clothes and those outlandish shoes, so she hasn't eaten yet. Last I saw, she slept soundly."

Soaking a chunk of crusty bread in the broth, Robert said, "She needs the rest. I can imagine her shock when she stumbled onto an ambush. No woman should have to witness the like."

Nell again made a sympathetic sound as she set a tankard of ale before him. "Mayhap 'tis best if she sleeps, as you say. Food we have aplenty. I'll see her fed when she awakes."

"Then I'll leave her in your capable hands. I won't bother her."

If he could put the woman from his mind he might yet accomplish something this day. Robert had farm accounts to review, a dispute over straying cattle to settle, and he could ill afford to forget the Morlands. He didn't need to add Adelaide Shaw to his list of worries.

He said to Nell, "Have one of your maids tell Walter I'll await him in the solar. I am ready to face his infernal accounts."

"Don't forget the butler wishes to speak to you, too," she added.

In defeat, Robert sighed. "Send Jack along as well. 'Tis best I face all at once."

Another of Nell's sympathetic clucks rang out. "What you need, son, is a good wife."

Robert snorted. "You forget I already tried wedding. All Catherine brought me was more trouble than I imagined a man could have."

Nell shook her head. "Catherine was no wife to you. She was a child, spoiled and cosseted, who would not face life. You need a woman, one who will walk by your side through whatever the Good Lord lets come your way."

Robert raised a brow. "You're a fine one to give advice. Once widowed, and I have yet to see Mortimer dance attendance around you."

Nell's fair cheeks blushed becomingly. "Some men are not the marrying sort, and I fear my Mortimer is one of them. But you . . . you, Rob, are the marrying kind. The kind a woman can look up to, trust, and rely on. A true knight, honorable and decent and brave."

Chuckling, Robert bowed. "At your service, Mistress Bolton. Any time you wish to marry, I'll gladly be your man."

Redder than ever, Nell flapped her apron his way. "Get on with you. Walter and Jack have waited long enough."

Robert spent the remainder of the day poring over sums and lists of household goods that needed replenishing, never able to fully forget a pair of flashing gray eyes. The same gray eyes that continued to sparkle at him in strange, disjointed dreams through the troubled night. The same gray eyes that had begged him not to hurt a woman who might well have come to destroy him and his.

A shaft of brilliant sunshine stabbed at Addie's eyes, forcing her awake. She didn't want to rise just yet, as she felt her exhaustion clear to the bone. But slowly, inexorably, reality pressed upon her mind, urging her to once again take up her heavy burden of responsibility.

"Emmie," she called, hoping her sister wouldn't be as difficult to wake as usual. The Shaws were not known as early risers. Still, Mrs. Wilhelm had offered the girl a job at her bakery, and Addie considered the position an answer to her prayers.

Emmie had grown too old for school, but because of her fey reputation, no man had come calling on her. It seemed both Shaw women were destined to remain old maids.

Addie had never learned the coy games other girls played to attract young men. She had always been too forthright, speaking her mind freely. A most daunting habit when it came to the male of the species. They'd shied away from her directness.

After her parents' deaths, Addie was left with a disconsolate, ten-years-younger sister to care for. She'd poured her every emotion into helping sweet, fey Emmie return to her loving, cheerful self. She'd had no time for courting, even if a suitor had come forth.

Emmie . . . Well, a fanciful girl with a strange propensity for chaos did not a suitable future wife make. Or so everyone told Addie with tedious regularity.

When Addie's call for her sister received no response, she mustered up her strength and rose on her elbows. Or tried, at any rate.

Her eyes widened in horror when her gaze met with nothing familiar. She wasn't in her room or even in her own bed. Billowing high around her, a fluffy mattress with what looked like goose feathers poking out through the ticking gave under the slightest pressure, making it even harder than usual for Addie to get up.

With trepidation, she glanced all around and saw a small, stark room, furnished only with the bed she lay on, an ornately carved chest at its foot, a three-legged stool near a narrow window, and on the wall near the bed, a crude lamp fashioned from some sort of dead plant material, extinguished at present.

Where was she?

Where were the children?

Where was Emmie?

"Hello . . .?"

Dreading who—or what—might respond, Addie fought her way out of the mass of mattress. When she stood on her feet, the icy cold of the bare stone floor caught her by surprise. Goodness gracious, who would neglect to lay down at the very least a braided rug by the bed in such a room?

She debated whether to crawl back into bed or search for shoes but never reached the conclusion of her consideration. The door to her left flew open, and a plump matron wearing a headdress reminiscent of some religious orders marched in bearing a tray with food.

Addie's stomach growled at the mingled scents of fresh bread and strong tea.

The woman grinned her way and made a comment in a foreign-sounding tongue.

"I beg your pardon?" Addie asked.

The woman repeated her statement, then set the tray down on the stool. Still chatting gaily, she came to Addie's side, grasped the skirt of the white linen shift she wore, and tugged upward.

"Hey!" Addie cried, fighting for her dignity as well as the garment. "I don't know who put this on me, but if it's yours, I'm afraid I need it more than you right now. You may have it back as soon as you return my clothes."

Giving Addie a pitying look and a shake of her wimple, the woman ignored her words, chattered blithely on, and grasped more of the linen in her hands. Up went the hem of the only thing that kept Addie from humiliating nakedness. She swatted at the woman, with no discernible effect. "I said I need this at the moment. Return my clothes if you want the nightdress."

As they struggled, another woman entered the room, this one carrying a basin and an urn, a length of white cloth over one forearm and various layers of yellow, cream, and brown fabric over the other. She had a pair of soft leather slippers tucked under her chin.

The first woman pointed at the newcomer. "Yer clothes," she said quite firmly and clearly.

Addie shook her head and folded her arms across her chest. "Not at all. I wore a white shirtwaist, a navy muslin skirt, white eyelet petticoats, corset, corset cover, drawers, and cotton stockings. I would like them back posthaste."

Another spate of indecipherable gibberish followed as the women spread the garments on the bed, placing the slippers on the floor. Much head bobbing and shaking and even more hand gesturing accompanied their words. Straining to understand—anything at all would do—Addie caught the word "blood" among many others.

Suddenly the horrors of yesterday exploded in her mind. She remembered taking her class outside to reenact the Battle of Bosworth, she remembered the creaking tree, she remembered her plunge, and worst of all, she remembered the men fighting, one slaughtering the other in a kaleidoscopic whirl of violence unlike anything Addie ever could have imagined.

She swayed, her stomach churning, her knees weakening, her head spinning.

Gentle hands caught her, and the older woman who had challenged her for the borrowed garment helped her down onto the bed. "Th-thank you," Addie murmured.

The woman *tsk-tsk*ed, then placed a cool wet cloth on her brow. "'Twas vile, I'd imagine," she said, her accent not quite so incomprehensible when she spoke slowly.

Again Addie remembered watching the one knight knock the other off his horse, battle him to the ground, and run a sword under his opponent's helm. Blood had spurted out from the severed vein, spilling onto the ground, and when the victor had pulled his sword from his victim, it had glistened red in the spring sunlight.

She gagged at the memory.

That very man, the one who had so efficiently slain another, had then come to her side, insisting on carting her off on his monstrous beast of a horse. She supposed she was now at his mercy.

"What about . . . the children?"

The wimpled woman gave her a quizzical look. "Children? I know naught of children, mistress. Mayhap Sir Robert can help."

If Sir Robert was the brute with the murderous sword and the Trojan-sized horse, Addie could certainly do without any more of his help. "I need to go home."

The wimple nodded, suddenly stopped, then cocked to one side. "Where is home?"

"In York."

"Then you're naught but a short ride away. You're at Swynton Manor, you know. When you've recovered your strength, one of the men will take you back."

Fighting nausea and that strange, light-headed feeling, Addie rose again. "I'm strong enough, and I insist on leaving right away. Fetch me my clothes and my new boots."

Clear blue eyes studied her, and Addie made sure her expression remained as firm as she could make it. She apparently won the battle of stares, since her accoster said, "As you wish, mistress."

"My name is Addie," she said, taking issue with the mistress appellation. "Addie Shaw."

"Very well, Addie Shaw, here are clean clothes." Gesturing for the younger, wide-eyed woman just behind her to come closer, the wimpled one again grasped Addie's nightdress and this time shoved it up well past her knees.

"What *are* you doing?" she asked, horrified by the woman's audacity. "Leave me alone this very instant, or I shall cry for help."

Her comment caused both women great amusement, and they giggled. Finally, when they'd relieved their unexplained hilarity, the older woman said, "I *am* your help, Mist—Addie Shaw. Sir Robert sent me to see to your needs, and 'tis what I will do."

"If you were sent to attend to my needs, then I believe you have done so. You have brought me food and drink, and, by your insistence, clean clothing. Since you refuse to return my original wardrobe and my boots—new boots, at that—then do me the favor of leaving so I can dress in private."

A silvery white eyebrow rose. "But I'm here to dress my lady."

Addie rolled her eyes. "If I'm the lady you speak of, I can handle that task. I've been doing it long enough."

"But—"

"I insist. I'm perfectly capable of dressing myself and I will do so as soon as you leave. Now go. I'm sure there is something else you should be doing."

Her unwanted helpers left, obviously chastened by her

adamant refusal of their assistance. As the door closed behind them, Addie released a relieved sigh and collapsed into the insubstantial mattress.

The fear she had fought to control burst into full life. She shuddered, and her hands shook. Bravado could only carry her so far, and this was as far as it went.

Where was she?

The woman had said York was nearby, but Addie had never seen, much less met the two who had just left. She knew she'd have remembered meeting the infamous Sir Robert had she seen him before their encounter yesterday.

Carefully thinking back over all she remembered of the day before, she came no closer to an explanation. Many foreign folks lived near and in York, and Addie had become adept at identifying if not understanding their various languages. What the wimpled woman had spoken had turned out to be English, but a form of the language strongly influenced by the accent of England—old England at that.

Their clothes and the wimple . . . Addie had recognized the medieval-style garments the women wore. Were they perhaps members of a religious order that had retained the habit of an early founder?

If that explained the clothing, then how could she explain the clanking armor of the barbaric Sir Robert? Of all the other men on that field?

And those horses. Good heavens, they were the largest beasts she had ever clapped eyes on. Never particularly fond of equine flesh, Addie felt horses were best suited to either grazing peacefully in fields or attached to buggies—of necessity, one had to travel, and the toothy, snorting, bucking creatures served excellently as the means to get you from one place to another. But that was it. Aside from their acceptable use, horses were unpredictable creatures that could do more harm than good.

Her parents were proof of that. A spooked horse had bolted while pulling their buckboard, causing both to fly from the vehicle and sustain untold injuries that eventually led to their deaths. Since then, Addie had made sure she maintained a respectable distance from the murderous beasts.

Speaking of killing . . . that Sir Robert was certainly guilty of it. Remembering, Addie again fought against nausea. How could anyone slice another's throat, then calmly go argue with a woman over her presence on a perfectly innocent field? At least, it had been perfectly innocent when she'd taken her students outside for their history lesson. By the time she'd come to after her as yet unexplained fall, it had become anything but.

She had to get out of here, certainly before the armored savage returned. And if she'd understood the women's words correctly, he was in charge of this place—whatever it might be.

Addie wrestled her way out of the bed, and with a jaundiced eye, considered the garments the wimpled one had brought for her use. Shaking them out, she found a lightweight cream linen dress, a richer yellow silk one, and finally a brown wool flannel gown of some sort.

Why had they brought her so many choices in clothing? And what was she to use as undergarments?

As she studied the pieces, an absurd notion began to take shape. She thought of the men in armor, the women's garb—that wimple, for goodness' sake. Glancing around again, she took note of the stone construction of the room, the narrow slit of a window. She remembered the floppy mattress, looked at the chest at the foot of the bed, studied the bunch of dead vegetation filling the holder in the wall. To her admittedly inexpert mind, the items looked as if they might have come straight from the Middle Ages.

Had she somehow wandered into an enclave of misfits who endeavored to keep alive the customs of a bygone era? Or had she somehow stumbled through the world she knew and come out in the past—

No. *That* was beyond irrational. She *really* had to leave, go home, return to life as she knew it, boring and humdrum—if difficult—as it often seemed.

Fantasy didn't make sense, and Addie prided herself on

her common sense. Real life was quite enough for her, thank you very much. Yes, boring and humdrum did her just fine. And with the number of responsibilities bearing down on her, she didn't have the time or patience to deal with a whole lot of make-believe.

It was well past time to go home.

Once again examining the clothes she had been brought, Addie decided they weren't all dresses after all. It would appear that one or another was an undergarment of some sort—although she sorely missed the familiarity of her drawers, petticoat, chemise, and corset. Since the silk piece felt soft and light, she decided it would do in a pinch as a chemise.

Addie removed the nightdress and shivered in the coolness of the room. Donning the yellow silk garment, she relished the flow of the fabric over her body. She had never been able to afford the luxury of real silk, and the fluid smoothness of the cloth afforded her a new pleasure. It rippled coolly over her breasts, slithered down past her waist, and flowed like gossamer gold over her legs. "Hmm . . . a woman could become accustomed to silk very quickly."

Noting how the garment hid nothing of her form, Addie blushed and quickly slipped the cream linen dress over her head. To her surprise, it fit tighter than the silk, but at least it covered her decently.

Approaching the narrow slit of a window, she noticed the lack of glass in the opening. "Well, no wonder it's so cold in here!"

True, the sun shone brightly outdoors, but as she stood in the shaft of light arrowing into the room, she felt the nip in the air. It was still spring, after all.

She wondered how warm the day would grow. Spring in York could bring many surprises. Often it went from near wintry cold to almost summer heat. It wouldn't surprise her if by noon the day became too hot to wear the woolen overdress . . . coat . . . whatever that was still lying across the foot of the bed.

As she debated whether to don the piece, a brisk knock

came at the bedroom door, and before she could respond, the panel of wood flew open.

In strode an imposing male, rich brown hair tousled, deep eyes haloed by a smattering of faint lines and underscored by dusky smudges. Despite his impressive presence, the man had not spent a good night . . . maybe more than one.

Addie recognized the expression in his gaze, the power in his stride, even if the first time she had seen him, he'd worn a full suit of medieval armor. Sir Robert, the man who'd coldheartedly slain another, who had forcibly carried her away, had come for her before she'd grasped the opportunity to escape.

As she gazed into darkest brown eyes, Addie found herself unable—unwilling—to look away. Half of her feared for her safety, the other half stared in fascination at the most attractive, intriguing man she had ever seen.

What did he want with her? What was to become of her now? Surely she wasn't about to meet the same fate as the fallen knight on the field . . . was she?

Chapter 3

UNWILLING TO ACCEPT the dictates of fate—whatever they might be—Addie prayed for courage and tipped up her chin. "Do you always force your unwelcome company upon a lady?"

Sir Robert flinched—to her amazement. His piercing gaze narrowed, and his lips tightened to a thin line rimmed in white. "When necessary," he said in a clipped, British-flavored voice.

He *was* a foreigner, and unfortunately displaying deplorable manners. "I don't appreciate such familiarity, sir. Kindly leave the room until I am ready to come out. As you can see, I'm nearly dressed, so I shan't be long."

A corner of his mouth tipped up, lightening his expression. Addie nearly gasped out loud. What a difference a smile—meager though this one was—made in his appearance. Why, if he weren't the ill-mannered, man-killing owner of a Goliath of a horse, she might find him irresistibly attractive.

Then she noticed his clothes. Oh, dear. He seemed to favor medieval garb when not in full armor.

A short, belted tuniclike item came down to his thighs, revealing powerful legs clad in strange, knit hose of some sort. Leather boots came up to his calves, but did nothing to conceal the thick muscles there. And nothing he might wear could disguise the breadth of his chest, his shoulders, the massive strength of his arms.

Sir Robert was a big man, strong, and from the looks of his expression, determined and accustomed to getting his way.

What would his way be when it came to her?

Addie was pretty sure she didn't want to find out, so she challenged him again. "Well? Will you kindly leave me to finish dressing?"

He cocked an eyebrow, and his grin widened. "Perhaps you should start over again, Mistress Shaw."

"My name is Addie, and as I told you, I'd like to dress. If you would *leave me alone* to do so, I'll gladly meet you somewhere—anywhere—else soon. A lady doesn't entertain a man in her room, at least, this lady"—she jabbed her chest with her index finger—"doesn't."

"I hardly think you are entertaining me, Addie Shaw. And if you think you are nearly dressed, I'd say the shock from yesterday is greater than I initially feared. You, madam, have your chemise on over your dress!"

Addie glanced down, frowned at the thought of putting the rougher linen against her body, then shrugged. Clearly she wasn't an expert in medieval garb. "Does it matter, sir? I am covered and decent. What did you want?"

"Answers."

"What kind of answers?" she asked, hoping for the opportunity to ask questions and receive answers of her own.

"Why were you on that field at that precise moment? Did Morland send you? And what had you hoped to gain? Were I a less honorable sort, I might have run you through with my sword."

Addie shuddered, and bile clawed up her throat again. "No need to remind me of your deadly actions," she forced out through the haze of nausea. "I saw you kill that other man."

The brown eyes narrowed, suspicion in every line of Sir Robert's face. "What you saw does not seem to have made you particularly docile, cooperative, or respectful, much less frightened." Despite her glare of outrage and spate of sputtering, he went on, "There's no need to feign innocence, madam. You know perfectly well that was Edwin himself I killed. Before he killed me, I might add."

Glad she hadn't yet eaten a bite, Addie faced the misery of sickness brought on by his repeated reminders of what she'd witnessed. "I don't need to feign a thing. I took my students out to the woods for a history lesson, and the next I knew you were slaughtering men left and right. Just so you understand, I don't know an Edwin or a Morland or you for that matter. I only wish to go home."

"Where is home?"

"York."

"Not far, then. When you prove you are no Morland spy, and that your freedom will not cost me any more men, Mortimer will escort you back. Until then, consider yourself my guest—regretfully unwelcome."

"Since I'm unwelcome, shouldn't I just go home? You'd be rid of me in no time."

His square jaw tightened, and his rough-chiseled features took on a dangerous cast. "You shall be out of my way, regardless. I have wounded to attend to, farms to see to, and a ruthless enemy to guard against. I scarce believe he would use a woman in his plans against me . . . no, I *do* believe it. It appears my wife's cousin has no honor, no shame."

Addie graced Sir Robert with a scathing look. "Might I suggest that if you don't want to be like him, you should not use a woman in your own plots? I can go home, and you can forget all about me."

He shook his head. "A few days is all I need to make sure you mean no harm to anyone who matters to me. And I cannot spare Mortimer just yet."

Hoping against hope, Addie argued, "But I can find my way home on my own. I don't need your man to escort me.

I simply cannot stay away any longer. Too many responsibilities await me."

"You should have considered those responsibilities before joining efforts with the likes of Morland."

Over the thudding of her heart, Addie let out a frustrated gust of breath. "How can I make you understand? I know no Morland, I have no connection to the man, I wish no one any harm, and I *must* go home. Now."

For a moment Sir Robert hesitated, his brown eyes boring into hers as if they could penetrate her most private thoughts, reach her very soul. Then he ran his hand through the tousled strands of his long hair. "I cannot let you do that. I bear much responsibility myself, and the main one is to my people. I cannot release you until I know you mean them no harm."

Since it had become irritatingly clear that she would get nowhere arguing with the hardheaded brute, Addie tried a different tack. "How long, then, do you intend to keep me here?"

"Days, mayhap a week or two."

"Impossible. I must return home immediately. In fact, I'm not even sure how long I have already been gone. When did you bring me here? What is today's date?"

"I brought you to Swynton Manor yesterday afternoon. Today is the fourth of May, in the year of our Lord 1485."

Addie's eyes widened at the man's words. 1485, he'd said. "Oh, stop! Stop, stop, stop, stop, stop. You're mad, totally, completely so."

A dark slash of eyebrow arched again.

Addie continued, "This is absolutely ridiculous. I don't know why you dress the way you do, why you speak with such a frightful accent, or why you've built this house with slitted windows and no glass panes, but I'm good and sick of it. This . . . medieval nonsense might amuse some, but not me. What is today's date, please? And don't treat me to any more of that 1485 foolishness, sir. I'm not a child, I'm a teacher. A sensible one, too."

The other eyebrow rose as well, and amusement returned

to Sir Robert's face. "I daresay you are in need of more rest. Mayhap a tisane for your nerves as well. Nell can fetch something from Thomasine. This, dear lady, is the reason why women should remain at home, where they are unlikely to witness sights that might affront their sensitive natures."

Addie gave him an arch look. "I'd say most right-minded folks would find slaughter revolting. And I was minding my business when I took the children outside. I gave them their lesson, then when things got out of hand, I sat to reconsider my instructions . . ."

Addie's voice trailed off as she recalled the events that had led to her current situation. "Then I sat against the oak," she said, pacing the room. A clear picture formed in her mind. The oak, with its area of darkened bark, became vivid, distinct, and detailed. She whirled on Sir Robert. "Of course! It must have been the tree."

"What tree?"

"Why, the one against which I sat. When I put my full weight on it, it made a frightful creaking sound. It must have been rotten or something to give way like that, because all I knew after that hideous noise was the fall."

"What fall?"

Addie huffed impatiently. "I'm trying to tell you about it. Please don't interrupt again. My memory of the incident is quite hazy, and I keep losing my train of thought when you ask your questions." As she spoke, images and impressions whirled through her mind with a speed that left her breathless. "It was dark and hot, and I felt myself falling. My skirts flapped up against my legs . . . and I grew light-headed. It seemed as if the fall would never end."

Sir Robert now wore a bewildered expression. "But it did end, did it not?"

"Of course, but I can't remember exactly when. I must have swooned—for the first time in my life, you understand. And I don't intend to do *that* again."

"I doubt it is something one can control," Sir Robert said, a humorous note in his words. "If you'll recall, you did so again when I carried you on Midnight."

Addie blushed furiously. "Regardless, I mean to do just that—control it. Swooning is . . . foolish, missish behavior, not practical at all. I don't have the time or inclination for such a thing. I deal in realities, the stuff of which life is made. And I don't intend to fall through another tree like that again, much less succumb to a silly swoon over it."

"And how does your fall through—a tree?" He gave her a mocking look when she nodded firmly. He then shook his head and continued, "How does that fall place you in the middle of an ambush, if not by Edwin Morland's instruction?"

"Oh, dear. So you're back to that again. I'm trying to explain. I simply . . . fell. When I came to after my . . . momentary lapse, I went to look for my students. Instead of a dozen children, I found you and your men . . . the swords . . . the blood. . . ."

Addie again felt weak, and something in her face must have betrayed it, for Sir Robert hurried to her side, clasped her elbow, and led her back to the bed.

"Here, now," he said, helping her down onto the fluffy bed. "You are assuredly not ready to go anywhere, much less York, and certainly not on your own. If you do not wish to swoon again, I would suggest you wait until you recover from the shock you sustained. I know not what you are used to, but at Swynton Manor we take care of those in need. 'Twould be most irresponsible of me to let you leave when you're so obviously unwell."

Addie propped herself on her elbows, her head again swimming. "I'm used to taking care of myself . . ." *And Emmie.* She dared not mention her sister, fearing Sir Robert might decide to seek out the girl to learn more about that Edwin Morland he kept mentioning. Not that Emmie was likely to know him . . . unless he, like her, was mad about flames. But that didn't matter at present. "Your sense of chivalry is fine and good, but somewhat outdated. I'm a thoroughly modern woman, accustomed to managing on my own, and I don't need to rely on a man who plays at being a knight."

Fire caught deep in those dark brown eyes. A muscle leaped in that lean cheek. Pride blared from the squaring of those broad shoulders. "Rest assured, madam, I play not at chivalry or knightly pursuits. I have proven myself worthy time and again. I pride myself on living honorably, since a man has, in the end, only his honor and his word."

Oh, dear. She had clearly offended her reluctant host. "I have no argument with your honor or the code by which you live, but don't you think your knightly pretenses—you know, the clothing, the armor—are a bit overdone for our time?"

Sir Robert's expression grew thunderous. "I already said I practice no pretense. I am who I am—"

"Yes, yes, but you don't need to solve your problems by jousting, nor do you need to dress like that anymore. If you have a dispute with that Morland fellow, you should simply take the matter up with the court. One doesn't slaughter those one disagrees with these days. Why, a body might get the impression you truly believe yourself back in the Middle Ages instead of in 1885."

Sir Robert astonished her by laughing. "You *do* need your rest, madam. 1885 . . ."

Addie narrowed her gaze. "Oh, that's right. You insist it's only 1485. Perhaps it's *you,* sir, who needs a rest."

Still chuckling, Sir Robert shook his head in bemusement. "Addie Shaw, I thank you for the best laugh I've had in months, perhaps years, but I insist you rest and recover. 1885 indeed."

Her pride piqued, Addie sat up, shoving down mounds of feather-filled ticking. "Are you insinuating that I'm somehow out of my faculties? I'll have you know I'm the most sensible woman you will ever come across. And as a schoolmarm, I *always* know my dates. If I say it's 1885, well, then, it most assuredly *is* 1885. *You* are sadly mistaken, sir, perhaps the one who has taken leave of his senses."

All sign of humor vanished. "I say it's 1485, and I know whereof I speak."

"It's 1885, and I know my dates."

"1485."

"1885."

He waved dismissively and turned toward the bedroom door. "Sleep is the only remedy for your temporary madness."

Addie sprang to her knees as if stung by a bee. "*Madness!* You're the one who is mad. Next thing I know, you'll try to persuade me I'm no longer in Pennsylvania, but somewhere else. Oh, of course. You'll insist we're somewhere in merry old England, that four hundred years of progress have all been figments of my imagination. If not that, then somehow I've traveled back through time."

Sir Robert frowned. "Of course this is England. Where else would we be? That Pensil . . .?" He shrugged. "That place you named . . . where exactly is it?"

Addie gaped. "Are you saying your knowledge of geography is as flawed as your methods of resolving disputes? *Everyone* knows where Pennsylvania is."

"I know enough geography to go where I need go, yet I know not where that Pen-place is."

A loud clanging suddenly rang outside. Masculine voices joined the racket, and Addie's mind flew back to the combat she had witnessed the day before. Swatting the mattress, she climbed out of bed, then ran to the miserly window. What she saw just beyond a low stone wall stole her breath. Men clad in chain mail and bearing swords and shields did battle again, a short, barrel-chested man at one side shouting encouragement and directions at a rapid-fire pace.

Spinning, she turned to Sir Robert. "*Do* something, because if you don't, *I* will. I cannot stand and watch yet more carnage without trying to stop it. If you live by the honorable code you alluded to earlier, you must not let the fighting go on unchecked. Stop it now, Sir Robert."

Again, her companion gave her a puzzled stare. "Of course I'll do naught to stop them. There is no danger on my practice field, Mistress Shaw. The men merely seek to hone their skills. Surely you know that."

"They don't look to me as if their skills need more honing. The bodies on that meadow yesterday were thoroughly dead."

With obvious patience, Sir Robert answered, "'Tis because my men practice every day that they live to do so again. They must keep their skills at the ready, or others better prepared than they will win the next contest."

Addie clapped her hands over her ears. "Oh, do stop the medieval nonsense. I'm not staying here a moment longer, and I'm going to find Mayor Noel. This kind of craziness cannot continue in a civilized city."

Again, she had attacked Sir Robert's pride. "Madam, we *are* civilized, even if I know no Mayor Noel. I understand you suffered quite a shock yesterday, but I cannot fathom how it made you lose your wits this way."

"Fine," Addie spit out, none too pleased by his erroneous assumption regarding her sanity. "They can practice how to murder others. If you insist, I'll accept your explanation. Now please tell me how I'm to accept your insistence that we're in England, sir. I live in Pennsylvania, I teach in a school just outside of York, and in America no one spends his days practicing to kill, much less pretending knighthood or any such nonsense."

"We *are* just outside York, Mistress Shaw, but I know not of this Pennsylvania, much less that America. For the last time, madam, no one at Swynton Manor pretends anything. And so that we have no further misunderstanding, 'tis indeed the year of our Lord 1485."

Addie took in Sir Robert's expression, intent and completely serious. She touched the cold gray stone wall before her and gazed out the narrow window at the mail-clad men outside. She spotted a sow and her brood rooting in the dirt just beyond the rehearsing warriors, and noticed a woman, dressed in clothes similar to those worn by the wimpled one, chase them away.

In a musing, perplexed voice she said, "1485?"

"Of course, madam."

With a look at her garments, Addie took in the rough texture of the linen chemise, as Sir Robert had termed the garment, then, glancing at the woolen dress on the bed, she studied its homespun weave. With her heart in her throat, she stared at the crude form of lighting on the wall over her head, the rough-hewn artistry of the chest at the foot of her bed, the slab of stone beneath her feet.

Turning her attention back to her unwilling host, she studied the unflinching gravity in his expression, the outmoded length of his hair, the cut and style of his clothes, the sheathed dagger at his side. "You're . . . serious, aren't you?"

"I have been from the start, Addie Shaw."

"And you're certain it's 1485?"

"As I am of my own name."

For a moment she tried to deny everything he'd said, but her mind had grasped his insistence and began to suggest the impossible. Of course it couldn't be . . .

Could it?

"1485?"

"1485."

Every ounce of strength again abandoned Addie, suggesting that indeed she needed more rest. For if what Sir Robert said was true, and if what her imagination was busy flirting with was also true, then she'd either lost her mind or . . .

In awe, she whispered, "I've traveled back through four hundred years' time."

Sir Robert's solemn expression changed to a wary one. "Impossible," he said, his tone inviting no argument.

Regardless, Addie argued back. "No more so than today's date being 1485." She glanced out the window at a fellow strolling past, a mattock hefted on his shoulder, apparently on his way to work the soil.

"One cannot travel through time," Sir Robert stated with such conviction in his voice that Addie wondered if he needed persuading himself.

She shook her head slowly, entertaining the impossible. "Yesterday morning I would have agreed with you, but today . . . I guess today I believe anything is possible. That being the case, a trip through four hundred years' time offers the only explanation for my presence here."

"In the name of God, begone, Satan!" Sir Robert cried out with vehemence. "Watch your words, woman. You blaspheme with your rantings."

Addie snorted. "I am not ranting and I no more blaspheme than you. If you insist we're in the England of 1485, and by some incredible twist of reality it turns out to be so, then I have traveled through time. Don't ask me how I did it, since I only know it had something to do with that blasted oak, but I started the morning yesterday in 1885 York, Pennsylvania. That allows for only one explanation, absurd though it might be. That explanation, Sir Robert, is that I've come back in time."

The more she stated her case, the more Addie liked the concept. As a teacher, she had always been fascinated by information, and she loved history best of all the subjects she taught. If she was in medieval England, she had been given a gift beyond all measure. She could now experience the past as she had experienced the future. Just imagine all she could learn, the questions she might ask, the information she hadn't had but could now take to the future.

That future with so many responsibilities. A future where her fey sister no longer had anyone to watch over her. A future where Addie was needed far more than in the past.

Discarding the mild sense of disappointment, and squaring her shoulders to again assume her habitual load, Addie said, "If it's 1485, then I don't belong here. It's time for me to go home where I *do* belong. Please don't oppose my efforts to return, Sir Robert. I have stayed in your time far longer than I should have. I must go back to 1885."

Sir Robert's mouth curled in obvious revulsion. "You're not mad after all."

Crossing her arms over her chest, Addie allowed herself a self-satisfied smile. "I told you so."

He nodded, his expression unchanged. Crossing himself, he backed toward the bedroom door. "Heaven help us all, you're . . . demon-possessed!"

Chapter 4

"OH, FOR GOODNESS' sake!" Addie exclaimed, sick of the entire, inane discussion. "If anyone here is demon-possessed, it certainly isn't me." She accompanied her words with a stare sure to leave him no doubt who she thought was. "If this is 1485, then to arrive here I had to travel through time."

Sir Robert glowered with repugnance. "Only one indwelt by evil spirits or one who dabbles in black arts would utter such heresy. What disregard for the Divine! I tell you, madam, we at Swynton are God-fearing, Christian folk. My sister Edythe is abbess of Saint Hilda's. We do not stomach sorcery, divination, or any other form of consorting with the devil."

Addie dismissed his argument with a wave. "I'm happy to hear that, Sir Robert. Since I'm a faithful churchgoer, we have no quarrel on that point. Besides, I have no patience for those who dabble in the foolishness of the occult. I'm no more demon-possessed than your sister, the abbess."

Her statement failed to alter the expression on the masculine mountain of mistrust barring the doorway. "Yet you insist on repeating that traveling-through-time nonsense," he said.

Addie threw her hands up in frustration. "How would *you* explain my presence four hundred years in the past?" As he opened his mouth to speak again, she cut him off. "Don't bother. You said it before. If I'm not demon-possessed, then in your mind I must be mad."

A small smile tipped up his finely drawn lips.

Addie bared her teeth, but *not* in a smile. "Tell me, Sir Robert, do *you* consider yourself mad? Demon-possessed?"

Outrage wiped the humor right off his face.

She continued, "From my perspective, *you're* the madman if not—"

"I suggest you measure your words," he said in a dangerously soft voice. "Such talk is risky indeed. You could be chained and whipped to drive out the demons that, in spite of your denials, have assuredly taken up residence in your soul. *I* am not the madman here, much less what you would insinuate."

Since Sir Robert continued to stare at her as if he expected the aforementioned demons to fly from her mouth at any moment, Addie gave up trying to persuade her unwilling host of her spiritual purity. Her frustration grew, and her desperation with it. What was she going to do? After all, if the man was right, Christopher Columbus wouldn't discover the New World for another seven years—but she didn't make the mistake of telling Sir Robert *that* bit of news.

She sighed, breaking the uncomfortable silence. "Since you insist we're in the year 1485, I don't know what will become of me. My home in York—York, Pennsylvania, that is—won't be there for another four hundred years, so I can't stroll down the road and run into Market Street—*if* you're right. I suppose I'll have to return through time the same way I came."

At the renewed curl of Sir Robert's lip, Addie decided she would do well to drop *that* subject, too. "Oh, fine," she said before he spoke again. "Since I find myself in need of rest, I would greatly appreciate your leaving this room. And don't return unless I invite you—which, you can rest assured, will never happen."

A strange expression crossed his handsome face. To Addie, it looked like bitterness. "'Twill hardly be new to me," he muttered, then turned on his heel and strode from the room.

The thud of the closing door reverberated in Addie's head. Bits and pieces of the bizarre conversation they had just shared whirled in and out of her thoughts.

What *had* happened to her? And how? Had she really traveled through time?

She approached the slit of a window and gazed outside. The men still lunged at each other, their weapons catching the glint of the sun as they slashed and sliced the air. To their left, the pigs still rooted for food, while a hen flapped her wings and cackled to their right.

Leaning further into the opening, Addie noted the extreme thickness of the stone walls. She glanced far to her left, then gasped. More than anything else, what she now saw convinced her Sir Robert had been telling the truth.

It was 1485.

An arched gateway broke the solid expanse of stone wall that encircled the courtyard where the men still went through their paces. As Addie watched, a pair of yoked oxen moved away from the opening, and a truly medieval-looking iron portcullis dropped into place, closing out whatever enemies Swynton Manor might have.

She stumbled back to the bed, collapsed into the feather-cloud mattress, and closed her eyes. *Dear God.* What was she to do now? How would she get back home?

What would happen to Emmie before she did?

Running a hand down his face, Robert considered his situation. It appeared he harbored a heretic and perhaps a witch as well. Such an action could have terrible consequences, as he well knew. The Church took exception to such foul beings. Jeanne d'Arc had been burned at the stake under suspicion of those very sins. But if he did not keep her under observation, what would he do with Mistress Shaw?

He dared not turn her out. If she was a sorceress, 'twould do those who lived nearby more harm than good to set her loose, to leave them at her mercy. If, on the other hand, she was mad, then 'twould be the utmost cruelty to free her to wander and babble nonsense among sensible, perhaps less tolerant, folk. Someone might attack her, take advantage of her. It wasn't in him to endanger Addie like that.

Unless she'd come to Swynton at Edwin Morland's behest. In that case, Robert would have to devise adequate punishment for her. She and her allies had cost him the lives of two good men. And could still cost him his.

But how did a decent man punish a treacherous woman?

Frustrated, he joined Mortimer on the practice field to watch his men's exercises. They were skilled; he and Mortimer had seen to that. Satisfaction filled Robert as he admired Harold and Jamie's swordplay.

"How is our guest this morn?" asked Mortimer.

Reminded of his troubles, Robert ran a hand through his hair. "I know not with certainty. She appears well, but what she speaks . . ." For a moment he sought a way to describe the conversation he'd had with Mistress Shaw. Then he gave up. 'Twas impossible, and Mortimer might think *he* had suddenly gone mad himself. "She speaks nonsense. It could stem from her experience on that field yesterday afternoon, or . . ."

"Or?"

Robert shrugged. "She may be a spy for the Morlands. Were that the case, then it could prove deadly for us to keep her here."

"What will you do now?"

A tight shake of his head accompanied his sharply indrawn breath. "How can I know what would be best?"

Mortimer scratched his grizzled beard. "Why not send her to your sister?"

"To the abbey?" Robert asked, horrified in view of his suspicions. "Saint Hilda's is *not* for a woman like her."

Bushy gray eyebrows beetled across a lined forehead. "And why not? They take in widows and others no one wants. She looks sturdy enough. I trow she would earn her keep."

Robert refused to meet his man's gaze. Since he still had to uncover the truth about Addie Shaw, it seemed prudent to keep his suspicion from Mortimer. "Think you Edythe would appreciate my sending her a spy?"

"Think you the lady is a spy?"

Robert remembered clear gray eyes, how they'd shot fire when he questioned her motives, when he'd suggested her presence on his land bespoke ulterior motives. Addie Shaw's response had seemed innocent enough then.

But he also remembered her words. ". . . *I have traveled through time. . . .*" Try as he might, he failed to fathom what might make a woman conceive such a preposterous tale, even if intelligently and soundly stated. Unless she had treachery to hide. No one risked the ire of the Church lightly, but saving her hide might give her good reason.

"I cannot assure you she isn't one," he finally said.

"Which brings us round to where we began, lad. What will you do with her?"

Slowly Robert shook his head. "I've yet to decide. But I'll keep an eye on her until I do."

Mortimer chuckled. "Be glad she's not a homely one. 'Twon't be a hardship to watch over her."

Robert frowned. Was Addie Shaw a comely woman?

She was no beauty, certainly not as lovely as Catherine had been. Although Addie possessed masses of medium brown hair, and the stuff looked fine enough, it didn't strike him as particularly special. Surely not as splendid as Catherine's moonbeam tresses.

As to Addie's features . . . they were regular, unremarkable. Her nose was neither small nor large, her mouth neither wide and merry nor budding and pouty. Her face was neither of a long or broad cut, and although her height was somewhat remarkable, her figure, endowed with the normal curves and valleys, seemed just as average as the rest of her.

Then the sudden image of flashing silver eyes leaped to life in Robert's mind again. Ah, yes. Mistress Adelaide Shaw possessed two outstanding features. Large and framed by long, curling lashes, those eyes spoke more eloquently than her oddly accented tongue. While he had only seen them spit daggers of anger or darken with fear, Robert found himself wondering what they would look like when she laughed, when she kissed, when she yielded to—

Nay. He could ill afford to entertain that kind of thought. Addie Shaw was not the woman about whom he should entertain it. She might well prove deadly.

"Care to go a round?" asked a breathless Harold, having just vanquished Jamie, a sword in his outstretched right hand.

Robert shook his head to clear away the distracting visions. Perhaps he should take up the lad's invitation. A good bout might well ease some of his frustration and worry. "Give me a moment to don mail, then prepare to lose."

Full of the headiness of victory, even if only on a practice field, Harold chuckled. "Beggin' pardon, m'lord, I trow not. I've worked steadily, improved regularly. Besides, I've youth on my side."

Robert answered with his own laugh. "Ah, lad, 'tisn't youth that always wins. Wisdom oft counts for more."

Today, with a probable enemy in the bosom of his home, Robert needed all the wisdom he could muster to prevail. His life might just depend on it.

As she lay on the overly soft bed, listening to the sounds of mock battle outside, time weighed heavily on Addie. She had never been one for inactivity, and with all manner of bizarre thoughts rushing through her head, the last thing she wanted was to face more empty hours.

Although she couldn't be certain, she didn't remember Sir Robert locking the bedroom door behind him. While she assumed he would believe her too exhausted and shocked to do more than lay in bed, such behavior went against her nature.

She had to find something to do to keep from going as mad as her grim host believed her to be.

Escape would be nice.

With the idea of action firmly entrenched in her will, Addie punched her way out of bed. She donned the soft slippers the wimpled one had left behind and approached the rough-hewn door. Pressing her ear to the slab of wood, she heard nothing on the other side.

Cautiously she drew it open, then closed it again as she left the room. Partway down a narrow hallway, within an ample alcove, she saw an arched fireplace, and down a ways beyond that, three more round-arched doors—all closed. "Now what?" she asked herself out loud.

Hesitating, she breathed a prayer for courage, which she sorely needed, since she found herself in the most unfamiliar of situations, in a place utterly foreign to her, one where she'd been told her presence was not welcome. And she only wanted to go home, to her sister. There had to be a way to accomplish her goal—*without* dealing with Sir Robert again.

Silently, since her soft slippers made no sound against the flagstone floor, she went to the far end of the hall. There she found a narrow, winding stairway leading both up and down. Her choice was easy. She wanted down and *out*.

The dark stairwell smelled dank and musty, making the chilly but dry room where she had slept incredibly appealing. Her need to return to her responsibilities, however, proved greater than her need for physical comfort.

At the next landing, where another set of steps led farther down, a cry of pain caught Addie's attention. Immediately she remembered the skirmish of the day before. She shuddered, the red haze of blood returning to her memory, and hurried, eager to leave the scene of those memories well behind.

But another restless moan—another whimper—rang out, and Addie's compassionate heart wouldn't let her proceed. She had never turned her back on any creature in need of assistance; she had to try to relieve the victim's suffering.

She smiled sadly, remembering Mama's frequent complaints during her childhood. *"Addie, child. It's only a bird. There's little you can do for it."*

And yet Addie had always tried, despite poor odds in her favor, and had accrued, over time, an impressive list of recuperations.

Shortly after her parents died, mindful of the Shaw girls' reduced means, Doc Horst had taken Addie under his wing, needing a good hand to keep his records up to date. Spending one day a week at the surgery, Addie developed an efficient system, then took advantage of his willingness to teach. She soaked up every drop of knowledge the older gentleman had ever learned. In short measure, he had informed anyone who cared to listen that a finer nurse than Addie Shaw did not exist. He'd often told her she would make a fine physician.

Her life was full and satisfying, if busy and challenging. During the week, she shared the knowledge she dug out of book after book with the children at school, while on Saturday she helped Doc.

Then last year matters grew a bit more complicated when Emmie's eccentric tendencies mushroomed into massive concerns. Mrs. Mahoney, who had watched Emmie while Addie helped Doc Horst, declared the young girl too much trouble for the pittance Addie could afford to pay, especially since Emmie had taken to lighting every scrap of fabric she could get her hands on. Matters came to a head when Emmie set Mrs. Mahoney's ample drawers ablaze one fine Saturday morn.

Addie was forced to take on an undesired and useless assistant—her fey sister. It hadn't been a perfect arrangement, but she had managed to prevent calamity while still working with Doc Horst.

Now . . . Emmie was alone. She would lack all restraint as long as her older, more sensible sister remained lost somewhere in the past. Anxiety curled in Addie's stomach.

Yet another wail of misery pierced her thoughts. Addie vacillated. Her love for Emmie and her more practical, sensible side compelled her to hurry, to run to the woods and find the tree that should, by all rights, take her home.

But her nurturing, emotional side, the side that would never forget her mother and father's pain-filled final hours, kept her feet planted on those dark, damp steps. Mama and Papa had suffered terrible injuries when their horse bolted, throwing them from their rig.

As York had no hospital, Doc Horst had had the elder Shaws brought home. Addie had tried to care for them, but her lack of training had frustrated her. She'd sat at their side, helpless to ease their pain. As Mama lay dying, Addie vowed to learn everything that might help those in need. Doc Horst's offer had seemed an answered prayer.

Addie's hunger for knowledge had served her well, and she had learned everything the kind doctor had shared. Now that long-ago promise to her mother turned Addie's feet toward the sound of suffering.

Moments later, after rounding a screen just inside an arched doorway, Addie entered a vast, vaulted-ceilinged hall with an impressive window bay at one end. Along the sides of the chamber, arches led into what appeared to be a honeycomb of alcoves, and in the middle of the left wall, a cavernous fireplace blazed with lively intent.

Some feet before the window, a raised dais held a table, behind which sat a massive wooden chair. Elsewhere, trestle tables and benches told her meals were taken here. Underfoot, gluing a mess of what looked like dirty straw, she saw—and smelled—the remnants of those meals. Addie's sensibilities complained as her stomach churned.

Between the tables and the arches, she found the source of her concern. A number of dingy cloth pallets lay over the straw on the floor, each holding an injured man. Some tossed and turned, some whimpered; two others, more frighteningly, lay immobile, their eyes shut.

To Addie's disgust, a pair of hounds wended among the wounded, sniffing at bloody bandages, licking indiscriminately at injuries that needed no canine care. Worse yet, a huge black cat, weighing perhaps twenty pounds, sniffed at one of the patients, nudged him in the thigh, then climbed up the man's belly and settled to wash itself on his chest, its loose hairs raining down on a filthy, bloodied bandage.

"Oh, for goodness' sake!" she cried, then charged the menagerie masquerading as medical minions. As she confronted the first displeased dog, she heard footsteps approach.

Spinning around, she saw the wimpled one bustle toward her; a tiny, thin woman, similarly garbed, was at her side. "What are you about here, mistress?" she asked. "These men need their rest, God save their souls."

Addie planted her fists on her hips. "Of course they need rest, but they also need clean bandages, medicine, and they *don't* need animals dropping fur and dirt and who knows what else all over them! I was chasing away the beasts, that's what I was about."

With a shooing motion, the woman said, "Well, now you can go back to your room. Thomasine is here, and she'll be carin' for the men. She's the finest healer in the land."

Not from what I can see! "I couldn't bear another minute of lying about," Addie said. "I've spent years helping Doc Horst back home, and I have two hands to offer Thomasine. In fact, if she would find me a stack of clean linen bandages and you could fetch me boiled water, I'll make the men more comfortable—as soon as the animals leave."

Either Addie's statement threw the wimpled one off guard, or her determined stance convinced her of the futility of arguing. Turning to the woman at her side, she asked for more rags in her heavily accented Old English.

Thomasine shot Addie a murderous glare and spat a response at her friend.

Addie didn't quite catch the healer's words, but her sentiment came through clearly. "Look," she said, hoping to placate the antagonized woman, "I don't mean to offend, but there's much I can do to help. I've years of experience, and we should make use of it. Since you're such a fine healer, you must have plantain leaves. I'll need a quantity for poultices."

When she mentioned the well-known plant, Thomasine's look of outrage eased fractionally, and the compliment could only have helped. Apparently Addie's knowledge of common herbal practice convinced the woman she knew something about the matter. "Oh, yes. Carbolic, or even brandy or whiskey would be helpful as well."

The two women gazed at her quizzically, then turned to each other. They murmured back and forth, then faced Addie again. "I'm afeared we don't know those plants," said the wimpled one. "Thomasine has betony, birthwort, houseleek, lungwort, Solomon's seal, and woundwort. Should she fetch them as she has not the others?"

Addie frowned. No carbolic? No whiskey? Or brandy? Then she remembered. These were—supposedly—medieval times. Those three common items of her day wouldn't be available for some time yet. She sighed in frustration. "Bring me what you have, and we'll see what we can do. Oh, yes. Willow bark. I'll need plenty of that. Wine, and lots of it, won't hurt, either."

With a nod, the wimpled one gave Thomasine a gentle push in the direction they'd come, and the two exited the hall, each dragging a baying hound in her wake.

Addie breathed a sigh of relief. Until she remembered the cat. She approached cautiously, well aware that its claws could do her harm. To her amazement, the beast had fallen asleep, and purred enthusiastically from its spot on the felled warrior's chest.

Despite the absurdity of the situation, Addie knew what she had to do. Crooning gently, she slipped a hand between beast and bed, waking only the cat. It opened a baleful green eye and *mrrowed* in protest while puffing up its fur.

"Oh, no, you don't," she murmured, rubbing her cheek against the animal's head, keeping its claws well away from bare skin. "You're a fine one indeed, only not for medical purposes. You'll just have to find yourself somewhere else to sleep."

Casting a look around, she noticed a cloak draped over the arm of the large chair on the dais. Still whispering silly words to the feline in her arms, she nudged the woolen garment onto the broad seat, and lay the animal within its folds. "You'll be more comfortable here than on that poor fellow's chest. He needs to breathe, and you need your nap. Sleep well!"

Picking cat hair off her borrowed garment, Addie looked around for somewhere to wash her hands. She found nothing that might conceivably hold fluid. As she remembered what she knew of medicine's past, unease tightened her middle.

Textbooks told how in the Middle Ages sanitation was haphazard, at best. Most folks rarely bathed, and most injuries led to death from poisoned blood. Lack of cleanliness played a great part in the high mortality rate. As Addie stood and studied the room, the men on the floor, the furniture, the lack of amenities, she remembered Sir Robert's contention.

"1485 . . ."

She had babbled about time travel when confronted with his insistence on that date, partly to rid herself of his unsettling presence, and partly because the concept held such wonder for someone with her insatiable hunger for knowledge. The chance to study the past firsthand appealed mightily. But a part of her hadn't wanted to accept it as true.

Again, however, she faced evidence she couldn't easily discount. Had she really traveled through time?

"Here y'are, Mistress Shaw," said the wimpled one, holding a deep basin against one hip and a large tankard in her other hand. "I've the boiled water and the wine you asked for. How will you use them?"

Addie called up her best teacher's voice. "Why, the water's to clean their wounds, of course. Such injuries might turn putrid if left unwashed, causing blood poisoning in no time. We cannot let that happen, you understand. And the wine, well, that's so the men don't feel the pain when I work on their injuries, since I doubt you have ether."

The wimpled one set her burdens on the nearest table, then faced Addie. "Can you keep the cuts from festering, mistress?"

"Please call me Addie, and I'd appreciate knowing your name, too."

"I'm Nell Bolton, Sir Robert's cook, but when there's need, I give Thomasine a hand with the care of the dying—"

"Hush!" Addie cried, dismayed by the woman's attitude. "You mustn't say that where they can hear you. We're going to do everything we can to keep them from dying. That's what they should hear, not a gloomy prognostication."

Nell crossed herself, then bustled to the table, gathering the basin of—Addie fervently hoped—boiled water. She approached the nearest pallet and was greeted by the injured man's feeble attempt at a smile.

Setting the basin on a bench to Addie's right, Nell asked, "How do we do it, mistress—er, Addie?"

"Let me examine his wound." Uncovering her patient, Addie noted the crusted blood on his dirty bandage. She shook her head. "I'll need to soften the dried blood on the linen first."

She went to work, carefully dripping small amounts of warm fluid onto the rag. A scant minute later, Thomasine returned, clutching a wealth of clean cloths. "I sent young Squire Andrew to fetch fresh plantain, mistress—"

"Call me Addie," she said, cutting off the unappealing term. "And I hope he returns soon." Turning to Nell, she asked, "Where can I find soap? We all need to wash our hands, especially when going from patient to patient."

The two women gave her surprised looks, then glanced at each other and shrugged. "I'll fetch the soap," said the cook, "and from the sounds of it, more water."

"Boiled, if you please."

"Aye, mist—Addie, boiled."

Turning to her patient, Addie went back to the unsanitary bandage, and soon eased the soggy cloth from the man's chest.

"Why do ye take his bandage off?" asked Thomasine, as she leaned over Addie's shoulder.

Noting the woman's fresh, herbal scent, Addie felt slightly better about the fate of her patients. "Because we must cleanse his wound. It can grow septic if dirt remains in the broken flesh."

"But ye'll let the body's humors escape," argued the medieval healer.

"Let's worry about one thing at a time," Addie answered, not knowing how else to respond. She didn't know much about body humors; she just knew the men on the pallets would likely die if left as they were.

Huffing, Nell arrived with the second basin of steaming water and handed Addie strong-smelling lye soap. "As you asked."

"Thank you." Briskly washing her hands, Addie urged both women to follow suit. Then she directed her companions to uncover and cleanse the other men's wounds, finally turning back to the foul bandage she'd begun to remove.

Dismayed by the reddened, swollen flesh she uncovered, Addie heard heavy footsteps at the entrance to the hall. She kept working despite the urge to see who had arrived.She didn't wait long to know.

"What the devil are you doing to my men?" bellowed the lord of the manor. "Was it not enough to help Morland ambush and kill two? By my troth, I knew you for a spy from the first! That 1885 business was naught but a poor effort to divert my attention. It failed to work then, as it surely will not again."

Taking her arm in a steely grip, Sir Robert hauled Addie upright. "You'll remain in your room until I decide how best to deal with a woman spy. Hanging's too good for the likes of you. You'd do well to pray none of these men die, since you'll pay for that life with yours."

Chapter 5

FEAR FILLED ADDIE'S stomach at Sir Robert's threat, but she couldn't let him see it. "If you lock me up, your men will certainly die," she said with more bravado than she felt. "They need good, modern medical care, and I'm the only one here who can offer it. Let me see to their needs."

For a long, silent moment, she held Sir Robert's gaze, again noting the concern in his frown and the fear in his eyes.

"I can help them," she said, softening her tone, entreating his consent. Sir Robert apparently bore a heavy burden. If he was responsible for all these folks, Addie could well believe such responsibility had etched the intriguing crinkles that fanned from his eyes and the faint twin lines between his brows.

"I really can," she added when he still didn't respond. "I helped Dr. Horst back in York."

Sir Robert scoffed. "Now you say you're a healer as well. Which shall it be, Mistress Shaw? Doctor? Teacher? Or do you use the words interchangeably?"

"What is wrong with that? A doctor can be both."

"Perhaps, but not a woman. Every time we speak you change your tale. Who can believe a word you say?"

Indignation burning through her, Addie said, "Believe this. I don't lie. I've been trained by a physician, and if I don't help your men, your fears will come true. More will die."

Pain twisted his features. "I cannot let you touch them. You helped Morland put them where they are, and you'll not have another opportunity to harm them again."

"Oh, for goodness' sake! Stop your foolishness. Let me do what I can—what I must. Besides, Nell and Thomasine are here. They'll make sure I do nothing to hurt your men."

Suspicion replaced Sir Robert's pain. "Who is to say you'll not use your black arts on the women?"

For a moment Addie tasted defeat. "So we're back to that again."

Sir Robert arched a dark eyebrow. "Did we ever leave that topic, madam? Or have you finally decided to tell the truth, to renounce your foolish tale of travel through time?"

Addie didn't know how to respond. If she said yes, he would use the recantation as proof of her having lied at the outset. If she said no, he would indict her as demon-possessed or who knew what other nonsense. In the meantime, his men could die without her help. "Fine," she said, "I won't say a thing. If you fear my actions so much, then stay and watch me. You can stop me as soon as you see me attempt anything suspicious."

With a yank, she pulled her arm free and returned to her task. While she soaked a rag in the boiled water, she instructed Thomasine to give their patient a hefty measure of wine. She hoped the drink worked fast enough to lessen the pain the man would surely feel.

A young boy then entered the chamber, bearing a thick wad of plantain leaves. He handed the vegetation to Thomasine, who turned to Sir Robert. "She asked for plantain," she said. "'Twill not hurt a soul, milord. I've used it many a time."

Addie again met her captor's gaze. The silence grew. A

ripple of awareness swept through her, and she wondered if that dark stare could see all the way through to her heart. If it did, what would Sir Robert think of what he found there? The fear, the confusion, and beyond that, the years-old loneliness, the yearning. . . .

"Flapdoodle," she muttered, irritated by her atypical, impractical, fanciful thoughts. More than likely, Sir Robert merely meant to intimidate her.

As Addie wiped a warm compress across the tortured flesh of the man at her side, he cried out. With a nod, she urged Thomasine to again dose him with wine. Murmuring words of comfort, she made herself ignore her host, focusing instead on her patient. At the moment she dared not even think of the man who held her fate in his hands.

"Fine," Sir Robert suddenly stated as he watched her deliberately careful, benign actions. "Help them if you can. But remember, Mistress Shaw, you'll pay with your life should any of them die."

A shudder racked her. "I won't forget, even if I cannot promise I will save them all. I haven't examined the others yet. But I can promise to do everything in my power to prevent more deaths. Beyond my best, the result lies in God's hands."

At her words, both Nell and Thomasine donned devout expressions and crossed themselves.

Although Addie could feel Sir Robert's seething restraint at her back, she breathed easier when he didn't accuse her of some other ecclesiastic faux pas. At least he didn't throw the word heresy her way again.

Studying the swollen flesh around the neat row of stitches an inch below her patient's ribs, Addie turned to Thomasine. "Did you bring the willow bark?"

"Aye, mistress—"

"Addie, if you please."

"Aye, mis—er . . . Addie. I gathered some yesterday morn, and 'tis already well soaked. If you wish, one of Nell's kitchen maids can bring it to a boil."

"That's precisely what we need."

" 'Twon't take but a breath of time," said Nell, who'd obviously followed every word.

Addie shot her a smile. "Make sure the water comes to a rolling boil and the bark steeps well. We need a strong decoction today."

Nodding, Nell left the hall. Addie returned to her work. Taking a bit of the plantain the boy had brought, she crushed the leaves and pressed them against the nasty cut. As she applied gentle though steady pressure, she asked Thomasine, "Have you any marigold ointment?"

A smile spread across thin features. "Indeed. Last week I boiled the powder with a good pound of lard. I keep it in a crock at the spring."

Relief washed through Addie. They did *not* need rancid lard. "Would you fetch it for me, please?"

"Of course, but how about him?" Thomasine asked, gesturing toward the man she'd been treating.

"I'm here, and Nell should be back soon. We will need that marigold salve."

" 'Tis well it works."

As she rose, Thomasine's knees objected audibly. When she walked away, a limp to her step, Addie diagnosed rheumatism and determined to help the older woman before she returned to Pennsylvania. Surely between the two of them they could come up with a good treatment for those knees.

The very thought of going home breathed life into thoughts of her sister again. As fear for Emmie grew, a sudden rustle of activity at the dais caught Addie's attention. A loud, indignant *Mmrrrreowwww!* followed.

Sir Robert cursed, then said, "What the—"

A heavy piece of furniture scraped against wood, accompanied by a prolonged litany of imprecations. A black streak shot past Addie, another yowl flying along with it. She fought a grin.

"What is this rat-catcher on my chair?"

Still struggling against the urge to laugh, Addie turned. "I do apologize, Sir Robert. I thought the furniture a better bed for the cat than one of the men whose injuries worry you so."

"*You* put him here?" he asked, smoothing the garment over an arm. "On *my* cloak?"

Addie shrugged and turned to her patient when she felt him tug on her sleeve. "Mistress . . ." the man whispered.

"Call me Addie."

A weak nod acknowledged her request. "Could I've more o' the wine?"

"Am I hurting you?"

"Nay, but I'm parched."

"Plain water would be best, and all I have here is hot . . ." She looked around, but the boy had gone, and neither Nell nor Thomasine had returned. She and her unhappy host were the only able-bodied souls in the room. Although she feared he would put up a fuss, she had no alternative but to ask him for help. "As you can see, Sir Robert, your man needs a drink. Would you please have Nell cool a quantity of that boiled water?"

Silence met her request, thick and ominous.

"Well?"

After another, lengthier pause, the metallic clink of mail came close. "What assurance give you that Ned and the others will still draw breath when I return?"

Exasperated, Addie blew a gust of breath out of the corner of her mouth. "None beyond my word. I guess you'll have to trust me, won't you?"

He knelt across from her, the injured man between them, and caught her chin in his broad hand. The heat of him penetrated her skin, winnowing through her. Addie trembled, not knowing if from fear of the threat in his gaze or from his enervating touch.

"By all that's holy," he said, his words clipped and sure, "if any die before I return—"

"I know, I know. It's my life for theirs. How stupid do you think me? I don't want to die, certainly not before I can see to Emmie—" Addie clamped her lips shut. She didn't want to talk about her sister, certainly not to *him,* and not when he was threatening death.

What if, after learning of her greatest weakness—her sister—he went for Emmie to force Addie to do his will, whatever that might be? She wouldn't put it past Robert Swynton to travel through time himself if doing so served him well—no matter what accusations he hurled her way.

Another shudder ripped through Addie. She had to beware around him. The alternative was too hideous to contemplate. "You needn't threaten me. All I want is to spare them pain. I will do what I can to keep your men alive."

Apparently her sincerity penetrated his suspicion, for Sir Robert stood slowly and threw his cape over his shoulders. With measured steps, he strode to the screen at the far end of the hall. As he walked, Addie spotted something out of the ordinary on the dark woolen cloth. Despite her host's repeated threats, she smiled.

The cat's claws had left their mark on the cloak. Dozens of long, loosened threads quivered and flapped with Sir Robert's every movement, marring the rich nap of the wool, the dignity of his walk.

Somehow that tiny detail lifted her spirits. She didn't feel utterly trounced in this latest match.

Hours later, after Addie had seen to all the wounded, cleaning, medicating, then bandaging their injuries with clean linen rags, she allowed herself to collapse on a bench. The tension that had carried her through her efforts suddenly leached from her, leaving her weak, shaking.

A gentle hand landed on her shoulder. "'Tisn't good for you to wear yourself so, mistress—"

"Addie."

"Aye, Addie," Nell conceded in her richly accented voice. "'Tisn't good at all, if you truly mean to help us tend the hurt. You need to eat, to rest. You suffered much yourself but yesterday."

"You would offer hospitality to the woman who supposedly caused all this?" Addie asked, bitterness in her words, her hand waving weakly toward the pallets on the floor.

For a moment Nell didn't respond, and Addie's heart plummeted. Not her, too!

Then the older woman said, "Nay, my lady, you caused naught at all. If you were at the field, then you were there for some reason of your own. One who works to save a man's life didn't try to take it first. Come to the kitchen. I've stewed rabbit and bread. 'Twill do you good to eat."

To her surprise, Addie's stomach growled. She grinned at Nell and rose. "I hadn't realized how hungry I was."

"Nay, lass, you thought but of them," Nell said, bobbing her rounded chin toward their patients.

Addie shrugged. "I couldn't let them suffer since I knew I could help. It was the only decent thing to do."

"The Good Lord'll bless you for your goodness, my lady."

"But not the lord of the manor."

Nell chuckled and pushed Addie toward the screen at the far end of the hall. "I'll grant you, Sir Robert is a difficult one. But he's no fool. He knew enough to let you do what you could. You'll see, my lady, he'll come around once he learns how well the men fare."

After exacting a promise from Thomasine to fetch Addie should any of their patients need her, she followed Nell down the narrow stairwell. As they walked, she explained the need for cleanliness, remembering the day Doc Horst explained Joseph Lister's revolutionary teachings. "If we keep the flesh clean and dry, the chance of putrefaction becomes much less. Then the body can begin to heal. That's when the willow tea and the marigold salve become truly useful. But first and always, one must keep the injury perfectly clean."

Nell murmured something agreeable, and Addie decided she'd instructed enough for one day. Especially since they'd entered a cellarlike place where she could hear a horse whickering, could smell the mustiness of the damp earth beneath her feet, could see all manner of barrels and containers storing who knew what, and could feel the bustle of activity around her.

The people rushing to and fro were dressed much like Nell and Thomasine, reminding Addie of pictures she had seen in various history books. They chatted in the same thickly accented Old English Thomasine and Nell used. By all indications, their walk had led them to what Addie assumed was the ground level of a castle or large manor house.

Moments later, the two women emerged into the sunlight, which blinded Addie momentarily. Then, when her eyes worked again, what she saw left her speechless.

They'd emerged into an enclosed courtyard—a bailey, in medieval terms. Against the stone wall enclosing the bailey stood an array of buildings, two of which emitted smoke from the roof, one that rang with porcine squeals, and others that susurrated with the sounds of fowl.

At the far end, a stately stone building bore a cross on its peaked roof, and just beyond the chapel, a large shed housed two wagons.

Addie blinked to clear the visions away, but when she stopped fluttering her eyelids, the view around her remained the same. The thatched roofs, the ancient layout, the enclosed common area, the solid manor house, the men wearing mail and carrying swords, seemed real enough. It looked as if she had found her way through a tree into the Middle Ages after all. 1485, as Sir Robert had said.

Questions, thousands of them, rushed to her mind, most pertaining to everyday life and customs and equipment particular to the era. Revealing as the answers would be, Addie squelched the questions, not willing to lose the support of Nell, her only ally. And since it appeared that she *had*—impossible though it seemed—traveled to medieval England, she needed every friend she could make to survive and find her way back home.

She felt a tug at her sleeve. Nell *tsk-tsk*ed. "You need food and rest, in that order and right away, Mistress Addie. I'll not hear a word of argument from you."

"Mmm . . ." Addie had no intention of arguing at the moment; she was too busy cataloging the sights and sounds around her—even the clash of weapons against mail drew her attention. While walking in Nell's wake, she watched two men thrust and parry, lunge and retreat, their exertion accompanied by masculine grunts.

The battling men handled their weapons well, the taller one clearly having the upper hand. Addie slowed her steps and watched, horror mingling with fascination. The tall knight moved with impressive strength and a grace that, although deadly, possessed a raw beauty all its own. His helmet caught the late-afternoon sunlight, reflecting it in a halo of sparks. He moved easily despite the mail shirt he wore, his sword an extension of his powerful body.

He thrust. His opponent countered, lunging forward in his own attack.

The tall knight dodged the thrust, catching the deadly edge of the other man's weapon on his own. A battle of wills—and muscle—ensued, neither man indined to yield. Ropes of sinew showed through the men's hose, as they alternated an intimidating stance with one of rebuff. Neither gave an inch.

Then might exerted itself, and slowly, implacably, the larger man's blade lifted and repelled the other. With a sudden jerk, the weaker warrior's sword flew from his hand; he stumbled backwards and fell to the ground. The victor pressed his knife's edge to the vanquished's throat.

Addie flew forward, screaming, "Nooooo . . .!"

Throwing herself across the felled man, she stared at the ruthless knight above her. "I will not stand by and watch. You'll have to kill me first."

Silence descended in heavy layers over the bailey. Not a soul moved, not even the pigs or the hens nearby. Every human eye, and some animal ones, too, clung to Addie. Expectation felt thick enough to touch.

Then with rough gestures, the winning knight sheathed his weapon and tore his helmet from his head. A familiar pair of brown eyes beneath an equally familiar, formidable frown met Addie's gaze, and she groaned.

"What in all that's holy do you now, woman?" Sir Robert demanded.

"What do you think? I'm trying to save this man's life."

A snicker sounded to Addie's left, but she dared not glance that way just then. Who knew what the beastly lord of this manor might do next?

Clasping his helm under his arm, Sir Robert ripped off his gauntlets, then ran a hand through his flattened hair, ruffling the long waves. Indignation blared from his every pore. "I challenge this sudden display of mercy, especially from a spy."

"I'm not a spy," she spit out.

"That remains to be seen."

"I've spent hours trying to save lives in there"—Addie gestured toward the manor house—"and now I put myself in danger by your own sword to prevent another murder. Why must you see me as some foul villain?"

"Think of when and where I found you, madam. You'll have your answer then. 'Twould be a fine way to persuade me of your goodness with all these efforts were I a green youth."

"A reasonable man, you mean."

"I'm as reasonable as the next, given reason to believe."

Addie stood as did the man whose life she'd saved. "And what am *I* to believe about *you*? You rant about the danger I supposedly pose, but I had to keep you from killing again as you did just yesterday."

Her harsh indictment garnered a gasp from those gathered around them.

To her amazement, Sir Robert laughed, as did the man she'd saved. "I had no intention of hurting Harold," said the lord of Swynton Manor. "He's one of mine, and he'd challenged me earlier. I beat him, but he would not let that outcome stand, so he challenged me again. All in the furtherance of his skill and to settle a wager between friends." With a shrug and a smug grin, he crossed his arms over his wide, mail-clad chest. "The results were the same."

"But not for long," answered Harold, rising and removing his helmet to display a cocky grin. "Youth will win out sooner than you think, my lord."

"Wisdom, lad. 'Twill win every time."

As the two men bantered, the fear and outrage left Addie, her limbs suddenly weaker than the newly hatched chicks pecking at the dirt not five yards away. Her knees buckled, and she began to wilt. Before she knew it, bands of steel broke her fall, and she found herself flying up through the late-afternoon, spring-fresh air. Her flight brought her nose-to-nose with her reluctant host.

"By my troth, woman, you're more trouble than you're worth. I should let you leave as you insist on doing."

Sudden hope infused her with a modicum of energy. Addie squirmed in Sir Robert's arms, trying to get down. "Of course you should. It's the only reasonable, sensible thing to do. Let me go home. As I told you before, responsibility awaits me. I cannot stay away a minute longer."

The chest cradling her rose and fell with his deep sigh. "Were I a less cautious, less responsible man, I would do just that. But I cannot let you go. Not until I know you mean no harm."

Despair hit Addie with the strength she'd seen him wield with his sword. Dear God, what would happen to Emmie? Taking a shuddering breath, she asked, "What will you accept as proof of my innocence?"

For a moment, Sir Robert studied her face. He stared into her eyes, then raked her every feature with his penetrating stare, as if again he sought her darkest secret. Slowly, the suspicion in his gaze faded, questions following in its wake. Finally, the questions faded into . . . something different, something Addie couldn't define, but which frightened her almost as much as his comfort with violence.

A flush crept up his chiseled cheekbones and reached his brow. His eyelids dropped, shielding her from his scrutiny.

Addie noted the length of his lashes, the angle of his jaw,

the stubble of his beard, the line of his well-formed mouth. A tremor shook her, and again she was struck by how attractive Sir Robert truly was. She feared if she remained in his presence too long, she might come to appreciate his physical attributes more than she should.

After all, no one had ever carried Addie as if she weighed less than one of the doves that cooed in the cote to her right. And this was already the second time the knight had held her, his strength abounding as hers diminished. His arms assured her she wouldn't fall; his chest offered shelter—even to a woman he wouldn't trust.

There was something terribly appealing about such a man, but Addie could ill afford to appreciate his appeal.

Drawing a deep breath, she said, "Fine. Since you won't let me go home, then put me down so I can eat. Or do you mean to exact my surrender by letting me starve?"

A look of outrage bloomed not a breath away from her, its power stunning. Then that foreign something glowed hotter in Sir Robert's eyes, that dark and potent something she now believed more dangerous than his suspicion, more thrilling than his strength, more appealing than his masculine good looks. "No, Addie Shaw, 'tis not starvation I want for you. . . ."

Since he'd skirted the issue of surrender, Addie wondered just exactly what he wanted for her.

With her.

Chapter 6

AFTER UNCEREMONIOUSLY DUMPING Mistress Adelaide Shaw onto the only chair in Nell's kitchen, Robert had fled her side as if all the hounds of hell had come nipping at his heels.

He'd scented danger the moment he first saw her, but nothing like what he now feared. As he'd held her in his arms after her attempt to protect Harold's perfectly safe hide, her huge gray eyes had again begged him to let her go. But he had felt her moist breath against his cheek, cradled her warmth and weight against his chest, breathed her sweet, womanly scent all the way into his soul. No power on earth could have made him release her right then.

He wanted her. Not as his captive, not to protect himself or anyone else, but for the feminine pleasure she might afford him, for the softness he had never known in a woman's arms, for the delicious oblivion other men told of finding in the joys of female flesh.

That realization had shaken him to the core, making him question his sanity. Evidence led him to believe the woman had come as a spy for his avowed enemy.

Still, those silver eyes had alternately flashed and beckoned, turning him inside out. He could not have her—would not have her. But then . . . how should he handle a woman he feared yet wanted with a hunger he had never known before?

Why now?

Why her?

He'd stormed from the kitchen, cursing his own foolishness. Perhaps Mortimer was right. Men were not cut out for celibacy, ancient knightly tenets be damned. Perhaps one maid would be as good as another. And Robert certainly had plenty to choose from, since nearly every female on his land had made private—and some not so private—offers since the day Catherine breathed her last.

He'd been a faithful husband, believing in an outdated code of honor, but it had gained him naught save embarrassing encounters in his wife's bed where she'd cowered and cried.

Robert had come to suspect all the nonsense about physical games was just that: nonsense. He'd devoted himself to managing two large demesnes and had managed to ignore the nudgings of the flesh.

Until he met Addie Shaw. And wanted her. And failed to understand why.

He'd decided to ignore her as he had those other occasional sexual urges. In the days since their most recent encounter, Robert had avoided her, but he hadn't avoided reports of her exploits.

The woman had been making herself indispensable at Swynton Manor. From what Nell had said, that first visit to the kitchen had inspired Addie to promote yet more use of soap and water, as she had done with the victims of the Morland ambush. Instead of eating then resting, as Robert had expected his troublesome guest to do, she had bullied and cajoled all of Nell's kitchen maids into a cleaning frenzy.

Now, a scant fortnight after her arrival, the stench of old grease was gone from the kitchen, replaced by scents of the next meal. Kettles were scoured after each use, pails kept dry and ready, linen boiled and dried twice a week, quantities of soap stored close at hand. Incredibly, everyone did as Addie asked—even strong-willed, independent Nell—without question.

How had she done it?

Robert refused to entertain the question seriously, fearing the answer would be one he, a godly man with an abbess for a sister, could not accept.

"Good mornin' to you, Sir Robert," called out Lissa, a kitchen maid.

"And to you," he responded. Jabbing his chin at the raucously protesting fowl in her hands, he asked, "For supper?"

Lissa shrugged. "Dunno. Mistress Addie asked for hens, and 'tis what I'll give her."

Robert frowned. "And do you always do as Mistress Addie asks?"

"Nell said we should."

"Does *Nell* do what Mistress Addie asks, too?" Robert still couldn't picture Nell abdicating control of her kingdom.

"Mostly."

He narrowed his gaze. "How goes it since one and all began taking direction from Mistress Addie?"

A smile split Lissa's freckled face. "Fine, sir. Most fine. She does know aplenty."

"Such as?"

"Oh, cooking and cleaning and healing things."

"More than Nell and Thomasine?"

"Oh, aye. Never seen the likes before she come to us."

Unease prickled at the base of Robert's neck. "None of the wounded has died."

Lissa shook her head. " 'Tis true, but Willis fares poorly. Mistress Addie's fretted much over him, knowing not what more to do. She fears the Good Lord will be taking that one soon."

The news saddened him. Willis was strong and swift, and his fall to the ground during the contest with the Morlands had dismayed Robert. Then it occurred to him to question his guest's actions. Was his man dying from wounds inflicted by known enemies, or was the snake within Swynton Manor poisoning Willis while she pretended to treat his injuries? As Robert had feared.

He refrained from voicing his thoughts, since Lissa ought not hear them. "What says Thomasine?"

"'Bout Willis?"

"Of course, about Willis."

"We all know 'tis but a miracle he's lasted this long, m'lord. Thomasine thought he'd die but a day after the fight. Mistress Addie has done much for him, and he hasn't gone yet. She's an angel of mercy."

Robert's frown deepened. More than likely an angel of death. A canny one at that, since she had made allies of the women. "What say the other men of Mistress Shaw?"

Lissa donned a sly grin. "Why, they're besotted, sir, pleased to be alive, and 'tis thanks to her they are. Half have asked her hand in marriage."

Robert's eyebrows flew upward in surprise. So she'd charmed his men as well. Despite his determination to avoid the woman, as lord of Swynton Manor, he had to look into the situation himself. He trusted no one to give a fair and accurate report of Addie's activities—especially if she had resorted to casting spells. He had suspected sorcery from the first.

He gestured toward the kitchen. "Go on, then. We mustn't keep Mistress Shaw waiting for those chickens," he said, struggling to keep the sarcasm from his voice.

Aye, he would investigate, and he would learn what about Addie Shaw had his people crowning her with halos and seeing wings on her slender back. At the same time, he'd be sure to learn her response to those proposals of marriage.

He dared not question why he cared to know; he simply knew he cared.

"Save the feathers you pluck, Lissa," Addie said, pleased by the maid's choice in hens.

"Aye, Mistress Shaw."

Addie had given up trying to break everyone of the habit of calling her that, even if it made her feel old, passed over, a spinster well beyond hope. To these women, she was just that. In medieval times, a girl would wed by fourteen or fifteen, or enter a convent instead. Although Nell and Thomasine now called her Addie, the undermaids never would. They used the term as one of respect.

"You call the dish potpie?" asked Nell for about the tenth time. "It has no crust, so how is it then a pie?"

Addie shrugged. "I don't know why it's called that, but it's a favorite recipe from home. It's simple, too. Watch!"

Addie gathered flour, eggs, a basin of water and a deep crockery bowl. She poured a measure of the flour into the receptacle, added beaten yolks and enough water to make a paste. Mixing it all with a generous portion of salt, she kneaded the mass until it felt just right.

Turning it onto the tabletop, she rolled it thin. "These are egg noodles," she said in her teacher's voice, "and for potpie, we must cut them into squares. They'll cook in the chicken broth and taste so good."

"Noodles . . ." Nell tried out the new word.

Addie nodded. She'd been homesick for the fare from Pennsylvania, where many of the folks were German. She remembered the kettle of chicken potpie Mrs. Meyers had brought after the deaths of her parents. Addie had welcomed the simple food, as she'd been too grief-stricken to cook. After that, she had associated Mrs. Meyers with the dish, since over the years, she'd taken comfort in her neighbor's many kindnesses and countless bowls of stew. She wished she could do so now.

A tear threatened, and Addie concentrated on her preparations. Nell again remarked on the odd name, and Addie remembered asking about the pie name. Mrs. Meyers hadn't been able to explain that part to her.

What needed no explanation was the tender, stewed chicken with onions and carrots and noodles in rich broth. Simple and nourishing, the dish offered a taste Addie turned to when she craved consolation, as she often did these days.

She needed something familiar, something to remind her

of life before her fall through the tree. And nothing did so as well as the foods of her native Pennsylvania.

She missed her home, her routine. Oddly enough, she even missed the trouble Emmie relentlessly made. At the thought of the unsupervised sixteen-year-old, Addie's throat tightened and tears scalded her eyes. Who was watching out for her sister? Was she well? Had she set anything on fire of late?

Although Emmie possessed that one odd quirk, Addie loved the girl dearly. She'd been born when Addie was already ten years of age, and the tiny, golden-haired infant had stolen her older sister's heart. Sunny-natured and always ready with a song or a fanciful tale, Emmie had been the joy of the Shaw household. Until her fascination with fire developed. Then, everyone did their level best to protect the child.

After their parents had died, the two girls had clung together, sharing their grief, halving their pain. Emmie had been inconsolable for weeks, listless and weeping. Although she had avoided trouble during those days, Addie had worried over her sister's condition. When Emmie's smiles returned, bringing a resumption of her incendiary pursuits, Addie had breathed a sigh of relief—and redoubled her efforts to watch over the girl.

But now, while she remained in this distant past, Addie knew of no one who would look after Emmie. Her anxiety deepened, and misery welled within her. No amount of potpie was going to cure what ailed her. And even the satisfaction she'd found in helping the wounded, in teaching Nell and Thomasine the value of soap and water in the treatment of the ill, wasn't enough to cancel her need to return to her normal life.

True, there were many more things she could teach the women if she was forced to remain in this backward time much longer. After all, weevily flour and spoiled, overseasoned meat went beyond Addie's tolerance. The people of Swynton Manor didn't need to tolerate such conditions either. It would do them immeasurable good to take advantage of Addie's advanced knowledge.

In turn, she would gather a treasure trove of medieval knowledge totally inaccessible from her time. Imagine what she could teach her students—even the experts—once she returned. . . .

"Addie?"

Startled by Nell's insistent voice, Addie realized she'd again indulged in thoughts she shouldn't entertain since she could do nothing about them. She had missed what her friend had said.

Shaking her head at her foolishness, and stifling a pang of apprehension over her situation, Addie said, "I'm sorry, I wasn't listening."

Nell chuckled. "I know. What ought we do with your hens now?"

"Stew them with onions, carrots, parsley, and pepper. I'll cut the noodles and let them dry a bit. When the meat is tender, we can add them to the broth. Supper won't take long after that."

As Nell bustled off, Addie heard a masculine voice to her right. Turning toward the kitchen doorway, she found it blocked by the lord of the manor himself.

To her dismay, an odd ripple of awareness ran through her at the sight of the imposing, disturbing man. Honesty forced her to admit it wasn't the first time she'd responded to him that way.

Although they hadn't spoken in the past few days, she had found herself looking for him when she went outdoors, when she glanced out windows. She'd caught herself listening for his deep baritone voice despite her decision to avoid him. And most mortifying of all, at night he had filled her dreams, all of which started with him wearing his suit of armor, holding her against his massive chest.

She had dreamt of his intriguing eyes, his powerful body, his finely cut lips. Before the dream progressed too far, the suit of armor always vanished.

The memory of her vivid nighttime visions made Addie

blush. She had no business entertaining those kinds of thoughts—even while sleeping—of a man so brutal as to kill, to keep her hostage to his whim. How could she prove she wasn't a spy? How would she prove her innocence?

No one in 1485 could vouch for her.

"Good morning, Mistress Shaw," said the man, disturbing her peace.

"G-good morning, Sir Robert. And please, I've asked that you call me—"

"Addie, aye. I remember."

"Thank you. What brings you here today?"

"Tales of your amazing feats."

"Amazing feats?"

"*Too* amazing, perhaps. So much, that I insist on accompanying you when you visit my injured men this day to view them for myself."

Remembering his threat and Willis's deteriorating condition, Addie knew fear again. Gulping against the lump that knotted her throat, she sought to hide her shaking hands by wiping the flour onto her apron. "I'll be ready in a moment."

Addie doffed her covering then hurried to wash, all the while conscious of Sir Robert's stare at her back. She felt that gaze as if it had been his hand touching her instead.

His attention only served to make her awkward, nervous, and she dropped the length of linen toweling. As she bent to retrieve it, a broad, tanned hand reached the fabric first. She glanced up only to find herself scant inches from the eyes that haunted her dreams.

Those eyes stared into hers, peering deeply, making Addie wonder what he saw when he studied her that way. Could he see to her very heart? Could he hear it pounding like a Fourth of July band each time he came near? Did he realize the effect he had on her?

At that thought, Addie straightened abruptly. Robert Swynton could never know how he affected his unwilling guest. If he did, Addie feared he might use the knowledge against her. She couldn't imagine how or to what purpose, but he had extraordinary power to unnerve her.

"The towel, sir," she said, her brisk voice cool as the predawn wind.

To her surprise, a shudder ran through him, and he seemed caught as off guard as she had been by him. "Aye," he said in a rough voice.

Although he'd agreed, he still held the towel firmly in his grip. Addie tugged on the cloth. Tension mounted, then fled when she yanked in irritation. Was he trying to rattle her? Or worse?

Had Willis reached the end?

Was Robert Swynton about to carry out his threat of exacting her life for that of his man?

Addie found none of her answers on Robert Swynton's rugged features. Shaken to the core, she stumbled backwards and returned the towel to a peg on the kitchen wall. Feeling as if she were headed for her own execution, Addie stepped to the door. "Shall we?" she asked.

With a nod, Sir Robert came her way. She escaped into the May sunshine.

Fearing it might be her last time, she breathed the fresh air, listened to the sounds of life around her. She had grown used to the grunting of the sow and her brood, the clucking of the chickens, the cooing of the doves, the whicker of the horses—as long as *they* kept their distance, of course. She knew the men who called out ribald jokes as they went about their chores. She had come to know the women who bustled to and fro outside, their tasks never ending.

At that moment, she realized she'd accepted the routine of life in 1485, hard to believe though that seemed. When faced with the inevitability of her circumstances, she had made the best of her situation. Although the need to return home still burned inside her, this simple existence had stolen her heart. If it weren't for Emmie, Addie wouldn't object to living out her days at Swynton Manor.

If she was allowed to live.

Something inside her rose in rebellion, hating the unfairness. She hadn't harmed a soul—ever. Instead, she'd used her talents to help everyone she came to know.

Yet this near barbarian thought her capable of plotting to kill his men. What fools men could be.

Women took what life gave them and made the best of it. It was, after all, the only sensible, practical thing to do. And Addie had always been eminently sensible.

The brooding, silent man beside her, however, was the least sensible human she had ever come across. As they approached their destination, his dark disposition threatened to consume her, to steal all hope from her heart. But Addie couldn't simply give up and die. She had to try to lighten Sir Robert's mood.

"Mark Whetstone went home yesterday," she said, hoping the good news would help.

"So I heard."

"Four more have likely gone already today."

"That is good to know."

Then why did he speak with no satisfaction in his voice?

Addie tried again. "Considering their condition when I first examined them, it's a miracle they didn't all die."

That brought expression to Sir Robert's face, if not the kind she wanted. Menace deepened his frown. "'Tis to your advantage that none die, madam."

Lacing her shaking fingers, Addie said, "So you say, but even you must realize how unreasonable that is. I cannot control everything. I can, as I said before, only do my best."

"Your best had better be good enough. I mistrust your word, and even more, your care of my men."

"But you will admit my efforts helped them recover."

For a moment, they walked in silence. As they entered the darkened lower level of the manor house, its damp, subterranean chill, so different from the bright, balmy air outside, pierced Addie. When her companion seemed unwilling to respond, she darted in front of him, forcing him to meet her gaze. "Well?"

Sir Robert sighed. "Very well, Addie Shaw, I'll grant you've helped. But as I have also said before, you could have merely worked to disarm my natural caution. I cannot let down my guard."

"Oh, you . . . you are the single most stubborn, unreasonable, ridiculous man I've ever known!"

At that Sir Robert arched a brow. "And you've known many, have you?"

Addie flushed violently. "I resent your implication, sir. Of course I haven't known many men. But of those I've met through casual encounters, none has been as . . . as . . ."

He gave a wry chuckle. "You need not overexert yourself, since you so eloquently stated your opinion already. But it bothers me not at all."

Addie sniffed and turned, heading toward the stairs. The man was insufferable. And unrepentant.

Lord willing, Willis would pull through—even if Addie couldn't see how. A dagger had found its way beneath his armor, cutting deeply into his side. The poor man had lost quantities of blood, and his flesh had been swollen and hot to the touch when she first examined him. No amount of cleansing, ointment, or willow bark had broken his fever, and he'd spent hours tossing and turning in agony. Finally his exhausted body had fallen still, his mutters fractured and disjointed. Despite her best efforts, Addie believed Willis's death a certainty.

She climbed the stairs at a steady pace, as if approaching a gallows. Each step she took tightened her nerves, bringing them to violin-string tension. That strain then slowed her progress to a near halt.

When Sir Robert pointedly cleared his throat behind her, so close that she felt his heat along her back, she picked up her speed somewhat. Her pulse pounded in her ears, and fear dampened her palms. Still, holding herself straight, proud, Addie refused to allow the lord of Swynton Manor the pleasure of witnessing her fear.

When they reached Willis's side, Addie's heart twisted. The mortally wounded man seemed shrunken in his massive, once-powerful frame, eyes closed, face pale, chest scarcely moving the blanket over him. As he labored for his next breath, Addie prayed for mercy.

"I fear he has not long," whispered Thomasine.

Addie nodded, compassion for the suffering man overwhelming her. "It will be a blessing when the Lord takes him from this. . . ."

Thomasine nodded, then clasped Addie's hand. "You mustn't grieve so for him, dearie. You've done more than I ever could. 'Tis clearly God's will."

"The result of violent acts, you mean," Addie said, unable to keep the bitterness from her voice. "If Sir Robert prepared his men to resolve trouble by means other than combat, if he didn't insist on that blasted battle readiness he so pompously speaks of, then there would have been no clash with the . . . oh, yes, Morlands. They might have resorted to discourse, to working out their differences peaceably, reasonably. And Willis would be fine, able to face anything, rather than breathing his last."

"Ahem," said the man she'd just maligned. Addie drew back her shoulders, no longer caring what he thought of her opinion, just as he didn't care about hers.

"If we hadn't fought the Morlands, Mistress Shaw," said Robert Swynton, "I know not how many more lives we might have lost. They respect not women nor children nor those too old to work. They would have proceeded to the village and then within the manor walls. Everyone here would have been captured, tortured, or worse. Including the women you've befriended."

Addie glanced at Thomasine, who bit her lower lip and nodded. "But why fight?" she could not keep from asking. "Why not negotiate?"

"The Morlands settle matters by fighting to the bitter end. I owe it to all who depend on me to keep them safe, to protect them from the likes of your friends—"

"Oh, for goodness' sake! I don't know those Morlands—for which I'm eternally glad. If they're worse than you, why—"

"I see they leave you speechless, madam," he answered

with irony. "I answer to my king for everyone and everything on Swynton land. Richard Plantagenet knows a Swynton is loyal and true and cares for those under his protection."

"Richard Plantagenet?" she asked, thinking back to her knowledge of fifteenth-century English history. "Oh, that's right. You said it was May of 1485. Well, Sir Robert, if I were you, I wouldn't worry overmuch about Richard right now. Henry Tudor will take care of him soon enough."

Robert's dark eyes became pinpoints of accusation. "You dare tell me you know not the Morlands, yet speak thusly of our king?"

His vehemence stunned her. "What do you mean by that? Of course I don't know the Morlands. I've told you that a dozen times. And everyone knows Richard dies at Bosworth."

Robert took a step toward her. "What mean you, Mistress Shaw?"

Uh-oh. She should have taken greater care with her words. Still, seeing she knew what was to happen, she felt she should warn him, especially since so many depended on him, and in view of his dangerous allegiance to a doomed monarch.

In her best teacher's voice, she said, "In August of 1485 Henry's forces defeat Richard in the contest that becomes known as the Battle of Bosworth, bringing the Wars of the Roses to an end. Henry then establishes the Tudor dynasty. If you value your life, Robert Swynton, you'll keep quiet about your loyalty to Richard. Or you might also . . ." Addie wavered, unwilling to voice Robert's possible fate.

"You speak treason, madam," he said in a thunderous voice. "Henry lusts for the throne, but Richard is king. Like my father before me, I am Richard's man, and like my father, I shall fight to the death for my rightful sovereign. Not like those traitorous Morlands who back a pretender. Henry hasn't a chance to defeat Richard."

This latest history lesson was earning the same lack of

success as the one that had launched Addie's current predicament. She tried again. "Every book about England's past tells the tale of Richard's defeat. It will happen in August of this year."

Sir Robert's finely drawn lip curled in disgust. "Yet another blasphemy, woman. Will you now tell me you learned this in 1885?"

Uh-oh indeed. "Well . . . perhaps a bit earlier, while I attended school." When her words did nothing but make him step closer, Addie knew she'd brought trouble on herself again. Still, her conscience refused to let her slink away. She had to warn him. For if he continued with his current loyalties, Robert Swynton was doomed. And Addie couldn't bear to think that.

"Listen to me," she implored. "Everything I've said is true. Richard will die, and Henry will take the throne."

"You tell me now you know what the future holds?" he asked, his voice dangerously soft.

Addie held her ground. "I know what I've learned of the past. In 1885."

"But since 'tis only May of 1485, then August is yet to come—our future, of course."

Addie conceded defeat. "So be it. Future, past, it matters not one bit. In August, Richard will die at Redmoor near Market Bosworth."

"How dare you deny dabbling in sorcery while claiming to know the future?"

Addie bit her bottom lip. She was again caught in an impossible position. In a weary voice, she said, "I'm no sorceress, Sir Robert. I somehow landed four hundred years before my time in this infernal 1485 of yours. Against my will. And if you fight for Richard, then you will surely do so to the death this August next."

At her words, Addie heard Thomasine moan. Turning toward her friend, she found fear where she normally saw admiration. The older woman crossed herself and backed away from her side.

"Aye, Thomasine," Sir Robert said. "Stay away from her.

As far as you can. A higher authority than I will ultimately judge her, but as for me, her words are proof enough. I find her guilty of divination and witchcraft. We shall see what time in the dungeon will make her confess."

Chapter 7

ADDIE SAW HER life fly by as Thomasine hastened from the great hall in search of jailers. Her mind served a banquet of hideous visions—dungeons had a most unsavory reputation, doubtless deserved.

Heart pounding, fear coiling in her middle, an idea—a saving one, at that—came to her. "How can I help your wounded if you lock me up?"

Her question caught Sir Robert off guard. He looked startled, then narrowed his gaze and peered at her, the familiar suspicion back in his eyes. This time, however, something new tempered it. Addie wondered if it might be . . . admiration.

"You're clever enough to tempt me with what you know matters to me," he said, his voice firm as steel, "and your dark talents can certainly help you in that regard. But your argument does not persuade me."

"Isn't a man's life, regardless of how I save it, more important than being right?" she asked, determined to save herself from the dungeon. "I have never used evil means to heal. On the contrary, long ago I took to heart a lesson learned in church. *'Inasmuch as ye have done it unto one of the least of these my brethren, ye have done it unto me.'* I've lived by that for many years. Later, I was trained by a good physician, and I cannot watch another's pain without doing my best to help. That is why I achieve the success you've seen. *Nothing* would make me dabble with ungodly powers."

Her sincerity must have struck a chord with her captor since the taut lines of his face eased momentarily. His gaze became more curious, less accusatory. Sir Robert then studied Willis, as if to gauge the man's condition.

"He was doomed from the start, was he not?" he finally asked, the expression on his handsome face tired, defeated.

Addie looked at him with compassion. "The wound was mortal," she whispered. "I did what I could, but when a person loses that much blood, it's practically impossible for him to recover. Now, if I could have somehow replaced the lost blood with new . . . then perhaps he might have had better odds."

At that moment, the dying man opened his eyes. "Mistress . . . Addie . . ."

Dropping to her knees, she took his hand. "I'm here, Willis. How can I help? Would you like another drink?"

"Nay . . . 'twon't be long now. I want to . . . thank ye for your kindness. You're an angel straight from heaven, ye are."

Addie blushed at his praise and fought the tears that rushed to her eyes. He was right; the end was near. "Hush, now. There's no need for such gloomy thoughts. Don't talk and wear yourself out. You need to rest and regain your strength—"

He squeezed her fingers and stopped her words. "Nay, my lady . . . a man knows when his time has come. I'm just glad you're here with me."

One of those hot tears rolled down Addie's cheek. She had nothing more to say, no more comfort to offer, so she held tight to Willis's hand and began to hum. A weak smile curved his pale lips, and she felt him relax again.

Despite the sadness choking her, she sang the words to her favorite hymn. "Amazing grace . . ."

With every note, the grip on her fingers lessened. As she sang the last words of the song, she felt life leave her patient, his last breath escape his breast. Addie sobbed, yet thanked God that Willis's suffering had finally ended. Placing his hand on his chest, she offered a quiet prayer, then stood, ready to face her fate.

"One has died, despite my best efforts," she said, staring at Sir Robert through a veil of tears. "Will it be your dungeon or a noose?"

To her surprise, moisture glistened on his thick, dark lashes. He didn't immediately respond. Then two well-built youths, daggers unsheathed, ran into the hall, coming to a halt one on either side of her.

A scream of horror formed deep in her gut, but Addie refused to give it sound. Instead, she focused on Sir Robert, daring him to blame her for his man's death.

After an eternity, he shook his head. "Nay, Addie Shaw, 'twon't be either." Turning to the man at her right, he said, "Go on. She had naught to do with Willis's death. The Morlands are to blame, and, by God, they'll pay. There is no profit in locking her away. Others can benefit from her gifts."

As the two men left, hesitating every few steps to make sure their lord didn't change his mind again, Addie felt what she imagined a condemned man must feel at the news of a reprieve. Indeed, Sir Robert had condemned her to die, and for some unfathomable reason, he had suddenly changed his mind.

"Might I ask why the change of heart?" she asked, more curious than cautious.

He turned his back to her, waved a hand, then said, "I doubt you would have sung him to heaven if you had hastened his death."

"Thank you."

He shrugged off her gratitude. Addie dropped down to

Willis's corpse and covered his face with the sheet. "Who will see to the burying?"

"I'll have Father Anselm come, even if Willis did die unshriven."

"Not at all. Nell and I made sure he received communion earlier today."

"Thank you."

"I did it for him, not you."

"I know, and since he can no longer thank you, I do so in his stead."

Addie accepted his words with a nod. Then, glancing around her makeshift surgery, now empty of all patients save the one who had just died, she wondered if the lord of Swynton Manor would allow her to return to the kitchen and work at Nell's side again. There was much she could do to improve the living conditions at the manor.

"Since I've no one else to nurse now," she said tentatively, "I would like to help the women in the kitchen. Will you worry I might feed you poisoned food?"

His dark gaze captured hers. He held it for a moment, then shook his head. "I doubt you would do something so foolish. It seems your craft is more that of a soothsayer's than that of a witch."

"Why do you insist on such ridiculous things?"

"Why do you insist on speaking of time travel, on telling the future? A most gloomy one for King Richard. And how do you explain your charming ways? My people have taken to you despite my warnings. You have obviously cast a spell over all at Swynton Manor."

Irritation made her reckless. "If I had, perhaps I would have charmed you, too, sir. It's perfectly clear I haven't done that. Don't you think if I indeed possessed the powers you think I do I would have worked doubly hard to win you over?"

Sir Robert's jaw clenched tight. His brows collided over the bridge of his nose. His eyes again bore into hers, and Addie sensed confusion, turbulence within him. But he uttered not a word.

After long moments of perturbing scrutiny, he spun on his heel and stalked from the hall, muttering under his breath. If it weren't so utterly preposterous, Addie would have sworn he'd said, "Who says you've not snared me in your spell?"

Robert escaped from the great hall, furious with himself. How could he let that woman get to him this way? How could he let her appeal to his sympathies? He should have sent her to the dungeon as he had initially planned. At least that way he would be safe from the lure of those gray eyes, her keen intelligence, her kindness and softness of heart.

But he had been incapable of locking her up in that dark, damp cell. Not after she sang so sweetly to Willis, eased his last moments of life. Surely she wasn't all bad if she cared enough to remain at the dying man's side, to offer what comfort and aid she could at the end. And her tears had been genuine. Her failure to save Willis's life had deeply affected her.

She was a gentle, caring woman.

Was she also a Morland spy?

His certainty began to waver. Badly. Surely a spy had no scruples, no emotions that suffering might engage. No spy he had heard of hid willingness to help an enemy. Addie Shaw displayed an abundance of scruples, emotion, and will to help.

She also had an uncanny ability to capture his attention and hold it tenaciously. He couldn't stop thinking of her, regardless of what he tried. He had spent hour after hour practicing under Mortimer's curious scrutiny. He had assiduously avoided her presence. He had forced himself to pore over farm profits, records of all sorts. Still, each time he closed his eyes, he remembered how Addie had looked in his arms, her silver eyes filled with fear, her lips quivering with . . . he didn't quite know what. And he wanted desperately to know.

As he wanted to know why she had so captured his interest when she never should have. She wasn't beautiful, but she had something . . . something indefinable that stole a man's attention and would not let it go. At least, that was what she had done to him. And Robert despised the results.

"Accursed woman . . ."

"So that's what's got you working my lads to a pulp these days!" exclaimed Mortimer. Robert hadn't noticed the smaller man's approach. He had stormed out of the manor, his mind filled with thoughts of Addie.

" 'Tis the desire to prevent another ambush that has me training these days."

Mortimer snorted. "I've lived too many years for you to try to persuade me of that. She's a spirited one, is Adelaide Shaw."

Feeling his cheeks warm, Robert raised an eyebrow. "A man can't hone his skills these days without you assuming a woman is involved?"

Mortimer chuckled. "When his skills are sharper than his sword, and all he does is trump his opponent in seconds, one wonders what's behind his diligence. A woman explains much."

Robert knew when evasion would avail him no more. "Damn woman's a sorceress."

"Why say you that, lad?"

"Look around. She has Nell and Thomasine taking orders from her, and I've yet to meet two less tractable women. Then there are the men she healed. From what's been said, she has received no less than four proposals of marriage and an abundance of less honorable ones."

"So that's what ails ye!"

Robert scoffed and began striding toward the practice quintain.

Mortimer followed, sticking to him like a thistle. "You can run from me, but you cannot escape the truth. Adelaide Shaw has worked her way under your skin. By my troth, and 'tis a good thing to see. About time your heart found someone to lo—"

"I have found no such thing, and I'd much prefer we discuss our readiness for another Morland attack." For good measure, Robert leveled a quelling stare on his master-at-arms.

Mortimer spat in disgust. "We're ready for them, and you know it. They won't take Swynton Manor. Not while Mortimer Swift is your master-at-arms. And just as that's a certainty, so is Addie's presence in your home, in your head, and, sooner or later, in your heart."

Robert continued striding, refusing to acknowledge what he feared had already become true enough.

After her unexpected but much appreciated reprieve, Addie had kept to the kitchens. She'd had much to teach the women there, and was happily reaping the fruits of her efforts. No longer did the table at Swynton Manor threaten the lives of those who supped there.

She had taught Nell the joys of making conserves. Taking advantage of the berry brambles surrounding Swynton Manor, they had sent five little girls to gather strawberries, elderberries, and wild raspberries. Although their stained faces bore evidence of the quantities consumed before the fruit reached the stoves, the kitchen had smelled of sweet, simmering fruit for days.

Now, rows of beeswax-sealed crocks lined a shelf in the pantry, while Addie kept an eye on the apple, pear, and plum trees blooming outside. More bounty to be processed was sure to come from them.

When one of the men found a buck dying from a broken leg, Addie had claimed the meat for the kitchens. They'd roasted some, and over Nell's objections, she had taught the women to corn the meat using saltpeter. The days were warm, unseasonably so, and she'd feared the meat would simply spoil if she didn't preserve it somehow.

She had also taught the women to slice the venison for jerky, then rub it thoroughly with salt. She'd sent the strips to the smokehouse, which, thanks to the abundance of apple and alder trees in the vicinity, was well stocked with fragrant fuel. When the meat strips dried, she'd had them hung in sacks from the rafters to keep out the ever-present rodents.

The work had surprisingly satisfied her.

Only yesterday Thomasine mentioned that even the village women had heard of Addie's rules of cleanliness, and the cases of "flux" had gone down appreciably. Many digestive ailments could be avoided, as Doc Horst had taught her.

With an hour to spare before the evening meal, Addie did as she'd taken to doing of late. She slipped out the gate, darting nervous glances behind her, hoping no one noticed her departure. Especially not Sir Robert Swynton himself.

She hadn't seen him since the day Willis died. But she'd felt his presence a number of times. He was clearly avoiding her, which was fine with her. She didn't need to hear any more outlandish accusations.

What she needed was to find the oak with the darkened bark to go home to Emmie.

With another furtive look toward the Swynton gate, she allowed herself a deep breath, certain no one had seen her. She scurried to the woods, which were mercifully not too far away.

Under cover of the spring-garbed trees, she rolled her neck and shoulders, releasing some of the tension that built up every day as she lived with the knowledge of her imprisonment.

She relished the blessed relief.

But only for a moment. She had business at hand.

From her pocket she withdrew the piece of burnt wood with which she marked the trees she tested after making sure they didn't get her where she wanted to go.

She was going home. It didn't matter how long it took her to find the tree, but she was going to do it. Who knew what kind of trouble Emmie had found, who she might have hurt in the process? Besides, Addie had no desire to stay in a time or place where her every action, her very existence, was suspect.

By a man who had killed right before her eyes.

At that thought, Addie searched the shadows for Robert's men. She saw nothing but trees, heard nothing but the song of robins up above. Still, remembering her encounters with the lord of Swynton Manor, she knew he had someone watching her. He was, perhaps, even watching her himself.

Gasping for breath, little Mick Hoskins ran up to Robert. "M'lord! I came as fast as I could, like you said I should. She's a-leavin' the bailey and goin' off to th'woods."

Sudden anger in his gut, Robert turned from his steward and stalked off, leaving Walter openmouthed. Every step he took cursed him for a fool. He'd let silver eyes lull him into easing his vigilance. Yet he'd known better than to listen to Addie's protestations of innocence. No innocent woman wandered the countryside on her own. Certainly not when, coincidentally, the Morlands ambushed his party.

He approached the thicket of trees with caution, not wanting to alert his prey. Taking care not to step on a twig or rustle the dead leaves on the ground, he went deeper into the shade. As his eyes grew accustomed to the reduced light, he heard a familiar voice muttering, clearly in disgust.

"I *know* that blasted tree is here somewhere," Addie groused. "It didn't just disappear. Now, which one is it?"

To his amazement, Addie stomped up to a massive oak, plopped down at its foot, leaned against the trunk, closed her eyes, and . . . waited.

"Come on, come on!" she cried. "Drop away. I know you're the right oak."

But no matter how fervently she implored, the tree did nothing of the sort. Not that Robert had expected it to do anything at all. But it was obvious *she* did.

Bemused, he scratched his head and donned a crooked, indulgent grin. Did she honestly expect the tree to budge? Surely not.

Did she?

Fascinated by the odd scene, Robert remained hidden, silent. He wanted to see what she would do next.

To his astonishment, she stood, swiped roughly at a tear that gleamed at the corner of one eye, then took a piece of burnt wood and drew a large *X* on the trunk.

"Another one down," she said, her voice revealing her frustration and exhaustion. She then turned and peered directly at him.

Robert caught his breath, fearing she had discovered his hiding place. But it seemed she hadn't, for she marched with determination to another oak, this one just a few feet away from him, and went through the same procedure all over again.

When she stood, more tears ran down her rosy cheeks. Amusing though her actions were, the evidence of her misery tugged at Robert's heart. Evidently she *did* believe she'd gone through a tree. And her failure to repeat the feat was causing her great distress.

"Oh, Emmie," she moaned. "I hope you haven't done anything foolish. I hope you haven't hurt anyone . . . especially not yourself."

Who was Emmie? Robert wondered, then cast the thought aside as Addie came closer to his tree. She sat under another oak, and when she leaned back with her eyes squeezed shut, he took the opportunity to put distance between them.

He watched her repeat her actions over and over again, each time with more tenacity, less sadness, more anger in her movements.

"I know you're here," she finally cried out, fists clenched at her sides. She turned in slow circles and glared at the unyielding trees. "I'm going to find you. Even if it takes the rest of my life. I'm not mad, I'm no sorceress, and I *did* fall through an oak tree."

After her preposterous declaration, she marched toward the edge of the thicket, clearly intent on leaving the woods. Robert watched and waited, unwilling to reveal his presence. He didn't know how she would react.

Then the oddest thing happened to this most peculiar of women. She fell. For no apparent reason. She just . . . fell, crying out in obvious pain.

As Addie lay on the ground, writhing and clutching an ankle, Robert forced himself to wait. Then, when he could no longer bear to watch her suffer, he emerged from the woods a short distance from where she lay. He ran toward her, then slowed as he came within a few steps.

"What happened?" he asked.

She started, then when she saw it was him, said with a sob, "I don't know. I was . . . walking in the woods, and when I stepped past these trees, something caught me across the front of my legs. I fell."

Robert gave the area she indicated a brief inspection but found nothing out of the ordinary. He knelt at her side, then reached for her injured leg. "May I?"

She blushed, nodded tightly, tears still squeezing past her lids.

He lifted her skirts, and noticed the swelling above the edge of her slipper. He pressed the puffy flesh with gentle fingers, seeking to learn the extent of the damage. She winced at his touch but didn't cry out. He continued his exploration.

"This would never have happened if Nell had given me back my boots," she said. "They're sturdier and grip the ground better than these flimsy slippers she insists I wear. They're the proper footwear for a lady, she says. My boots are better, I say. Besides, they were practically new. And I paid a pretty penny for them."

"Nell likely felt those strange boots you wore when I first found you might cause you trouble when you walked. They had those exaggerated stacks at the heel."

To Robert's dismay, the memory of slender ankles in lace-trimmed boots leaped to his mind, affecting him in a way they should not, especially when one of the ankles in question was hurt. He made himself think of the dent the shoes had poked into Mortimer's armor instead of how alluring they'd made Addie's legs look. He smiled and focused on the injury.

As Robert prodded the center of the swelling, Addie cried out, and another tear ran down her face. "The bone appears sound," he said. "But I doubt you can walk on it."

She drew a shaky breath. "I suspect it's sprained."

"What is that?"

"A wrenching or twisting injury to a joint," she said in a somewhat condescending tone. Did she think him stupid? A child?

He studied her pained expression and decided 'twas the effects of her injury that caused her to address him in such a manner. "It does look that way. Regardless, you cannot walk on it. I'll carry you home."

She averted her gaze, then gave a tight nod. Robert slid his arms around her and brought her close. With ease, he stood, again marveling at how little she weighed. Although taller than other women he knew, Addie was slender, willowy, and caused him no strain.

As he stepped into the June sunlight, he admitted to himself how much he enjoyed cradling her in his arms, pressing her firm, womanly body close to his. She wrapped her arms around his neck, fixed her eyes on his face.

Again awareness rippled through him and, to his dismay, pooled in his groin. Difficult to understand though it might be, Addie Shaw heated his blood like no other woman had.

Robert wondered if his response came as a result of the danger she represented, if somehow his perverse desires enjoyed flirting with disaster in the form of a treacherous woman.

He'd had the experience of finding himself fully aroused in the midst of violent combat, but other men assured him that was common. This . . . unruly desire for a woman who might have entered his life seeking to end it seemed madness of a most extraordinary sort.

But no matter what he thought or feared, he found it impossible to tear his gaze from her face, her soft, parted lips. Hunger for her taste overtook him, stunning him with its intensity. At that moment, he noticed the expression on Addie's face. It seemed the same web of need tangled around him had caught her in its gossamer yet undeniable hold. Her eyelids swept languidly down her pretty eyes, her skin donned a hint of flush over her high cheekbones, her moist lips quivered, and her breasts rose and fell with a gentle sigh.

Nothing could have kept him from acting on his desire.

Robert brought his lips down on those so sweetly calling to him, and as hers molded to his, he marveled at the wonder of kissing Addie Shaw.

Chapter 8

THE LAST THING Robert saw before his lips touched heaven was the shimmer of tears in pools of liquid silver. Then he drowned in incredible softness, lost himself in a gentle giving unlike anything he had known before.

Addie had tensed in his arms, but as his lips wooed a response from hers, she relaxed and now lay pliant against him, her lips parting on the softest of sighs.

He deepened the caress, and sweetness overtook his senses. The richest confection couldn't taste half as sweet as did Addie Shaw. Surely she was a sorceress, an enchantress. This kiss assured him of that, for as he grew acquainted with the silky smoothness of her mouth, Robert no longer cared whether she was a witch, a soothsayer, or even a Morland.

He only knew he wanted to kiss Addie forever. As he delved into her mouth, she tightened her clasp around his neck, molded her body to his. His arms pulled her closer still, and her breasts pressed against his chest—his unshielded chest. He had worn armor or mail the other times he'd held Addie, but now he felt the warmth of the woman, the round fullness of her flesh.

His blood caught fire. If he'd wanted her before, madness

now stole over him, as need for this stranger who had landed in his care ran rampant through him.

With a wriggle she pressed tighter against him, and Robert nipped at her full bottom lip. Its satiny texture gave under his assault, making him wonder how it would feel to have her yield to a more intimate invasion. The taste of the woman intoxicated him; her spicy sweetness tempted him to relinquish his habitual control.

Hungry for more of her essence, Robert allowed himself to lick at the corner of her lips, but this time, mingled with her natural flavor, he tasted the salty tang of tears. He remembered why he held her in his arms. Still, even though he knew her pain, he couldn't bring himself to end the kiss. Instead, he deepened his exploration, delving into the secret cavern of her mouth.

At the touch of his tongue against hers, she started, stiffening again. He murmured low in his chest, refusing to let her break the connection between them. He hadn't yet had enough. And it suddenly occurred to him that he might never have enough of Addie Shaw.

That thought doused his ardor.

He pulled away, opening his eyes only to catch himself on her silver gaze. Bewilderment hovered in those depths, and the flush deepened on her cheeks. Then she lowered her lashes, ending her scrutiny. Robert shook his head and took determined steps toward home and sanity. Still, he couldn't help wondering what went through her mind just then.

Addie felt as though someone had taken her world, shaken it, then plunked it back down, the elements still swirling as if they hadn't yet realized they'd hit solid ground again.

The pain in her ankle had faded to nothing under the flood of sensations Robert's closeness unleashed. And then . . . his kiss. Nothing Addie remembered came close to those indescribable feelings.

Heat.

Hunger.

Need.

His lips, softer than she had thought a man's mouth would be, had pressed against hers, sending shafts of warmth straight to parts that had never known such fire. And he'd gone farther, breaching the seal of her lips. The intimacy had shocked her . . . initially. Then, sensing his pleasure, she had yielded to his exploration. Waves of piercing intimacy had broken over her, threatening to drown her in pleasure.

The touch of their lips, the rub of their tongues, the press of her breasts against his chest . . . Addie had felt brand-new, and she had wanted the experience never to end. Robert's kisses were better than worrying over her sister, over what the future might hold. In his arms she felt like a woman, all woman, for the first time in her life.

And for that she had this man to thank, a man she didn't dare trust, this man who had killed without remorse.

This man also cared deeply for those in his keeping. She remembered the glisten of tears on his lashes when Willis breathed his last. And she couldn't discount his tender touch when he had examined her ankle only moments ago. Addie knew that although he didn't trust her any more than she trusted him, he hadn't had the heart to cast her in a dungeon, even if his change of heart had come against his better judgment.

Robert Swynton was a good man.

And he had an undeniable talent for kissing a woman senseless. Addie couldn't believe she'd allowed him such liberties. She couldn't believe she'd given free rein to her urges, entertained such crazy thoughts. About a man from 1485. A man who held her fate in his hands as long as she remained an oddity out of time.

"Put me down!"

At her command, he tightened his grip and kept walking.

Addie slugged his shoulder. Robert didn't flinch. She repeated her demand.

"Nonsense," he said, exasperation in his voice. "You cannot put weight on that foot."

Tipping back her head, Addie glared down the length of

her nose—as best she could, considering she lay in his arms. "I'll not have you manhandle me again."

He arched an eyebrow. "You deny you enjoyed my kiss?"

"Oooh, you cad!" she cried, furious as the heat of a blush swept up her cheeks. "Of course I do. You took advantage of my injury."

Robert laughed. "I can't deny that, but you could have stopped me. I wonder why you now protest so. Is it perhaps because you enjoyed it too much?"

His dark gaze remained fixed on her, again making Addie wonder if he could see straight to her soul. She looked away before he could discover how right he was.

Injecting as much starch as she could into her voice, she said, "I can hobble to the manor. Why, I'll crawl if I have to. What I will not do is allow you any more intimacies—unwelcome at that."

To her amazement, the always-in-command Robert Swynton stumbled. Her gaze flew to his face, registering the wrinkling of his brow, the chilling of his gaze, the tightening of his jaw, the clamping of his lips.

Conversely, his arms loosened around her, and for a moment she feared he might drop her.

Then he squared his shoulders, snugged his hold on her again, and in a clipped voice said, "I've half a mind to let you find your way back on that damaged ankle, but my conscience works overmuch. Madam, you have made your feelings perfectly clear. In the future, I will refrain from forcing my *unwelcome* attentions on you. I have a wealth of practice doing just that."

The bitterness in his voice made Addie wonder what had happened in his life, but the chill in his demeanor kept her from asking. Was he saying he made a habit of forcing himself on unwilling women?

She nearly snorted with laughter. There wasn't a woman at Swynton Manor who hadn't voiced her wish to satisfy her lord's most intimate needs, so Addie couldn't imagine one rejecting his advances.

Besides her. And she had done so for good reason. *Very*

good reason. "Then do us both a favor and put me down," she said, fighting her most unreasonable longing to stay right where she was.

Robert kept walking as if she hadn't spoken. "We're nearly there, and I will gladly relieve you of my presence as soon as Thomasine sees to your foot. Until then, I pray you find the sense to say nothing more."

Stung by his words, Addie felt the urge to argue, to fight him, but embarrassment—and pride—kept her silent.

He had made his feelings abundantly clear. He didn't want her on his property, even if he felt responsible for her while he remained uncertain of her intentions toward those he cared for.

An imp at the back of her mind reminded her that he'd kissed her. Soundly.

Why?

Well, that really didn't matter. Did it?

She didn't want to be here either. She would leave as soon as she found that confounded oak. As soon as her foot was well enough for her to resume her search, she would return to 1885 and stay there. Then neither she nor Robert would be forced to endure the other's unwanted presence.

They would never have to see each other again.

But as Addie silently repeated that sentiment, a twinge of conscience reminded her to be honest, at least with herself.

She *had* enjoyed Robert's kiss. More than anything else in her lonely life. And the thought of never seeing him again left a hollow feeling in her heart.

So she didn't want his kisses, hadn't liked them, she'd said. Then why had she pressed her breasts against him, wrapped herself around him like a lithe and deadly snake?

What kind of game did Addie Shaw play? Was she one of Morland's spies, out to destroy him and all he held dear?

Although the evidence pointed toward treachery, something visceral rejected that possibility, made Robert hope Addie was innocent of his suspicions, if thoroughly mad.

"Damn the woman," he muttered, kicking a rock in his path.

"I tell you, lad," Mortimer said, startling Robert. "Worked her way under your skin, she has, and there's only one way to deal with a woman like that."

He glared at Mortimer, irritated to again be caught off guard. When had the rotund little man become so silent in his approach? And when had Robert become so engrossed in thoughts of Addie that he might have missed the approach of an enemy army?

That thought made him angrier still. "What gem of wisdom do you offer to remedy my condition?"

Mortimer chuckled, his cheeks red with mirth. "Why, lad, you must bed her. 'Tis the only way, you know."

Remembering Addie's rejection, Robert set his jaw against another surge of desire. "The lady wants me no more than I want her."

At that, Mortimer's laughter rang out in seemingly endless peals. Finally, wiping his eyes, he said, "Have you tried a touch of persuasion? A kiss or two?"

Robert vividly remembered the caresses he and Addie had shared, but he had no intention of letting Mortimer know exactly what had transpired. "Of course not," he said, perhaps blustering a bit. "Neither wants the other."

Wicked glee twinkled in Mortimer's knowing blue eyes. "Then the fire in your face matches not that in your staff?"

Robert rammed a hand through his hair. "She's a spy! Think you I'm so rash as to satisfy an itch with one who will likely off me while I sleep in her arms? Not that she would have me. Or I her. As she—er—*I* said."

"Aha!" crowed Swynton's master-at-arms. "So you've tried, she said nay, and you gave up. Funny, I've never known Robert Swynton as a quitter. Exceptin' when it comes to women . . . like Catherine Morland and now Addie Shaw."

Humiliation burned in Robert's gut. What was it about him? He'd married a woman who came to hate his touch, and now his loins burned for another who, although she caught fire in his arms, demanded he keep his distance.

Which he should do, rightly enough. He trusted her not at all. But he wanted her. And feared for his sanity, torn as he was between reason and passion.

He caught Mortimer's concerned look and stood tall, shoulders square. "A quitter? A man wise enough to avoid those who despise him is hardly a quitter."

"Mayhap more a fool instead," suggested his friend. "A man who sees not what's before his nose is a fool. You've been scenting that woman since you found her, as a stallion does a mare in heat. And like a mare, she's dancing skittish. 'Tis the stallion who decides the outcome of the dance. He either quits or he persists."

Ignoring the hot, graphic image Mortimer's comparison drew in his mind, Robert scoffed. "I have not time, energy, or interest to dance—"

"Sir Robert! Sir Robert!"

At the sound of his name, Robert turned and saw a mail-clad Neville Smith drop from his horse and run to his side. "Yes?"

Panting, the man paused momentarily. "I've news of the Morlands. 'Twould appear Michael is leading them toward Wales. Word has Henry Tudor about to set sail, and he aims to land there."

Everything in Robert chilled. Just two days before, he'd received word from the Commissioners of Array in Yorkshire, ordering him to prepare troops to do the king's service upon an hour's warning, should the need arise. Richard's dread of Henry continued to grow and, if this man's message was true, with reason aplenty. Danger was nigh.

As Addie had indicated.

For the first time in a very long time, Robert felt fear, true, deep, gut-wrenching fear. Not of the future, of the possibility of upcoming battle, not even of death, but of Addie's unholy knowledge.

Had he welcomed a demon to his home?

How had she known of Henry's imminent threat? What

else did she know that could harm his king? His people? Himself?

At that, Robert's fear turned to anger, becoming a swirling red rage that propelled him forward. Ignoring the messenger's question and shrugging aside Mortimer's restraining hand, he started toward the kitchen.

Striding into the open doorway, Robert turned on Nell. "Where is she?"

She faced him, frowning. "Who, son?"

He frowned at the woman who had raised him, and chafed at the knowing look in her eyes. "Addie Shaw, of course."

Nell's scowl deepened as she broadcast her displeasure at his tone of voice. He suspected she also objected to the thunderous expression he knew he wore, but Robert didn't care. Not right then. He only cared to hear the truth from the witch's own lips. "Well?"

"She's in the buttery storing the elderberry wine she made. What want you with her?"

"That's between Addie Shaw and me."

"But . . ."

Robert knew his behavior was uncharacteristic, unreasonable. Later on, after he'd had his say with Mistress Shaw, he would return to Nell and beg her forgiveness. Right now he had to acknowledge the awful truth. His body craved the tender mercies of a soothsaying witch, one who likely had formed an unholy alliance with his king's greatest foe.

He ran to the manor, not bothering to respond to the greetings his people sent his way, his focus on the buttery and the woman he would reportedly find there.

The woman he nearly ran down when he took the last three steps to the first floor in one lunge.

"Oh!" she exclaimed. "I didn't know anyone was there—"

"Tell me now," he demanded. "How did you know?"

Puzzlement appeared on her face. "How did I know what?"

"About Henry. And Richard."

She waved. "Oh, that. I told you I've read a number of history books. In school, you understand."

The red rage turned deeper, darker. He saw nothing, heard nothing but his blood pounding in his head. "Do not lie! I want to know where you gained your knowledge."

Addie huffed, then donned that disgusted look she so often used on him. "I—just—told—you," she said slowly, carefully enunciating each word as if he were a dunce. "I dearly love history and read much at school."

In frustration, Robert grasped her upper arms and fought the urge to shake her. "There are no history texts telling tales that have not happened yet, tales that smack of treason. Speak the truth, woman! The Morlands sent you to distract me while they prepare to help Henry usurp Richard's throne, did they not?"

She rolled her eyes and tried to shake off his grasp, but Robert's emotions ran too wild, too powerful just then to yield to her silent request. He held firm.

She glared. "How many times must I tell you I don't know any Morlands? I know about Richard and Henry because everyone in 1885 can read of their feud if they wish. I told you the other day that Richard will die at Redmoor, near Market Bosworth, on August twenty-second, 1485. The conflict will become known as the Battle of Bosworth, and the Tudors will rule England for centuries. Richard is the last Plantagenet monarch."

"I'll hear no more foolish talk of books. What know you of Henry's intentions? I must send word to Richard of the pretender's plans."

Again Addie tried to free herself, but the more she strove against him, the more determined Robert grew to keep her captive. "I told you, I'm no expert in medieval history," she said. "I don't know any more than I've already said. Now, if you would be so kind as to let me go, Nell is waiting for me in the kitchen."

"The punishment for treason—"

"I'm not a traitor," she spat, eyes flashing silver daggers of rage. "I'm a teacher. I'm lost in the wrong century. I soundly object to your behavior. Unhand me, please, so I may return to the kitchen."

"How long will you use this foolish tale of traveling through time to excuse your actions? 'Tis bad enough you consort with Satan himself to learn the future—*if,* as you say, you don't know the Morlands."

Her expression grew mutinous. "I'll insist I've traveled through time until the day I die. I *know* where I grew up, I know where I taught school, I know my neighbors, my town, my country, my name. I *know* where I came from, even if I don't quite know how. Could we please not discuss this again?"

"Once I know you'll do no harm with your unholy knowledge."

"Oh, for goodness' sake! An education doesn't qualify as unholy knowledge, and I have *never* consorted with"—at this, she shivered delicately, and the tremor ran from her arms to his hands, affecting him more than it ought—"Satan."

Robert could see she wasn't about to divulge a thing. He would have to resort to stronger measures. "Perhaps the dungeon will persuade you to speak the truth. I can have you watched there at all times."

She snorted in a most unladylike but most Addie-like fashion. "As if you hadn't been doing that already."

"What mean you?"

A look of extreme forbearance blossomed on her face. "Someone follows me everywhere I go."

"Do you accuse me of that?"

She shrugged.

"I haven't the time to pursue you, madam."

"Then someone does it for you. I'm not mad, and someone is never more than a step behind me. I feel him watching every move I make, listening to every word I say. In fact, I'm certain someone followed me into the woods the day I turned my ankle. I wondered often enough if it wasn't you."

"Think you I would do that?" Robert asked, fighting the flush that threatened to fill his cheeks with guilt. He'd had Mick Hoskins watch Addie, but the lad hadn't gone into the woods. Robert had been the only one there.

Addie sniffed. "I wouldn't put anything past a man as suspicious as you." A haughty tilt of her nose accompanied her words.

"I didn't . . ." He let his words trail off in defeat. He had been in the woods. Following her.

She smiled in triumph as he flushed in mortification. "Did you set the trap that tripped me, too?" she asked, challenge in her silver eyes.

That shook him. "What trap?"

"The one stretched between the two trees. The one that caught my legs and made me fall."

Her words stunned him. "'Twas no accident that day?"

"Precisely."

Her assertion so astounded Robert that he momentarily loosened his hold on her arms. She took advantage of his distraction and ran down the stairs. "Wait!" he cried, questions thundering through his head.

"For what?" she tossed back, never slowing her descent. "More of your irrational accusations? Next thing I know, you'll paint me the author of Henry's feud against Richard, neither of whom I've met, since I've only recently come to their time and place."

Perhaps he had pushed her too far. "I'll agree to set aside the time-travel nonsense if you explain your reason for suspecting foul play."

She didn't pause at the foot of the stairs but headed straight for the outdoors. "I don't normally trip over my own feet, sir. I am the most cautious, practical woman I know. I don't entertain silly notions, as I've always had to concern myself with reality, and rely on nothing but common sense to weigh matters. Something caught my shins and caused my fall."

As Addie made her outlandish declaration, she ran out into the bailey and paused, blinking. The bright afternoon sun set off the sheen of her brown hair, making it look silkier, softer than usual. For a moment Robert stared at that thick, sleek mass coiled into a loose, fluffy knot at the crown of her head, soft tendrils kissing her neck, her temples, her ears. 'Twas surely the most ridiculous hairstyle, and she refused to cover her head as other women did—no cauls or wimples for Addie Shaw—but Robert secretly relished the freedom to admire her thick hair and wonder how it would feel spread across his chest as they labored to reach the pinnacle of pleasure—

"Look up!" cried Mortimer, panic in his voice.

Doing so, Robert ran out and saw the boulder teetering on the roofline of the manor. The rock tipped over the edge and began to fall.

Addie stood in its path, frozen by fear.

Robert lunged at her. *"Addie!"*

Wrapping his arms around her frozen body, he threw every ounce of his strength into moving her to safety. They fell to the cobbles, rolling with the momentum of his leap. A thunderous crack sounded at his back, and the earth shuddered beneath them.

Robert's heart stopped, aware they had just defeated death.

Everything around them was silent, even the pigs, the doves, the chicks.

For a moment he lay there, his body covering Addie's, scarcely daring to breathe, hearing the renewed pounding of his heart, feeling the rush of blood through his veins. Robert grew painfully aware of that very life he suddenly treasured, his every sense acutely sharp. He felt the soft body beneath his, heard the stuttering spurts of Addie's breath, smelled the dirt on the cobbles mixed with the gentle spice of womanly flesh.

Then Mortimer cried, "Go up there! Find who did this. Posthaste, men!"

Out of the corner of his eye, Robert saw Harold fly by, Jamie at his heels. Ned followed, as did others who could do so thanks only to Addie's help.

Then she shuddered. "Are you hurt?" he asked.

She shook her head, and a raw sob broke from her lips. Slowly he rose on his elbows. He raked her with an assessing stare, verifying the truth of her denial. Not a speck of blood showed on her clothes, and although he weighed many pounds more than she did, he didn't think he had crushed any delicate bones when he stole her from the jaws of death.

Again she sobbed, and the sound cut straight to his heart. He rolled over, then wrapped his arms around her, settling her on his lap. For long moments, he simply held her, his hand smoothing down her back, wiping away the dirt and straw she had picked up as they avoided disaster.

Still, her weeping continued. "Hush, now, you're fine," he murmured.

"But I might not have been."

He smiled at her contrary statement. How very like her. "Don't entertain such thoughts. They can only disturb you more."

Tear-filled eyes sought his, begged his understanding, and Robert felt her need in the deepest corner of his heart.

"You don't understand," she said, her voice gaining strength. "I nearly died. Moments after you accused me of plotting against your king, against you. Will you also accuse me of somehow rigging that rock to fall on me as I left the manor? Do you honestly think I've come to cause you harm? When all I've done is help? It seems to me I'm the only one who's been hurt of late."

As her words sank in, Robert was forced to accept the truth in them. If she was a spy, she would never risk injury. She would protect herself so she could work her evil. She wouldn't be the victim of her efforts. And if Addie was indeed a soothsayer, then surely she would have foreseen the danger about to befall her.

Would she not?

Chapter 9

AS ROBERT DRIFTED off to sleep that night, he continued to ponder the puzzle that was Addie Shaw. If she was a sorceress, then she was a peculiarly inept one. While she insisted she knew when and what harm would befall King Richard, she had yet to foresee trouble meant for her.

As had become the norm, he slept poorly, his dreams filled with visions of Addie: a fiery Addie standing up to him; a warm and yielding Addie, lips beckoning; a compassionate Addie, fighting to save the lives of his men.

As had also become frustratingly common, he awoke the next morning painfully aroused. What personal flaw made him want women who rejected him?

As Robert splashed cold water on his face, hoping to wash away his pointless thoughts, he again vowed to avoid Addie at all cost. Too much and too many depended on him; he could not let her distract him again.

After breaking his fast, he had Cuthbert, his squire, help him don armor. He had to face facts. Someone had tried to hurt Addie. Twice. He knew not why.

And she was under his protection, regardless of who or what she was.

A twinge of conscience challenged him to admit the entire truth. Beyond his sense of responsibility toward everyone at Swynton, including his uninvited guest, he had feelings for Addie Shaw. Feelings he ought not feel.

That weakness irritated him. Enough that, when he reached the practice area, he attacked the practice quintain with a vengeance, digging his broadsword deep into the wooden post.

Cursing fluently, he fought to pull it out, his thoughts on his situation rather than the task at hand. His temper flared, and his efforts proved futile. At least he had not lashed out at one of his men in a mock duel. He might have done irreparable harm—if not of the physical sort then to the respect he needed to command.

Muttering yet more imprecations, he wrestled with the sword.

"You can't still think her a Morland spy, can you?" asked Mortimer as he pushed Robert away from the quintain and easily pulled the sword from where it had become lodged.

By damn, he'd again been too deep in thought over Addie to hear his man's approach. He needed to exercise more care, else he would soon join Willis at Morland hands. "I know not what to think of her."

"But you no longer deny thinking of her," Mortimer chortled. "Aplenty."

Robert shrugged, then, realizing his gesture most likely had gone unnoticed under his armor, said, "No."

"And you agree someone tried to hurt her."

"Of course."

"Then what's brought you out in such a fine mood?"

Robert doffed his helmet and studied his master-at-arms. He knew no man more trustworthy than Mortimer Swift. Still, he felt an odd reluctance to reveal what Addie had said.

With a sigh of defeat, he chose to confide in Mortimer—somewhat. Ofttimes two came to more profitable conclusions than one. "Addie insists that come August, Henry will kill Richard at Redmoor near Market Bosworth."

"And . . . ?"

Mortimer's equanimity surprised Robert. "Do you not find that suspicious? Even when we have word to prepare to defend our king? That the Morlands aim to meet Henry in Wales?"

The older man shrugged. "Henry and Richard have been at odds for years. What's to keep a woman from weaving a tale of what might happen between them? Would you feel better had she said Richard would kill Henry instead?"

"I'd much rather she hadn't claimed to know the future."

"So you, too, believe the tales I've heard about our guest. You think her a witch, a soothsayer."

The accusation in Mortimer's words shot a shard of discomfort through Robert. "Think you not remarkable that of a dozen injured men only Willis died? The strongest of the lot? There were others with serious wounds."

A frown wrinkled Mortimer's brow. "Do you suggest she . . . charmed them back to life?"

Robert shrugged. "I cannot say, but she does possess strange powers. Think how she has Nell doing her bidding. I've yet to see you win a battle of wills with my cook."

Mortimer flushed. "Woman's led me a merry dance indeed. Wants me to wed her, but I'm not a marrying man. I'm a fighter, not a farmer like she needs. She's been widowed once."

Robert saw the opportunity to tease his friend as Mortimer often did him. "But you'd like to bed her, as you've often said. And she hasn't let you."

"Yet."

" 'Tis years you've spent arguing your point."

Mortimer grinned. "Not just arguing, lad."

Sly fox! "Still, the results are the same. She does not your bidding, yet she surrendered her kitchen to Addie Shaw upon her first request."

"You can't argue against Addie's results."

Robert chuckled when his friend turned the topic. "Nay, her cooking is tasty, and 'tis more pleasant in the hall with the floor coverings she braided. The rushes were a mess, and the hounds . . . well, they're likely better off elsewhere."

Mortimer chuckled. "We've all looked for them with a scrap in hand a time or two. Even you. But Mistress Shaw will have no more tossing of food on the floor."

Robert grinned sheepishly. "I'll grant she's done well there." He grew serious again. "But that means not I'll accept all she says."

"You think her a witch, then."

"She has cast a spell over Swynton Manor."

"And its lord."

Robert glared at his companion. "I did not say that."

"But you're charmed and can't deny it. I've seen the way you watch her."

Cursing the heat on his cheeks, Robert said, "She *must* be watched. If Henry is on his way, then we must defend the crown. And if the Morlands have openly allied themselves with the bastard, then our caution must be that much greater."

"Won't argue there, lad. 'Tis true enough about the Morlands. A pack of deadly snakes they are."

"Yet another reason to hate and fear Catherine's family," Robert said, bitterness again eating at him.

"You regret that marriage."

"Every day."

"Your father—God rest his soul—was wrong to demand it. I never thought 'twould bring the peace he sought. It's only brought more fear and death."

"And if Michael Morland has thrown in with Richard's foe, the future looks grim indeed. It could still cost us more. It could make Richard question our loyalty by association if word of a Morland allegiance to Henry reaches London. My family-by-marriage must be watched. Mistress Shaw as well. And we must get word to Richard of what we know."

"What exactly do we know?" Mortimer asked shrewdly.

"That the Morlands mean to join Henry, who prepares to attack Richard."

"Richard knows of Henry's actions. 'Tis why he sent word through the Commissioners of Array."

"Aye, but he knows not the outcome Addie foresees."

"Think you to warn him of that?"

"After we make certain of Henry's plans."

"How will you do that?"

Robert ran a hand through his hair. "We will dispatch a spy of our own. Perhaps Harold would do best. And I shall send Neville to Richard with the message he brought us."

"Think you this will avert disaster?"

"If not, I'll at least have done my duty by my king. I mean to keep the pretender from taking Richard's life at Market Bosworth."

"*If* Addie Shaw is correct. Fear you she might be?"

For a moment Robert wavered. Then he shrugged. "I dare not act as if she's not. Until I'm certain, I will watch her every move. I cannot shirk my duty to Swynton. Or to Richard Plantagenet."

Mortimer gave him a penetrating look. Then he smiled. "'Tis a splendid idea, that. Follow Mistress Shaw as if you were her very shadow. I'll wager you'll find answers to all your questions soon enough if you do."

Later that afternoon, as Robert finished his midday meal, Walter Reeve, his steward, ran up to the head table.

"A group of Swynton Village folk demand an audience with my lord this day."

Robert frowned. "Has there been trouble?"

The man cast a furtive look toward the screen that shielded the buttery from the great hall, then faced Robert again. "'Tisn't for me to say, sir. They wish to speak with you."

"Very well. I shall see them as soon as I've finished here."

A short while later, a nervous gathering stood before him, made up mostly of farmers and a few of his trades folk. Mary, the alewife, a large, loud woman, appeared their self-appointed leader.

"We've come to tell ye, Sir Robert," she said, "that you've a heathen witch in the bosom of your home. We cannot stomach that, for sure, and the Good Lord'll punish us for her bein' here."

A knot tightened in Robert's stomach. "Who do you accuse and why?"

" 'Tis that Addie Shaw ye brung wi' ye the day o' the ambush," ventured a toothless crone. "She's consortin' wi' the de'il hisself."

"What makes you say so, Jillie?"

The old woman came forth, baring skinny legs and knobby knees. "I was so stiff I couldna' walk for two years. Yer Mistress Shaw gave me daughter a potion to rub on, and here I'm a-walkin' agin."

Robert sought to hide a smile. "An ointment sounds innocent enough. No one has charged Thomasine with witchcraft before."

"Thomasine's potions don't allus work, m'lord," Jillie retorted. "I've heard naught but what Mistress Shaw's magic's what makes *her* potions work."

Robert frowned. "I shall look into the matter. Any other problems?"

The alewife dragged her unruly son forward. "Rufus's hound allus has fleas. Thomasine has me soak the beast in pennyroyal, but they only leave for a day or two. Mistress Shaw gave Rufus a string to tie round the dog's neck an' now the fleas be gone. A string, Sir Robert, naught but a piece of hempen rope she done somethin' to. I ask ye, how could a rope rid a hound of fleas?" She waited for a heartbeat, then said in a sage tone, " 'Twas witchcraft, ye know."

Robert again fought against laughter, not seeing much to damn Addie from these reports. "Any more?"

A rustle of movement broke out in the gathered group. Dylan Finch, Robert's massive farrier, stumbled forward, his cheeks red as fire. The normally ebullient, forthright man shuffled from foot to foot, clearly mortified.

"Go on, now," ordered his wife, jabbing a finger into his solid side.

Dylan scowled fiercely. "She's took care of me. . . ." He glanced around, blushed even more, then spit out, *"Piles."*

Solemn nods stole the last of Robert's composure. His laughter burst out, rolling over his people, astonishing some, inviting others to join him. When he could again speak, he said, " 'Twould appear Mistress Shaw has done naught but improve your lives. And you've cause to complain?"

" 'Tis man's lot to suffer in this life, m'lord," said Mary, her tone pious. "Father Anselm says 'tis the way to heaven. I'll not be wanting Mistress Shaw's spell-castin' to send me ta hell."

He had to speak—convincingly—before this frightened, superstitious group did something regrettable, and to do so he had to set aside his own doubts about Addie. When voiced like this, they sounded foolish indeed. "Mistress Shaw has been trained by a physician. Surely that is from whence her knowledge comes. I'll speak with her and take care of the matter. Go back home and to your work in peace."

Doubtful looks came his way. Robert understood the fear; Adelaide Shaw was a most confounding woman. He wished his sister's abbey was closer to Swynton. Surely an abbess would know whether demons possessed a woman, whether she was a witch or a well-trained healer instead. But St. Hilda's and Edythe were days away.

Twelve years Robert's senior, Edythe had helped Nell raise her brother after their mother's death and before their father fostered him at Morland Castle.

Still, the strong bond between brother and sister had remained, and Edythe's vows merely made her more trustworthy in her brother's eyes. She *had* warned him against wedding Catherine Morland.

That, more than anything else, made his decision for him. He would send for Edythe, beg her to come home as soon as she could possibly manage. 'Twas a matter of life and death. His people's, his own, and perhaps even his king's.

And although he would never admit it out loud, 'twas truly a matter of the heart.

"Where go you?" Robert asked Addie a few days later. He'd seen her leave the kitchen, a reed basket over her right arm, and had silently come to her side.

She stumbled, then turned. "I've nothing more to do in the kitchen for the moment. It's a pleasant afternoon, and I thought to go to the woods. For a walk, you understand."

He understood. Mayhap too much. "Despite your accident last time?"

Her expression grew ferocious. "It was no accident, as well you know."

"Then 'twould seem wise to avoid the woods."

Addie lowered her gaze. She caught her bottom lip between her teeth. "I can't," she finally said, her voice low.

"Why not?"

She took a deep breath, squared her slender shoulders. "Because I must find that oak. I must go home before—"

When she abruptly stopped speaking, Robert waited, his patience lasting but seconds. "Before . . . ?"

"Before . . . trouble arises."

Robert again felt the urge to grab her arms, to shake the truth from her. But he knew 'twould only make her more guarded. "You cannot wander the woods alone. Twice now the area has proved dangerous, once to my men and once to you."

Her eyes met his, defiance in their depths. "You will not stop me. I *must* go back."

Reluctant admiration rose in Robert again, despite his equally strong determination to keep her safe. "I offer you one solution. That you not go alone."

Dismay melted her set expression. "You would expose me to more of your people's unfounded fears? I know what they say, what you've led them to believe."

The unfair comment made Robert want to argue, but perhaps letting Addie believe as she did would keep her alert, ready to protect herself when the need next arose. "Then I shall escort you."

"But—"

"Nay, Addie. If you go to the woods, then you'll do so with me. Only with me. Make your choice."

Addie stared at the immovable man before her, knowing

he would keep her from her objective if she refused his condition. The threat of the dungeon was never far.

Yet she had to find the tree. She had to return to York and Emmie. She had been gone too long.

"Fine. But don't be too surprised when I disappear through the oak," she said, then headed for the main gate.

Robert kept apace her, walking silently for a few moments. As they left the enclosing barbican behind, he said, "God's truth, Adelaide Shaw, nothing about you surprises me anymore. Even those of my people who've come to like you fear you."

"Not enough to stop coming for help."

"I'll grant you that."

Pride made her add, "I know what I'm doing."

"That, too."

"Then what is their complaint?"

"You're naught but a witch, and we worry for our mortal souls."

At his faintly humorous tone, Addie shot him a sideways glance. He didn't look as worried as he did bemused. "You don't appear particularly frightened right now."

He chuckled. "I've begun to wonder if you have not told the truth. Perhaps you *were* taught by a master. The tales my people tell don't speak of unholy arts, but rather rare knowledge and keen ability."

"But you still believe me a spy."

He shrugged. "You know too much."

"I don't know the Morlands—"

"Enough," he cut in. "I agreed not to discuss that again and I will keep my word. I always do."

"As do I," Addie assured her companion. "And I swear by all that's holy that I have nothing to do with them, much less with Henry Tudor, witchcraft, or any other such nonsense."

"Yet still you seek an oak to help you travel through hundreds of years—as you insist."

It was Addie's turn to shrug. "I can't deny that."

"Then let us search for this oak of yours."

Addie knew he doubted her, if not mocked her silently,

but she wouldn't—couldn't—let him distract her from her goal. She had to go home. She had to get back to Emmie.

With her customary, methodical deliberation, she scanned the trees she had yet to test. Many trunks displayed markings, natural stains, and splotches, and although she remembered the one she'd leaned on had had a darkened area, she doubted she could identify the mark just by looking at it. She figured she would have to test tree after tree until the right one gave way.

She spotted a massive oak, its trunk several feet thick, its branches tall and luxuriantly garbed in green. "Here," she said to her companion, thrusting her basket at his chest.

Robert took it without a word.

Taking care to arrange her skirts around her legs, Addie sat at the foot of the tree, determined to ignore the man who stood just inches away, to achieve her goal, to go home. Concentrating, she leaned her weight against the trunk, closed her eyes, and prayed. *Dear God, let this be the one. Let him see I've told the truth.*

But as she sat, the only sounds that met her ears were the songs of birds, the breeze dancing through the leaves overhead, the easy breathing of her protecting knight.

No creak, no crack.

The tree remained as solid as ever against her back.

Sighing, Addie rose. "Must not be the right one after all."

Robert murmured something she couldn't quite make out. Addie refused to glance his way right then. She didn't want to see an I-told-you-so look on his face.

She drew an *X* on the tree with her piece of burnt wood, and turned toward another oak. She repeated her motions, again achieving the same results.

Tree after tree said nothing to her; not a whimper escaped the wood at her back.

Addie repeated her motions, again and again, each time hoping to prove Robert wrong. She had to show him she had come through a tree, and the only way to do so was to go home the way she'd come here, crazy though the notion seemed even to her.

But the trees refused to cooperate.

And her temper grew apace her frustration.

Finally, after testing a dozen oaks, she stood, whirled on the unmoving plant, and kicked the trunk soundly. "Ouch!"

To her dismay, a chuckle sounded behind her. In her anger, she'd forgotten her companion, and now Robert had seen her do the most ridiculous thing she'd ever done. Kicking a tree—how utterly absurd and foolish. Impractical and silly. Yet somehow satisfying, if completely unlike herself. Her normal self. But perhaps that was because that self she'd always known had been forever changed by the events of the past few weeks.

As an eminently sensible, practical woman, during those recent weeks Addie had experienced moments where she had questioned her sanity. Everything in her assured her time travel couldn't exist, it just couldn't happen. Trees didn't open up and swallow one, only to disgorge one in a different time and place. Yet . . . that was precisely what had happened to her.

And Robert Swynton had no right to laugh at her. "Stop!"

He did. "What have you here?" he asked, lifting the basket he gingerly carried.

"Cookies and fresh milk."

"Cookies?"

"Er . . . sweet biscuits. A recipe from home."

"Perhaps you should take a rest from your search. Refresh yourself."

Addie shrugged. The snack would be pleasant, but she hadn't planned on sharing it with Robert when she'd packed it. "There's not a lot."

"We don't need a lot. 'Tis just the two of us here."

Suddenly the air around them changed. Addie felt the woods close in on them, the air grow charged, as if the world had narrowed to encompass only the two of them. Her perverse memory brought back thoughts of the kiss they had shared.

Flushing, she set out the miniature feast. As she reached

for the basket, her fingers grazed his, and awareness crackled up her arm. Her gaze flew up, his down.

Tension sparked in the scant inches between them, the memory of a wild kiss alive and powerful.

"Oh, for goodness' sake," she muttered, shaking herself. She couldn't afford to think such thoughts, much less give Robert the idea that she wanted to repeat their embrace.

But honesty forced her to admit she did.

Even if it was the most unwise thing she'd ever wanted.

"Here," she said, trying to break the mood. "Let's sit by this tree, since we know it won't go anywhere."

He murmured something that sounded like, "Nor will the others," but she didn't give him the pleasure of rising to his taunt.

Burrowing under the napkin, she found the sugar cakes she had baked earlier that morning despite a heated discussion with Nell over the scarcity of sugar. Even knowing how rare the commodity had been in medieval times, Addie had again needed something familiar, something from home. Pennsylvania Dutch sugar cakes had been precisely what she craved. "Have one."

Robert took the treat and said, "Thank you."

"You're welcome," she answered automatically, noting the husky tenor of his voice, how his eyes seemed to take in every detail of her face, how his smile carved dimples in his cheeks. When she realized where her thoughts had sped, she nearly kicked herself as she had the tree. It seemed neither her words nor her cookies could dispel the energy that surrounded them, the energy she remembered they had generated when they'd kissed.

"Mmm . . ." he murmured, his gaze flickering to her mouth.

"Do you like it?" she asked, absurdly pleased if unnerved by his perusal of her lips. As she watched, Robert licked a sprinkle of sugar from his bottom lip, and Addie again felt the pressure of his mouth against hers—impossible though that was.

"Very much. 'Tis almost as sweet as you—"

"What was that?" she suddenly asked, unwilling to hear the rest of his thrilling if dangerous thought, relieved to hear a strange chirp from the other side of the oak.

"What?"

"That cheep. It sounds like a bird on the ground. That's most unusual, and probably means it's hurt." Taking advantage of the momentary distraction, Addie scrambled to her feet, putting distance between them.

"More than likely 'tis a sparrow," Robert said dismissively. "We've too many around, and certainly naught to worry over."

Addie cast him a disparaging look, then cautiously peeked around the trunk. "Oh, look! It *is* a sparrow. A tiny one, too. Must have tried to fly and failed."

Dropping to her knees, she ignored the scoffing sound Robert made. "Its wing is broken, Robert. It can't return to the nest. Oh, dear."

"By God, Addie, 'tis only a *sparrow.* One of thousands and thousands. If you've need to fret over something, then think of yourself. You've been the target of two attacks, yet you've returned to the scene of the first and act as if naught had occurred."

Gingerly running her fingers over the bird's body, she found its rapid, fluttering pulse. She clearly frightened the poor mite, but knowing it would die if she didn't help it, she persisted in her examination.

"I'm fine," she said, "but this little one isn't. And, Robert, even God considers the sparrows. St. Luke's gospel says, *'Are not five sparrows sold for two copper coins? And not one of them is forgotten before God. But the very hairs of your head are all numbered. Do not fear therefore; you are of more value than many sparrows.'* He matters, and since I matter more, I'll worry about him and let God worry about me."

Robert stared at Addie, stunned by her words. What kind of sorceress spoke as his sister or Father Anselm would? None he'd ever heard of. Especially in the fervent, sincere tone Addie had employed. The more he thought about her, the better he came to know her, the more he thought her assertions true. Addie Shaw didn't strike him as a sorceress, merely a tender-hearted, experienced healer. And not of the pagan sort who might resort to dark arts, the kind the Church and society couldn't countenance. Surely Edythe would agree.

As Addie cradled the tiny clump of feathers in her palm, warmth filled Robert's heart. Not the heat of passion that oft struck him when in her presence, but a deep, rich sense of rightness, of indulgence he'd never before known.

He shook his head. "I suppose you'll insist on taking him to Swynton."

The look she gave him said it all. "As if there was anything else to be done," she added needlessly.

Robert grinned, a foolish, silly smile that he feared revealed the depth of feeling flooding through him for this woman.

A sibilant hiss whipped by his ear, accompanied by a spit of air, followed by the thud of metal against wood. Every muscle tightened to readiness. Then Robert saw the arrow. Horror filled him, and he threw himself at the woman before him.

"What . . . ?" Addie asked, dropping the bird. Then Robert's solid, muscular chest crushed the breath from hers, and she could say no more.

As they rolled over the damp forest floor, she fought for air. Blinking, she saw only darkness broken by bursts of sparks. She grew light-headed, fought to breathe again. Panic like what she'd felt the day she fell through the tree stole her thoughts, and she feared she would asphyxiate, death only seconds away.

Slow, painful seconds away.

Oh, Emmie . . . Robert . . .

Finally Robert moved a fraction, and air rushed into her starved lungs. Drawing in blessed lungfuls, she tasted the round fetid smell of wet earth and rotten leaves. It was mercifully real.

As was the heat of Robert's body pressed all along hers.

His legs braced hers, his arms cradled her, his hips met hers so intimately that she shivered, senses heightened, alert.

She knew danger.

It surrounded her, filling her middle with apprehension, chilling her to the heart. It was alive, achingly so, but Addie didn't know if it came from the man atop her or from some other unknown source.

Wondering what had caused Robert to act so strangely, if he'd really tried to kill her, Addie glanced back to where she had sat only a moment before. The feathers on an arrow's shaft shivered sharply, its tip buried not an inch away from where her head had been.

Someone had tried to kill her.

Again.

Chapter 10

THAT REALIZATION, UNQUESTIONABLE this time, hit Addie with greater strength than had Robert, large as he was. Every sensation, every sound, every beat of her stampeding heart became exquisitely clear, agonizingly sharp, devastatingly dear. She didn't want to die, especially without knowing why someone wanted her dead, and who that someone might be.

She only knew Robert hadn't tried to kill her.

He'd hurled himself into the path of danger twice now to prevent her harm. Even if he had threatened her any number of times, Addie felt as if the gears and wheels spinning in her heart suddenly fell into place. Robert was an eminently decent, honorable man. If he had a quarrel with one, one would know. If he wanted one dead, one would also know that. The surreptitious attacks on her had not been perpetrated upon his command. Straightforward and sincere, Robert had not an ounce of cowardice or subterfuge in him. He would never operate in such a way.

Addie opened her eyes and again allowed herself a moment to admire the strong male face a mere breath away from hers. Mirrored in his eyes she saw the fear and rage she felt. But something else glowed there, too, something she remembered from the day they'd kissed, something dark and heady and dangerous in its own special way.

That something in his gaze then caught fire, smoldered, and burned in an unusually intense way.

He murmured her name as he captured her lips.

For a moment Addie allowed herself the joy of that caress, the warmth, the heat, the desire that rose fast and wild inside her. She relished the firm pressure of his mouth, the sleek possession of his tongue, the sharp nip of his teeth.

Then sanity struck with sickening power. Someone had used her for target practice, and that someone could still be near. As she and Robert lay tangled beneath the trees, they made a perfect mark for their unseen enemy. He could efficiently rid himself of two with just one shot, and Addie had no desire to end her life skewered to the ground like the fly she once pinned to a board for her pupils to study.

She pushed against Robert but found her effort futile. The man was strong and determined to kiss her senseless. Had they been anywhere else, she might have accommodated his desire, but at the moment, in such precarious circumstances, Addie preferred to keep on living so they could kiss again another time.

When he didn't budge despite her efforts, Addie groaned in frustration. Robert must have taken the sound as encouragement, as he deepened the kiss, letting his hands roam over her body.

Addie gasped at the surge of need that rose to her skin everywhere those large, warm hands touched. She returned his impassioned kiss, stroke for stroke.

When he groaned deep in his chest, Addie allowed her hands to do some exploring of their own. She molded her palms to his biceps, verifying the strength of the sinew she'd seen bulge and flex there. She let her fingers run the width of his shoulders, again marveling at Robert's sheer size.

A sound of pleasure rumbled somewhere in his chest, and his caresses continued, growing more intimate, more arousing. To Addie, who had convinced herself she would never know the pleasure of a man's desire, the moment brought a revelation. She would never again consider herself destined for spinsterhood. She could inspire a man to touch and kiss and want her as any other woman could, and if Robert's reaction to her inexpert touch was anything to go by, she gave pleasure in the same measure she received.

Yet another bit of self-knowledge told her she wanted to bring pleasure only to this man from a time long past. A man who mistrusted her. A man who could easily get her killed with his suspicions, even if he didn't shoot the arrow that did it himself.

That thought brought her plummeting back to reality.

Addie resumed pummeling Robert's back, wriggling under him like an earthworm after a spring shower. He grunted his objection, but only tightened his arms around her.

Frustration and fear grew, stealing away every vestige of passion. Hysteria rose, and an inappropriate laugh burned in her throat. What an absurd fix to be in. Addie would have to resort to more drastic measures, since she didn't want both of them pierced by a madman's arrow. She kicked Robert's shins as she pulled on hefty handfuls of hair.

He tore his lips from hers with a roar. "What the devil . . . are you mad, woman?"

Addie gulped and giggled wildly. "No, but you have obviously taken leave of your senses." More chuckles left her, and she pushed harder against him. "There's a most unfriendly person in these woods. While your kisses are very nice, indeed"—she ignored the smug smile he flashed—"I would think you'd want to leave here alive."

The grin vanished, and he shuddered. "You're right, Addie Shaw. I . . . I lost my head there."

It was her turn to smile in feminine satisfaction.

"But," he said before she could revel in the knowledge, "we must hasten back to Swynton. I've much to do if I intend to keep you safe. And alive."

Addie frowned. "How about you? How can you be so sure whoever shot that arrow meant it for me?"

He rolled off her, leaving her somehow bereft, a greater loneliness than she had known before sharp in her heart.

"Had they meant it for me," he said, "I would be dead by now. It would have gone through my back, and we would never have known who did it. That arrow only narrowly missed your head."

Nodding when another rough shudder ran through her, Robert turned toward home. "I will learn who is behind these attacks. But you must do as I say. There can be no more jaunts through the woods until the danger is past."

Addie cried a wordless objection, but at the implacable light in Robert's eyes, she bit her tongue to refrain from arguing. He was right. She couldn't afford to die in her efforts to go back home. It would be more sensible and logical to wait until it was safe to resume her search.

In the meantime, she would have to pray for Emmie's safety. And wonder when Robert Swynton would kiss her again.

He would never kiss Addie Shaw again. The woman had the power to distract him even at the most unlikely moments. Someone had shot an arrow at her. He'd seen it pierce the trunk of the oak inches from her stubborn head. Then, moments later, he'd forgotten every sensible thought, every cautious consideration, and lost himself in the pleasure of her lips.

She had returned his kisses, by damn, fervently and with more passion than he had suspected she possessed. Why, if his admittedly limited experience was anything to go by, Addie had as sensual a nature as he did, one equally untapped as of yet.

The mere thought of being the man to plumb the depths of her desires set his blood afire, made his body rigid, ready for delving of a most intimate sort.

And that was precisely why Robert could never kiss her again.

He had to keep his mind on important matters, on matters of life and death. Hers, his, and King Richard's.

Still, he'd never forget her gentle touch and concern for the tiny sparrow. He'd wondered fleetingly how it would feel to have someone care for him that way. But he'd immediately—wisely—set that thought aside.

Especially in view of her mulelike, obstinate insistence on bringing the thing home. And what did she intend to do with it? Why, she'd spoken to Arletta, who wove the finest baskets in Swynton Village, asking her to fashion a cage for the scrap of down. Addie meant to keep the wounded creature in her room, tending to it, feeding it, as if it were a babe.

The thought of Addie, infant at the breast, had haunted Robert ever since. Predictably he'd managed scant sleep. A fact which had him starting the new day as miserable as a dog with fleas.

Now, as he stood to leave the head table after breaking his fast, a commotion at the entrance to the great hall caught his attention, preventing his departure.

Although Mortimer did his level best to keep a band of Swynton retainers from entering the chamber, they would not be stopped. Cyril Woodhouse stepped forward, his lean face set in stubborn lines.

"I would be beggin' m'lord's pardon for interruptin' yer day like this," said the man, "but 'tis a serious matter we bring afore ye."

Robert frowned, remembering the last time a group of his people had sought an audience with him. They had come to accuse Addie of sorcery, and he feared today would be no different.

Waving them into the room, Robert returned to his chair. "Speak your mind, Cyril."

Casting a glance at his companions, Cyril approached the table and cleared his throat. A flush bloomed on his cheeks as he lowered his gaze to the braided-cloth floor-covering Addie used in place of rushes.

"Well, man, say what you came to say. I assume you've plenty to keep you busy. 'Tis planting season, is it not?" asked Robert, growing warier by the second.

Lifting his head and squaring his shoulders, Cyril met

Robert's gaze. "Aye, m'lord, 'tis that indeed. And 'tis a serious matter we bring afore ye today. That . . . that Mistress Shaw, sir. She's . . ."

He then glanced around the room, and Robert assumed he looked for the woman he'd come to discuss. Addie hadn't appeared to break her fast, and Robert envisioned her fussing over the damn sparrow. He nearly smiled, remembering her defense of the poor thing, but the dour faces before him stole the pleasure from his vision. Certainly it would never occur to the woman to sleep later than usual after the shocking attack on her life.

"She's a witch," Cyril said, "an' she must be burned at the stake."

Dear God. "Such a charge is serious indeed. One I hope you make not lightly."

"On the contrary, m'lord. We've known about her since ye brought her here. We haven't said a word out of respect for ye, since she's your guest. But we can hold our peace no more. Not after last night."

A murmur of agreement rippled through those flanking him.

Dread filled Robert's gut, mixing unhappily with the bread, cheese, and ale he'd only minutes earlier consumed. "What happened last night?"

"Ye knew Percy's wife was . . . breedin' again?"

Robert nodded. Nothing strange there; every spring Mistress Goodling provided her husband with yet another mouth to feed.

"Well, Marthy's time came, and Thomasine went to help. After three days, she still hadn't birthed the child, and we heard they were not long for this world."

"Aye," murmured a woman to Cyril's right.

"'Tis so," said another to his left.

"'Twas Marthy's time to go," offered the one behind.

Robert experienced a deep sadness; the Goodlings were a hardworking, honest lot, if fertile as hares. He would miss Martha's pleasant smile and greeting next time he went to discuss affairs of the farm with Percy.

"When's the funeral mass?" he asked.

"'Tis just it, sir. 'Twon't be a mass. Marthy didn't die. Thomasine called yer witch to help, and she . . ."

Everyone in the group made the sign of the cross in unison.

"Mistress Shaw *cut* the child out of Marthy, and . . ." Cyril again crossed himself. "Saints preserve us, *neither one of 'em died.*"

Robert started. "What say you?"

Cyril nodded somberly. "Just that, m'lord. She cast a spell on Marthy an' put her to sleep. She cut down Marthy's middle, took the baby out, then sewed her back up. Both are with us yet this day."

"She cheated Marthy out o' heaven!" cried a woman from the rear of the crowd, anger in her voice.

Although Robert knew the Church taught that Eve's original sin cursed womanhood with the horrors of childbirth, he wasn't certain that an early death promised anyone more glory than achieving a ripe old age. Others believed the great number of deaths among birthing women proved that thought.

But to accuse Addie of using witchcraft to keep someone from heaven?

He remembered the times she had spoken as his sister would, her determination to help others, even a lowly sparrow. Slowly Robert shook his head, rejecting what he had just heard. "That cannot be. Surely you're mistaken."

A dozen heads shook. More than a few hands again made the sign of the cross.

Cyril harrumphed, then went on, "If we were in York proper, the guild would take care of her. She's no physician, surgeon, or barber, nor does she work for any of the like. The guild would investigate, lock her up and fine her, and the Church would burn her. Here in Swynton, we have no guild. We've naught else to do but burn the witch ourselves. We cannot keep her here."

The thought of immolating Addie repulsed Robert. He had twice faced death himself to keep her safe. Now his people came with clear and punishable evidence, and he feared this time no amount of arguing on her part or protective action on his would keep her from death.

His heart ached at the thought.

"Thomasine!" he cried.

Slowly, reluctantly, the slender healer came out from behind the screen by the buttery entrance. "Aye, my lord."

"Were you there?"

"Aye."

"Does Cyril speak the truth?"

A tear rolled down her thin cheek. That single, silent drop drove certainty through Robert, making his meal sour in his stomach, his feelings for Addie burn in his heart.

"Aye," said Thomasine yet again, her voice scarcely more than a whisper. "She cut the babe from Martha's womb, and both still live. I've never seen that before, not even Richard Wasdale—God rest his soul—could have done it, and he was a truly fine member of the guild in York. I should know, for I helped him leech patients many a time."

Robert's already depressed hope plummeted. "Think you as Cyril that Addie did this through black arts? Think you not she might have learned from a greater master than even Wasdale?"

Thomasine refused to meet his gaze. "I know not, sir. She had me grind together equal parts of opium seed, mandrake root bark, and henbane. Then she dipped a cloth in the mix, set it over Martha's nose and brow—"

The group gasped as one.

Nodding sagely, Thomasine continued, "Aye, 'tis true enough that mix can kill. But it didn't when Addie used it. 'Tis then she took the knife and cut. I know not what to think."

A ray of hope rose in Robert. "Surely she learned all this . . ."

He let his words fade as Thomasine met his gaze, pity in her eyes. "Perhaps. But, my lord, they *live*. No potion I know can keep someone alive who's been cut open like that.

'Tis what Wasdale did with cadavers to embalm, he cut them apart, but after they'd died. I saw it with my own eyes."

A delicate shudder ran through Thomasine, the woman who had attended every birth in the nearby area for longer than Robert remembered. She crossed herself, then said, "I like her. Very much. And I've learned much from her. But this . . ." She shook her head.

A rumble began behind Cyril. Robert caught the word "witch" in many different voices, all filled with horror, some even with hate.

Part of him acknowledged the danger—spiritual and from the Church—in harboring a suspected sorceress. The other part of him could only think of Addie's sweet taste, her gentle giving in his arms.

He remembered her tears when she failed to save Willis's life. And only yesterday she'd sought to save a mere sparrow. He could see her facing the loss of a woman and child in childbirth. Possessed with such great knowledge, ability, and compassion, Addie could no more have let Martha and her child die than she could have killed Willis.

But was her knowledge demonic?

He remembered her familiarity with the Word of God.

"Wait!" he cried, hoping for sanity from the panicked mob. "I will speak with Mistress Shaw. I will see what she has to say for herself. Then I will decide her fate."

Silence suddenly blanketed the room, ominous and dangerous.

"What is it?" he asked, perplexed by the accusatory looks he spied on a few of those before him. "What is wrong with my proposal?"

Mary the alewife stepped forward, her square, jutting chin leading the way. "'Tis said ye've taken the witch to bed. How can we know she has not charmed you with a spell and won't sway ye've with her favors or her arts?"

Rage roared in Robert. "'Tis a lie! I've no more bedded Addie than I've bedded you. What manner of man do you think me? Think you I am so easily led?"

Again that chin pushed out. "A man like all others, sir.

And we all know how Alice Perrers enthralled poor old King Edward with effigies, enchantments, and incantations. Besides, ye've not taken up any woman's offer since yer wife's own death."

"That should prove I can refuse even Addie's favors, should she offer, which she hasn't."

Some put off their disbelief. Others retained the remnants of doubt. He went on, "I am Robert Swynton. My word is law here. When I say I will learn what is behind Martha's recovery, you can trust me to do so. If Mistress Shaw is guilty of witchcraft," he said, swallowing the bile that rose in his throat, "then she will face the consequences of her sin. If she is innocent, then you shall owe her an apology. And your respect. Now begone. There's much I need do, not the least of which is learn the truth about Adelaide Shaw."

Murmurs of dissent followed the group as they left the great hall. Thomasine remained behind, then came to stand across the table from him. "If I can help prove Addie innocent, I will do so. She's a good woman, is Addie Shaw, but I heard her speak of Henry and King Richard that day. . . ."

Robert sighed. "Aye, Thomasine, 'tis that which worries me, too."

As he sat in the silence of the empty hall, Robert dropped his head into his hands. What should he do?

As a godly man, he could not countenance a sorceress, much less tolerate an attraction between them. Yet the feelings he had for Addie grew greater each day, and he feared he might be falling in love with her.

A Christian could never bind himself to a practitioner of the black arts; 'twould mean eternal damnation.

Was Addie Shaw a witch? A necromancer? A soothsayer as well?

He remembered her stating in that firm, sensible voice of hers, "I'm no more demon-possessed than you."

Dare he believe her? The woman he burned for? The woman who sweetly welcomed and returned his kisses, his touch?

The woman who insisted she had traveled through time.

* * *

Without ceremony, Robert threw open the door to Addie's chamber and strode in, questions boiling in his mind.

"Don't ask," Addie warned, turning from the sparrow's cage on the window ledge.

"Ask what?"

She snorted. "Your innocence is patently false, and I don't care to indulge it. There's talk of what I did last night. I knew there would be, but . . ."

Robert's jaw tightened, resembling a granite sculpture. "But what?"

Summoning every ounce of dignity she possessed, Addie said, "I thought I could help."

"What exactly did you do?"

"I performed a cesarean section to deliver the child," she said in her precise teacher's voice. "I assisted Doc Horst once, and although I wasn't sure I would succeed, I could not let them die without trying. Thank God, all went well."

"You invoke God when all around you link your name with Satan's?"

Addie marched right up to the ridiculous man. She poked her finger into his rock-hard chest, seeking to control her anger. "Now you listen to me. I told you any number of times I'm not demon-possessed, I don't practice any form of witchcraft, and I'm a Methodist by affiliation, a Christian by faith. If I remember correctly, however, God's Word states we are not to judge, since judgment is for Him alone."

Robert flushed. "I know not what a Methodist is, but—"

"But nothing," she said, gratified by the embarrassment on his cheeks. "I've been well trained, even better than I thought. I have always been curious about all the learning disciplines. When Doc Horst needed help in his surgery, I leaped at the chance to learn more about medicine and the wonders of healing. I cannot bear to see anyone suffer."

She didn't often speak of such personal matters, but perhaps this was the time to do so. "When my parents' horse bolted and injured them, Doc Horst had them brought home for nursing care. I did what I could for them, but because I lacked medical training, I felt helpless. I hated that feeling. Their wounds were grave, and I watched Doc treat them. As Mama lay dying, I vowed to learn all I could to help anyone who needed care, no matter who they might be. I have always remembered the biblical admonition, *'Inasmuch as ye have done it unto one of the least of these my brethren, ye have done it to me.'*"

This time, Robert nodded awkwardly and grinned sheepishly. "You sound like my sister."

"Well, if she agrees with me on caring for those who need help, then I regret not knowing her."

His expression lightened. "Oh, but you might yet. I sent a message to the abbey inviting her home, and perhaps she'll find the time to come."

Addie considered the possibility. "I would like that very much. And perhaps she will succeed where I have failed. She might well manage to rouse your common sense."

An eyebrow rose. "Oh?"

"Yes. If she can successfully run an abbey, she is likely a practical, sensible woman. I doubt she'd spend time worrying about demon possession and witchcraft and other such nonsense. She would surely see I'm no more a heretic than she."

Robert's gaze narrowed, and Addie wondered just exactly what he thought. But he didn't satisfy her curiosity. He turned toward the door, then paused and said, "Perhaps she will."

As he left, closing the door behind him, Addie thought she heard him add, "I surely hope she does."

Hours after that frustrating parley where Addie again denied demonic influence in her actions, hours filled with disturbing thoughts, Nell and Mortimer approached Robert, their features revealing their deep concern.

Nell twisted nervous fingers, then asked quietly, "Might we speak with you, Rob, my son?"

"Speak your mind," he answered, surprised by her solemnity.

Mortimer glanced at the kitchen maids clearing the remains of the evening meal from the trestle tables in the great hall. "Not while everyone else can hear."

"What troubles you?" Robert asked, afraid he knew only too well.

Mortimer shook his head, his rotund face set in unyielding lines. "Nay, lad. What we've come to say must be said in private."

Surrendering to the inevitable, Robert gestured for the couple to follow him. He led the way to the solar. Once there, he sat on his bed, crossed his arms over his chest, and raised an eyebrow. "Well?"

After a gentle squeeze to Nell's shoulder, Mortimer stepped forward. " 'Tis certain you are that someone tried to kill Mistress Shaw in the woods yesterday afternoon, right?"

"As I am of my name."

"And the arrow was meant not for you?" Nell asked, her normally smooth forehead pleated with worry.

"Aye."

"How mean you to keep the girl safe?" asked his master-at-arms.

"I've her promise not to leave the manor until we know who is behind the attacks and why," Robert answered defensively.

" 'Tisn't enough, son!" cried Nell. "Someone sought to crush her with a stone here at home."

Robert nodded, rage curdling yet another meal in this miserable day, helplessness sitting with him as poorly as always. "I've spoken with Addie, and she denies all accusations, save the one that attributes Martha's and her child's lives to her. As to the culprit, I will question everyone at Swynton. If I've reason to misbelieve anyone's innocence, they'll find themselves in the dungeon before nightfall."

Mortimer shook his head. "A lot can happen between now and daybreak. By then, Addie Shaw could well be dead."

Ice flowed through Robert's veins. Mortimer had just voiced his greatest fear. One he hadn't had the courage to put into words. "I won't let that happen."

A steely expression tautened Nell's soft, round face. "You will not succeed by asking a multitude of questions. Lies come cheap, son. You must do more, and I trow you know what you must do to keep her safe."

Apprehension knotted in his middle. He had spent the day pondering that very thing, and the only conclusion he had reached was one he didn't want to face. But it seemed his two most loyal retainers wouldn't let him shirk responsibility. "I suspect someone truly fears her talents and has decided to rid Swynton Manor of the witch they believe lives here."

His companions nodded.

Robert rammed ten fingers through his hair. "I want to believe her, but I've seen the results." He'd gone to the Goodlings' cottage, seen mother and child, been shown the evidence of Addie's actions.

When Mortimer and Nell went to speak, Robert raised a hand to halt their words. "I doubt Addie has malicious intent, and I suspect she truly has been well taught. Yet I am responsible for her while she remains among us. 'Tis up to me to protect her, and the only way I know to do so is to . . ."

He hoped he was doing the right thing. For his sake and that of everyone else. Including Addie. "The only way to protect her is to wed her. To give her my name as proof of my trust. I know no other way to show one and all that they've naught to fear from Addie Shaw."

But I do. The thought formed before he could stifle it, and with it came vivid mental pictures of the moments they'd spent in each other's arms the day before.

Followed swiftly by her rejection of his advances.

Aye, he had plenty to fear from Addie. He feared he might lose his lands, his sanity, his life.

He chuckled ruefully. Worse, infinitely so, he feared he might lose his heart.

Still, deep inside, where he'd so diligently sought to stifle his response to Addie, excitement leaped through him at the thought of taking her to wife.

To bed.

That still hopeful part of him, that incautious, impetuous part came back to life, igniting hope that perhaps he would now learn the joy other men found in the arms of a passionate, willing woman.

Perhaps he would finally come to know the pleasure to be found with a sensual woman like Addie Shaw.

Chapter 11

THE SUN SHONE bright on Addie Shaw's wedding day.

At times she wondered if she wasn't playing some kind of make-believe, or creating a fantasy like those she often conjured for her students. But as Addie took slow, measured steps toward the altar in Swynton Manor's chapel, she could no longer question the truth of the assertion.

In minutes she would marry Robert Swynton.

The sweet perfume of lilies and beeswax teased her senses, and the light streaming through the narrow windows illuminated the crucifix with a shaft of summer sun.

In minutes she would become Robert's wife.

The thought sent thrills of excitement through her, only to have her more sensible nature quell them each time her nerves took up their merry dance. Robert had insisted this would be a marriage in name only. He'd offered his name for protection, since he believed whoever had tried to kill her had done so out of fear of her supposed occult powers.

It seemed the very folk Addie had most helped had not only labeled her a witch, but now demanded her death at the stake. Robert, out of his sense of duty, was determined to protect her. His honor had led to his proposal.

Addie couldn't help wishing his feelings had inspired it instead, especially since hers for him were definitely there, if thoroughly bewildering. How could she possibly be attracted to stubborn, overbearing, lord-of-the-manor Robert Swynton?

Her—a modern woman. To him—a medieval barbarian.

Surely her love of history had led to her bizarre interest. After all, Robert Swynton was a living, breathing slice of the past, of a time that was truly fascinating, one she had known little about and that she could now study through him to her heart's content. He brought to life what until then she had known only through records in dusty books.

There was nothing musty or dusty about *this* knight of the realm.

That had to explain the irrational, impractical, nonsensical appeal the most unlikely of men held for her. Nothing about *him* personally could interest a modern woman like her. It couldn't be love or any such foolishness.

Not at all.

Robert was the most unreasonable man Addie had ever met. No amount of arguing on her part had changed his opinion about her situation, much less convinced him their union was unnecessary. Addie believed that with time, logical explanation, and plenty of evidence of her medical training—and nothing more sinister than that—she could persuade the folks of Swynton and the surrounding countryside that she was no witch.

But no. Robert wouldn't hear of it, so certain was he that her life was doomed if she didn't marry him—posthaste at that. And when she'd demanded additional reasons for their wedding, her feminine pride stung by his lack of emotion over their upcoming nuptials, he hadn't offered any beyond his blasted duty to protect her.

Still, that stony jaw, that burning conviction, that very immutability made her wonder about his motives.

She *had* taken part in those wild kisses in the woods. He couldn't deny he had wanted that intimacy at least then. Addie both feared and craved the repeat of such encounters, but she had agreed that their marriage would be a matter of logic, of cautious protection. A most practical arrangement.

Then she'd foolishly asked him what he expected to gain by marrying her. Robert had paused momentarily, and hope had leaped to life. But then he'd crushed it by citing the improvements she'd made in the manor, and yes, he'd agreed that the healing gift that had caused so much trouble thus far would be a boon.

He wanted a housekeeper, for goodness' sake! He even wanted her to accompany him to Morland Castle, the property his first wife had brought to the marriage, in the hopes that she would establish order there as well.

Perversely, although his persistence in considering only her practical gifts continued to bruise her pride, Addie's heart refused to relinquish hope that personal interest might also fuel his determination to marry, even if he didn't admit it. And even when she'd acknowledged that her own interest in him sprang only from the opportunity he provided to study a time long past.

As it positively did. Since she couldn't possibly be interested in him as a man or husband. Not at all.

Even now, Addie's ridiculous hope kept her moving forward, no matter how many times her more practical side argued against it. It seemed she'd inherited some fanciful traits herself, traits she'd never before identified, traits that thoroughly dismayed her. This wasn't the time to lose her head, much less her heart. Certainly not to such an inappropriate man.

Addie straightened her spine and strengthened her resolve. She had to get back to York—York, Pennsylvania, that was—and Emmie. Too much awaited her there to let a passing attraction disrupt her goals.

Robert Swynton couldn't matter to her.

When she reached the altar, Robert extended his large, warm hand. She placed her fingers on his and felt his strength as he clasped them tightly, gently, decisively. Again that current of energy that always flew through her at their slightest touch threw her off guard. She looked into his eyes, enigmatic and penetrating. A shiver, born of either danger or excitement, ran through her. Neither of them spoke while holding the other's gaze. The moment grew, and Addie couldn't help but wonder what their union would bring.

Then Father Anselm cleared his throat. They turned and faced the priest.

No matter how hard Addie tried to concentrate on the age-old, eternally meaningful Latin words of the marriage rite, her only thought was of their union, the weaving of two into one. She stared at their joined hands, noticed the fingers laced together in a knot. Could their marriage someday turn into a lovers' knot?

She forced herself to turn her attention back to Father Anselm, to the event unfolding around her, to the improbable situation in which she found herself. She looked up. As she stared at the crucifix hanging behind the altar, Addie could no longer lie to herself.

She hoped, more than just about anything else, that their marriage would change, grow, become something wonderful, even though she knew it shouldn't—couldn't.

Still, hoping against hope, she longed to someday become Robert Swynton's wife in more than name. She hoped to someday become his lover, too.

Immediately after the ceremony, Robert introduced Addie to his elder sister Edythe, the abbess of Saint Hilda's. The nerves that had yet to raise their unruly heads struck Addie right then.

"I've heard tell of your gifts, Addie Shaw," said her new husband's sister, keen brown eyes scouring Addie's flushed face.

She grimaced, but in her usual fashion addressed the situation head-on. "I'm certain what you've heard proclaims me a heretic at best, a witch at worst."

In a gesture identical to her brother's, Edythe raised an eyebrow. Then she smiled. "You're most direct. I'm surprised."

Addie chuckled. "What would be the point of avoiding

the matter I'm sure is uppermost in your mind? Your brother mentioned summoning you here, and I'm afraid you've been disturbed on my account."

It was Edythe's turn to laugh. " 'Tis true my routine at the abbey was disturbed, but I would not care to miss meeting Robert's new wife." Glancing toward her brother, she sobered. "I warned him against the first. To my dismay, I was right to do so. I cannot deny I've concerns for his happiness."

Addie winced inwardly. "I doubt happiness carried any weight in his decision to marry me. Robert's sense of duty extends to anyone he believes depends on him, even a woman he considers an enemy, so long as she is a captive in his home."

The two women strolled from the stone chapel to the manor house in Robert's wake. Edythe lay a gentle hand on Addie's forearm. When Addie glanced at her companion, she noticed the frown beneath the pristine edge of the abbess's wimple.

"Answer truthfully," Edythe requested. "He has not kept you in that gruesome dungeon, has he?"

Addie covered the long fingers with her own. "No, but he's threatened to do so a number of times."

"The scoundrel!" Edythe exclaimed, a sly grin on her lips. "He could no more treat a woman that way than he could fly. But I fear he made you think yourself in danger, did he not?"

Addie narrowed her gaze. "You mean he was all bluster? No teeth to his threats?"

"No-o-o . . . I would not say his threats were totally empty. He will protect his own, regardless from whom he must protect them. But I suspect he would struggle with the thought of mistreating a lady."

Addie thought back on the various times she and Robert had clashed. True, he'd always shown himself a stubborn man, and a powerful one, but he'd yet to turn that power and strength against her, even when his temper raged. She nodded slowly. "You know, I think you're right."

Edythe sniffed delicately. "Of course I am. I've known

my brother forever. And he has acted true to his nature by wedding you."

"Why do you say that?"

A momentary discomfort obviously silenced Edythe. Addie held her breath, praying the abbess would speak her mind. Then, after another of her piercing stares, Robert's sister nodded. Apparently she had reached a decision about Addie. She held her breath.

"He felt," Edythe said, "and I must agree, that he had no other means to save your life. Even as far away as Saint Hilda's, gossip has it he beds a witch."

When Addie made a sound of outrage, Edythe raised her hand to forestall any comment. "Listen to me, please. Robert has feared your talents from the start, but if he knew you guilty as charged, he would already have administered due punishment. My brother is a devout man."

Addie shuddered, and opened her mouth to defend herself. The look in Edythe's eyes stopped the words forming on her tongue.

"'Twould seem," the abbess continued, "Robert's honesty prevents him from punishing a woman he cannot prove guilty of grievous sins beyond a doubt. Adelaide Shaw—"

"Adelaide Swynton as of today," Addie inserted, tipping her chin skyward.

Edythe smiled, her gaze growing more intense, more like Robert's by the minute. "Aye, 'tis true enough. I ask you now, Adelaide Swynton, as Robert's sister and as a nun, are you a witch as you stand accused?"

Addie met the dark gaze of her sister by marriage. "Not at all, Edythe. I'm as Christian as you and Robert, merely trained in medicine. A physician near my home needed help in his surgery. When he learned of my desire to help, not just him but those he treated, he began to teach me what he knew. I cannot bear to stand helplessly by and watch someone suffer without trying to relieve their pain."

The two women stood face-to-face, silver eyes staring into darkest brown. Minutes crawled by, and Addie felt an unexpected urge to squirm. She had never been subject to scrutiny such as the Swynton siblings delivered. She knew who and what she was, but they, coming from a time fraught with prejudice and superstition, might not see past the absurdity of the claims against her to the truth of her integrity.

She didn't want to burn at the stake.

The day was warm, and beneath her multiple layers of clothes, Addie began to perspire. Dear God, was Edythe Swynton, abbess of Saint Hilda's, the one who would determine her fate?

Robert's voice sliced the silence between them, "What think you of my lady wife, Sister?"

Addie flushed. Leave it to her new husband to get right to the heart of the matter. But although every fiber of her being clamored to present her defense, pride kept her lips pressed shut, her spine straight, her shoulders back, her chin up, her gaze firm.

A soft chuckle suddenly left Edythe's lips, and she saluted Addie with a dip of her crisp white wimple. "I trow, Brother, this time you have met your match."

"No sorceress, is she?" he asked, a smile curving his lips.

Edythe waved an elegant hand, dismissing the claim, then brought her fingers to rest on her brother's arm. She nodded toward the door to the manor. "We have a marriage to celebrate. Give your wife your arm, and let us show your people you've chosen well."

Addie's knees wobbled, and she realized how desperately she'd needed to hear herself proclaimed innocent. She took a step forward, but her legs buckled, their consistency suddenly resembling that of overcooked potpie noodles.

A steely arm caught her by the waist. Her gaze flew up and tangled with Robert's. What she saw in her new husband's eyes caused her to falter again.

He took his other arm from his sister's clasp and cupped Addie's elbow in his large hand. The arm around her middle remained firmly in place. "Shall I carry you again?"

Addie's chin shot ever higher at the memory of those earlier times. "Absolutely not. I can walk on my own two feet."

"Pity."

She shot him a questioning look.

In a voice too low for his sister to hear, he said, "I've come to appreciate the more pleasant aspects of having the witch of Swynton Manor well in hand."

Addie tore out of his grasp. "I thought you'd decided I was no witch. You even said so to your sister, and she believes you chose well when you decided to marry me. Why must you persist in accusing me of witchcraft?"

"I suppose there must be different kinds of witchcraft," Robert said with a chuckle. "'Twould seem you've charmed us all."

Addie caught her breath at the smile on Robert's lips, the simple humor on his rugged face, his willingness to banter with her—something he'd never done before. Did he suddenly believe her because his sister gave her approval?

Or was Edythe right in saying Robert must have been unsure from the first? Even if he'd been her first accuser.

His words rang again in her mind. *"'Twould seem you've charmed us all."* Then, before she could stop herself, she blurted out, "Even you, my lord?"

Robert blinked, clearly taken aback by her forward question. Then his surprising, devastating smile broke out once again. "'Twould seem so, my lady wife."

As she stood transfixed by his smile, Robert took her hand, placed it on his arm, and led her inside the manor house.

Addie's thoughts, however, remained on the words spoken on the bailey grounds. Did Robert believe her now? And if so, did he believe because of *her?* Only her? Or because his sister had given her approval?

Time would tell. Suddenly Addie found herself wondering how much time she had left to find out.

She needed to return to Emmie, but now she was of two minds. While she loved her sister as much as always, now her heart craved to learn just exactly what Robert Swynton had meant.

What was she going to do?

* * *

Nothing, it seemed, since, true to his word, Robert kept his distance after the wedding. His gaze, however, followed Addie without fail. She scarcely moved without him watching, studying her with that dark, piercing stare, flustering her. His constant attention made her question his insistence on keeping the match one of convenience and practicality, since he'd finally seemed to relinquish the witchcraft and spy nonsense.

Dare she hope he might possibly care for her?

To distract herself from the awareness of his perusal, and especially to forget the distance he had built between them, Addie busied herself with running the manor. She came to know Walter Reeve, Robert's steward, quite well.

Her mornings began with worship in the chapel, Father Anselm saying the daily Mass. Then the members of the household would break their fast in the great hall, now much improved thanks to her efforts. She'd replaced the foul rushes on the floor with braided rugs she'd taught the women to make. Frugal as always, Addie had used garments she'd found in chests throughout the house.

Then Robert retired to the solar to discuss farm matters, only to emerge a short while later and head for the practice field.

Addie hated the sound of battle, be it real or not, but she dared not object, as she knew what he would say.

"We must be ready to join our king at all times," he'd said the first time she'd complained after their marriage. "'Tis a matter of honor, Wife. When Richard became king, I traveled to London and swore allegiance to him. I vowed to support him with men and arms. He has called his nobles to prepare to stand against Henry Tudor, and I do just that. 'Tis a matter of honor."

Addie couldn't argue that point, so she'd determined to keep her thoughts to herself. She hadn't, however, rid herself of her fear for her husband. Or for the men who so lustily engaged in the exercises outdoors.

She couldn't bear the thought of having to patch them back together again.

Unable to alter her circumstances, she'd familiarized herself with the running of Swynton Manor. Practical as always, she'd organized the work by season, by month, by week, and day. She drew up a series of lists, determining who would do what and answer to whom, and was about to pass them out to the women who would carry out the tasks.

"Do you think they are clear enough?" she asked Walter, showing him the parchments with their neat script.

A dubious look deepened the furrows on the steward's forehead. "Methinks, Lady Addie, you'll find few who can follow them at all."

"But why? I've made them perfectly simple, direct, and I've divided the work equitably."

"Aye, you have, but 'tisn't your organization that's in question, madam, 'tis the women's ability to read. Not a one can."

Addie gaped in horror. "You mean . . . they're completely untaught?"

Then she remembered what she knew of England's late Middle Ages. Nobles schooled their children, teaching them to read, write, and cipher, but the general populace, as a rule, had remained uneducated until much later. Books had been available in the fourteenth and fifteenth centuries only to the wealthiest.

"A deplorable situation," she stated, "but one I can easily remedy. I believe my husband has not yet left the solar. He and Mortimer always have much to discuss. I shall speak to Robert about this immediately. I appreciate your help with the lists, and I think things will run much more smoothly from now on as a result of our hard work."

The man murmured acceptance of her gratitude, but left her room still wearing a doubtful look. Addie would entertain no doubts. Why, what better way to fill her hours than to teach the women to read—now that as Lady Swynton she was no longer welcome to work in the kitchen with Nell and the maids. She would also teach the children, once again putting to good use her love of knowledge and her desire to share what she learned.

Excitement bubbled up inside her. If her memory served her correctly, the Wycliffe translation of the Bible had been available around this time, as was Chaucer's *Canterbury Tales,* Mallory's *Morte d'Arthur,* William Langland's *Piers Plowman,* and the anonymous *Gawain and the Green Knight.* Medical texts and Psalters could more than likely be obtained as well, making up a suitable source of material for Addie's prospective students.

She had always devoured all sorts of texts: history, literature, science; it all fascinated her. Then she would feel fit to burst if she couldn't share the nuggets of wisdom she unearthed with those around her. She couldn't wait to resume her teaching career.

In the flush of her renewed zeal, she left her room and ran down the stairs, again cursing the flimsy footwear she'd been forced to wear since she had arrived in this time. She often wondered what Nell or Robert or whomever had taken her boots had done with them. She'd inquired many times as to their whereabouts, but Nell never had a real answer to give and always changed the subject. Robert merely shrugged, stating that Nell had cared for her that night.

"One of these days," Addie muttered, rounding the corner to Robert's solar, "I'm going to pin you down, Nell Bolton. You're going to give me back my new boots."

As she approached her husband's private chamber, she heard the sound of agitated male voices. Hesitant to interrupt, she paused by the doorway, then heard the name that no longer failed to curdle her blood.

". . . Henry Tudor," said Mortimer.

"Aye," Robert concurred, "they've gone to meet him, or so we hear. Yet we know not how many remain behind. If we're to travel to Morland Castle in relative safety, now is the time to do so, while those scheming traitors are on their way to join the pretender in Wales."

"I cannot talk you out of going?" asked Mortimer.

"Nay," answered her husband in a tone she knew brooked no argument.

"But what about . . . ?"

"Addie?"

"Aye, lad. Your lady wife."

"She must come. I need her talents to establish my presence there. We must put in place retainers who are loyal to me. And Addie has a way with folks. She can charm even the most intractable."

Mortimer chuckled. "Like my Nell."

"Aye, just like Nell."

Anger flared in Addie. She marched into the room. "What do you want with Morland Castle?" she demanded of her husband. "Do you have a death wish? They tried their best to kill you not so long ago, and I have not forgotten the men they hurt. The men I worked to save. And especially the one I couldn't save."

Robert spun to face her, his broad cheekbones tinting with red. "Morland Castle belongs to me," he said, his voice inflexible, his footsteps toward her decisive and steady. "'Twas the only reason I married Catherine, and I've paid enough. I will not so easily surrender my right to what is mine."

Addie had never known rage like this before. She took another step toward him, staring unflinchingly into those dark eyes. "Will you risk the lives of more men just for the sake of pride? A pile of stone? A plot of land? What value do you place on human life?"

Eyes flashing, her husband came within inches of her nose. "A great one, especially on mine, yours, and that of my retainers. Should I not establish my authority over what is mine, the Morlands will attack us again and again. Not only do they want to regain Morland Castle, but they also want Swynton Manor in their coffers. By swearing allegiance to Henry, they've declared themselves our enemies to the end. They'll not hesitate to burn, pillage, and destroy everything in their path to achieve their end. 'Tisn't Henry's right to the throne they fight for, 'tis the power the alliance will give them if they win. They crave Swynton wealth to bolster that power."

"Money is what's important to you, then?" she asked, disdain in her voice.

"Nay, Wife. 'Tis the power to protect what's mine that matters. And honor. I cannot stomach the thought of Henry Tudor stripping Richard of the crown. I'll not discuss this further. We leave for Morland Castle within the week. You will accompany me, so choose the maids who will come with you."

"Just like that? You'll order me to do what you want? With no consideration for me?"

"Nothing matters more than establishing myself at Morland Castle. For my sake, and to support Richard's cause."

Addie's heart plummeted at the steely glint in her husband's eyes. "You said you were marrying me to protect me, yet now you're prepared to sacrifice everyone and everything for the sake of your pride and your lands."

He averted his gaze. "Aye."

"Even me?"

Without looking her way, he strode to the doorway. "Like my father before me, I'll uphold my honor, defend my family's name."

How foolish she had been to hope Robert might someday care about her, might want her for herself. He'd only sought to protect her as a matter of his blasted pride—it would besmirch his confounded honor if she died while in his care. And those moments of passion they had shared had only sprung from the tension of the moment. Addie was sure of that now.

For here he stood, prepared to use her to enlarge his holdings, vast as they already were. She should have remained a spinster after all. She should have rejected his ludicrous notion of protecting her with his name.

Protection, my foot!

No sooner were they wed, than he exposed her to real danger, leading her straight to his enemies' den, the very men who had ambushed him once before.

She'd been a fool to hope to mean something to Robert Swynton someday, to think she might someday become his lover in truth. But the pain in Addie's heart told her the most foolish thing she'd done to date was to fall in love with the miserable man.

Chapter 12

SHE COULDN'T LET him merrily waltz to his death. No matter how little she meant to him.

"Wait!" she cried, running after the man who had just broken her heart. "You cannot do this. You're going to die!"

Robert turned at the head of the stairs, a bemused look on his face. "We all are, madam."

Addie ran to him and grasped his forearms, digging her fingers into the taut, unyielding flesh. Just like his unwavering determination. "But there's no need to go seeking death. And that's just what you'll do if you continue to support Richard. Challenging Henry's nobles will only ensure your next king's wrath. You cannot afford that, if you put so much value on your responsibility to your people."

"I have scarcely finished speaking of what truly matters to a man. 'Tis my honor, my family name, that I have when all is done. If I betray those, I have naught. My word to my father and my king, Addie Shaw—"

"Swynton, if you please," she cut in. "By your insistence, if you'll remember correctly."

A quirk of amusement tipped his mouth crookedly. "I could never forget, Lady Swynton." The humor vanished again. "I cannot betray my father and my king. 'Tis a matter of conscience, and I mean to keep mine clear for the day I breathe my last."

"If you continue down the path you're aiming to follow, that day will be right around August twenty second."

Robert's expression grew thunderous. "We'd agreed not to speak of that foolishness again. You're in a precarious position, my lady, as my people wish to burn you at the stake. I cannot protect you if you insist on speaking rashly."

"But Henry will kill Richard at Redmoor—"

"And if he does, he'll do so through me."

Addie's heart constricted in her breast. Robert drove her to distraction with his archaic notions of honor and pride. He frustrated her at every turn, questioning the truth of her experience through time. But most of all, he brought to life in her heart the most incredible feelings she had ever known. And the thought of him dying, for something so foolish as pride—after all, *"A man's pride shall bring him low,"* the Bible said—caused her visceral pain.

She heard his footsteps descend the stairs, each one pounding reality deeper into her misery. Robert, the man Addie loved, would die on a bloody field in little more than a month.

Her throat burned from the desire to cry out again. Tears rolled down her cheeks. The bread she'd eaten a short while ago felt like a sickening lump of steel, immovable and intolerable.

Just like her situation. She would become a widow before ever truly becoming a wife.

Unless . . .

Unless she could keep the muleheaded, pigheaded, noodleheaded fool from his stupid, prideful path.

Now, if only she knew how to accomplish just that.

During the next few days, Addie pondered myriad possibilities, quickly discarding each one as implausible. How could she best reach Robert's common sense? Especially since she'd come to fear he didn't have any at all.

She couldn't physically restrain him; the very thought was laughable. Big and massive as a granite cliff, and owning muscles to rival those of his beastly warhorse, Robert was no match for a woman—not even most men.

He didn't lack wit or intelligence, so Addie knew tricking him would be . . . well, just that: tricky. Still, distraction seemed the only way to divert him from his suicidal path.

How should she go about it? How could she appeal to him in such a way that he would go along with her? And not drag up that absurd witchcraft nonsense again.

As she considered her options, Addie plowed forward with her plan to educate the folks of Swynton Manor. Once she had an outline of her program in mind, she sought the lord of the manor for the necessary supplies.

"I need help with something I very much want to do," she said after supper one evening.

Robert eyed her warily. She didn't fault him for that, since she'd refrained from speaking with him after their last, disastrous confrontation. It hurt too much to think of his days as numbered.

In her most academic tone, she said, "I have uncovered the existence of a deplorable situation here at Swynton. Your people cannot read. Or write. As a teacher, I can and must remedy the condition, but I need reading material for my future students."

Robert's expression changed as she spoke. It now displayed complete confusion. "But . . . why would they need to read? Or write?"

"It's something *everyone* should do. To help themselves, to learn things, to improve their lives. And I can teach them. All I need is books."

Robert shook his head, letting her know how foolish he thought her idea. "I have books, but I won't have you keeping folks from their tasks. Swynton is a large holding, and everyone must do their part, else all others will suffer."

"I'll take but brief bits of their free time."

"Few have any free time."

"Then perhaps their taskmaster is too harsh."

Robert's eyes narrowed. "I work equally hard."

"I didn't say otherwise, just that perhaps you need to . . . oh, perhaps give up your fighting nonsense and put your men to work more productively at crafts or farms or commerce of some form."

The look of horror that filled Robert's handsome face almost made Addie laugh. Almost.

"They're men-at-arms, woman! Finely trained, at that. I cannot waste them on fields of corn or at a forge. As if any would go were I to order them. Mortimer would rather die than give up his broadsword—"

"As he likely will, come August next," she spit out.

"Enough!" he roared. "We've had this discussion oft enough. We shan't waste the time again. I'll fetch the books, and you may use your time any way you wish. Should you interfere with my men's readiness, however, Wife—"

"I won't, I won't," Addie hastened to say, the look in his eyes quite persuasive. "I'll teach the children and those women who wish to learn. I won't disturb the running of the manor, the farms, or any other work you deem necessary. The choice will be the people's. I'll simply make myself available to them."

With clear reluctance, Robert nodded. "Walter will bring the texts to you on the morrow."

"Fine. And thank you."

His rare grin flashed, surprising her with its sudden appearance, its stunning effect. "'Twas hard for you to say, was it not?"

Although she thought she knew what he meant, Addie tipped her chin high and asked, "What?"

"A simple thank-you."

"Why, not at all! I thank everyone all the time."

Bemusement filled his face. "'Tis the first for me."

"Impossible. It couldn't be—"

"But it is."

Addie fell silent, thinking back on all the times they'd clashed, all the times they'd spoken. It struck her he could very well be right. They hadn't had many opportunities to speak pleasantly, to do things that would lead her to give him thanks. And she wondered . . .

Were their differences, their frequent arguments, the reason he hadn't come to care for her as she had him? Why he didn't want her for a wife? A *real* wife?

Would friendship improve matters between them? Would he want that kind of bond? Would it lead to deeper feelings for her? Would Robert like to know her better?

She remembered the day they'd gone into the woods, the time the arrow had narrowly missed her. They'd spoken. He'd eaten her snacks. And he'd indulged her need to care for Cheepers the sparrow, now her pet.

He'd also kissed her. Twice. With a passion she would never forget.

He'd meant those kisses. Just as much as she had.

Perhaps that desire was a base she ought to build on. She'd give the idea a bit more thought, but at the moment it felt right, filled with possibility.

For the first time in a long time, hope surged in Addie's heart, real, rich, and alive.

By golly, it was going to work!

As Nell filled the reed basket with treat after snack, the oddest sense of calm surrounded Addie. She ought to be jumpier than a hare fleeing a hound, but instead she felt certain she was doing the right thing.

"Does me good to see you tryin' to get that boy away from his worries, if only for a while," Nell said, placing a skin of Robert's favorite wine in the basket.

Addie flushed. If Nell knew *all* she planned to try on that *boy,* she might not think that way. But she didn't, and wouldn't, know. "No one can spend all his time thinking of killing without it doing something to his head."

"Aye, Addie Swynton, methinks you're right. Look at Mortimer, fool he. The man loves me, of that I'm sure, but he feels he cannot wed, that his duty to his lord comes first."

"In the meantime the both of you grow old alone, when

you should be sharing your lives and reaping happiness instead."

"Indeed."

With a pat to the white cloth over the simple but generous repast, Addie slung the basket's handle over one arm. "We shall see how well I fare, Nell. Can't say a thing about Robert Swynton but that he's set in his ways."

"As he has been since he was a babe."

"You've known him that long?"

Nell chuckled warmly. "He suckled at my breast from the day he was born. My own little one—a girl—was stillborn. He's my son as much as if I had borne him. And I've never known him to have a scrap of joy in his life." The older woman gave Addie an assessing stare. "But since you've come to Swynton, I've begun to hope. Methinks you're the one to give him all he's lacked."

Butterflies swarmed in Addie's middle. "Perhaps, Nell. Perhaps." Then, shaking off the silly, fanciful thoughts, Addie made herself focus on her more practical goal. "At the least, I'll give him a moment of rest." *And maybe even save his tough, prideful hide.*

Knowing her husband at least a bit, Addie calmly strolled toward the barbican gate, waving to all who passed her, chatting pleasantly with those who paused.

"Good day, Lady Swynton!" called Lissa as she emerged from the dovecote, swatting feathers from her plain brown dress. "I wrote on the dirt outside yesterday until the sun was set. I can do most of the letters you showed me."

Addie smiled, sincerely pleased. "Keep at it, and soon you'll be scripting missives as beautiful as Walter Reeve's."

Lissa chuckled, shook her head, and held herself straighter, her accomplishment providing the pride she now bore so well. Addie again felt that sense of rightness, that knowledge that she'd done something good, of lasting value. It was what she always felt when she taught or helped someone recover their health.

As she neared the gate in the stone wall, Addie noticed

Mary, the alewife, rolling a wooden barrel out the brewing house door. "Good morning, Mary!"

The stout woman glanced up, narrowed her gaze, then muttered, "Good day."

"How is Rufus's hound? Do the fleas still plague him?"

Mary straightened and faced Addie. "Not so long as I keep using yer hempen rope," she said grudgingly. "Makes a body wonder what ye've done to it . . . what kind of power gives such results."

Addie knew trouble when she heard it. "There's nothing odd about my method. I soak the strings in oil of pennyroyal I obtain from Thomasine. The same pennyroyal you use to bathe the animal, if I'm not much mistaken."

Mary's brown eyes narrowed. "Then why does the bath not rid the beast of the fleas while the string does?"

"Because the pennyroyal in the bath wears off his fur in a short time. The oil on the string lasts longer. It's most simple, you see."

Mary nodded slowly, considering the explanation. "And ye do naught more to it?"

"No, Mary, I don't chant, conjure spirits, or cast spells on the string. It's merely a matter of how we apply the medicine. The oil lasts longer, and the string remains tied around the animal's neck. See?"

"I . . . see," the woman finally said, offering a tentative smile. "Well, then, if that's how ye do it, would ye tell me how ye've rid the Swynton kitchen of weevils? I've a fair plague, ye know."

Addie smiled in triumph. "Of course I'll tell you. And I'll send you a muslin bag filled with crushed cloves this afternoon. All you do is set it on the shelf where you store your grains and flour. The troublesome bugs detest cloves, so they'll stay away. But first you must rid yourself of the weevilly stuff. I'll have Nell send a kitchen maid with enough stores to replace what you throw out."

Mary hung her head momentarily. Then she met Addie's gaze directly. "Can ye forgive me, mistress? I've accused ye of witchcraft, and 'twould seem from what ye've said that ye're no more a witch than I. As yer good husband said."

Addie nodded and smiled. "Don't think of it again. Go clean out your shelves. You've much to do this afternoon. Oh, and if you have the time, I'll be teaching my reading class in the bailey at five tonight. You're welcome to join the rest."

A dubious look spread over Mary's stolid features. "Oh, I know not about that. Dunno what my Horace would say to me readin' and writin' and all. But thank ye, anyway, Lady Swynton. Ye're most kind to offer."

Addie started toward the gate, thinking again that if it weren't for Emmie back home and her fear for Robert's life, she would indeed be happy to live out her life right where she was. She had a mission, a true calling, that could greatly benefit those around her. One that brought her much satisfaction.

Now if she could only achieve happiness. . . .

Remembering her goal, Addie resumed her greetings to any and all who passed her way. Knowing Robert, the moment he heard she'd crossed the gates, he would be after her like a bird after a worm. He wasn't about to let her return to the woods without him—as he'd stated any number of times.

A sly grin on her lips, she stepped beyond the confines of the barbican wall. Without even the briefest glance over her shoulder, she ambled in the direction of the stand of trees. So confident was she of her husband's reaction that she began to hum a ditty, anticipation simmering in her.

Before she'd even gone halfway, she heard his yell.

Without responding, she glanced at him, took note of the flush on his cheeks, the anger in his eyes, the rigid set of his jaw, and waved. She never slowed her pace.

Seconds later, he grabbed her free arm, swung her around, putting a halt to her advance. "What think you to do, Lady Swynton? Were you not told to stay within the walls at all times until the danger is past? Yet you've left all protection behind for nothing more than a whim." He waved at her basket.

Hiding her nervousness, Addie gave him a glowing smile. "And a good day to you, too, Robert. As usual, it's a pleasure to see you. Of course, that's as it should be between married folks, no?"

To her delight, he flushed redder and averted his gaze, giving Addie the opportunity to break free from his hold.

" 'Twould be a fine day if you had stayed where you belong," he answered. "Why must you defy my order?"

Giddy with anxious energy, Addie twirled in a circle, feeling feminine, womanly. "Because the day is lovely indeed, the breeze is sweet, I'm sure the birds sing happily in the trees, and I'd like to have my picnic in the woods. The one that was interrupted by a vile arrow that other time."

From the corner of her eye, she saw the muscle twitch in his jaw. " 'Tis because of that arrow you should stay away."

"Ah, but you've come with me. Again."

"My presence did not deter the attempt on your life that last time."

"But surely whoever's at fault won't try the same thing twice. They'll try something else, since they know we're aware of their way with arrows."

Robert scoffed. "Spoken foolishly like a woman."

Addie snorted. "Nothing more foolish than a man who playacts war all day."

To her surprise, he didn't rise to her taunt. Instead, he stared at her for a long moment, then allowed a slow smile to spread across his lips. "You'll not lead me into another of your endless arguments, Addie Shaw—er, Swynton. You wish to stroll through the woods? Very well, then, we shall stroll through the woods."

Satisfaction again rippled through her. "What a gracious offer! How could I refuse, my lord? Thank you *ever* so kindly."

At his snicker, she glanced his way. The arch of a dark brow let her know he was only too mindful of his comment regarding her gratitude the other day.

She nodded in acknowledgment, still thrilled to have gotten this far. The cold mutton sandwiches, the wine, and the sugar cakes should do the rest.

In peace, they walked into the woods, and Addie commented on the expectant hush within the stand of trees. "It reminds me of church," she added.

Robert looked up at the soaring ceiling of green. "A cathedral, perhaps."

Thrilled to hear her husband chat pleasantly, Addie went on. "A natural one, at that. God's creation is magnificent indeed."

He nodded absently, and she caught him studying the basket on her arm. "Have you more of those cookies today?" he asked.

Success! "Aplenty. And you'll be pleased to know that Nell packed fresh bread and mutton and a skin of wine, too."

Robert narrowed his gaze. "You expected company, then?"

Addie smiled sweetly. "Of course."

His brows crashed over the bridge of his nose. "Whose would that be, my lady?"

Lowering her lashes and feeling a blush warm her cheeks, Addie murmured, "My lord's."

She didn't wait for his response but kept walking until she reached the spot she'd remembered from her earlier forays. The tree was massive, its base wide-spreading, thick moss blanketing the earth between knobby knees of root. Addie set down her basket and lifted the napkin cover. As she withdrew a length of linen, she dared a peek at her companion.

What she saw stunned her. Robert remained where he'd stood, arms loose at his sides, a thunderstruck expression on his face.

"Well?" she asked when it became clear he wasn't about to move, not even when she'd finished spreading the cloth over the ground. "Will you simply stand there and stare, or will you join me?"

He shook his head as if to dispel his thoughts, then approached. "I know not whether to feel flattered or outraged."

Addie waved and chuckled giddily, her nerves inciting the uncharacteristic sound. "Oh, flattered, of course. It's too fine a day for outrage."

"You dare much, lady wife," he said in a suddenly deeper, harsher voice.

Addie caught her breath. What would he say in about . . . oh, another hour or so?

But, no, she wouldn't let fear or shyness or anything else deter her. She'd decided on the most logical, practical strategy, she'd put it in action, and she was on the verge of seeing it bring forth fruit. "Perhaps I've come to know your bark is worse than your bite," she said with a bold wink.

He scowled, the ferocity in his expression patently false. "Respect, lady wife, is sorely lacking. Mayhap I must bite to prove I've teeth."

Addie remembered the time they'd kissed, how he'd nibbled on her bottom lip, sending sharp stabs of need right through her. She shivered in anticipation. Calling on all her courage, she murmured, "Perhaps."

Once again, the silence in the woods seemed to grow, deepen, enveloping them in an intimate cocoon. The very air around them thrummed with anticipation, as if the world itself awaited a significant occurrence, an imminent, momentous event. Addie glanced at her husband and, noting the fire in his gaze, sat on the cloth she'd spread for them. "Come," she whispered, patting the spot at her side.

Just then, the enormity of what she was about to do struck her. Was she mad? She'd never been the sort to interest men, much less lure one to a tryst, but here she was, doing precisely that. Judging from the expression on Robert's face, her attempt at seductive behavior had so far succeeded, but she wondered if she had the courage to see it through.

Then she thought of the alternative. She thought of Robert marching off to battle for Richard—a doomed effort, if ever there was one. She thought of herself, alone again, widowed and far from home, from Emmie.

Deep in her heart, a huge "No" arose, nearly bursting

from her lips. She bit down on the soft flesh to keep the word from ringing out.

She would do whatever it took to achieve her goal. She would know her husband's touch, she would keep him from giving his life in vain, and she would somehow get back to Emmie—without relinquishing anything she'd gained.

As she vowed to continue down the only path she could consider, she became aware of the hard, warm thigh at her side. She again met Robert's gaze.

She wouldn't let him die without a fight.

Clearing her throat from the sudden lump it held, she asked, "Would you like a—"

"Sweet," he said, cutting off her words.

"Of course," she answered and, flustered, rummaged in the basket.

A massive arm came across her middle, stopping the nervous movements in the depths of the woven reeds. "Not that kind," he said, then pressed a kiss on her cheek.

Addie's skin tingled at the touch of those warm, firm lips. Her breath caught in her chest. Her pulse pounded in her temples. With all the courage she owned, and knowing full well what she invited with her actions, she turned her hand, laced her fingers through his, and brought her lips a fraction closer to his.

"Oh, Addie . . ." he murmured and brought his mouth to hers.

Once again, feelings overwhelmed her. Not just the excitement of his lips against hers, the roughness of his stubbled skin against hers, the hard contours of his chest against hers, but the sense of being where she belonged, with this man, in this place.

Robert rubbed his mouth against hers, and Addie sighed her pleasure, warmth suffusing every corner of her self. This was Robert, her husband, the man she loved.

A tiny tremor shook her, and he molded his mouth more fully to hers. Addie responded shyly, yet willing to give him everything she had, everything she was. He didn't hesitate to accept.

As she clung to his one hand, she relished the deep, sensual kiss they shared and knew the moment his other hand curved at her waist. Her heartbeat sped ever faster, pounding so loudly in her ears that she wondered if he could hear its crazy pace.

And then nothing mattered, for that hand began to explore her body. Long, slow caresses swept over her, leaving fire and ice in their wake. How could that be?

Who cared?

Addie heard a strange sound and realized it came from deep within her. It must have pleased Robert, for he then dropped her hand and curved his arm around her back. With his body, he pressed her down to the ground, surrounding her with his presence, heating her with his passion.

The kiss never stopped.

Tentatively she allowed her hands to roam, curious and needing to know her husband as he clearly craved to know her. It was right, this they were doing! They were married, husband and wife. And these feelings, this glorious, maddening, ravening want she felt was just exactly what they were meant to share.

Lovers.

They were about to become that, in every meaning of the word, at least for her. And surely, with hunger such as he revealed with his kiss, his touch, it wasn't a mere physical act Robert sought. Addie's hope soared as his mouth left hers to trail kisses and broken whispers down her throat.

He touched her as if she were the most precious thing in life to him, as if she were fragile porcelain, worth more than all the riches on earth. He mouthed her name in a reverent voice, his lips gentle and devouring at the same time.

When he grasped the hem of her gown, Addie couldn't keep from whispering, "My husband. . . ."

Robert stopped. He lifted his head from the curve of her breast and met her gaze. "My wife," he replied, his voice deep and sure.

Addie's heart soared with joy when he removed her gown, leaving her bare to his gaze. For a moment she wondered how that could be. She, who had never been seen this way by anyone else, felt no shame, no embarrassment. Only a need to be Robert's ran through her, stealing every bit of the modesty that had always characterized her.

How could she not feel joy when admiration gleamed in his eyes, accompanied, she could swear, by the same joy she felt? She wondered just exactly what he felt.

How different Addie was from Catherine, Robert suddenly thought, as she lay before his heated gaze. Not once had she sought to avoid his touch, his kiss. And now that he had stripped her of all covering—something his first wife had never allowed—Addie lay beneath him, an invitation in her slumberous gray eyes.

She'd called him husband, respect and want in her voice. She gazed upon him with need and passion in her eyes. And to his amazement, she lifted her arms, curved them around his neck, and pulled him down to her firm, welcoming flesh. "My wife," he repeated, then lost the ability to think anymore.

He felt the silk of her breasts against his chest, the sleekness of her legs against the roughness of his, the shy touch of her mouth against his, and he knew their loving was meant to be.

He knew now what he'd missed before. With sudden clarity he understood that this time was different, because this time 'twas Addie with him, in his arms. Gently, wonderingly, reverently, he made them one.

Their joining rocked him to the very core of his heart. Emotion filled his throat, threatened to spill from his eyes, as he strove to bring Addie pleasure, as he sought to find his own. Her gasps, her moans, her sighs and cries, played sweet music to his love-starved ears. Robert felt ready to burst from the feelings surging through him, stealing his last rational thought, filling him with newfound joy.

He moved steadily, tenderly, and in a fireburst of sensation, he spun toward bliss with his wife.

Chapter 13

THE MOST INCREDIBLE thing had happened, really and truly. Addie had become a wife. After spending her adult life certain she would remain a spinster with only her younger sister to love, she now found herself well married indeed.

Her feelings for her husband amazed her, emotions deep and rich that bubbled to the surface as she lay at his side, her head cradled on his broad shoulder. A tear rolled down her temple, and she caught it on a finger before it bathed Robert's skin. Although he slept, she feared he'd feel it and think her unhappy by what had just transpired between them.

What exactly *had* happened?

They'd made love, rich, satisfying, unforgettably sweet love.

As she closed her eyes, remembering, joy again stole through Addie, leading her to place her hand over Robert's heart. She felt its beat through her palm, strong and sure and steady. Just like the man himself.

She loved him. Utterly, unwisely, and eternally.

That was why she couldn't let anything happen to him.

She had to find a way to save his life, even if she had to fight him to do so, which she feared was precisely what she would soon have to do.

But right then Addie could take advantage of his slumber.

Extricating herself from his embrace was no easy task. Each time she moved, Robert tightened his hold, first on a hip, then at her waist, then on her thigh. Addie waited patiently each time for him to sleep soundly again, smiling the last time when a quiet snore rumbled past his lips.

He wasn't as perfect as he would like to think, but rather human and as flawed as she knew him to be. Regardless, she loved him. And her love brought forth a ferocious protectiveness—even more powerful than what she felt for her sister, odd though that seemed.

Stealthily dressing, Addie glanced at the sleeping man again. Her body still felt his touch in all its intimate spots, and she blushed, thinking how wantonly she'd welcomed his possession. She blushed hotter yet when she thought how much she'd welcome it again in the future.

She tiptoed a ways from Robert's makeshift bed, taking care not to make a sound. Then, eyeing her surroundings, she found a likely candidate and approached the oak, determination at full pitch. "Are you the one?" she asked the lofty plant.

It didn't respond, and she took its mottled bark as a good sign. She knew the tree she sought had a discoloration somewhere near its base. She just couldn't remember exactly what it looked like, since she'd scarcely taken note of the tree when she sat against it that fateful day. Of course, she hadn't; who would have thought something so fantastical would happen mere moments later?

Arranging her skirts around her legs, she sat and leaned back, closing her eyes, thinking of York, home, her school, her sister.

Nothing.

Just the sound of singing birds, the soughing of the wind, the skittering of a squirrel not far away.

Disappointment rushed in, but Addie ignored it. More

than ever she was determined to find her way home, for now it wasn't just Emmie she worried about. Now she had to make sure that Robert survived. The only way she knew to accomplish that was to drag him back home with her through the blasted oak.

Even if he fought her through all four hundred years.

Despite his determination otherwise, Robert Swynton was married again. And this time he truly knew himself a wedded man. He smiled in satisfaction—satisfaction indeed. His lady wife was . . . he still knew not how to describe Addie. He simply knew she'd done something to his more rational self and stolen right into his heart.

She'd roused his passions to a fever pitch then satisfied them in the sweetest, most innocent manner, generously giving herself in a way over which he still marveled. He'd never forget her cry when he'd made them one. The awe in her gaze, the smile of ecstasy on her lips unforgettable minutes later.

He would never forget the quaking waves of pleasure that had swamped him as he'd reached a pinnacle he hadn't known existed. But it did. And he'd found it with Addie. His lady wife.

Now, as he watched Mortimer put his men through their paces, Robert found it nearly impossible to concentrate on his master-at-arms. All he could think about was joining Addie in her bedchamber later that night and again sharing the beauty and passion they had so recently discovered.

True, he'd spent a useless hour watching her test trees. But he hadn't had it in him to fight her right then, not when the memory of their loving lived fresh in his heart. Finally, when she'd cried out her frustration, he'd taken her in his arms, kissed her gently, and promised to return with her again and again, until reality proved to her the oak of her delusion didn't exist. He had no idea why he'd made such a foolish vow, but it appeared he had much to learn about being in love.

Love.

He'd never thought he would find it, especially since he had never believed it existed outside the words of bards and scribes, but he had no other word to express what he felt for his new wife. And so he called it love. As he suspected she did, too.

The emotion he had seen in her eyes, damp with tears, when he'd promised to help her look for her damnable tree, could only have been love; it so nearly matched what he'd felt while watching her sit under tree after tree, refusing to give up despite impossible odds.

Ah, yes. Robert Swynton had found wedded bliss, and he intended to explore it more fully—not to mention his wife's delectable body—once nighttime returned.

"Sir Robert, Sir Robert!" cried Mick Hoskins, panic in his high-pitched voice.

"What is it, lad?" he asked, fear for Addie clutching at his throat.

"'Tis Harold, sir. Neville has returned and bears a wounded Harold over his horse."

Icy hatred filled Robert's gut. The Morlands, damn their black souls. They'd struck again, bringing down a man he trusted like a brother, loved thusly, too.

"How bad is it?"

Mick shook his tousled brown head. "I know not, but me mum ran for Thomasine the minute she heard."

Mortimer bustled near. "'Tisn't Thomasine the boy needs, lad," he said, panting, "but your Addie."

With a nod Robert headed for the manor house. "Neville took him to the great hall, did he not?"

"'Course," answered Mick.

"Addie will be there," Robert called to Mortimer. "Let the others know. I'll see to Harold myself. And, Mick, after you've supped tonight, come to me. You've earned a reward for a watchman's job well done."

The boy's crowing cheer behind him, Robert loped toward home, knowing naught but anger, hate, dread.

He feared for Harold's life—and he feared a future where the Morlands might strike at will, unchecked should the pretender assume the crown, their greed forgiven by one as greedy as they.

He dreaded a future where he would have to deny Addie access to the woods.

As he took the last three steps to the main floor of the house, Robert careened into a soft, warm body that emitted a surprised "Ooof!" in a most familiar voice.

"So sorry," he said, catching his breath and his wife's linen-laden arms at the same time.

"Oh, Robert," she wailed, distress on her fine features, "Lissa said Harold's been hurt."

"Aye, Addie. He has indeed. I know not how badly yet, as I'm on my way to his side. Will you . . . will you save him?"

Addie glared and sought to escape his hold. "Why do you even ask? What else do you think I would do? Don't you know anything about me yet?" Shaking her head, she tried to wiggle free, but he held firm.

She sighed and turned those clear, sincere eyes up to meet his. "I can't promise more than I promised the first time, but you truly *should* know by now I'll do my best."

Robert smiled wryly, concern for his friend still strong within him. "'Tis right you are, my lady wife. Forgive my foolish words. They sprang before I gave them thought. Your best is good enough for me."

With a nod Addie tore away from his grasp and ran past the screen before the arched doorway to the great hall. "Don't get in my way," she warned, and Robert smiled crookedly.

If Harold had a chance, it lay in Addie's capable, determined hands. As Robert stepped around the screen, he watched her bend over his man's pallet, still holding the rags she'd carried. Anxiety filled her features, caring her voice.

When he reached her side, she turned to him and, thrusting the wad of cloth at him, said, "Here."

He clutched the mass to his middle and watched her prod the area around the bloody gash on Harold's right thigh. The young man winced. Blood spurted from the cut.

"What happened?" Robert asked, determined to learn the slightest detail of the attack.

Addie glared again. "I warned you to stay out of my way."

"I am out of your way, madam, but I can pose a question, can I not?"

"Not if you tax his strength," she answered, frowning at the renewed bleeding. "Fetch Thomasine."

Robert nearly smiled at her command. How very like his new bride. "She's on her way," he said. "Mistress Hoskins went for her the moment we learned Harold had been hurt."

"Thank God," she murmured. "We must clean and close this immediately. I'll need her help."

The wounded man made a sound. "Will I die, Lady Addie?"

"Not anytime soon!"

A small smile lightened his drawn expression. "Will I . . . lose the leg?"

"Not if I have anything to do with it." Turning to Robert, she said, "Why are you just hugging those rags? Please fetch me a basin of clean, boiled water from the kitchen. And my sewing basket. Nell's sharpest knife as well."

Knowing better than to argue, Robert went to set the bandages down. Then he heard familiar footsteps rounding the screen. "I've your water and the knife, Addie," said Nell, her breathing rough from exertion. "Didn't need to be told—I know you well enough by now. And I'll fetch the sewing basket from your chamber."

Moments later, Thomasine arrived, bearing herbs and creams and things Robert couldn't identify. Feeling ever more useless before the women's expertise, he nevertheless couldn't tear himself away from the scene.

As he watched, Addie competently sliced away the torn hose from Harold's leg, not in the least bothered by the location of the young man's wound. She cleansed his upper thigh impersonally, clearly unaware of her patient's abject, painful embarrassment. That, if nothing else, allayed the worst of Robert's fears.

If Addie's ministrations disturbed Harold thusly, then his

man would soon be well enough again. The question in Robert's mind, however, was whether the brilliant swordsman would again fight on that viciously cut leg. He had enough sense to keep the question to himself, and he smiled as he imagined the scolding his wife would give him should he think to voice it.

As his fear for Harold's life dissipated, discomfort at his wife's obvious familiarity with a man's body grew. She blithely swabbed a cloth disturbingly close to her patient's groin, discomfiting the man.

And him.

Moments later, Robert realized he wasn't merely discomfited by Addie's actions. He recognized the feeling in his gut as . . . jealousy. With a shameful dose of pettiness, he realized he didn't want his wife touching another male so intimately, if dispassionately, but him. He remembered her fingers coursing over him earlier that day, the effect those caresses had had on him, and he knew an irrational need to grab her and tear her from Harold's side, to forbid her to touch any other man but him, even if she merely meant to save the man's life.

Robert conceded he'd lost his mind.

Well, perhaps not so much his mind as his heart. To the maddening, fascinating woman who had stumbled from the woods near his home one bloody afternoon.

The woman who vociferously objected to the fighting that brought men to her in broken bits. The woman who would patch Harold back up, only to see him go out and risk injury again.

Robert finally understood her hatred of weaponry and battle. Not that he particularly enjoyed watching men kill or doing so himself, but he could see that with her need to heal, to help others, she would suffer more than most when the unthinkable came to pass.

A hiss of pain breached Harold's lips. "So sorry," Addie murmured, anguish in her voice.

"'Tis naught, my lady," her patient said between gritted teeth, clearly loath to appear weak before her.

Finally, when the leg displayed a long row of neat stitches, and Addie had wrapped her needlework with the linen strips Robert had held for her, Harold lay back, sweat gleaming on his brow, his upper lip. "Thank you, Lady Addie," he said, gratitude and more in his voice.

Robert looked sharply at the man and saw the same appreciation in Harold's eyes as he had seen in those others his wife had tended. He narrowed his gaze. "Methinks you've coddled him enough, my lady," he said, his voice sharper than he'd intended, jealousy burning through him. "He's a warrior, trained and tried, and as such has faced wounds before. I needs must speak with him. You women have other duties awaiting."

A mutinous expression darkened Addie's face. "I warned you, Robert Swynton, not to get in my way. You don't know a fig about medicine, so I'm in charge here. Harold is very weak as he has lost much blood. The next day or so are of utmost importance if he's to keep that leg."

When Harold blanched, she lay a gentle hand on his, patting gently. "Which he will do, if he does exactly as I say. You, too."

The sight of that hand clasping another man's turned something sharp in Robert's chest. What if she didn't care for him as much as he'd thought? As much as he hoped?

What had the tryst in the woods meant to her? As much as it had to him?

Come nighttime, he would find out. "I must know what happened, Addie, if I'm to keep others safe. Including you."

She arched an eyebrow. "You haven't called off that foolish trip to Morland Castle yet, have you?"

"I cannot."

"Of course you can. You just don't want to. And it's that prideful whim of yours that endangers us all. Including Harold."

"Addie . . ."

She nodded sharply. "Yes, I agreed we'd not discuss this matter again. Still, I have an opinion—"

"One I know too well. And need not at all."

With that characteristic, upward tilt of her chin, she graced him with a glacial glare. Perhaps his plan for the night would not come to pass. Pity. But Robert could not give in on this point.

'Twas a matter of honor.

"I'll be leaving now," she informed him in a haughty voice. "See that he doesn't move. And let him rest, for pity's sake. You'd have more than enough time to discuss what happened if you wouldn't insist on tomorrow's departure."

Before he could formulate an adequate reply, she was gone. "Fine woman," Harold murmured.

"Mine," Robert bit off before he could stop the revealing word.

"Ah, so 'tis that way, then."

Robert clenched his jaw against a withering retort. "Whatever way you think, remember this: she's my lady wife."

Harold lifted an eyebrow and said shrewdly, "Should *you* forget, others will gladly step in your stead."

"Not if they care to live," Robert said with menace, then stared at Harold's injured leg. "Or walk again."

"I understand, my lord. But you'll forgive an admiring man's gratitude for her mercy, will you not?"

"So long as it remains gratitude and naught else."

" 'Twould matter not to her if it were more."

"Oh?"

Harold laughed. "So you're blind as well," he said, shifting on the pallet. He gasped in pain and clutched his thigh just beyond its linen cover.

Robert cursed his unruly emotions for making him forget what truly mattered at the moment. "Forgive me, Harold. I know not what's come over me. What happened today?"

A tight nod acknowledged his apology. "I was attacked as I set off to follow the Morlands again. I thought I'd escaped their notice, moving slowly and far behind. But they left scouts in their wake. Someone must have reported my presence, the questions I asked."

"What did you learn?"

"Michael has indeed sworn fealty to Henry and means to join him in Wales."

"As we'd heard."

"Aye. But there's more."

"Tell me."

"They're enraged by your . . . marriage."

That dread chill again lodged in Robert's gut. "What mean you?"

Harold sighed. " 'Tis foul, milord. They call your lady Swynton's Sorceress, and they mean to keep her from stepping foot in Morland Castle. They want your first wife's dowry back, and if 'tis the only way, they'll kill you and Addie to regain what they believe is theirs. They fear an heir, you understand. She cannot live, much less bear you a son. They're the ones at fault for the attacks on her life."

"Damn every last one of them!" Robert growled. " 'Tisn't her fight at all. The scurrilous cowards won't face me squarely, but ambush and strike from behind. Now they target a woman, by damn! And they've betrayed the crown. I won't run from them. I cannot. And I'll keep her safe, here as at Morland Castle itself."

"Have a care, my lord, when you travel west in the morrow. They've left a few of their men along the way. Not many, but enough to attack when you least expect."

"Ah, but I'm forewarned. I'll watch for them every step of the way. I'll not see Addie harmed."

As evening approached, Robert struggled to keep his thoughts on anything but his wife. Apprehension surfaced with alarming regularity, especially since they'd be traveling into dangerous territory.

He had to claim Morland Castle, and do so decisively. For his own sake and that of King Richard.

Addie would help him establish himself there, and in doing so, she would be at risk. Now that he knew 'twas the Morlands behind the attempts on her life, he knew she'd been right when she'd accused him of using her for his own gain, for the sake of his pride.

He would do so, but he'd also keep her safe. How? He knew not just then, but he'd never failed those who depended on him, and he would not fail the woman he had come to love.

Even if he had to use her to attain his goals.

As they supped, she cast him odd glances, and he noticed how nervous she appeared. Thrice she dropped the silver-plate spoon she used for her soup, and twice she spilled ale when she grasped a cup in her unsteady hand.

'Twas unusual in a woman as steady and sensible as his lady wife.

His wife.

Addie.

The giving woman who had lain with him under cover of spring-green leaves just hours ago. The delightful woman he intended to bed just hours from now.

Anticipation roared through him, making him careless with a crust of bread. As he bent to pick it up from where it fell to the floor, a thought occurred to Robert.

Could Addie be thinking about the hours to come? Those hours he intended to spend at her side? In her bed? The hours he hoped would be a repeat of the spectacular experience of that afternoon.

He glanced sideways and caught her studying him. A blush tinted her fine cheekbones, and she lowered her lashes, hiding those magnificent, normally direct gray eyes from his gaze.

How unusual!

The only other time she'd appeared shy in his presence had been just before she'd given herself to him . . . and if he wasn't much mistaken, 'twas that she thought about right then.

To test his theory, Robert reached over and cupped her chin in his palm. Tilting her face so he could more clearly study her reaction, he heard her catch her breath.

Her eyes opened wide. Her lips parted softly. She looked much as she had earlier that day, and Robert couldn't stop himself. He rubbed his thumb over the line of her jaw, marveling at the smoothness of her skin, caressing her gently, enjoying the warmth of her silky flesh.

She was so different from him.

And so feminine, in a lithe, willowy way.

How could he ever have thought her plain? Had he been blind when he first saw her?

Her soft skin flushed gently when she grew flustered, which she clearly was right then, since roses blossomed on her graceful cheekbones. Tendrils of glossy brown hair framed her face in softness, inviting him to take the thick mass down and bury his face in it. And her eyes . . . he could easily drown in those flashing silver beacons that knew not how to dissemble, that always bared her deepest thoughts to anyone who cared to learn them.

As he did right then.

"Addie . . ."

"Y-yes?"

To his dismay, Robert realized he'd been about to comment on their earlier intimacy, not remembering where they were. He chuckled ruefully, saving his words for a more appropriate time. " 'Tis an enchantress you are, my lady wife." When she stiffened, he smiled ever more broadly. "And you've truly enchanted me."

Her lips, delicately drawn and delicious, as he now knew, parted, forming a perfect *O*. With his index finger, Robert traced that soft circle, noting the rippling of her flesh. He'd much prefer to kiss those ripples away, he realized, and leaned forward to do just that.

A breath away, she slipped a hand between them and exclaimed, "Robert! You mustn't. Not here," she added, waving toward the room full of people.

"Why not?" he asked, rare mischief urging him on. "We're but newly wed. 'Twould surprise not a soul to see us kiss."

Her cheeks burned redder, the color reaching up to her hair. "But it would embarrass me!"

"Why, my lady wife?"

She frowned, her lips tightening, concentration etched on her forehead.

"I've left you speechless, then."

Her eyes narrowed, and Robert smiled, knowing her about to retort with her usual verve, her normal wit. But instead she winced. Then she moaned and clutched her middle.

"What?" he asked. "What is it?"

"Oh . . ." She gasped. "It hurts. A twisting cramp. . . ."

Addie doubled over, her misery only too clear. Robert shoved his chair back, and at the sound the room fell silent.

"What ails my lady?" called Mortimer, hurrying to the dais.

Distressed, Robert shook his head, then knelt at her side. "Addie?"

She lifted her head, and Robert noted the paleness of her cheeks, her lips, the dampness on her brow. "I was fine all day . . . and hungry. This pain . . . this dizziness . . . suddenly overtook me . . . *Oh!*" she cried again, her eyes widening with fear. "It—it's . . . worse. . . ."

Robert took her hand between both of his. It felt clammy when she gripped his fingers. "I'm about to carry you to your bedchamber," he said. "You'll not fight me, right?"

She shook her head tightly, then closed her eyes. Robert beckoned Mortimer and slipped his arms around her. At his nod, his master-at-arms moved her chair from his path. As Robert brought Addie close, he realized his hands shook. Fear filled his throat. What was wrong with her?

"Thomasine!" he cried. "Someone fetch her. Quick. My lady fares poorly, and we need help."

Ned Whitesell rose and headed toward the screen. " 'Tis the least I can do for Lady Addie after what she did for me."

Robert held her tighter to his chest and noticed how weak she seemed. "Addie?"

She didn't reply.

"Addie?" he asked, this time more sharply.

He again got no response.

When he pressed her flush against him, her pulse felt

slow, weak. Her head lolled back over his arm. Her breath, shallow and thready, scarcely moved her breast.

If he'd thought he had known fear before, he'd been sorely mistaken. Naught he had ever felt compared with this gripping clutch at his heart, this twisting coil at his gut, this surge of bile in his throat. Had it not been for the scant beat of her heart, weak, aye, yet palpable still, Robert would have sworn his wife lay dead.

In his arms.

And he could not bear the thought.

Not when the possibility of losing Addie showed him how very much he'd come to love her.

Chapter 14

DEEP IN THE bowels of the hideous night, Thomasine and Nell banned Robert from Addie's bedside. He hadn't wanted to move, not until those silver eyes opened and met his again, until he heard those soft lips murmur his name once more.

But they'd insisted evil intent lay behind her sudden illness, Thomasine even suggesting the likelihood of poison as the cause of Addie's collapse. They'd sent him to learn the truth.

That possibility had wrought a tortured cry from deep in Robert's gut. If he proved their suspicions right, then he had failed Addie only hours after vowing to keep her safe.

Robert doubted his people had resorted to such a cowardly attempt on her life. They'd approached him honestly with their fears, they'd openly accused her of witchcraft, and just as openly accepted his word about her innocence.

Poison smacked of the Morlands.

And betrayal.

Someone in his household had played him false. His wife had paid the price—indeed still paid it, as she lay deathly pale, scarcely breathing.

Outside her chamber door, anguish overtook him, nearly bringing him to his knees. "They will not go unpunished," he vowed, fists clenched at his sides as he fought his emotions. "Before God, I will avenge this foul deed."

As the night had turned cool, he forced himself to go to the great hall for his cloak, having left it over the arm of his chair, as he was wont to do. 'Twas late, he knew, but he needed to speak with Mortimer, needed to seek his most loyal man's counsel, his help with the decisions he must make.

The scene in the hall left him cold, making starkly real what had happened earlier. The meal had not been cleared away. Trenchers lay on tabletops as the diners had left them, Nell having gone straight to Addie's chamber, refusing to leave her side. The kitchen maids had failed to finish the task their chief had left undone.

Robert strode to the dais, wondering how best to reprimand the women for their negligence. There he found the proof he needed, proof that Thomasine's fears had been right. His blood chilled.

His head still on Addie's trencher, Nell's enormous black tom lay lifeless, his tongue lolling thickly between his open jaws. Sadness mixed with rage as Robert remembered the day he feared he would strangle the beast himself after noting the mess the animal's claws had made of his fine woolen cloak.

Nell would be heartbroken, and more so much if her mistress met the same fate as her cat. Instead of donning the cloak as he'd initially intended, Robert took the garment, folded it into a generous square, and lay the stiff corpse in the center. With one corner, he covered the lifeless animal, then carried it outside.

Every step he took strengthened his determination. The Morlands would pay for their crimes. Aye, even the death of an innocent cat would come to bear when they faced justice. And Robert would mete it out.

He gently lay his burden beneath a fragrant shrub in Nell's kitchen garden, knowing she would want to be present when he buried the beast. Robert knew not why the death of the animal affected him so; he only knew it did.

Perhaps it was because he knew Addie might come to a similar—

"Nay!" he roared to the night, refusing to consider the dread possibility. She would not die. Was Thomasine not the most gifted healer between Swynton and the city of York with its surgeons, physicians, and barbers?

Well, no. Not any longer.

Addie was.

"Dear God," he prayed, humbled by the depth of his pain, "have mercy on me. Take her not now that I've just found her."

Anguish in his heart, Robert gave the stiff, wool-covered body a tender pat, and went toward Mortimer's cottage. Before he even came close, he noticed light inside the chapel windows.

Diverting his steps, he opened the door to the stone building and caught his breath. He had found the women he'd thought neglected their tasks.

The kitchen and dairymaids, Mary the alewife, Jillie, Martha Goodling, and countless others knelt in prayer, Father Anselm leading them from behind the altar table.

A knot formed in Robert's throat, and tears burned in his eyes. As he stood immobile, watching, a hush filled the room. "How fares the lady?" asked the priest.

"She . . ." Robert's voice failed him, necessitating the clearing of his throat. Embarrassment filled him at what he'd revealed to the faithful gathered in the church, then it suddenly mattered not. They prayed for Addie, and they cared what happened to her. They would not view his emotions as a flaw, but rather as evidence of his love for his wife.

"She's no different than when I took her to her chamber. But I found Nell's tom, dead after eating the remains of my wife's meal."

Sharp gasps hissed through the chapel.

Robert hardened his jaw. "Someone in my house poisoned Addie, and his days are numbered. I will learn who did this. He will answer to me."

Without waiting to measure the reaction to his words, Robert left, needing to act, to do something, no matter how futile it might seem, since Addie still lay abed, unable to know how much he cared.

He cursed himself for not telling her his feelings that afternoon. The last thing he wanted was for her to die without knowing herself loved. By him.

At least he had made her his. They'd both had that.

"By damn, and we will have more," he vowed, refusing to entertain a tragic outcome any longer. "The Morlands will never have another chance to touch her."

In seconds, he stood at Mortimer's door, his fist pounding viciously, as he wished to do to the one responsible for his wife's condition. The door flew open midpound, telling him Mortimer hadn't slept.

"How fares your lady?" Swynton's master-at-arms asked.

Robert strode into the cottage and slammed the door. "Thomasine believes Addie's been poisoned."

Mortimer's frown deepened. "Has she woken yet?"

The question stabbed Robert's heart. His eyes burned again. "Nay. She . . . she just lays still, scarcely breathing, scarcely liv—" He caught himself before voicing his worst fear.

The image of Addie as she'd looked the last time he saw her clung to his mind with tenacity. Impotent rage surged through Robert again, overcoming his anguish. "I will not let her die! I've decided to send her to MacTavish in Scotland the moment she can travel. Father always claimed Mac would do anything to help a Swynton. Well, 'tis time to make use of that loyalty. She'll be safe far from Morland scum."

Mortimer lit a beeswax candle, cupping the flame with his callused hand as it sputtered to life. "You'll give up on Morland Castle, then?"

Robert's eyes narrowed. He clenched his jaw. He paced.

"Nay. I'll have it all. The castle, the lands, and my lady wife as well."

"But you've decided against taking her there."

"Aye. She'll go to Mac when Thomasine agrees."

"So we leave not on the morrow."

"Not until Addie is well."

"Thank the Good Lord for that, lad."

"You think as she does?"

A shrug and a grim twist of Mortimer's mouth spoke eloquently.

"You'd have me betray my father, my king?" Robert asked, disbelieving. "Claiming the castle in Richard's name is the only honorable thing to do."

"Not at Addie's expense."

"Aye. Not at her expense, and 'tis why she'll go to Scotland. Then I'll do what I must."

Mortimer didn't respond. The small cruck structure rang with silence, long shadows cast by the guttering flame dancing on the wattle and daub walls, highlighting the long tree trunks that formed the three bays of living space. Robert waited, knowing full well his man would not speak until ready.

Minutes passed, slow, awkward ones, where he came to know he'd not like what Mortimer finally said. The older man rarely challenged him, but when he did, he did so after giving his position every possible consideration.

"If 'twere only a matter of honor, of loyalty to the crown," Mortimer finally said in a solemn voice, "I would question not your actions. But I cannot help thinking 'tis a more personal, less honorable cause you champion."

Robert rounded on Mortimer, stung in a private corner of his heart.

Mortimer held out a scarred hand. "Nay, lad. Hear me out," he said before Robert could argue. "You never accepted the hand dealt you in your marriage to Catherine. When her family accused you unfairly, 'twas your pride they pierced again. Then they sought to kill you, as they've now tried with your new wife. 'Twould seem you crave vengeance of a private sort rather than a righteous battle on behalf of your king. You've kept a record of each wrong done you, and you now demand payment in land you believe due you."

"Want you the truth?" Bitterness made his words come out sharp, ugly. "Then, aye, I want vengeance. I want the Morlands to pay for the misery they've brought me, for the years of wedded hell with Catherine, for the lies told about me, and aye, more than everything else, for what they've done to Addie. And no one—nay, not even you—will keep me from exacting it."

Before Mortimer could respond, Robert stalked to the door, yanked it open, and said over his shoulder, "Prepare the men. We leave for Morland as soon as Addie is headed north."

As he stalked toward the manor, he stifled the burst of conscience that suddenly challenged his resolve. He had been taught vengeance belonged to a higher One. But a man could only bear so much. No one would keep him from exacting revenge. No one.

The next day, Addie awoke, feeling as if someone had crammed her mouth full of stable straw—*after* it had been used. Her head throbbed wickedly, and her stomach lurched when she drew breath. But since she didn't relish asphyxiating, she slowly sipped blessed bits of air, wondering what had happened.

Opening one eye, she found herself in bed, daylight slicing in the narrow window on the stone wall. Cheepers fluttered merrily in the sunlit cage on the ledge. So she hadn't found the oak and returned to York yet.

Oh, and there was Nell, sleeping in a most uncomfortable position, her back against the stone wall, her ample rump overflowing the three-legged stool's seat, her small feet propped on the wooden chest at the end of Addie's bed.

What was she doing here?

"Nell . . ." she croaked and *really* wished she hadn't.

"God in heaven, you're alive!" exclaimed the woman,

tears filling her eyes, spilling down her plump, peaches-on-snow cheeks.

Addie closed her eyes. She blinked once, twice, then looked at her friend again. Chubby fingers clasped prayerfully at her breast, Nell smiled through yet more tears, her lips mouthing praises.

"What . . . happ—"

"Hush," Nell admonished, bustling to Addie's side. "You've had an ordeal. But you're alive, and 'tis all that counts. I'd best find Robert and let him know. Poor lad, he's been most distraught."

"But . . ." Addie let her voice trail away as Nell ran out the door. Moments later, Robert rushed in, his presence dwarfing the room.

He knelt at her side, clasped her hands in his. " 'Tis true, then," he murmured, kissing her fingers. "You live. How do you feel?"

"Of course I live," Addie retorted, dismayed to hear the words come out weak rather than sharp as she'd intended. What was all this alive foolishness? "Why would you . . . think otherwise?"

Robert glanced behind him, and Addie noticed Thomasine inside the room as well. The healer nodded. Her husband faced her once again. "You've been . . . poisoned, Wife."

Addie bolted upright, her eyes widening in horror. Then the nausea leveled her against the feather mattress again. She moaned in misery. "Poi—soned . . ."

"Aye," he said, " 'twould seem the Morlands have no honor."

"Oh, dear," Addie said. "Not them again."

"Who else?"

She shrugged, then decided not to do so ever again. Her head spun, and the wicked, wicked gnome banging at her skull renewed his onslaught with glee. She felt sick enough that the notion of poison no longer sounded preposterous. "But why?"

" 'Tis of no import," said Nell, dragging Robert upright.

From the corner of her eye, Addie caught the glare the former wet nurse gave her long-ago charge. "What matters now is for you to rest and recover. Thomasine and I will see to you, and Robert can again see to the demesne."

Although Robert left without further objection—strange enough in itself—Addie acknowledged her need for rest and succumbed to the older women's loving care. But before too many days had passed, that odd exchange at her bedside returned to her thoughts time and again.

When she felt well enough to put an end to the unnecessary coddling, she rose, dressed, and insisted on taking a walk around the bailey. Confinement could easily drive a woman mad, she thought, if not the excessive attention she'd received after some misguided fool had tried to eliminate her.

Misguided, for even Addie knew Robert's ire had been raised by that cruel act. He seemed ever more determined to shore up the manor's defenses, and his latest warning against trying to escape the barbican wall had assured her she'd not get away as lightly—much less pleasantly—as she had the last time.

"You now know what they can do. They'll not hesitate to strike again," he'd predicted.

When she'd asked him why they had repeatedly attacked her, he'd grown oddly silent, simply repeating his warning in that menacing tone.

But it hadn't been enough for Addie, and her natural curiosity had impelled her to learn more. So she had kept her eyes and ears wide open, as she'd known eventually she would have her answers.

To her relief, the answers she sought came rather sooner than later. That first walk around the bailey led her straight to the dairy shed when she heard riotous, raucous female laughter. She tiptoed to the entrance of the structure, pausing beyond the doorway, curious to learn the cause of the merriment, yet knowing her position as Lady Swynton would put an end to the pleasantries.

"'E's a foine man, 'e is!" crowed a buxom girl Addie knew as Daisy.

Jillie, the old woman with the rheumatic knees, cackled from her stool at a fat cow's side as she rhythmically filled the pail between her legs with rich milk. "An' ye'd know today, would ye not?"

Daisy smiled from ear to ear, a shiver of delight shimmying through her generously curved body. "Aye, 'tis true, 'tis true. I know. Has a splendid weapon 'tween his legs, the man does, and oooh . . . he knows how to use it right well! Best I've had, I'd say."

"An' ye've had plenty, ye have," called someone Addie didn't recognize.

"All what's got a weapon, I'd say," said another wryly.

"All but the lord of Swynton Manor," Jillie countered.

Daisy conceded with a shrug. "Not for lack of tryin'."

Addie blushed hotly, jealousy raging at the thought of the girl trying to lure her Robert to bed. She swallowed distaste at the crude comments while the other women asked for additional details.

When the graphic descriptions died down—during which Addie learned much she'd not known before—a voice from the far corner of the structure called out, "Fear you not for what you've done, Daisy?"

"Fear?" Daisy tossed her mane of blond curls. "I'll not be breedin'. I've been to Switha a time or two."

Addie caught the spate of crosses drawn at the mention of the name. She'd have to ask Nell about that Switha person. And Robert—if she dared—about the *other* things Daisy had described.

"Nay," said the woman in shadow. "Fear of what Sir Robert might do when he learns who you've lain with."

Daisy waved the concern away. "'Tisn't for him to decide what man I'll take."

"But when the man's a Morland—his avowed enemy—your master might have much to say."

Helpless to stop herself, Addie gasped. The women spun to face her. She stepped forward, rage burning at the treachery wrought against her husband. "Tell me, Daisy, who do you answer to?"

The dairymaid took a step back, her cheeks turning scarlet, but said nothing.

Addie, however, had plenty more to say. "The Morlands or Robert Swynton? Who owns the land that feeds you? Who ensures your safety? Who risks his life so you can entertain whomever you wish?"

Daisy tossed her head defiantly but had the grace to stammer. "I—ah . . . er . . . All I done was lie with a foine man, not smuggle 'im inside Swynton Manor or aught else, milady."

Addie narrowed her gaze. "Was that what he wanted?"

Daisy preened, jutting her mountainous breasts farther out. "He wanted *me* more."

Addie fought to tamp down her rage. "I wonder . . . do you know the Morlands tried to kill me? Three times? They've tried to kill Sir Robert as well."

Daisy shrugged. "You're neither dead yet."

"Yet?"

"O' course," Daisy said, flushing darker, sidling toward the door, her movements jerky, nervous. "And you likely won't be. Not for a long time. Right?"

"Daisy . . ." Addie said, mimicking her husband's warning tone. The girl stopped but wouldn't face Addie. Instinct told her Daisy knew far more than what she had divulged. Addie meant to learn it all. "If you've any wisdom to you, you'll tell me every last thing you said to that man, everything he said to you."

"Everything?" asked Daisy, a lascivious note entering her voice again.

Addie knew what the girl sought to do, and she wasn't about to let her win. "Not another word needs to be said about *that.* In the future, you'll keep such things private, as they should be," she said. "I meant everything that matters—really matters—to Robert and everyone at Swynton."

With a sigh of defeat, Daisy turned and collapsed on a milking stool. In halting bursts of speech, her tale of treachery spilled out, chilling Addie to the core. The foolish chit. To win the attentions of a handsome Morland buck, she had yielded every detail she knew of Robert's plans to travel to Morland Castle—plans she'd learned in the arms of a Swynton squire. She had promised the enemy entrance to the manor once Robert left.

It didn't take much genius to decipher the Morlands' plan.

And Addie didn't think Robert could be budged from his.

Still, she tried to persuade him to leave Swynton Manor, to forget Morland Castle, begging him to follow her into the future.

"'Tis that very kind of talk that will have you burned at the stake," he warned.

"I traveled through four hundred years, Robert," she stated, her voice as firm as her chin. "I know that just as I know that if you meet with and do battle for Richard Plantagenet, you will die on August 22, or perhaps days thereafter."

"Even if you came through time—which I do not say you did—do you expect me to run like a coward? To hide behind a woman's skirts when the time to act with honor comes?"

"But you will *die,* Robert," she argued, anguish bringing tears to her eyes, "for the sake of your foolish pride. Your presence on that field will not change the outcome. Despite your efforts, Henry Tudor will take the throne, and you'll merely die too soon. For nothing at all."

"Honor and duty are not nothing at all," he countered. "Would you have me betray my father's memory and my king by fleeing when I'm most needed? Even if 'twere possible—which it most assuredly is not—I will not plunge through time and run away when duty demands I go to war. My father did not raise a coward, and a coward did not pledge fealty to Richard. Nothing will make me betray them. 'Twas I who gave my word, the only thing a man truly has. While I would not come out in some future time, I will not evade my duty by going through your oak. Father laid down his life for king and country. I can do no less."

She wept then, huge, racking sobs that ripped through her. Robert said her name, then cursed and left her room.

Reasoning with Robert didn't work. So Addie devised a plan of her own. This time she vowed they'd not return to Swynton again. It was already August sixteenth.

"Please, Robert," Addie pleaded two days later. "I shall go mad if I can't go for a walk."

He scowled. "A few times around the barbican wall—*within* the bailey—offers all the exercise one could need."

"But it isn't *just* the exercise," Addie wailed. "I *really* need to find the oak."

Robert gave her a hard look. Addie didn't flinch; no amount of glares would deter her, but he didn't look ready to give in either. Addie only knew one way to get around her man.

One she'd tried before, with spectacular results.

Results he hadn't tried to repeat since, to her everlasting dismay.

Had he not enjoyed their loving in the woods?

She returned his stare, seeking to fathom what went on behind that broad brow, behind those dark, enigmatic eyes. Why hadn't he kissed her since the night she was poisoned? She'd thought surely they would share a bed like most married folks after their tryst in the woods.

But nothing.

Robert had spent his every waking moment in swordplay with his men, in consultation with Mortimer, or visiting his outlying farms. Nights had been lonely, as he'd sent her to bed while the men remained in the great hall, alluding to many demesne matters that required discussion.

If her instincts served her right, Addie believed her husband was trying to avoid a repeat of their loving.

She had to know why.

Just as much as she needed to know what that afternoon had meant to him. She remembered the fiery, intense look in his eyes as he'd poised above her, a mere second before making them one. His expression had been wild, drawn, the muscles in his arms corded tightly, bulging with his effort at control. She remembered how the breath had hissed from between his lips as he'd thrust, how he'd closed his eyes at the very instant she did, how he'd muttered her name with his every move.

She would never forget how he had lain over her, spent, replete, a satisfied smile on his talented mouth.

Oh, yes. Those memories proved he had enjoyed himself. As much as she. So Addie would use feminine knowledge again to achieve her goal. Time was running out. The situation was critical.

"You promised you would go with me until I found the tree," she said, playing her trump card.

" 'Twas before you were poisoned I promised, lady wife. Wish you to end like Nell's cat?"

Addie shuddered, saddened each time she remembered the poor animal. She much preferred to think of him as she had first seen him, sitting on Ned's solid-though-wounded chest. "Surely nothing will happen in the woods. They've tried that before and couldn't be so dull-witted as to try it again. Besides," she said, lowering her voice, "we spent a . . . special time there before."

Something sparked and caught fire in his gaze. Addie took note of the ruddy tinge that spread over his chiseled cheekbones, the flare of his nostrils, the shifting of his massive frame.

Victory! The memory lived in him, as potent as it did in her.

She waited. And waited. She remained silent, wondering exactly what was going through his mind.

Robert's body felt afire, so vivid were the images rushing through his mind. Every moment he had spent loving his wife had become indelibly etched in his memory.

Still, he couldn't let physical urges get the best of him. He knew his Addie too well. She had never backed down from a confrontation, yet he'd never known her to be this bold but once before.

'Twould seem she wanted a repeat of their tryst. Was that all she wanted? Only time would tell.

For the moment he would play along. If she craved another delicious tumble in the woods . . .

A slow smile curved Robert's lips. 'Twould be no hardship to indulge her. And if he planned things right, he could use her desire to accomplish his ultimate goal. " 'Tis another picnic you want, Addie?"

She blushed enchantingly and lowered her gaze. "Yes."

He tamped down the surge of desire that sent blood rushing to a suddenly lively body part, hoping they'd have time enough for what they both wanted before the more important matter was resolved. "Go, then," he said, gesturing toward the kitchen. "Pack your basket. We'll go within the hour. I've something to discuss with Mortimer yet, and 'twill give you time to prepare."

She gave him a radiant smile, then rose on tiptoe and kissed him sweetly on the lips. He instinctively reached out to clasp her waist, but she danced out of his grasp. "I'll pack us a feast," she called back, running toward the kitchen. "You'll see how wonderful everything will soon be."

Robert shook his head and wondered why he had thought it wise to avoid his wife's bed the past two weeks. True, she had been ill from the poison she was fed, but she had soon recovered, and he could have joined her many a night.

He'd feared how she would receive his advances. After all, Catherine had welcomed him to her bed the night they wed, only to fight him every subsequent time. He dreaded a repeat of his past failure to win his wife.

Still more, he had feared the overwhelming need Addie brought him with her merest touch. Robert feared he would lose himself in the joy and wonder that was Addie Shaw, Lady Swynton. Lose his sanity, his perspective, his heart. To his wife.

He had to keep his wits about him, else the Morlands would succeed. They would kill her, and more than likely him as well.

But today, with her invitation, Addie had allayed one of

his fears while giving him the perfect opportunity to ensure her safety. He couldn't let it pass.

Robert would make sure harm never touched his wife again, or he would die trying.

Chapter 15

AN HOUR LATER, his newest plan in place, Robert returned to the manor, as he and Addie had arranged to meet there. He carried his armor, for this time he refused to be caught unprepared. He would bring Midnight along with them. The stallion was swift and could elude what attackers might come after them. He had planned for every possible eventuality.

Or so he hoped.

Addie's life depended on his readiness.

"Oh, there you are!" he heard her call.

Turning, his heart picked up its pace when he saw her sweet face lit with that same radiant smile she had given him a while before. He noticed the basket over her right arm, the ridiculous cage she'd had built for the sparrow in her left hand. He frowned but chose not to say a word. " 'Tis time to go, is it not?"

Addie blushed becomingly. "Mm-hmm—" She stopped when she spotted his armor and sword. "What's that doing here?"

"I'm not mad, you know. I will accompany you to the

woods, but I will be prepared for whatever happens. No one will ever hurt you again."

"Bu—but—"

"But naught. 'Tis my sole condition. I go fully armed. And Midnight goes with us."

She blanched. He had expected that, but he hadn't expected her to sway. He reached out, caught her by the elbows despite basket and cage of anxiously peeping, wing-flapping bird. "Hold your argument, Addie. Midnight comes, regardless of how much you fear the beast."

That stiffened her spine. "Why, what on earth would give you the absurd idea your horse frightens me?" She tipped her chin skyward, and Robert nearly laughed. "I'll have you know I fear nothing, sir."

This time he didn't stop a chuckle. "Is that why you swooned when Mortimer handed you to me that first time?"

"Of course not," she cried, cheeks blazing. "I swooned, as you insist, because I hate the sight of slaughter. You'd just sliced another man's throat."

Robert grimaced. "Before he did the same to me."

She gestured with the hand holding the bird. The animal again cheeped in fright. "I know, I know," she conceded. "But that hardly matters now. I thought it would be just the two of us in the woods. Why would you take that beast along?"

"For safety. And now that I've responded, tell me why you bring that ridiculous bird?"

She lowered her gaze to the ground. "Oh, well . . . you see . . ."

Robert narrowed his gaze with suspicion. What was she about?

"Oh, yes!" Addie cried, again gracing him with that glorious smile he was beginning to dread. "Because the woods were his first home. I'm sure he'd like to visit again."

Robert closed his eyes. Hard. He rubbed his temples where a dull throb had just begun.

He had never heard a more absurd explanation, but since it came from Addie . . . well, he would have to let it pass.

For the moment. It mattered not what she did with the sparrow. What mattered was getting her to the woods at the appointed time.

He shrugged. "Take the bird if you must, as I will take the horse. But before we leave, you must help me don the armor."

Addie frowned. "I wouldn't know where to start. Where's your squire?"

"Cuthbert's with Mortimer, and I know where to start. Set your burdens aside, and I shall tell you what to do."

Moments later, he regretted the idea of having her help him. Her every innocent touch reminded him of that other afternoon, made him think of what he wished he were about to repeat, of what he craved more than anything else.

But he couldn't let passion blind him.

Addie's life mattered more than one afternoon's stolen loving. If events went as planned, they would have eternity for slow, sweet passion in their own home.

Still, her hands fluttered over him, arousing him to a fever pitch. He wondered if she felt as he did.

Nibbling her bottom lip, Addie wondered why she'd thought another picnic a good idea in the first place. Her decision to play on their memories of a passionate interlude had worked. Too well.

And backfired on her.

She couldn't keep her mind off the kisses they had shared, the passion they had discovered. And helping him put on this ludicrous metal carapace simply made matters worse. Each time she touched Robert's warm, solid flesh, she longed to do more, to mold her hands over his sculpted chest, twine her fingers with his waving hair, palm his firm, stubbled jaw.

She wanted her husband.

But she wanted him alive.

She would have to deny them the loving they both seemingly wanted today in the hope of ensuring their tomorrows.

Desire rendering her more awkward than ever, Addie followed Robert's directions. Her fingers performed like thumbs, while her thumbs behaved like toes. She felt as inept as she had when she'd tried to repair a china plate she'd broken at the age of six. Then, Mama had tenderly laughed away her clumsy efforts, discounting the importance of the dish.

Robert mattered more than a dish.

Finally he was fully armed. Addie was fully aroused.

As she gathered her basket and her bird, she glanced around the bailey, regretting she would never have the chance to bid her many friends farewell. She'd never know what Nell had done with her boots. Sadness filled her, as did a sense of finality. Somehow, deep inside, instinct told her she would never again see Swynton Manor and all those dear folks she had come to know.

She would sorely miss Thomasine and Nell. They had become the closest friends she'd ever had.

But she had to do this. She had to save Robert.

And there was Emmie to return to.

"Ready?" Robert asked, armor clanging as he clambered onto Midnight.

Tears filled Addie's eyes. She felt suddenly reluctant to leave a life that had given her so much. A meaningful cause for living, friendships aplenty.

A husband.

Love.

But Addie had no alternative. If she didn't find that oak today, Robert would die. In a very few days. As, more than likely, would she.

Then, too, Emmie would be alone. Forever.

She wouldn't—couldn't—fail the two people who meant everything in life to her. "I'm as ready as I'll ever be."

Stubborn as usual, Addie refused to join Robert atop Midnight's solid back. She marched at his side, chin high, shoulders square, swinging the basket of food and the sparrow's cage as she went.

Robert pitied the bird and hoped to talk his lady wife into setting the poor thing free. Yet he doubted his success. Addie was a most strong-willed sort.

Since the poisoning, she had tried, time and again, to persuade him to follow her into that mythical future from whence she still vowed she had come. Robert marveled at her tenacity.

Nothing he said, nothing she saw, not even her failure to find that damnable oak lo those many times she had tromped through the woods would budge her from her position.

Pride blazed from her sincere expression; certainty rang in her voice. Regardless of how mad her assertion was.

And she wept, her anguish only too real. Robert's every instinct urged him to hold her each time, to kiss away the moisture that bathed her soft cheeks, but he feared his weakness toward his wife. He feared that if he but touched her, she would sap his resolve, lure him to her bed, make him promise anything she wished, make him betray his conscience.

And he already struggled with that overworked part of him. Knowing how violently the Morlands opposed her presence at Morland Castle, and hating the foul title of "Swynton's Sorceress" they had given her, Robert knew he had only made her situation more precarious by wedding her. A fact that did not lay easy on his conscience.

His enemies hated him, and they wanted Addie gone, for she posed a double threat to them—a religious one as well as a legal one—since they wanted no heirs once they did away with Robert.

They feared Addie might bear him a child.

A blessing Robert craved but could not have. Not yet. Perhaps later, once danger was past.

He knew he could not leave Addie unprotected when he joined Richard. He suspected the Morlands would again attempt to ambush him en route, but this time Robert was ready for them.

What troubled him was the certainty that the Morlands would pounce on Addie the moment he left. They would rid themselves of the grieving widow before she became one, and thereby the potential mother of an heir to what they believed was theirs.

Robert knew MacTavish would care for her. His father had oft said he trusted the Scotsman with even Robert's and Edythe's lives, his two greatest treasures.

The day after the poisoning, Robert had arranged for Ned to spirit the incautious, somewhat daft Lady Swynton to safety in Scotland. When she invited him to yet another of their futile searches for her imaginary oak, Robert saw the jaunt as the perfect opportunity to set his plan in motion. He'd had not a moment to spare, since he would claim Morland Castle for Richard, then join the monarch forthwith.

A hooded Ned would meet them in the woods within the hour, bearing a blanket and hempen rope with which to truss Addie and secure her to his mount. Robert's wife would not otherwise ride a horse.

She still refused to do so, causing her to march at his side, making him feel like a boor. Still, it had been her choice.

"Won't you join me?" he asked again, knowing full well her response.

She spared him not a glance, instead picking up her pace.

Robert chuckled. Addie remained, as always, true to herself. She might be a mite touched, but she was also honest, sincere, and always direct.

As they neared the spot she seemed to prefer in the stand of trees, Robert called out, "Go on a bit farther. I'd much prefer to tie Midnight out of sight of the road. As a precaution."

Nodding, Addie walked faster still. Then, with a nervous glance over her shoulder and a nibble to her bottom lip, she said, "Daisy from the dairy has given her . . . favors to a Morland."

"What!" Robert's temper boiled instantly. "How long have you known?"

She shrugged. "Two days."

"Thought you not to tell me?"

With another leery look at Midnight, she said, "What for? The harm was done."

"She could do much more."

"I was poisoned already, wasn't I?"

"Is that the worst you think the Morlands will do? 'Tis an innocent and a fool you are, Wife."

She spun and came to a standstill. Anger sparked in her silver eyes. "I'm no fool, Robert. I know precisely what I'm doing, which is more than I can say for you."

"I protect what's mine, Addie, and neither Daisy nor you will keep me from it."

Silence fell between them, heavy and charged. Mayhap 'twas best this way. She might be easier to manage when Ned appeared if she focused on their argument rather than other things. Like her accursed tree.

But no. It seemed naught would deter Addie from her goal, as Robert learned once he tied Midnight to a solid oak just yards inside the woods.

With her usual determination, and more than usual desperation, Addie darted from tree to tree, sitting, leaning, closing her eyes, demanding he follow her to each.

"Why do you do this to yourself?" he asked, pity in his heart. "'Tis futile, you know."

She again turned on him, eyes blazing, nostrils flaring. She was magnificent. If fey. "No, I *don't* know that it's futile. I came through an oak and I will prove it to you, even if it's the last thing I do. Now come, help me test this tree."

Robert shook his head but did as commanded, knowing refusal would lead nowhere. His helmet firmly clasped under his arm, sword secured in its sheath, he followed her to yet another tree, wondering what made a woman so dogged, so firm in the face of monumental odds.

Addie sat beneath another oak, refusing to consider, even for a moment, that she might fail. It *had* to be today. She knew from questioning Daisy that the Morlands were close. Those who had stayed behind when the larger group had gone to Wales had begun to move in preparation to kill Robert before joining the Lancastrian forces.

August 22 was only four days away.

If she couldn't find the tree and drag Robert to 1885, he would die, either at the hands of the Morlands or when facing Henry Tudor.

"Botheration!" she muttered when yet another trunk failed to budge. Scrambling upright—a job in itself when holding a birdcage in one hand—she plastered a bright smile on her lips.

"Not this one," she called out to her husband. "Let's try that one over there."

Robert glanced in the direction she indicated, and started walking that way. When he'd gone but a few steps, Addie heard a sound that curdled her blood.

A piece of wood cracked to her left, something that could only happen when someone stepped on a branch or a twig. Since she had yet to see an animal larger than a squirrel during her many forays to the area, Addie felt certain the sound presaged danger.

"Hurry!" she said in an urgent whisper. "We *must* find the tree. I just heard . . . something over there."

Robert shrugged. "'Twas nothing, I'm sure."

Addie couldn't give credence to what she'd just heard. The man who had ranted endlessly about the threat posed by the Morlands, and who believed she took her life in her hands each time she came to the woods, appeared utterly unconcerned when she finally heard something truly menacing.

"Robert Swynton, you have taken leave of your senses!" *And more than ever, I need to get you out of danger.* "Let's try this tree."

Desperation swelled inside her, growing steadily with every tree she tried. Addie ran from oak to oak, refusing to consider anything but finding the one with the distinctive dark area.

She *would* save her husband.

She *would* take him to a safer time.

His honor be hanged.

To Addie's horror, footsteps approached again, this time from her right. "Robert—"

"Hush!" He crammed on his helmet, shoved up the visor, grabbed her forearm, and dragged her toward the edge of the woods. The change in his demeanor proved to Addie what she had suspected. The Morlands were coming.

No. The Morlands had arrived.

Latching in turn on to Robert's solid arm, Addie pulled in the direction of yet another massive oak. "We haven't tried that one," she said, her voice sharp and high with fear.

Robert swung his head to face his wife, dismayed to hear her still cling to the foolishness of her tree. "Woman, can you not let that be? Danger surrounds us now, as I'd feared. We must leave the woods, we must alert the guard at Swynton, we must go for help. The time for your imaginary tree is long past."

"*No!* The tree is real. I'll find it. One more. *Please.* I—I beg you. Just one more."

Although she dug in her heels, Robert continued to drag her behind him. "Nay, Addie. 'Tis gone on long enough. We must go." Hope of meeting Ned in time to spirit Addie to safety in Scotland began to fade, and Robert lost his patience. He swooped her up into his arms and flung her over his shoulder. "I've made provisions for your safety. I'm ready to meet the Morlands."

"*No!*" she cried again, fighting wildly.

Robert ignored her efforts, armor-clad as he was. "Ease up, woman! You'll fall, hurt yourself."

She pounded on his helmet with her free fist, since she had yet to relinquish the absurd birdcage. "I can't! Don't you see? You'll die if I don't—"

"*You* shall perish if you persist in your foolishness," he muttered, despite ears ringing from her high-pitched, panicked voice and continued beating on his helm.

"It isn't foolishness!" she cried, kicking his well-protected middle. "I know what I'm doing. Let me go!"

She fought like the madwoman he feared she had in fact become, and to his horror, she wriggled free, thanks to the slick metal of his armor.

He hurried after her, awkward in his covering. "Addie, come back. We must ride Midnight—"

Panting roughly, she turned to face him. "Please, Robert. Just this one more tree."

He met her wild gaze, noted the tears flooding her face, the shaking of the fingers she held out, the way she clung fiercely to her bird's cage. She might be mad, but he loved her. And she truly believed she had to try yet one more time.

Robert darted looks around the again silent forest. He saw and heard naught out of the ordinary. Mayhap she had only heard Ned coming close. Both times.

'Twas unlikely, true, but since he saw no imminent threat, he would indulge her one last time. He couldn't bear the suffering he saw in her beloved face, the anguish in her huge, haunted eyes.

Perhaps they would have enough time to escape. Enough, if she surrendered after this final try. "Promise 'twill be the last one," he demanded, knowing full well she wouldn't go back on her word. She was too guileless for that.

Hesitantly Addie turned a circle, apparently unsure of which tree to choose. In a trembling voice she said, "I promise, Robert. Just let me choose well."

She walked a few paces to her right, and Robert felt time fly by. He sensed danger approaching. He had not heard aught else, but instinct told him 'twas time to seek safety.

Then she gasped and gave out an excited little cry. "I found it!" she exclaimed. "This is the one. I just know it. I do, Robert, I do."

"Hurry, love," he said, his voice urgent. "We must not waste a second more."

She jerked her head around and met his gaze, and he realized what he had just said. He smiled crookedly.

She did not.

Squaring her shoulders, she approached a massive tree, its trunk mottled and stained with age. To his relief, Robert noticed 'twas the one to which he had tethered Midnight.

"While you test this most likely one," he said, trying to mollify her, as he could not deter her, "I shall untie Midnight. Then we can leave once you have seen if 'twill budge for you."

Addie tipped up her chin. "You'll see, Robert. This is *the* tree. The one I fell through."

"Splendid," he growled, thinking 'twas anything but. He slipped the reins from round the limb and brought the massive horse to scant feet away from his wife. The moment Addie faced the truth, he would scoop her up and somehow mount the horse, hoping she, for once, did as expected. He prayed she'd swoon the minute he reached Midnight's broad side.

"Robert," Addie called.

"What now?"

She held out her free hand. "Please. Hold me. Just for a moment."

Knowing refusal would only delay their escape, Robert approached in resignation. As he held out his gauntleted fingers, he heard the arrival of death.

"Swynton!" called a miserably familiar voice.

"Addie," he urged, "'tis Michael Morland, uncle to my late first wife. We must leave! Now."

"Please," she begged, sobbing, silver eyes swimming in tears.

"Damnation!" he cried, knowing himself truly damned if a pair of watery eyes could make him risk his hide for a mere, mad whim. With great clanging of armor, he leaned toward her. "'Tisn't the time to play silly games."

"Close your eyes," she implored.

"Why?"

"Don't ask. If you're in such a hurry, just do it. If it's Michael Morland, you've even more reason to listen to me."

Shaking his head, wondering how much longer they would live, Robert tugged on Midnight's reins, bringing the beast closer yet. "Here, but for no more than a second—"

A vicious crack rent the air, deafening Robert, stifling the words he had been about to say. He clasped Addie's slender hand, feeling it convulse in turn.

As their fingers knotted tightly, solidly, the earth shook beneath his feet. Midnight reared, neighing wildly. In the cage Addie held, the sparrow flapped its wings and cried piteously.

Suddenly Addie fell backwards, the hand bonded to his dragging him in her wake. Robert fought to keep his footing but failed. With great clanging of armor, he tumbled, his gear preventing him from rising again.

Disoriented, he looked up and saw the tree's green canopy sway madly from side to side. Then a face contorted with hate appeared in his line of vision. Robert knew he and Addie were as good as dead.

"*Dear God, no!* Save her, please!"

At that moment he heard a piercing whine above him, not human, not animal, unlike anything he had ever heard. And as the sound roused panic within him, he felt himself fall again.

This time he didn't hit the ground. He kept falling . . . falling, gaining speed.

He hurtled through a void. Hot winds buffeted him. He realized he still held Addie's hand, Midnight's reins. He heard her sobbing, the horse's shrieking, the bird's cheeping. Behind it all, he heard the rush of air around them, surging past them.

Terror clawed his throat. So this was death.

Not at all the peaceful end Anselm had always preached.

Time seemed to stop when nothing else did. Farther down they went, and dizziness overtook him. Thoughts swirled through his mind, memories of his childhood, his father, Edythe, and Nell, and Catherine. His land. He relived the day he felled Edwin Morland, when he first saw Addie Shaw. He remembered kissing her, making her his. At that glorious memory, he strove to breathe yet one more time, hoping to keep that vision alive until the end. For Robert had accepted the inevitable.

He would never see his wife again, would never kiss her, bed her, confess his love for her. They would never make a child, hold it, raise it. Robert's heart broke into a sob of unutterable agony. He had found everything he had ever wanted in Addie, his wife, but they would never live long enough to relish it.

He stopped fighting the inevitable, the darkness.

He embraced death.

Chapter 16

OR . . . MAYHAP NOT.

Hearing songbirds overhead a lifetime later, Robert wondered if such were the sounds of heaven, those very earthly sounding chirps and trills, if 'twere indeed paradise where he had landed after his fall.

Every inch of him ached, and he did not recall Anselm ever saying that heaven held pain for those who attained it. To the contrary, Robert had always heard that glory meant no more misery, no more troubles, naught but joy and peace and comfort throughout eternity.

But he most assuredly did not feel comfortable, and he had experienced enough pain in his mortal life to know what it felt like. His head throbbed with his every movement, his chest burned with every breath he took, his back ached in four spots, and a slicing pain bit through his right leg.

Then he heard it.

"AAAaaahhhh!"

The piercing female shriek broadcast such fear, such panic, such abject terror, that Robert knew instantly he had not died. That was no response to achieving everlasting life, and furthermore, the voice sounded entirely too familiar.

A second scream followed.

"NOOoooo!"

That one cry lay all doubt to rest. Fighting his reluctant body, Robert wrestled his unwieldy armor, his lingering dizziness, his reluctance to move, for his wife needed help.

"Addie . . ." he said in a voice so rusty he scarcely recognized it as his own.

"Go!" she screamed inexplicably.

Robert tried to lift his visor, as he could scarcely see through its narrow opening, but found it jammed, dented in the center. He ripped off his gauntlets and began to work the damaged piece upward, unwilling to relinquish the helmet's protection while the Morlands were still about.

Addie yelled again, "Go away. *Now!*"

What did she mean? "Addie," he called, turning his head from side to side, hoping to spot her through his crushed visor. "'Tis but me, Robert."

"Oh!" she exclaimed, relief in the word. "Then, thank God, we're not in hell after all. Hurry and help me."

Giving up on the visor, Robert ripped off the helmet. The sudden light blinded him for a moment, but what he could make out looked much the way it had when they'd arrived at the woods earlier that day. "Hell? What mean you?"

"No, no, no, *no!*" she cried again, and Robert turned toward the sound of her voice. Then he understood.

Midnight's muzzle hovered mere inches from his wife's pert nose, the horse clearly curious about her. He chuckled, shaking his head.

"How dare you laugh?" Addie asked, indignant. "I was certain I'd died and gone straight to hell when I opened my eyes and saw this great monster of yours preparing to have me for his next meal."

Robert laughed louder. They were most certainly alive.

His laughter did not please his lady wife. "Stop it! It isn't funny. Not only did we travel through four hundred years, tremendously taxing in itself, but arriving to find enormous teeth about to nibble on necessary body parts does not amuse me."

Robert choked back another bark of laughter at her ludicrous comment. "Must you persist with that time-travel nonsense? I know not how we were spared death at Michael Morland's hand, but we must take advantage of our great good fortune and make for safety. Get up." He held out a hand.

Remaining flat on her back, Addie glared at him. "Get your confounded horse away from me—*far* away from me—if you wish me to stand. Then I'll prove to you we did indeed travel through time. I'd wager anything we're in York, Pennsylvania, and that the year is 1885."

"Midnight will not hurt you," he said. Then, choosing to ignore her other statement, he added, "But the Morlands will. We must go."

Knowing the reason for her fear, however, he went to his horse. To his dismay, he noticed the animal's reins were ragged, and the saddle bore gouges and rips. What had happened?

"Oh, Robert," she said in a long-suffering tone, "you really should listen to me. The Morlands are four hundred years away. In England. We're in Pennsylvania. We need not fear them anymore. Now, your horse's teeth . . . well, they're another matter altogether."

Robert bit down against sensible argument and diverted Midnight's attention from his wife. As he tethered the horse to a nearby elm, Addie rose gingerly, wincing and rubbing her back.

'Twas then he noticed the tattered condition of her garments, the filth smeared on her cheeks. Her hair fell in wadded streamers to her shoulders, and her hands were scratched and bloody. She had obviously fought an attacker, but who? Michael Morland?

Nay. If the man had indeed attacked her, she would never have survived. 'Twas strange, very strange. Robert knew not if the current calm was but a new twist in the Morlands's plot. 'Twould not surprise him if they lay low, letting him and Addie think themselves safe, to then come in for the kill when both were fully aware of what was about to happen.

"Wait here," he ordered. "I shall scout around, make certain Michael and his do not linger. Then we must ride to safety." Pray God, Swynton had weathered well the attack he doubted not Michael had launched.

Addie crossed her arms across her chest, huffed a breath to blow a clump of hair from her right eye. "I already told you, Robert, they aren't here. But if you must, go ahead. I'm sore and tired, and I'll gladly rest right here."

With that, she plopped down on an old stump.

As Robert turned, he heard the distant lowing of cattle. The sound reassured him. Perhaps Mortimer had spotted the enemy's approach and dispatched them to perdition.

If 'twere so, then why had his master-at-arms left him and Addie unconscious on the forest floor? Unease trickled into his gut. As a precaution, Robert unsheathed his dagger, then patted the hilt of his sword in its scabbard.

Aside from the sound of the cows and the occasional bird-call, the woods resonated with their normal silence. Still, Robert knew his foes full well. And he feared their cunning.

As silently as possible, considering the clanging of his armor, he made a sweep of their immediate surroundings. He found naught but dead leaves, sprouting shoots, and a plump hare who skittered for shelter far from Robert's side.

Circling around, he returned to Addie's stump. " 'Tis safe, so far as I can tell. But we cannot count on the Morlands being gone. We must hasten to safety. I will not risk your life again."

Addie smiled her dazzling smile and stood. "That's very sweet, Robert," she said with a pat to his cheek. "I appreciate the sentiment, but there's no longer any danger from the Morlands. You'll see. Let's go home."

Robert again clamped his teeth down on a retort. He awkwardly clambered onto Midnight's back, wishing for Cuthbert's aid since he was laden with metal, then leaned and offered Addie a hand once in the saddle. "Come. We'll make better time if you ride with me."

She sniffed and tipped up her chin. "We've no need to

hurry, and I won't climb on that beast. It is anything but safe up there."

"Addie, love, you must get beyond your fear of horses. What happened to your parents was unfortunate, but 'twas an accident and only that. Midnight will not hurt you. He nuzzled you out of curiosity earlier. He's gentle, if courageous and strong."

"Splendid! You ride him while I walk. Besides, I have Cheepers to carry."

At that, Robert groaned. He hadn't noted the presence of the sparrow, but now he could not miss it. Battered and with many broken reeds, the cage seemed scarcely more than a handful of kindling. To his amazement, the bird still fluttered its wings and cheeped as if aught had happened.

"Won't you let the poor thing loose while we're still here?" he asked, waving toward the trees.

"Of course not. Cheepers is my friend." Jabbing her determined chin forward, Addie began to stride toward the edge of the woods. "Let's go home. I must find Emmie."

Robert again wondered who Emmie might be, as he had heard Addie mention the name a time or two. Knowing his wife, however, who was hastily departing the area, he supposed she would inform him in her own good time. Since he also knew her stubbornness, he allowed himself to be led. After all, she did know the way to Swynton.

When they emerged from the woods, Robert experienced a moment of disorientation. Nothing seemed familiar, and Swynton was not where it always had been. He could not quite place where they had come out.

Still, Addie cried out in joy and ran toward a small red-clay-brick building near a dirt road. "See?" She faced him momentarily. "My school. It's closed for the summer, but here it is. Just as I said it would be."

Robert nodded, choosing to humor Addie. If she wanted to believe them in that Pen—Pensil—place of hers, he would let her do so until she no longer could, until reality made facts perfectly clear.

"We'll follow the road into town," she called, then turned

in the opposite direction from where he knew Swynton Manor stood.

"Addie, you head the wrong way."

"Not at all. Now we're in my time, in my place, so you'll need to trust me."

Trust her? Dear God, how could he? The events in the forest had clearly stolen what scant reason she'd had left. 'Twas sad—tragic, really. Still, tenderness and sympathy mingled in his heart, and as he saw no immediate threat, he allowed her the delusion.

For the moment.

Then a black, boxy carriage appeared down the road. Addie waved enthusiastically at the equally somber-garbed driver. "Mr. Reisinger! How are you? How does Nathan feel these days?"

To Robert's surprise, the long-bearded man acknowledged Addie's greeting by gaping openmouthed, his horse's reins growing slack in his hands. As the horse continued clopping down the road, the man's gaze remained fixed on Robert, his head craning around as far as it could.

Addie never received a response.

Worse, Robert didn't recognize the astounded man.

Unease curled in his middle. Could she possibly be right . . . ? Nay. There was no such thing as travel through time. They had merely taken the road in a different direction than he normally did, and had come across a foreigner to these parts.

Of course. That explained everything. The man had likely been amazed to see Addie so disheveled, as well as hearing her blither nonsense about that Reisinger person. 'Twas the only explanation Robert would accept.

"How rude!" his wife exclaimed. "And Hans Reisinger has always been the epitome of politeness. What could have come over the man?"

Robert made a neutral sound, knowing not what else to do.

They continued down the road and soon approached a

number of buildings. What Robert saw stunned him. None of the Swynton farms had ever looked like this!

Instead of cruck cottages, many of the structures were of stone, looking as though the building material had been gathered straight from the fields. Others were of the same red-clay brick as Addie's school. But what most amazed Robert was the roofing on each house. Costly slate rather than thatch topped the structures ranging down either side of the road and coming now with greater frequency.

His unease returned, proving more difficult to shake than the first time.

Although he found not a Morland in sight, Robert saw no one he recognized either. The longer they traveled, the busier the thoroughfare grew. He turned and stared at every unfamiliar sight. To one side of the street, he saw an establishment with the name Peter Weist emblazoned across the front. It had an expanse of glass that must have cost a king's ransom, and through which Robert could view a quantity of unidentifiable items.

He stared at the place, wondering what sort of commerce went on there, but continued riding Midnight along Addie's side. As they went down the road, more carriages rolled by, some as plain as Mr. Reisinger's, others showy and lavishly decorated. Flat carts loaded with unrecognizable goods also coursed the street.

"Four hundred years of advances . . ." Addie had once said.

Robert's unease turned into apprehension. Could she have been right?

"Nay!"

Addie glanced at him, but he shrugged, determined to put aside all ludicrous thoughts—especially those inspired by her rantings. He was too rational and refused to entertain her wild tales.

A few minutes later, another structure caught his attention. From the looks of the men going in, since the sun made its way down the horizon, Robert assumed it to be a tavern. A tankard of ale held great appeal just then.

But Addie kept on walking. He followed, despite his thirst.

Robert again marveled at the number of buildings with elaborate glass on their fronts. Like the one approaching on his right. This one displayed no less than nine windows—four at ground level and five more over those—across its front, all glass. Above the lower windows were the words PHILADELPHIA MILLINERY. From what Robert could surmise, they traded in extraordinary headgear within, as he could see from samples behind the plate glass.

He glanced at Addie. Back at the store.

Mayhap . . .

Nay. He *would* not let his feelings for her affect his sanity—any more than they already had.

As he rode on, a woman emerged through the doorway of the millinery, wearing a . . . thing—a hat? a hood?—on her head similar to the ones arrayed in the store, replete with flowers and, if he wasn't much mistaken, even a bird. Her garments resembled the ones Addie had worn when he'd first seen her, the gown fitted tightly to her upper body then belling narrowly over the hips and down to the ground. Most bizarre, however, was the draping of fabric over an exaggerated, round protuberance where the woman's posterior should be. He wondered about the odd deformity, sadly noting that the attempt to conceal it had not worked.

As they traveled farther into the town, they passed greater numbers of people on foot. Addie nodded to everyone, but no one responded in kind. To Robert's astonishment, they all did as the man on the outskirts had done, gaping dumbly at them, as if there were something odd about him and his wife.

Well, Robert knew plenty was odd about her—take her foolish attachment to a sparrow, if not her laughable belief in travel through time—but not enough to make everyone stop in their tracks and stare.

Then he noticed the oddly fashioned clothing the men wore. Instead of hose, they had on garments with loose leg coverings that flapped as they walked. Unusual, boxy tunics garbed them to below the hip, while flat-topped cylinders rode their pates.

"Addie?" he said hesitantly, again feeling that uncomfortable sense of dread building in his middle. She couldn't be right. . . .

Could she?

She didn't respond, but called out, "Melanie! It's a pleasure to see you. Have you finished the quilt we started for your sister's wedding? I hope not. I'd so love to help you some more."

When Robert looked in the direction Addie had addressed her question, he noticed a dark-haired young lady also dressed much like Addie had been the day she appeared in the woods. At her side, a small girl shuddered, whimpered, then hid in the woman's gown, obviously frightened. The mother, eyes wide with terror, pushed the child more fully behind her, then glared at Addie. She backed into the doorway of the building she had just exited.

Turning, Addie called, "Mrs. Birdwell!" Her voice bore the sharp note Robert had come to know betrayed fear. "How is Stevie coming along with his summer reading? He needs to practice if he means to keep up with the others in class. Do let me know if I can help."

As she bustled down the roadway, the line of his wife's spine grew so stiff and straight he wondered how she managed to walk. But she did, head held high, pride in every line. She continued to turn to each side, to offer cordial comments to those she found there. They all responded as one.

They stared in horror, disdain, shock.

True, he and Addie were dirty and exhausted, but Robert could not imagine what made these strangers behave so rudely. Nothing about him and his wife was particularly remarkable. 'Twas the onlookers who dressed oddly and behaved just as strangely.

He refused to consider any other possibility.

Then a small boy threw a rock at Midnight, causing the animal to shy sideways. Women shrieked, men yelled. The other conveyances on the road pulled over to the sides.

"Go 'way!" yelled the boy. "Sure an' you're scary, mean."

"No, he's not, Liam," countered Addie. "This is Robert, my new husband, and you know me well enough. I'd best not see you throwing rocks again, or I shall have to speak to your father."

"Faith an' 'tis a wicked sword he carries. He'll slice me head off with it before I can run away."

Addie shook her head, and the murmur of the bystanders grew to an agitated buzz. "Robert wouldn't hurt you. He has never hurt me."

Robert waited, expecting her to mention Edwin Morland's demise, but to his surprise, Addie said not a word.

Then a man yelled, "Fetch the constable!"

Another scurried away.

"He's armed and dangerous!" cried a woman, hysteria in her shrill voice. "Who knows what he's threatened Addie with. Of course she'll say anything."

"And she's been most negligent of late."

" . . . unconscionable behavior . . ."

"Husband? What husband?"

" . . . spinster. Addie's too old for any man to take her."

"She left that fey Emmie all alone . . ."

" . . . can't be trusted . . ."

"Now she's brung a savage to town."

"A madman, most likely crazed like the rest of the Shaws."

Glancing at his wife, Robert saw anguish in her silver eyes. "Addie . . ."

She met his gaze. Then, to his amazement, she stretched a hand toward him. "Help me up," she said, her voice tight, controlled.

When he clasped her fingers in his, they shook, fear very much a live thing within her. "Are you certain?"

"As I've ever been."

"Put your foot on mine and lift yourself when I pull."

She did as asked, breathing in shallow pants, darting scared peeks at Midnight, clearly mistrusting the beast. Robert feared she would swoon. But Addie's determination prevailed, and she sat before him on his damaged saddle, leaning slightly against his chest, broken birdcage still firmly in her clasp.

"Listen, everyone," she called to those who still stared. "May I present my husband, Robert Swynton? You have nothing to fear from him. You've known me all my life and know I have never hurt a soul. You know I always help anyone in need—be it medical, schooling, or any kind of help. I would never wed a dangerous man."

Addie darted looks in all directions, but Robert saw she met only with stony stares. She continued, "We may look strange, but we have just endured a . . . frightful ordeal. You know you can trust me and you can now also trust my spouse."

When her words merely garnered disdainful sniffs, turned backs, and additional mutters, Robert wrapped a bolstering arm around Addie's middle. "Hush," he said, feeling her tremble. "No more. You need not humble yourself any further. We ride for Swynton now."

She shook her head tightly. "We're not in England. We must go home—*my* home. I've been gone long enough. Continue down Market Street, then turn south on George. We'll be home shortly."

Robert knew he ought not listen; common sense told him they would be best served if he turned and left the way they had come. Then he would ride for Swynton, have Thomasine brew his wife a tisane, and Nell would put her to bed. He could then pray her wits would soon return.

But Robert dreaded causing Addie further anguish, and surely if he did as he ought, his actions would do precisely that.

And so, contrary to his instincts, he followed her directions. The sights he saw amazed and repelled him at the same time. Row upon row of slate-roofed, red-clay-bricked, plate-glass-windowed buildings lined the road—Market Street, Addie had called it—interspersed irregularly with the odd stone structure.

Nowhere did Robert spot a fortification, nowhere did he

see a man prepared to protect his own. A stray comment of Addie's fluttered through his mind as he stared. *"One doesn't slaughter those one disagrees with these days. Why, a body might get the impression you truly believe yourself back in the Middle Ages instead of in 1885. . . ."*

Could she have spoken the truth?

Nay. 'Twas just an odd city, this. It *had* to be, he would accept naught else. "Where say you we are?"

"York," she answered, the word scarcely audible.

" 'Tisn't York at all," he argued. "I've been there many a time."

"Not York, England, Robert," she said, some of her normal vigor returning to her voice at last. "This is my hometown. York, Pennsylvania. Believe me, we *have* traveled through time."

Regardless of what he saw, Robert rejected his wife's statement. Travel through time was absolutely impossible, heresy. It went against all God's laws. But something uncomfortably like fear again wallowed in his middle.

He argued no further but took in the strange sights around him. In the distance, the sun continued its descent; the day grew late.

As he approached a wide, busy crossing, Addie squealed, "Here! Turn here. This is George Street. We must go right."

Robert guided Midnight into the right turn Addie requested, when to his horror, four bursts of light, brilliant enough to rival midday, exploded overhead. They met at a pole bearing a striped and starred red, white, and blue banner.

Drawing back hard on Midnight's reins, Robert cried, "Addie, beware! 'Tis the end of time. God's come down from heaven in a blaze of glory."

"What?" she asked, turning.

He crossed himself, then took his gaze momentarily from the spectacle above to gaze into her dear face—surely for the last time. "Up there!" He pointed. "If Edythe were only with us . . . she would dearly love to witness this."

To his amazement, his wife chuckled. "No, Robert, it's

not the Rapture—at least, not yet. Those are electric arc lights. York is a most progressive town. Soon every home and every street will be lit like this."

Over the frenetic thumping of his heart, he asked, "Electric arc lights?"

Addie patted his hand at her waist. "I cannot explain quite how they work, but we can find someone who will. Marvelous, aren't they?"

"Frightful," he muttered, fearing the electric lights would soon shower the innocent below with flames. Surely brilliance like that, suspended from the sky, was not natural, safe, or to be trusted.

Could it truly be of the future?

They rode south on George Street as Addie insisted, but Robert cast the occasional look back at the terrifying lights. He shook his head. If he stood a chance of getting his way, he would turn back to the tavern they had passed not long ago. Or stop at the establishment up ahead. It bore a sign identifying it as the Reever House, and had the look of a place where a man could purchase strong ale and hearty food.

But he dare not leave his wife alone in this extraordinary town. Who knew what might happen next?

Across the street from the Reever House, Robert spotted a tall, thin man dressed in black, carrying a long beam on a shoulder. He approached one of the metal posts set at measured distances down both sides of the road. Pausing, the fellow nudged a metal piece jutting out near the top of the post, and a flame flickered to life within the glass cage there.

"By my troth!" Robert exclaimed. "What is he about? More of those electric lights?"

"Who?" Addie asked. "Where?"

"The man with the fire and the stick."

Addie chuckled and waved dismissively. "Oh, he's a lamplighter. He does this every night at dusk. Those are gaslights, and they're the ones that will be replaced by the electric ones." She turned partway in the saddle before him and gave him a satisfied smirk. "I *told* you we were four hundred years away from Swynton, from the Morlands. Do you believe me now?"

Robert refused to believe or respond.

Minutes later, he sensed Addie's change in posture. "Turn left here."

She sat straight, tense. Her breathing came shallow and fast. She stared straight ahead and to their left.

"Dear God," she whispered. "I'm home. At last."

Robert followed the direction of her stare. He noticed the small, neat wooden house about fifty yards away that apparently captured her attention. It had an odd, roofed front with cutout walls above waist height, something Robert had never seen before . . . before today, that was.

This cottage also had a slate roof, and its plate-glass windows were flanked by black planks. The door was also black.

A forlorn look clung to the place, as if it had been abandoned for a time. Weeds abounded at the base of the walls, and the walkway that led from the road displayed yet more worthless growth.

"Hurry," she said, urgency in her voice. Then she added, "I'm scared. It doesn't . . . look right."

He kneed Midnight to pick up his pace and gave Addie an encouraging squeeze around the middle. But he knew not what to say.

Robert's mind swirled with questions, doubts, fears. 'Twould seem he had indeed brought Addie home, but where? And how?

When they came to a halt before the sad little house, Robert again wished for Cuthbert to help them dismount, but managed to get down from Midnight's back without mishap. The moment Addie's feet touched ground, she flew away.

"Wait!" he cried, not knowing if 'twas safe to let her enter the cottage without ensuring its safety.

"I can't. I've waited too long already."

Before he could say another word, she dodged under the

steps leading to the unusual platform and rummaged about. "Here it is!" she cried, holding up a small brass object.

She then ran up to the door, paused to use the key, for 'twas what the tiny item had been, and vanished into the darkened house, calling, "Emmie! I'm home, I'm finally home."

Robert followed much more slowly, the steps a major challenge. Clanking and rattling, he made it to the platform, determined to capture his wife and make her help him out of the gear. Inside, he heard her run to and fro, crying in dismay. She repeated her call for Emmie.

He would not again forget to ask who Emmie was, for every time Addie said the name, she sounded more alarmed, distraught. Emmie meant much to his lady wife, enough to bring her back onto the jutting part of the house, silver eyes swimming in tears, anguish on her face.

"Oh, Robert," Addie said on a sob. "She's not home. Emmie's gone."

Chapter 17

SHE CRUMPLED. RIGHT before Robert's eyes, Addie melted and flowed onto the ground, sobbing, huge tears bathing her cheeks. "Oh, Emmie, Emmie, Emmie . . ."

The litany held such misery, such anguish, Robert felt it in his very core. Unable to stand by and witness his wife's suffering, he leaned toward her, awkward in armor, and slipped his hands under Addie's arms. He lifted her and, cursing his unwieldy protection, sought to comfort her as best he could. He brought her close, patted her back, letting her pour out her agony.

When the tide seemed to ebb somewhat, Robert wiped her cheeks with an uncertain finger. "Who is Emmie?" he asked, hoping his question would not set off another bout of misery. "You mentioned the name a time or two, but you've never said who she is. And now . . ." He gestured helplessly.

"She's—" Addie hiccuped. "She's my sister, my younger sister, just sixteen years old, and she's—" Addie stopped abruptly, staring at her hands.

Robert tipped up her chin. "Go on, love. I need to know."

"Oh, you likely won't understand," she said, a hint of anger in her response. "Emmie . . . Emmie's different. She always has been. Most little girls like dolls and playing house, but Emmie never did. She preferred to sit before the hearth, watch the wood burn."

Puzzled, Robert said, "True, 'tis a mite odd, but . . ."

When Robert's words failed him, Addie took a deep breath. "It would have been a mere oddity if all she'd done was look." She shuddered, remembering the various episodes over the years. "As Emmie grew older, she grew more and more fascinated by fire. Eventually she took to . . . lighting her own."

Addie darted a glance at her husband. Alarm bloomed on his rugged features, and she realized he still wore his no-longer-necessary armor. "Here," she said, reaching for his breastplate. "You don't need this any longer. There's no danger to you now."

Robert frowned but evidently chose not to argue. As Addie helped him strip off the clumsy, noisy gear, he exclaimed in dismay when he noticed its condition. "Mortimer shan't be pleased! He takes much pride in maintaining Swynton armor. He purchases the finest metal, employs the best armorers. This . . . this is a disgrace!"

Addie smiled thinly, relieved for the brief respite from her troubles. "Travel through time takes a toll on one's garments, be they cloth or not."

"Addie . . ."

"What will it take to persuade you?" she asked, growing impatient with his warning tone. "You've seen the city of York, the gas and electric lights. No one carries swords on their hips, and no one wears armor. The year is 1885, and you simply *must* believe me. I have given you every reason to believe, especially since I never lie."

Out of arguments, Robert averted his gaze. "We shan't discuss it further," he said. "So tell me more about your sister."

Addie's stomach clenched. "Well . . . she loves fire. And she's the most fanciful person I've ever known. She spends days weaving tales in her head, tales of adventure, excitement, and . . . well, fire."

"She sounds a most unique sort, but why would that make you weep?"

With a shuddering breath, Addie sat on the porch railing. "When she makes fire, Emmie is not always particular about what she burns. She's been known to light bits of wood, scraps of paper, odds and ends. But . . ."

"But . . . ?"

"She once took Mrs. Mahoney's petticoats, hung them on the wash line, and set them aflame. She . . . wanted to watch the fire dance on the wind. Then there was the time she stole our kitchen grease crock."

"Hmm . . ." Robert murmured with a raised brow.

"Indeed. Unfortunately Emmie gathered kindling in the woods behind the schoolhouse—the one I showed you earlier today, the one where I teach—and with the help of the grease, built a most lively blaze too close to the chicken coop of a neighboring farm."

"It, too, burned?"

"Spectacularly," Addie answered dryly. "No one could forget those poor hens, cackling and squawking around the yard, waving their singed wings, unable to fly or escape the blaze, scared out of what scant wits the Good Lord ever gave them. Oooh, and the smell of scorched feathers." Addie wrinkled her nose.

"The farmer was not pleased."

She *hmmph*ed. "I nearly lost my job that time. Which would have been disastrous, since my wages are all we have." Sighing, Addie remembered those days before she'd decided to take Emmie with her to Doc Horst's surgery. "I can't turn my back on Emmie, even though she's all of sixteen. She ought to be thinking of marriage and suitors and her future, but instead she only speaks of gunpowder, matches, blazes, and fire."

"Dangerous, is she?"

"Not maliciously," Addie hastened to say. "But she could hurt herself."

"And others as well, 'twould seem."

She sighed in defeat. "That's my greatest fear. And why

I've been so determined to return. Now you understand why I continued to search for the blasted oak that started all this." She pointed to his armor, to Midnight tethered at the hitching post by the street. "I had to come home to keep Emmie safe. I love her, and she's been my responsibility since Mama and Papa died."

"Instead, you've come home to find her gone."

Another sob escaped her control. Addie nodded.

Robert slipped a comforting arm around her shoulders. "Mayhap a kind soul has taken pity on her, given her shelter, food, kept her safe."

She swallowed hard and shook her head. "I wish I could believe that, but most folks are frightened of Emmie. They fear she will do something wild, destroy their homes as she did the henhouse, hurt them and theirs."

"From what you've said, they've reason for their concern."

"But Emmie's just a girl!" she cried. "A wonderful, witty one, at that. She tells the most marvelous tales, sings like a bird, laughs and dances and hugs everyone she meets. She's the most loving sister a woman could want. And I failed her. I stayed away too long."

Running a hand through his hair, Robert ruffled his sable waves. "Why did you not tell me your sister needed you? We could have searched for her earlier."

Addie glared at her knight. "I tried to find the oak. I told you I needed to, but you insisted on keeping me at Swynton. I said time and again that I *had* to come home, that I had too many responsibilities to play lady of the manor to your knight in shining armor."

Her knight glowered back. "As I oft repeated, I play not at what I do. I've distinguished myself in battle and have sworn fealty to Richard. I am a knight of the realm, and Swynton is my manor. When you married me, you became our lady."

"Then surely you'll acknowledge now that I traveled through time to arrive there. As you have now done as well.

We're no longer in England, and the year is no longer 1485. You saw the evidence yourself."

"I agree to naught save that you've a sister to find," he snapped. "Where shall we search first?"

Addie gave her husband an assessing look. "Ah . . . er . . ."

"Yes?"

"We have a minor matter to attend to before we go back out to the streets of York."

"That would be . . . ?"

Addie waved. "Your clothes."

That dark eyebrow rose. "What is wrong with my clothes?"

Addie stifled a smile. "Nothing—for 1485. But everything for 1885. I'm afraid if you go into polite society wearing that hose beneath your short tunic, the ladies would be scandalized. And the men, well, let's just say they would not find your garb especially masculine."

Robert's stormy frown reappeared. "Do you question my maleness?"

Shaking her head, Addie hastened to say, "Of course not! But no one here is prepared for the way you dress. You saw the men on the street today. What do you think?"

That gave him pause. He set his jaw against his wilder thoughts. "They *were* oddly garbed."

Addie sighed in exasperation. "They're not the ones wearing strange clothes, *you're* the one in fashions four hundred years out of date. . . ."As she spoke, she noticed the clenching of Robert's fists, the stiffening of his stance, the narrowing of his gaze. "What—"

He withdrew his dagger. "Be still, Wife. A pair of those peculiarly dressed men are on the approach. Quick! Get behind me."

Refusing to scoot behind Robert, Addie turned and saw Pastor Wright and another gentleman giving Midnight a wide berth. "Put that thing away!" she urged, pointing at her husband's knife. "Pastor Wright is a man of the cloth. You wouldn't greet Father Anselm with weapon drawn, would you?"

Robert's jaw jutted, and Addie knew resistance when she saw it. "He wears no churchly vestments, no chasuble, no surplice, no cassock, no cowl. And I see no rosary beads or cross on him."

As the men came up the front walk, Addie lunged for her husband's sword, grabbing it a second before he did. She concealed it in the folds of her gown.

"He's a pastor not a priest," Addie answered. "Different from Anselm in certain aspects, but of similar Christian faith." How did one explain Martin Luther, the Reformation, and centuries of Protestantism to a medieval knight?

Yet another future lesson for her misplaced husband. At the moment she prayed he accepted her inadequate explanation. "Trust me, Robert, he's a man of the cloth, so *hide that dagger.* I don't know the other fellow, but Pastor Wright is the kindest, most godly person I've ever known. Here in *this* York, of course. Back in yours there was Father Anselm and your sister Edythe—"

"Adelaide, my dear," called the black-garbed reverend as he ascended the steps to the porch. "I'm much relieved to see you again. We'd begun to wonder if tragedy had taken you as well."

Moonlight illuminated the preacher's solemn expression. His words skittered a chill down Addie's spine. "As well?"

Distress showed in the man's pleated forehead. "Oh, my. Could we perhaps go inside? I'm afraid this isn't the sort of news one gives outside like this. . . ."

Addie knew the moment the elderly preacher spotted her brand-spanking-new spouse. His words dried up as fast as dew in the August sun, his jaw dropped, and he backed away. "Who . . . what . . . ?"

There was no getting around it. "Pastor Wright, allow me to present my husband, Robert Swynton. We were wed while I was . . . away."

For a moment Pastor Wright remained frozen—all but his eyes. In the moonglow Addie saw faded blue orbs dart up and down, cataloging Robert's unorthodox—to 1885 standards—appearance.

"He . . . he gotta . . . knife," stammered the preacher's companion in a heavily accented voice.

Robert stepped forward, holding said knife at the ready.

With a swish of skirts, Addie darted sideways, inserting herself between visitors and knight. Out of the corner of her mouth, she spit, "I warned you. Civilized folks do *not* threaten others when they come calling. Put that thing away!"

Robert dropped a heavy hand on her shoulder. "'Tis my duty to protect you, wife. I intend to do so." He nudged her away.

Addie resisted. "You have nothing to fear from these men. Do you see a sword? I don't."

Applying more insistent pressure, Robert tried again to move her, but she refused to be budged. To Addie's dismay, he stepped around her.

"Disarm," he demanded.

Pastor Wright stumbled backwards, shaking his head. "We have no arms. I'm a man of peace, a man of God."

"I no do nothing," said the other, his voice quavering. "I no fight nobody, not now, not when boy."

Alarmed by the rapidly deteriorating situation, Addie again darted around Robert and took the preacher's arm. "Pay no mind to Robert. He's . . . ah . . . oh, yes! He's been . . . making a . . . museum exhibit . . . on medieval battle equipment. That's right. And he's frightfully devoted to his work. It consumes him at times, you see."

Pastor Wright gave the glowering knight a doubtful stare. "Evidently, this is one of those times."

The man who had come with the reverend suddenly trotted up to Addie and, clutching her free arm, nodded respectfully to Robert.

Until he spotted the sword in her hand.

"Aaack!" he cried.

"What—oh, this?" she asked. When he nodded, shaking like custard, she relinquished her hold on Pastor Wright and patted the man's shoulder in reassurance. "Just another part of Robert's display, I'm afraid. And the remainder of his armor is in that corner of the porch. Fascinating, if that sort of thing interests you. I've always loved history, and I find the English Middle Ages particularly fascinating."

As she passed her spouse, he muttered, "Never lie, do you?"

"I'm trying to save your neck," Addie retorted, then led their guests into the house. Addressing them, she said, "I'll just be a moment turning on the lights."

She turned the pin on the lamp nearest the door. To her dismay, it did not light. The pastor cleared his throat. "Adelaide, dear, I'm afraid the gas service has been stopped," he said in a gentle voice. "You've been gone a long time."

Addie frowned, tamping down the anxiety that burgeoned. "But Emmie was here. Surely no one would be so cruel as to leave her in darkness just because I was away."

Silence followed her comment. In the darkness of the room, Addie saw nothing more than the shadowy outlines of the men and Robert's hulk filling the doorway.

"This is silly," she forced out, trying to regain a semblance of normalcy. "I have candles in the kitchen. I'll be right back."

She ran to the rear of the house, rummaged in a drawer, and found the candles and the box of matches she kept there. Taking deep, even breaths, she tried to regain her equanimity. As she trotted back to the unlikely trio in her front parlor, she prayed for strength, for peace.

Striking a match, she applied the flame to the candlewick. She heard Robert's hiss behind her, and added matches to the mental list of future lessons. It was a good thing she loved to teach.

"Gentlemen," she said, placing the candle in a glass holder she withdrew from the glass-fronted curio by the front window. "Shall we take a seat?"

The two modern gents did as asked. Robert remained in the doorway, but mercifully slipped his dagger back in its sheath. He then folded his arms over his chest.

Addie gave him a smile. "Now," she said, making her voice purposely cheery, "what brings you here tonight, Pastor Wright?"

The aged preacher shot a worried glance at Robert, then withdrew a handkerchief from his suit pocket. He held it out to Addie. "I'm afraid, my dear, I'm the bearer of tragic news."

Her heart lurched. "Tragic?"

"Indeed." Pastor Wright waved the square of white linen, and Addie took it warily. He went on. "You see, after you left—without word to anyone, I might add. A trifle unusual for you, was it not?"

Addie blushed and shrugged, twisting the handkerchief in her fingers. She couldn't explain the outlandish circumstances under which she had disappeared.

The reverend cleared his throat and gave her a disapproving frown. "As I was saying, after you left Emmie was disconsolate. She stopped going to work at the bakery and wept for days, which in a way must be seen as a blessing, since she found no mischief while she grieved."

"Thank God," Addie whispered.

"Not so fast," the stranger snapped.

Addie frowned. "Excuse me, Pastor Wright, just who *is* this gentleman?"

"Patience, please. I'm getting there."

As he sat on the edge of the settee, the spindly preacher reminded Addie of a crow—not a comparison she would have made before tonight, but anxiety filled her, altering her perspective. "Go on, then. Clearly you've come about my sister, and I've been frantic about her."

A skeptical look filled the reverend's face, but nevertheless he refrained from commenting—for which Addie rejoiced.

"Many of us were alarmed," he said, "but . . . well, you know how Emmie frightens folks. And she refused to move in with Mrs. Wright and me. Short of arresting her, we couldn't forcibly take her away."

"Then where is she?"

Pastor Wright averted his gaze. "Since Mrs. Wilhelm still needed help with the dough, she was afraid to hire someone else. Emmie had no form of income. It struck many as a trifle irresponsible on your part, you know. You may find the town's opinion has turned against you in your absence."

Addie clenched her jaw, unable to explain the reason for her delay. "I will deal with that when I must. Tell me about my sister, if you please."

Pastor Wright pursed his lips in disapproval, then harrumphed and said, "She was forced to seek employment, as she wouldn't take help. That's where Mr. Palotti comes in. He owns a fireworks manufactory on the southeast side of town. He's been here less than a year."

"Business been good," Mr. Palotti commented. "I give work to many people."

Addie slowly faced him. "Please don't say you hired Emmie."

Mr. Palotti shrugged.

Pastor Wright continued, "Indeed he did. Your sister insisted she was old enough and capable of keeping a job. Mr. Palotti needed workers." The reverend gestured helplessly.

Addie stood, her stomach churning sickly. "What did Emmie do?"

"You'd better sit," suggested the preacher.

"I can't. Just tell me. Now."

With obvious reluctance, Pastor Wright resumed his tale. "Once she began working for him, Emmie begged to be taught how to make and ignite the explosives. Mr. Palotti, being new in town and not knowing of her . . . *problem*, agreed, pleased by her interest in his business."

When the preacher paused, Addie's temples began to pound, but she said nothing and waited.

"Early the morning of July fourth," he then said, "Mr. Palotti stored all the pyrotechnics he planned to use for the celebration in the back of his shop. With so much to do, all the employees worked that morning but were to leave by midday."

Addie began to shake. "And Emmie . . . ?"

"Didn't. Or so it would seem. At half past two, when Mayor Noel began his speech, the most horrific blast occurred in the rear of Mr. Palotti's building."

"Fire spoiled Four July show," mourned the fireworks maker.

"No," Addie whispered.

"I'm afraid so, my dear. When they finally put out the blaze, they found nothing but ashes."

"No more factory," bemoaned Mr. Palotti.

Crushing pain hit Addie with the strength of a locomotive. She backed away from Pastor Wright, as if by doing so she could escape the news he had given her. A hideous image, all fire and flames and smoke, filled her mind.

"Emmie," she moaned. "Dear God, not Emmie . . ."

Then the pain exploded into sobs, violent heaving bursts of misery that tore through Addie, leaving her gasping for breath. Scalding tears rolled down her cheeks. *"No!"*

Pastor Wright came to her side and placed a hand on her back. "We gave her a Christian burial, even though we didn't turn up as much as a fragment of bone in the rubble. The blaze was so great it left little behind. Mr. Palotti paid for everything."

Whimpering, Addie shook her head and held out a trembling hand. "Please, no more. I can't bear it."

At Addie's words, Robert stepped forward and, grasping each man by the arm, led them to the door. "You've heard my lady. She can bear no more. Mayhap tomorrow or the day after that you can say more. When she is ready to listen. Go now."

Without argument, the men departed. Robert faced his wife, feeling more helpless than ever. "Addie . . ."

She turned on him, tears of anguish turning into a grimace of rage. "You! It's all your fault. If you hadn't kept me from finding the oak, this wouldn't have happened. I would have come back to my sister where I belonged."

Fists doubled, she came at him and pummeled his chest. Robert sought to capture those weapons, but her strength surprised him, as did her agility.

"Don't you touch me!" his wife screamed. "You wouldn't believe me, and this is what happened. I hate you! I hate, hate, hate, hate you!"

He reared back. Although Robert realized she spoke out of grief, her words wounded him deeply. Images burst in his mind. That spectacular afternoon in the woods came into focus, vivid, haunting, perhaps more real than any other moment in his life. He remembered Addie's every touch, her every sigh.

In a sudden flood, he relived the feelings, recognized his love for her. Yet she hated him. As had Catherine before her. Agony filled his heart. Another wife; another failure.

"I—hate—you," she repeated, her words deliberate, crushing.

He believed her. He should have expected it. 'Twasn't new for him.

Yet he yearned to hold her, change her feelings with his love. But she would not even let him comfort her.

"I did what I knew was best," he said, disillusionment in his heart. "I cannot let you wander the woods while the Morlands remain a threat. I don't want your death on my conscience."

Tears spilling again, she shouted, "You've my sister's there! You kept me from my duty, you who talk so much about your responsibilities, your blasted honor. And now, because of you, my sister's dead."

Addie's voice broke, and Robert's heart with it.

"I wasn't here where I should have been. I failed her. All because of you!" Ripe bitterness saturated her words.

Robert ached, her agony wrapping itself around his throat, making it difficult to speak, to breathe. "I could not have known. You said naught but that you wished to go home. I did not know of Emmie until now."

She again came at him, punching wildly, landing only the rare blow. "I told you I had to find the tree," she wailed, her roiling emotions tearing at him as her nails did his flesh.

Her misery was such that Robert feared for her, knowing

in her grief she could hurt herself while she sought to hurt him. He tried to reason with her.

"Come, now," he said softly, lovingly, his heart in tatters. "Hitting me cannot change a thing, but you might hurt yourself. And I—I cannot bear the thought of harm coming your way."

Clapping her hands over her ears, she cried, "You've done all the harm you could! You've hurt me more than the Morlands could have. They might have cut me with swords, killed me even. But you . . . you kept me from my responsibilities, my duty. You and your blasted honor. You should have understood when I said I had to go. My sister needed me, and I failed her."

"Ah, Addie, love, death comes when it comes. Mayhap 'twas her time, no matter where you were."

"She was only sixteen!" Tears flooded her face as Addie stood stiff and hurting.

Robert reached for her and, taking advantage of her momentary stillness, wrapped his arms around her. "I could not let you leave. I answer to Richard for everyone at Swynton. Even a suspected enemy. I could not dishonor my word to my king."

"Yet you made me dishonor mine to my sister, who I had promised to help and protect. Was that an honorable thing to do?"

Anger flared. "No less than what you ask of me."

"What do you mean?"

"You ask me to abandon my king when he has summoned me. You ask me to betray my oath and leave. See you now why I cannot follow you? Why I must go back?"

Addie's head snapped up. "Go . . . back?"

"Aye. Richard needs me."

"But . . . but you can't."

"Of course I can. And I will, once I ensure your safety. I'll ride Midnight back the way we came, meet Mortimer and the others, then travel on to meet my king."

"Ah . . . Robert," she said tentatively. "Remember the oak? The fall through the darkness? Your dented armor?"

"Aye, of course I remember all that. It has naught to do with my fealty to Richard."

Addie would not meet his gaze. "I'm afraid it has everything to do with it. You can*not* just ride down the road to Swynton. We're no longer in England. Your lands are nowhere near. And Richard . . . well, he died four hundred years ago. I wasn't lying about that. The only way to go back—*if* it's possible at all—is to find the oak. It took me months to find the right one. I'm afraid you won't be going to England any time soon. Not in time to meet Richard. The Battle of Bosworth is only days away, and who knows how long it will take to test the oaks behind the school."

She paused, took a deep breath, and met his gaze. "I had to bring you with me. I—I couldn't bear to see you die."

Rage tasted sour when it came on the heels of heartbreak and betrayal. "You rail at me because you feel I kept you from your duty, yet you admit you've sought to keep me from mine? What manner of honor have you, Wife?"

Up went Addie's chin. "It was the only way I knew to save your life."

"My life is worth naught without honor," he rasped.

Bruised by grief, she met his gaze. "Honor counts for nothing once you're dead."

"Not true," he countered, steeling himself against her pain. "My father died for his king and his country. 'Twas an honorable death. Yet you try to keep me from doing the same. Mayhap 'tis I who should accuse you of all you accused me. For you've made me betray my king."

He stared at the blotched, tear-stained face of the woman he loved, the woman who had played him false. "Mayhap 'tis I who have cause to loathe *you*," Robert said with quiet menace in his voice.

Chapter 18

HE'D DRAWN THE line between them with words. Addie gasped, and Robert could not back down—his honor would not let him.

His wife had voiced her hate for him and confessed her efforts to have him dishonor his vow to his king. He had no alternative but to kill his feelings for her. He could never love a woman who had betrayed him.

After a long, silent moment, Addie seemed to close in on herself, putting up a nearly tangible wall between them. She stood, waved toward the padded bench where the two men had earlier sat, and said, "I need rest—alone. If you're tired, sleep there."

With that, she vanished up the steps against the right wall of the chamber, and moments later the house echoed with the sound of a slamming door above stairs. Robert blew out the candle, then collapsed onto the furnishing, certain he would never sleep on such a short, narrow thing.

'Twould matter not. He doubted his milling thoughts and shattered emotions would allow him any rest. What was it about him that caused women to reject him, to betray him?

Especially Addie.

He had loved her, and it truly anguished him to see his feelings come to naught again. How could she have given herself to him so sweetly then turned on him so cruelly? To strike at his honor was more devastating than if she'd sought to use even the witchcraft she vowed she did not employ.

It occurred to him in the darkness that Catherine's outright rejections had been much easier to accept. But Addie . . . oh, Addie had welcomed his touch, his tenderness, his lovemaking. Robert could not doubt that.

'Twas why her treachery struck so deeply, hurt so savagely.

Turning to yet another contorted position on the uncomfortable bench, Robert strengthened his resolve. He would not allow his emotions to subvert his commitment. He would leave on the morrow, join Mortimer and his men, ride to meet Richard, and fight Henry when the time came.

Love be damned.

Well before he was ready to relinquish his hold on slumber the next day, a bolt of sunlight struck Robert's tired eyes, rendering further rest impossible.

He cautiously unfolded his long body from the instrument of torture in which he had lain, his every muscle objecting to the effort.

"Damnation!" He felt much worse than when he had finally dropped off to sleep.

Then he heard a sharp *tap-tap-tap* crossing overhead. The brisk sound rang out on the stairs, and Robert braced himself for whatever it meant. He first spotted the pointed tips of the odd shoes, much resembling the cream-colored ones Addie had worn that first day—the shoes Nell had seized out of fear for Addie's safety. These were black.

At what he imagined must be ankle height, Robert saw a froth of white fabric, held safely away by a pair of familiar, white-knuckled hands. A slender waist followed, and soon painfully straight shoulders appeared. Addie's graceful neck held her head stiffly upright, and the expression on her sweet face was anything but.

Angry eyes met his momentarily, then she averted her gaze, sniffed, and descended the final few steps. Without a word, she turned and headed toward the rear of the thin, quadrangular house, her shoes still marking that sharp tattoo.

He muttered a curse, then strode to the narrow door through which they had entered the night before and twisted the ball knob. "I shan't subject you to my unwelcome presence any longer," he said in a flat voice. "I'm off to Swynton, and won't come this way again."

The tapping flew toward him. "Oh, dear! You cannot go outside like that. You'll cause a stir, a scandal. If you insist on going, even though I assure you Swynton is nowhere near, at least wait until I find you decent clothes."

Robert stiffened. "My garments are fine. I'll only trouble you to assist me with my armor."

Addie's eyes widened. "*No!* You can't do that. Wait. Please. I'll be right back."

Running lightly out the front door, she proceeded to the street and there turned left. Robert followed her to the . . . porch, she'd called it, and watched her lithe form hasten away. To his dismay, he had to fight the feelings that surfaced—warmth, longing, desire.

What was it about the strong-willed, contrary woman that so affected him? Even after what she had done? What she had said?

As he scratched his stubbled chin, pondering the matter, Robert noticed movement in the street. A group of children—mostly boys, but he could see a girl or two—stood ten feet or so away from where he had tethered Midnight to the ringed metal rod Addie called a hitching post. Fingers pointed, heads came together, and sibilant whispers soared on the morning breeze.

Mostly they stared at the beast as he nibbled on a pile of hay within his reach. Had Addie done that for his horse? If so, when? She would have had to pass by his uncomfortable bed to reach the animal, and Robert remembered naught from the night. More importantly, did she care enough about him and his beast to see to the animal's needs despite her fears?

A flicker of hope kindled in his chest, especially when he thought back on her actions of the day before. When the child had attacked Midnight, when passersby had called for the constable, she had set aside her feelings toward horses and shown her support by riding with him.

Then Robert remembered the look on her face as she screamed her hate at him. Nay, he was not that great a fool. 'Twas likely a kindly neighbor who hadn't wished to see a horse go without feed.

Addie cared not even enough to respect his integrity.

Turning, he entered the wooden cottage again. He ought to leave, but something deep inside would not let him, not until he saw her again. He had to bid his wife a final farewell.

She returned sooner than he'd expected, bearing an armful of black and white fabric. "Here," she said, thrusting it at him. "Get dressed. Then, if you insist, try to find Swynton Manor. You'll soon see I did not lie."

Robert clutched the wad of cloth, biting down on a retort. Their acquaintance was old enough by now that he knew better than to object. He instead turned to the stuff in his arms and frowned. "What are these? Whose are they?"

"Doc Horst is the only one in town whose size comes close to yours. He's not quite as tall, but who cares if the trousers are a mite short? At least you'll be decently covered."

Robert frowned. "I've always been decently covered."

When her eyes widened and her cheeks reddened, Robert realized what his words had done. They'd brought memories to life, memories neither wanted revived. At least not any longer.

But there they were, heated and real.

Unutterably beautiful.

"Robert—"

"Addie—".

She flushed darker when they spoke at once, then she

shook her head. "Just get dressed. The long things with two ends are trousers. You can put those on first. Then the white shirt. The black coat goes on after your shirt. You needn't bother with the tie, since you're in a hurry to be gone."

With a tip of her chin, she spun and headed back to the rear of the house. Robert laid the three garments on his erstwhile bed and gave them a slow perusal, finding them heavy and ungainly in appearance. Although he was most reluctant to don them, he remembered Addie had worn what Nell provided while at Swynton. He could do no less.

Mayhap she was right, and 'twas best to dress as others in town did.

Following her instructions, he stripped to his under breeches, then shook out the item she had indicated was meant for his lower half. It looked cumbersome, certainly unusual, and had a slit that ran from the top edge to between the legs. The one side of the opening had small, flat buttons and the other, holes. The buttons would fit through the slits, but he knew not if 'twas the front or the rear of the garment.

"Addie?" he called reluctantly.

"Yes," she answered curtly.

"In the item with the legs," he began, inserting all the dignity he possessed into his voice, "does the part with the buttons go forward or back?"

To his disgust, he heard her snicker. "Addie . . ." he said in a warning tone. " 'Tisn't humorous at all."

"You found it funny when I didn't know what went where. Even though I was not amused. It's the front, Robert, and they're called trousers. Only men wear them."

He bit down on a sharp comment and slipped a leg inside one of the tubular parts. He did the same with the other, then pulled all up. The trousers were loose—*very* loose around the waist and hips, even after he had buttoned them, and his legs brushed oddly against their flapping fabric casing.

He doffed his torn and filthy tunic, taking up the white shirt. That posed him no trouble, and with newfound confidence, he proceeded to what she had called a coat, but which, aside from having arms and bodice, resembled none he had ever seen.

He cleared his throat. "I'm dressed as those strangers were last night, and I assume I shall now create no scandal. I'll bid you farewell, my lady."

A long moment of silence met his words.

"Addie? Will you not wish me Godspeed?"

"Just go," she said in choked voice. "You'll be back sooner than you think. Swynton isn't where you expect it to be. You're not in England anymore."

A red haze of anger exploded in his head. "Very well. I'll leave. On unpleasant terms, since you so wish. 'Tis not the way I would part from my wife, but you've made the choice."

He thought he heard her sob. Then nothing more.

He took that as his wife's bitter adieu.

Robert stalked outside, filled his arms with armor, and went to Midnight. He gave a gentle pat to the animal's withers, murmured soft words. The horse was his only friend right then.

After mounting, he gave the tall, narrow cottage Addie called home a final glance, then turned, setting aside the pain of her betrayal.

He retraced his path of yesterday, knowing he would never forget their ignominious entrance into his wife's town. Nor would he forget the extraordinary sights he had seen.

It mattered not how intriguing the sights here were. He had given his word, and regardless of what Addie wanted, what she had tried to make him do, Robert Swynton was a man of honor. Richard Plantagenet's man. He would meet his monarch, do battle for him, shed his blood, die if need be. As had his father before him.

Head held high, Robert proceeded through the town and on down the road to the outskirts. Before long, he spotted the small red structure Addie had identified as the school where she taught. He knew not what to believe of her assertion, as he had never known a woman tutor. But in a land as peculiar as the one that had produced Addie Shaw, he might conceive of such a thing.

As she had often said, a dense stand of trees stood but a short distance behind the building. Robert directed Midnight's steps that way. Entering the green-topped area, he breathed a sigh of relief. The blessed hush of the woods was achingly familiar, the first thing that felt thusly since he had closed his eyes to Michael Morland's vicious face.

He sought to find his bearings, turning in the saddle to study his surroundings. He could not recall where they had emerged the day before, but he knew Swynton Manor did not lie anywhere near where he had just come from.

He was loath to leave the comfort of the woods, to go where strangers might spot him and fear Midnight. He dreaded a repeat of yesterday's rock-flinging incident. Choosing to ride just inside the edge of the forest, he cautiously guided the horse with gentle nudges and soft words.

Despite the utter unfamiliarity of all he saw beyond the woods, Robert persisted doggedly. The sun climbed to its zenith, heating the day, yet still he continued his quest.

His stomach growled, reminding him he had eaten naught since the midday meal the day before. They'd had Nell's roast pigeons, bread, and tender beans from the kitchen gardens. Just the thought had him salivating.

But his determination proved greater than his hunger, and he pressed on. For hours, lonely, silent hours.

Late in the afternoon, he made an unsettling discovery. He had spent the day riding in a circle and now stood directly behind Addie's school once more. Naught he'd seen during his travels even remotely resembled the road to Swynton.

As the sun began to make its way back down the sky, Robert conceded defeat—for the moment. Aye, his lady wife had apparently been right. He would indeed return to her. He had nowhere else to go.

But he would be back on the morrow. He would find his way back home. Even if it meant seeking that damned oak she spoke of, the accursed tree he had refused to believe existed, the tree she had found as Michael Morland appeared, the tree through which they had come to her town.

Four hundred years in the future—or so she said.

After trudging an entire day around the woods, Robert was ready to consider—consider, not accept—the remote possibility that Addie might not be mad.

The town, the people, the lights, the unfamiliar terrain where the road home ought to have been. Something had happened to him—he knew not what, but something had.

Mayhap Addie was right about the time . . . the year. For a second, the possibility intrigued him. Then he frowned. He was beginning to think like Addie.

A most alarming thought.

Robert rode home at a measured pace, again noting the attention Midnight garnered. At least no one threw anything at the animal today, and when he passed under the arc lights at the corner of Market and George streets, they mercifully remained unlit. 'Twasn't as late as yesterday.

His heart picked up its beat as he approached Addie's home. His head, however, warned him against tenderness. She had betrayed him. He needed but a place to rest and a meal, not a traitorous wife. He had offered her hospitality in his home, she could do the same for him now.

After dropping his armor in the corner of the porch, Robert went to the door. He paused, steeling himself against the sight of the woman who meant too much to him. Then he knocked. Hurried, tapping footsteps approached.

When she saw him, she gave him a knowing look. "Do you believe me now?"

He grimaced. "I believe I'm a stranger to these parts. I also believe I'm near starvation and death by thirst. Surely you will take pity on a husband in need."

Stepping back, she gestured for him to enter. "I have company at the moment, but you are welcome to eat and drink. I never deny basic necessities to even the cruelest sort."

"Addie . . ."

She slammed the door, then rounded on him. "I do not appreciate that tone of voice, and while you're in my home you shall refrain from using it." She paused, took a deep breath, and appeared to regain her composure. "Follow me to the kitchen if you wish to eat."

Swallowing a response, Robert marched behind her and fisted his hands. They itched to grab her shoulders, to shake some sense into her, but 'twould do naught, he feared.

Nay, he thought with sudden certainty. 'Twas not the futility of the effort he feared. He fought the impulse to touch her because of the feelings such contact might arouse in him again. He could never forget Addie had asked him to betray his vows.

She bustled from one end of the room to the other, pausing before a vast black metal device with doors across the front, flat circles on its surface, and a fat round pipe that climbed to the ceiling. From on top of the . . . thing, she took a silver-toned pot and set it on the table in the center of the room. She returned to the . . . was it a hearth, a kiln, an oven of some sort? She returned to it, opened a door, withdrew another covered vessel, and placed it, too, on the table.

Then she turned away another time, and when she returned, she slapped a white plate down on the tabletop. She gave him an impatient stare. "What are you waiting for? Take a seat. I have chicken, mashed potatoes and gravy, fresh carrots, and biscuits."

Moments later, she had piled fragrant food before Robert. He eyed the mounded white mush drenched in golden brown gravy with suspicion. "What is that?"

She smirked. "Those are the mashed potatoes. England did not have potatoes until . . . oh, about a hundred years after your time. We in America often enjoy them. They won't poison you, so give them a try."

The scents entrapped him. Forking up a bit of the soft potatoes, Robert gave them a try. The mellow flavor, mixed with the spicier taste of the sauce, burst delightfully in his mouth. He savored the bite, his vacant middle urging him to hurry.

A clear glass vessel filled with water appeared at his right hand. "I mentioned I had company," Addie said in a crisp, impersonal voice. "Mr. Palotti has waited while I fed you. You may join us in the parlor once you've finished, but only if you leave your weapons behind. He has come to offer condolences."

She left, and the soft sibilance of conversation soon reached his ears. A blissful Robert ignored it—as he did the damned sparrow's cheeping from where Addie had hung its cage at a nearby window—while he consumed every scrap of the banquet she had served him. When replete, his thirst quenched as well, he again grew aware of the presence of the stranger in the adjacent chamber. Remembering Addie's words, he decided to humor her and left his dagger on the table.

Curiosity led him from the kitchen.

Mistrust halted him in the parlor.

Mr. Palotti, far younger than Pastor Wright, had a cozy arm around Addie's shoulders, while his free hand patted her knee most familiarly.

Possessiveness roared to life in Robert. It mattered not that they'd had words the night before. It mattered not that Addie had betrayed him. It mattered not that she had said she hated him.

She was his wife.

And another man dared touch her.

As he hadn't in days. Weeks.

If she were to be believed, in centuries.

He reached for his dagger but found an empty sheath. "Damnation," he muttered, knowing he ought not have listened to his wife.

"I see you've finished your meal," she said, her voice thick with tears.

"'Twould seem your guest is about to enjoy one of a different sort," he countered, glaring at the man's hand on her knee.

"Robert!" she cried. "Mr. Palotti's a guest. Mind your manners."

Mr. Palotti bolted upright, nearly unseating Addie in his haste to put distance between them. "I no do nothin'. Miss

Shaw's sister, she my worker. I came for to say sorry she died. I no do nothin'."

Robert approached the much smaller fellow. "Touching my lady wife was enough. Methinks 'tis time for you to leave."

"Robert!" she repeated, clearly appalled.

As was he. He had never experienced the slightest bit of jealousy while married to Catherine, but then again, Addie was no Catherine. She had crawled under his defenses when he had sworn never to marry again, and now everything about her mattered. Too much.

"A man has a right to choose his guests—"

"Perhaps in his own home, but here, even you are my guest."

Robert arched an eyebrow. "Will you demand I leave?"

"If you offend my guest again."

"Ahem!" said Mr. Palotti, darting toward the door. "You busy. I be go now. Miss Shaw, I very sorry about your Emmie sister. Very, very sorry."

Addie slipped her hand through Mr. Palotti's arm, giving Robert a quelling look. "*I* appreciate your efforts," she told the transgressor. "You must excuse my husband. He's not from around here. York natives are much more welcoming and polite."

She led her guest to the door, and shook the hand he awkwardly extended. Trust Robert to turn a simple condolence call into something totally unbearable.

When she closed the door, she heard him approach. She spun and faced him, choosing offense as her best defense against his potent effect on her system. "Well, sir. Are you happy? You intimidated that poor man. And he only meant to show kindness."

"'Twas interest rather than kindness he showed—in your knees."

Something in Addie sparked to life. Perhaps Robert cared enough about her to feel jealousy, enough to forgive what she had done.

Then she mentally scolded herself. There was nothing to

forgive. She had saved his life, while on the contrary he had cost her sister hers. Addie couldn't care for him. He had prevented her return home when Emmie most needed her.

And he called her a liar.

She hadn't lied.

"What did you find in the woods today?" she asked, knowing well what he hadn't found. "Not the road to Swynton, I'm sure."

Robert turned away. "I found no familiar road, as you say. But I will try again on the morrow. I will keep my word to Richard."

"You want to find Richard Plantagenet?"

"I want to meet up with him before the pretender attacks."

"Here." She stalked to the bookshelf against the parlor's left wall, yanked out a history of England, and slapped it against his middle. "You'll find him here. You can read about him, Henry Tudor, the Battle of Bosworth, and the four hundred years since. Perhaps then you'll believe me."

"I believe you've gone mad with grief," he shot back.

"I was not in mourning when we first met."

"The blood of battle offended your sensibilities."

"I can't deny that."

"'Tis that which made you concoct your tale of travel through time."

The urge to punch him struck Addie again, and she acknowledged how frequently the uncharacteristic impulse came while in her frustrating husband's presence. "How do you explain the gaslights on my parlor walls? The arc lights in Center Square?"

His jaw grew granite hard. "I need not know all that goes on far from my home. You've ingenious citizens here."

Addie threw her hands up in surrender. "I can't go through this anymore. Just read the book. If you must, go back to the woods. You'll never find the road to Swynton, for it's not there. The best you can hope for is to locate the oak. I wish you well, since you're determined to join Richard in death."

"I'm determined to honor my vow."

The memory of a candlelit chapel brought anguish to her heart. "And your vow to me?" she cried. "Have you forgotten that one? You made it before Anselm and God. You're to love, honor, and cherish me, you're my husband, and I don't want you dead."

He refused to meet her gaze. "I pledged myself to you for so long as we both should live," he said in an oddly hollow voice. "If I perish at Richard's side, then I honored my vow and you until my death."

"Then read the book," she said, tears again rising to her eyes. "If you insist, go seek the oak, but I won't help you. I've spent years learning to save precious lives."

Through her tears, Addie saw her words hadn't moved him. Gathering her courage, she went on. "I dragged you with me—yes, against your stubborn will—to prevent your unnecessary death. I will not help you throw your life away for nothing more than foolish pride."

Chapter 19

HE READ THE book.

He looked for the oak.

He tested tree after tree, sitting, leaning, kicking, cursing.

After spending the miserable day in his futile search, Robert headed back toward Addie's cottage, defeated, bitter, broken in spirit.

As he rode through town, his head swarmed with questions, all relating to the impossible, implausible events of recent months. How could a tree give way and eject first Addie in 1485, then the two of them in 1885?

Was his original suspicion of sorcery correct?

Nay. Aside from her unnatural mode of travel, Addie seemed quite what she said, an ordinary, devout woman who had been thrust into extraordinary circumstances.

She bore no blame in that.

She was, however, guilty of trickery. To lure him into the woods, she had played on his desire for her. Like a fool, he had followed. She had shown no respect for his need to honor his vow to the Crown, and had, as she confessed, dragged him through time, far from where his duty commanded he go.

He would never forgive her treachery.

Upon arriving at Addie's home, Robert found the door unlocked, and he strode in. Without hesitation, he went directly to the shelves from where she had taken the book last night. There he found a number of other tomes on the history of England and methodically paged through each and every one.

They all told the same sad tale. Richard Plantagenet had met his death at Redmoor near Market Bosworth, the battle taking place, as Addie had said, on the twenty-second day in August of 1485. The Lancastrian forces soundly defeated the Yorkists, and Henry Tudor ascended the throne.

After hours of reading, Robert dropped his head onto the high back of the bench Addie termed a settee and closed his eyes.

That was where Addie found him when she came home after a most frustrating and bitterly disappointing day. As Pastor Wright had said, most people in town had turned against her, accusing her of negligence toward her sister, blaming her for Emmie's death.

As a result, a new teacher was being sought.

Addie had no means of supporting herself.

Now she had to deal with Robert, who had apparently spent time in historical research, if the books strewn across the settee and the small table before it gave any indication.

She sighed. "Do you still accuse me of lying?"

He rose slowly, then faced her, his eyes haunted. "Nay, 'tisn't that your sin. You've admitted to trickery—*that's* unforgivable. A man is only as good as his honor, and flight is anything but honorable. You subverted my intention to fight for my king as my father did—"

"What good would dying on that field have done?" she demanded. "None to Richard, none to England, none to you, and none to me."

Robert shrugged. "You cannot know. I might have slain Henry before dying myself. What I cannot accept is that you kept me from living up to the standards my father set. By doing so, I failed the many loyal Swynton retainers."

Addie twisted her fingers in anguish at the thought of Thomasine, Nell, Mortimer, Lissa. Contrary to what he might believe, she had thought of them. "I couldn't bring them all with me. I—I had to make a choice. I chose you."

Anger blazed in his dark eyes. "You should have let me meet my destiny. 'Twas as lord of Swynton Manor I should have died. What think you their fate will be at Morland hands? Michael has wanted Swynton lands all along, and now with Henry about to ascend the throne, God only knows what atrocities he will commit on those who resist. Mortimer will not easily yield to Michael and his men."

"I warned you what would happen to Richard," she said helplessly. "You could have chosen to remain neutral."

"A man doesn't choose to honor a promise only when he knows the outcome will favor him," he answered with disdain. "At least, an honorable man does not."

Despite resenting him for his part in her sister's death, Addie felt the need to ease his misery. "Perhaps now that you've gone, the others will remain neutral to the battle for the Crown. And you've said the Morlands are snakes. Surely Henry will soon see that. He should recognize the value of treating the people of Swynton decently and winning them to his side."

"Mortimer was loyal to me, and I was Richard's knight."

"But was Mortimer bound to fight for Richard? Would he have led Swynton's men against Henry? Was Mortimer Richard's man as well . . . or merely yours?"

That gave Robert pause. She watched him wrestle with the concept.

"Mayhap you're right," he said at length. "Mortimer would follow me to hell itself, but I know not how he might act without my lead, if he would support Richard in my absence."

Addie sighed in sudden relief. She waved expansively. "Well, there you go. I'd wager all at Swynton fare just fine. Mortimer hadn't sworn allegiance to Richard, so common sense would have it that he stayed home to guard Swynton against the Morlands. You ought to thank me instead of cursing me. I probably saved your people by getting you away. I told you it was the only sensible, practical thing to do. I will always do what I must to save lives—any lives, even yours."

At first her husband looked dumbstruck. Then he blinked. Repeatedly. Finally his brows crashed over the bridge of his nose, and he came toward her.

Addie backed up.

She went no farther than the front window seat, which caught her behind the knees, sending her sprawling over the chocolate-colored upholstery.

Looming over her, Robert said, "I'd decided you had not lied to me, even if I understood not how the time travel occurred. I had come to believe you when you denied practicing black arts. Now, however, I find myself questioning *my* sanity, which I never before found cause to do."

Puzzled, Addie said, "Why?"

He rubbed the frown lines in his forehead—hard—then shook his head. "Because for one wild, crazed moment, you made sense, with the most nonsensical explanation a man has ever heard. You dare much to suggest I should thank you for thwarting my intent and causing me to dishonor a vow, for making me abandon my duties, my heritage."

She attempted a smile and a lighthearted wave. "You should thank me for keeping your people out of the Battle of Bosworth, and maybe even safe from the Morland threat. I'm certain Mortimer did such a fine job managing things after you left that Henry kept him on. Perhaps he finally married Nell, too."

Closing his eyes, Robert again shook his head. "Stop, Addie. What you did was wrong, and no amount of storytelling will change that. You kept me from Richard's side for that decisive battle, from laying down my life as my father did before me. I'll never forgive you that."

Addie winced as if he'd struck her. "As I'll never forgive you for keeping me from my sister. Whereas your people most likely did not suffer, Emmie died."

To her satisfaction, he flinched as well. "I can only say in my defense that you spoke not a word of Emmie during all those months you were my guest. You, however, knew how I felt."

He crossed to the door. "I've no stomach for any more of this. I must see to Midnight, as I would prefer not to leave him in the street again. I mistrust the children after one cast a stone at him unprovoked."

Addie swallowed hard, knowing there was no winning their argument. Both had clearly lost. "You can take him to Sweitzer's Livery. They'll board him there."

"With directions, I can find it. No need to trouble yourself on our behalf."

Scant moments later, after she had sketched a rough map, he left. Addie closed the door behind him and leaned her forehead against the wood. What had she done?

By seeking to save the life of the man she loved, she had killed any chance of happiness for them. Although he had never spoken of love, he had desired her, and she had hoped to build on that passion, that need. Now all she saw when he gazed at her was anger, resentment, even the hate she had assured him she felt when she first learned of Emmie's death.

But she didn't hate him. She never could. She loved him, even though she shouldn't. He had made her fail her sister, and Emmie had died.

She had saved his life by bringing him to her time. Now he was here, in an unfamiliar setting, wishing he had never come. Worse, he probably wished he had never met her.

Addie's heart broke yet a little more. "Dear God, what should I do next?"

Sweitzer's Livery welcomed Robert with the familiar smells of horse and hay, the well-loved sounds of snuffling and whickering.

"*Guten Abend,*" called a rotund man with a shiny pate as Robert led Midnight through the wide-open stable doors. "Vat I help you with?"

Robert responded to the greeting with a nod. "My horse

needs stabling, food, and water. I'm . . . a stranger here, and I cannot leave him tethered in the street as I have done the past two days."

The gentleman clucked and shook his head. "You *kommen* to right place. Hans Sweitzer"—he jabbed a thumb at his well-padded chest—"take *gut* care of very, very fine horse." He ran an appreciative hand down Midnight's powerful neck and shoulders, and patted the animal's flanks. "Big horse, *ja*?"

Always at ease around admirers of fine equine flesh, Robert smiled more easily than he had in days. "Quick-witted and gentle, as well. He was a pleasure to train."

"*Ja, ja!* Smart, big horse. Strong."

Hans knelt, expertly inspected Midnight's ankles and hooves, then shot Robert a grin. "I haf fine mare, *ja?* Ve mate them. Make *sehr gut* babies."

Robert laughed. He shrugged. "I know not how long I'll remain in town. We can see when the time comes."

Hans stood and stuck his hand out at Robert. "Ve haf deal. When mare ready, ve talk again."

Robert shook the man's hand. "Have we also an agreement for the horse's care?"

The stable owner nodded, then mentioned a number. *"Ja?"* he asked expectantly.

Staring blankly at the man, Robert wondered if that was the cost of caring for a horse. "I fear I'm unfamiliar with your currency. And short of it at present."

Hans's blue eyes narrowed. He studied Robert minutely, discomfiting him. How could he explain his bizarre situation to a man who dealt in the realities of horses?

Then his companion surprised him. "Maybe ve make *ein* more deal. You haf no money, but you haf fine horse—"

"Midnight is not for sale," Robert said, his voice firm, allowing no discussion on the matter.

Hans shrugged and grinned. "Fine. You haf work? You make money working? To pay Hans?"

Robert nearly laughed at the absurdity. Back at Swynton *he* asked the questions. But he was no longer there. He would need employment, and soon. "No, I have no work. Yet."

A radiant smile burst on Hans's round, red face. *"Gut, gut. Sehr gut.* You work for me! You big man, like horse. Strong. Help with shoe-making, the forge."

The thought of working with horses held a measure of appeal. 'Twas something he knew well. And although he had never made a horseshoe, surely he could learn. "We again agree, Hans—I may call you that, no?"

"Ja, ja! And you . . .?"

"Robert. Robert Swynton."

Again, the pudgy yet strong hand darted out, and Robert shook it. 'Twasn't what he might have envisioned in his future, but the arrangement brought him great satisfaction. "Shall I start on the morrow?"

"Tomorrow, *ja.* Six o'clock."

"Six o'clock, then." He'd always been an early riser, and the prospect of again engaging in productive work would give him an incentive to leave his wife's home. "Thank you kindly, Hans."

"Velcome, velcome, Robert. Today is *gut* day for Hans Sweitzer. New man for work, and new horse for Philomena."

Robert chuckled. "If I'm still in town when she's ready."

Hans gave him a sage look. "You vill be. I know."

Laughing without humor, Robert turned to leave. "We shall see what the future holds," he said, then strode through the doors.

The immediate future brought a frigid homecoming. Addie had clearly taken their last confrontation as reason to retreat from him. When Robert entered the front door, she descended the stairs.

"There is food on the table," she said, "but I must warn you. I have very little money left and no employment at present. If matters don't change soon, I stand to lose the house. I'll have no more meals—not for me, not for you."

"You may congratulate me, then," he responded. "I have been employed by Hans Sweitzer to work at his livery. I begin on the morrow."

Addie's eyes opened wide. "I thought you went to find lodging for your horse."

"Hans has plans for Midnight and his mare, Philomena. He also needs another hand at the business. 'Tis a man's place to provide for himself and his wife, so you need not fear losing your home or going hungry. I may no longer have my lands, but I have my pride."

She frowned. Robert braced himself.

"I don't much like that pride of yours," she said. "It stood in the way of my coming home to Emmie. I cannot accept what you offer. I—I don't even know how married I can be to the man who caused my sister's death because of his overblown pride."

The memory of a spindly, overly familiar stranger fondling his wife's knee exploded in Robert's mind. "Aye, 'twould appear you prefer the mouse who employed your sister—and failed to protect her."

Addie gasped. "You couldn't know that! You weren't there."

"True. But I've been responsible for the well-being of many for years. 'Twas his duty to oversee his workers, and Emmie was one. Where was he when the explosion occurred? Why would a man leave a young woman alone in such a place?"

"What a foul accusation! I thought you had more integrity than that, Robert Swynton. You cannot shift your guilt onto another. You must accept it."

"I bear no guilt in this!" he roared. "You never explained your situation, and I was not the one who failed to ensure Emmie's safety. Do not be fooled by your grief, Wife. You who always speak of common sense seem sadly lacking when it comes to judging what has happened. Find some and use it rather than blaming me falsely."

Addie gasped, then opened her mouth. Shut it again. "Fine," she finally spit out. "You ask me to use common sense, and I shall. It tells me to leave the presence of a man who refuses to face facts. Good night, sir."

Her smart steps ascended the stairs. The tapping crossed

the upper floor of the cottage. A door slammed toward the rear of the house.

Robert sighed. 'Twould seem, if he wanted company, he'd have to go to the kitchen and chat with Cheepers, the sparrow.

He went to the settee and sat. Perhaps he had allowed jealousy to cloud his perspective, but something about that Palotti fellow struck him as odd. Mayhap 'twas the way he had first mourned the loss of his building, then appeared most moved over Emmie's death just one day later.

Or mayhap Robert just hated the way Addie had let the rodent touch her. As she hadn't let him touch her in days . . . weeks.

He ought not want her. She had betrayed him.

Yet despite his bitter resentment, his righteous anger, he wanted her. Loved her.

Cursing himself for a fool, he rose and went to the kitchen, ate the simple but savory repast to the tune of a sparrow's song, then returned to the miserable settee. By candlelight he again pored over his wife's treasury of books, reading about the most fantastical things.

He learned of the discovery of another half of the world, of wars and inventions and progress. If all were true, and he had no reason to doubt the books, then Addie's world was indeed a fascinating, exciting place to live.

But he missed his home, all that had been familiar to him. He missed the security of knowing himself lord of Swynton by birth, by right. His very identity had vanished when he traveled through time. 'Twas a most disconcerting, rootless feeling.

One that urged him to find the oak and go home again. Soon.

As he turned the pin to extinguish the gaslight, a noise from above stairs caught his attention. Unlikely though it had to be, it sounded as if Addie was weeping.

He held his breath, hoping to hear the sound again.

Long moments later, he released his breath, thinking he had imagined the sound. Grimacing, he folded himself onto the settee, wondering if the Holy Church had had it built for the Inquisitors he had read about.

As he hovered between wakefulness and slumber, Robert heard the sound again, distinctly enough to know he hadn't dreamt it. Addie wept, her misery breaking from her in deep, soul-wrenching sobs. Despite everything that lay between them, all the issues separating them, the love his heart stubbornly clung to forced him to go to her.

Knowing his wife would not appreciate his actions, Robert nevertheless did what he had to do. He opened the chamber door at the rear of the house and approached her bed.

She lay curled into herself in a puddle of moonlight, looking unusually small, vulnerable, very unlike the strong woman Robert had come to know. Her entire body heaved. Guttural sounds burst from her parted lips.

Confronted by his wife's suffering, Robert's heart broke yet a little more. "Addie, love," he said as he sat at her side and placed a hand on her shoulder.

She gasped and stiffened. "How dare you?" she asked in a frosty tone. "I did not invite you into my room. I remember telling you not to enter it uninvited again."

He remembered, too. Remembered the many times Catherine had sent him from her bed, cursing him for being a man. He remembered Addie's rejection, echoing his first wife's repeated spurns.

Robert felt the blade of pain slice through what remained of his heart. The sour taste of agony rose in his throat. He stood and walked away. "Forgive my misguided desire to comfort you, Wife. I vow 'twill never happen again." He closed the door on her silence.

He wrapped disillusionment around himself on his mean bed.

The sun rose bright the next morn, 22 August, in fact. Robert acknowledged its arrival with sadness. He mourned this day. He grieved for the death of his king and the end of an ill-conceived marriage.

During the sleepless hours of the night, he had reached a decision. He could no longer stay in Addie's house. He could not bear all she brought to mind each time he saw her.

Betrayal. Death. Heartbreak.

And love.

Impossible love.

Knowing Addie cared not for early morn, Robert spared no time gathering his belongings. This time he wanted no farewell. He would be gone before she began her day, relieving both of the awkwardness sure to be between them.

She knew where he would work, where he would stable Midnight. If she wanted to see him again for any reason, she could find him at Sweitzer's Livery. Otherwise, he would honor her wishes and leave her alone.

His broken heart could bear no more pain.

He left the small cottage with its porch and neat black shutters for the last time and made his way to the livery. He had expected to wait awhile for Hans to open up, but when he arrived, the wide doors were already flung ajar.

"*Guten Tag,* Robert," called the rotund man upon spotting him.

Despite the heaviness in his heart, Robert gave a smile. "You open for business early," he said.

"*Ja, ja.* I like morning *sehr gut. Es ist nicht gut* to lay in bed all day."

"I agree with you, Hans. 'Twould seem we shall get on very well indeed." Squaring his shoulders, Robert did what he had to do. "I'm in need of lodgings. Have you a corner in the stable where I could sleep?"

Hans narrowed his gaze and peered curiously at Robert, but surprisingly asked not a thing. "I haf room. Full of crates and stuff, but if you want, it's yours. Frau Sweitzer *ist gut* cook. You want meals, too?"

"As a part of my wage, you understand."

"*Ja, ja.* You work for keep. *Ich bin* lucky you come."

With a wry smile, Robert shrugged. "We shall see once I begin to work. Mayhap I won't take to the farrier trade particularly well."

Hans gestured dismissively. "You big, strong. You vill learn *gut. Kommen sie mit mir,*" he said, gesturing for Robert to follow him. "We put 'way your things. Eat first, work then. *Es ist ein sehr guter Tag.*"

To Robert's amazement, the day did proceed pleasantly enough. Hans had abundant work that needed doing, work that kept his mind from wandering too frequently toward his troubles.

He learned that Sweitzer's Livery was a prosperous enterprise, and he met a number of regular customers as the hours rolled by. When the sun went down, the flow of business slowed to a trickle. He went to pay Midnight a visit.

After checking the horse's water and feed, Robert brushed his long mane and told the beast many of the things he had learned. After a while, he heard Hans walk past the stable, chatting in his thickly accented English to yet another customer.

"You come from Lancaster, *ja*?" asked Robert's employer.

"Just arrived, and as we entered town, my horse threw a shoe. I was told you would help."

Hans clucked. "Herbert White shoe your horse?"

"How did you know?" asked the stranger.

"I fix many of his mistakes."

"I . . . see." From the man's tone, Robert gathered he did not see at all.

"Ja, ja. Herbert greedy. Take too much work for one man. *Es ist nicht gut* to work so fast. Careless. He need helper. Like me. I haf *gut,* strong man to help."

Robert smiled.

"Hmm . . ." murmured the stranger. "You know, I saw the oddest thing when I last went to Herbert's place. He had taken on a helper, but she was a woman, little more than a girl. I doubt she could lift a mallet even."

"Huh?" asked Hans, indignant. "Girl no *gut* for forge. You need big man, strong man."

"I thought so, too, but I saw her there, using the bellows to feed the flame. Seemed to enjoy her duty right well, you know. Chuckled each time the fire flared higher and hotter. Sure looked like she loved that blaze."

Robert's curiosity was piqued. He'd only ever heard of one other girl who loved fire, and that girl was dead. Could there be two such women in the area?

He wondered . . . and wondered.

Chapter 20

SHE'D LOST EMMIE.

She'd lost Robert.

Well . . . to be perfectly accurate, and Adelaide Shaw—er, Swynton—was always accurate, she had sent him away from her side. But that was a mere technicality.

It was good she had brought Cheepers back with her through the tree. He was all she had left.

Evidently she had been right all those years when she'd believed herself utterly inept and unwise in matters of the heart. She was meant to be a spinster after all.

A spinster schoolteacher. Now more than ever she possessed unique qualifications to teach, especially history. Medieval English history. And, blast it all, teach she would.

She had cried enough.

Bolstering her resolve, Addie hurried down the stairs, wondering if Robert had already left for the livery. More than likely, since he was perfectly happy to rise with the dawn.

She shuddered. Mornings had never been her strongest suit.

He wasn't in the parlor, and so Addie broke her fast with a leftover biscuit from last night's supper and a cup of tea. Without wasting time, she donned her plainest straw hat, straightened her neat, navy skirt, and hooked up her black walking boots.

Addie Shaw—er, Addie Shaw Swynton—was on a mission.

She was going to get her job back.

Knowing she would need an ally, she met with Doc Horst, who grabbed his hat and coat and followed her to Pastor Wright's office for the planned meeting. When they arrived at the church, as Addie had expected, they found a healthy gathering of parents and business leaders. Even Mayor Noel was in attendance.

"What should we do?" asked Pastor Wright as Addie and Doc slipped inside the crowded room. "It's much too late in the summer. Most good candidates are contracted elsewhere." He waved three sheets of paper. "Those who have applied lack the credentials we want."

"Sure an' we hire the best o' the lot," said Sheila O'Shaughenessy. "My wee ones cannot walk that many miles to the other schools."

Murmurs flourished as people discussed the situation.

"But," interjected the mayor, "is it in the children's interest to hire an inexpert, unqualified teacher?"

Erma Martin, childless and long widowed, but always in the thick of things, sniffed loudly. "What could be worse than having had that irresponsible Addie Shaw teach them for years?"

Addie recognized the time to take action. "What did I do during those years to merit that accusation?"

Every head spun toward her. She heard gasps from every direction. Then murmuring resumed.

" . . . hussy . . ."

"Brazen!"

"Brave."

" . . . courageous."

So she had supporters in the group. That knowledge gave

Addie the impetus she needed. "I had an . . . accident one day as I taught my students a history lesson. As a result, I was unavoidably detained out of town and could not even send a message. I assure you I did everything I could to return."

Whispers again swarmed the room.

"Accident?" a woman in plum serge questioned.

"Amnesia, perhaps?" volunteered a gentleman in gray.

"Hah!" scoffed Erma. "Mark my words, a man's involved. . . ."

Addie squared her shoulders. "You're right to a certain extent, Mrs. Martin. I did marry while I was away, but that had nothing to do with my leaving. And it certainly has no bearing on my ability to teach. Which is why we are all here, right? September is just around the corner, and you've stripped me of my position. Who will teach the children?"

Sheila O'Shaughenessy wended her way between various clusters of whisperers to reach Addie's side. The two women embraced warmly. "Faith, an' 'tis glad I am to see you, Addie Shaw. Maeve and Sean refused to listen when I said ye'd not be back."

"I *am* back, and ready to resume my duties."

Erma and a handful of the men frowned ominously. Before any spoke, Addie continued, "Doc Horst offered an excellent suggestion, which I would like you to consider. Allow me to return on a trial basis. You can assign someone—anyone—to check on me regularly. If you observe any sign of trouble, I'll step down. Just don't make the children suffer because something unexpected once happened to me."

Her offer caught everyone off guard. Addie saw it in the surprised expressions all around her. Then the mayor cocked his snowy head. "You'd be willing to work under those circumstances?"

Squaring her shoulders, she met his gaze. "To teach again, I'll work under whatever restrictions you choose."

At Addie's left, Doc harrumphed loudly. "What happened to Mrs. Swynton—that's Addie's married name, you know—is a private matter. No one's business but hers. Now, what happens at the school is everyone's business. And we won't find a finer teacher than her. You know how much she loves the children, and many of you have benefited from her efforts in my surgery. How you could accuse her of negligence is beyond me."

Crossing his arms over his broad chest, he glared at the crowd.

Mayor Noel leaned toward Pastor Wright. Both whispered briefly, then nodded. "I was never in favor of hiring any of these last-minute candidates, Miss Shaw—er, Mrs. Wynton is it?"

Addie gulped at the knot that rose in her throat every time she thought of her ruined marriage. "Mrs. Robert Swynton."

The mayor nodded. "Thank you for the correction. I believe Mrs. Swynton's offer is by far our best option. It will allow school to start on time, and with an experienced teacher—"

"But you can't forget she left that crazy, fire-lovin' sister of hers all alone to burn up that building!" cried Erma. "What if she has another 'accident' while teaching the children?"

Silence descended on the group. Addie saw her hopes fade, until Sheila nudged her right side and Doc her left. Mentally scrambling for an argument, she said, "That's why I offered to have someone keep an eye on things at the school. Anytime—*all* the time. You can't choose a teacher believing he or she will never have an accident. That is not a practical, sensible way to act."

The mayor glanced at Pastor Wright, who looked to Doc. All three nodded as one. "Addie Shaw Swynton will return to her post when school starts in a week's time," Mayor Noel declared in a voice that allowed no further discussion. The matter, as far as he and everyone in an official capacity was concerned, had just been declared closed.

Addie breathed a prayer of thanksgiving. All had not been lost.

* * *

In the days that followed, Addie worked ceaselessly to prepare for the start of the school year. All those things she would normally have done during the summer months she was forced to do in a very brief week. Having regained her job, however, and with it something to think about besides her tragedies, she dug in with relish and accomplished everything, much to her surprise.

Only the nights were bad. Robert didn't return to her home; evidently he had taken her at her word when she'd asked him to leave her side until invited.

As she lay in bed in the dark, the tears returned, bathing her face in misery. To her great shame, grief over her sister's passing didn't spawn her tears, but rather it was longing for her husband, his touch, his kisses, that tore her apart.

"Oh, Robert . . ." she sobbed.

The loneliness she had once been resigned to suddenly became unbearable. She missed arguing with him, missed seeing him—even at a distance. She especially missed his voice, his laughter, his overbearing need to protect everyone from every last thing.

She missed Robert.

With every fiber of her being.

Inexplicably.

She hadn't forgotten his refusal to listen to her. He hadn't believed her. And so she had failed Emmie.

Robert had married her, but only to save her from a superstitious group who had wanted her burned at the stake as a witch. Her, of all people.

On her part, she had given her heart for the first and, more than likely, only time in her life. A woman couldn't love like this more than once. This much emotion, so deep and visceral, could only happen once. It demanded every drop of feeling in her, leaving her void when it came to an end.

Even knowing she shouldn't love him, she did. Richly and passionately, as she had never thought she would love. But he thought her a liar, a traitor.

And Emmie had died.

Now loneliness filled Addie's nights, nightmares her sleep, establishing a pattern that continued even after school began. Although glad to be working again, Addie quickly became exhausted. Teaching children was taxing work. Especially for a woman whose broken heart made sleep a thing of the past. Especially when that woman's students wanted to reenact the Battle of Bosworth one more time.

"No, no, Liam," she said when he again begged her to let them become knights of the realm. Everything in her recoiled from the thought of reliving the moment that had launched her misadventure through time. "We already did Bosworth and should study another battle, one far more interesting than that. Waterloo! We can do Napoleon, right?"

A classroom full of little heads shook somberly from side to side.

"Bosworth, Mrs. Swynton," said Carl Fieldhouse. "We want to do Bosworth again. We never got to kill Richard Plantagenet because of your accident."

Trust Carl to aim straight at her heart. "How about the Spanish Armada?" she offered, desperate to avoid her memories—at least during the day, since they so persistently haunted her nights.

Carl's dark eyes bore into hers. "We want to do Bosworth."

The child's doggedness brought to mind someone she would much rather not remember right then. "Tell me, Carl, do you have English ancestors?"

"Mama says we came from Yorkshire, ma'am. The Fieldhouse name's common there."

Addie gasped and blushed. Could this scamp be distantly related to a stubborn knight of the realm? "Oh, dear! I merely meant to make a joke, but it's apparently on me."

"What do you mean?" asked the boy, curiosity in his dark eyes.

She shook her head. "Lesson time, Carl. Let's think about a new battle. History has seen many important contests.

Why, any number of major ones were fought during our very own Revolutionary War. How about the Battle of Saratoga?"

Carl crossed his arms over his chest and shook his head. "Bosworth, Mrs. Swynton."

Addie sighed in surrender. "Bosworth it shall be. But," she added, shaking a finger, "you must listen to the me much more closely this time. You cannot smack anyone you want while you're being knights. You mustn't smack anyone at all. You're to duel with the 'swords' as the troops would have done, and only engage members of the opposite force. They were deciding political differences, and that's what you must learn."

Carl grinned and shrugged. "We'll listen if it means we get to play knights."

Once again, the boy's innocent words speared straight to Addie's heart, reminding her of yet another tense moment between her and Robert. Clearly knighthood meant much to her husband, and by accusing him of playing at it, she had deeply wounded him.

As he had wounded her by questioning her integrity, accusing her of witchcraft, of lying to him.

Struggling against tears, she forced a smile onto her lips and continued teaching for the day. But by the time she returned home after hours, she felt drained, too exhausted even for food. She closed the front door behind her and hurried up the stairs, unwilling to catch sight of the settee where Robert had slept for a couple of nights.

Certain she would finally sleep as a result of her bone-deep fatigue, Addie doffed her school clothes and collapsed onto the bed in chemise and drawers. Sleep, however, proved elusive.

When she returned to school the next day, Addie was forced to face myriad painful memories. Beginning with yet another lesson on the Battle of Bosworth. Knighthood and fealty. Richard Plantagenet and Henry Tudor. All while her mind replayed a collage of images she would never forget.

Images of a country manor in medieval Yorkshire, England. Images of its devastatingly attractive lord.

Her husband.

Addie's very own knight.

"*Ja, ja,* Robert," Hans said with a smile. "Go. You no take time off since you start working *mit mir.* Weather is no *sehr gut* today, people no travel much. Horses fed and watered. Everything is *gut.* You go."

Armed with determination, Robert set off for the western outskirts of York, his destination only too familiar. He had decided to find the oak and return home. There was no reason to remain here.

He could not forgive Addie, and she hated him.

Although he enjoyed working with Hans, it didn't make up for all he had lost, all he hoped to recover once he found that damnable oak.

When Robert approached the red-brick school, he found the children and their teacher filing out the door. He drew back on Midnight's reins, unwilling to let Addie see him.

He thirstily drank in the sight of her.

Why was he cursed to love her and resent her at the same time? Why could he not have come to love an easier woman, a more convenient, medieval one? Why had Addie crashed into his life, only to turn it out of kilter?

He watched her walk toward the woods, her slender figure moving gracefully. The gentle sway of her hips caught his gaze and reminded him of moments he ought to forget. As did the mass of hair piled atop her head, crowning her sweet, oval face in shiny, brown glory. That hair, silky and smooth to the touch, filled a lover's hands as gold did a miser's. Robert's fingers itched to tear out the pins that held it in place.

But he could not. She had sent him away—wisely, at that.

As the dull ache in his heart again threatened to become acute, he saw Addie distribute stripped branches to her students. More bewildering yet, she gave out pieces of what looked like parchment, then helped the children don them.

Nudging Midnight forward, Robert caught bits and pieces of her conversation. He heard her say, "Richard Plantagenet was king . . . Henry Tudor wanted the throne . . . they fought at Redmoor near Market Bosworth . . . August 22. . . ."

He groaned. Did she make a regular habit of this? Worse, would she then go find that blasted oak and return to Swynton? If so, he intended to go with her, even if they argued all the way through four hundred years' time. 'Twas best not to let her out of his sight.

To prevent her leaving without him, of course, not because he craved the very sight of her. Even though he did.

As Robert urged Midnight closer still, Addie divided the children into two separate groups, obviously Yorkists and Lancastrians. Then she gave the order to engage.

The children squealed with glee and brandished their branches enthusiastically. For a moment Robert wondered if Addie had truly read all those books in her home, as it seemed none of the youngsters knew for which side they should fight. But slowly, guided by his determined lady wife, the factions became more distinct, and the Lancastrian side began to exert dominance over the Yorkists.

As he watched the crude reenactment of the decisive battle in the Wars of the Roses, snippets of material he had read in Addie's parlor returned to Robert's memory. Addie's voice wove in and out, her many warnings while at Swynton figuring prominently in his mind.

"Richard will die, and Henry will take the throne," she had said, and four hundred years later Robert learned she had been right.

"You will die for the sake of your foolish pride . . . your presence on that field will not change the outcome . . . you'll merely die too soon." As he watched the mock battle, the fighting stripped of all nuances of duty, honor, or pride, Robert realized Addie would more than likely have been right about that as well.

"What good would dying on that field have done?" she

had demanded, and as he watched a diminutive Henry Tudor repel an equally small Richard Plantagenet, Robert was forced to agree with his wife. His death would have done no appreciable good, not to Richard, to England, to him or to her—as she had said.

By coming forward through time, he had been granted a reprieve, he had been given a new beginning, a second chance at life. Now he had to decide how to live it.

He knew how he wanted to spend that new lifetime, and with whom, but he was not certain 'twould be possible at all.

Harsh words lay between them.

As did the death of a girl.

Addie smiled at the improved effort of her students. Had they tried this diligently to follow the history books the first time around, she would never have sat beneath that blasted oak. She would have been spared the heartache that now followed her more assiduously than her shadow.

"Good, good!" she exclaimed, dragging her thoughts away from forbidden territory. "Now, Yorkists, you and I know you are brave and stalwart knights of the realm, but you're about to be defeated. Remember the lesson. . . ."

A blur of movement down the road a ways caught her attention, and she let her words die off. Silhouetted against the gray-clouded sky, Robert and Midnight rode toward town. Addie drew a harsh breath, wondering if he had seen her, if he had witnessed her reenactment of that accursed battle.

She stared hungrily at his back, feeling her heartache more acutely than she had for days. It came at her with the force of a destrier, the sharpness of a lance. It left her gasping, not knowing how she would live with such pain. Tears filled her eyes at the futility of loving the man who had caused her sister's death as surely as if he had run her through with his own sword.

All around her the sounds of her students tore at her, reminding her she could not give in to her pain. She could not break down and mourn her one lost chance at happiness. She had to go on, despite the need to wrap her arms around herself and cry out her grief yet one more time.

The day fit her misery well with its overcast sky and the scent of incoming rain heavy in the air. Behind her, the children continued to clash, their imaginary strife a reflection of the turmoil between her and Robert.

The rumble of thunder sounded near, and Addie cast a glance at the horizon. Sure enough, a slash of orange lightning ripped down the darkening slate expanse to the west, followed by another thunderclap.

"Come along, boys and girls," she called, relieved to put an end to the exquisitely painful exercise in remembrance. "The weather is turning nasty, and we can no longer stay outside. It's time to return to the classroom."

"Oh, no, not yet!"

"Please, Mrs. Swynton, just a little longer."

"We haven't kilt all them Yorkists yet."

"It's not even raining."

The chorus of childish complaints matched the woebegone faces before her. Torn between allowing them their fun a bit longer and the need for caution in the path of a storm, Addie wavered.

Carl, unanimously elected to portray Henry Tudor, marched up to her and announced, "I have yet to kill Richard. Then we can go inside." The dark eyes turned beseeching when she didn't reply. "Please, Mrs. Swynton."

With another glance toward the menacing swirl of storm clouds, calculating the distance and speed of the storm, Addie relented. "Five more minutes. Then we must run for cover."

"Yay!"

"Whoopee!"

"Let's go!"

The battle resumed, Lancastrian troops intent on their mission. Watching the pleasure the children garnered from the event, Addie thanked God for the opportunity to teach again. She had come so close to losing even this, all because Robert had kept her from her search.

Another roll of thunder brought her thoughts back to the matter at hand. "Did you hear that? The storm is coming. We must leave now."

More grumbling ensued, but the two factions made their way to the school building—albeit reluctantly. Addie sighed in relief. She hated refusing the children the opportunity to continue the reenactment until its logical end, but their safety came first.

Especially since a most disapproving Erma Martin had been appointed to monitor her.

The thought of the unpleasant woman spurred her to gather up the laggards, Carl being the last one. "Hurry, boys. Those clouds mean business, bad business, at that. We don't want to get caught out here by the lightning. We're right at the edge of the woods."

Carl glared. "You said we would finish the battle this time, that nothing was going to stop us."

"I can't control a storm and I won't let you get hurt."

"But you said we could—"

"When I made that promise, I did not know it would storm today. The woods are dangerous right now, so I cannot let you stay. We will battle another time, on a better day, when the weather is nice and clear."

"But—"

"You heard me, Carl. We will come back once the danger is past. Go to the school now."

As the boy opened his mouth again, lightning slashed jaggedly across the sky, much closer than the last bolt had done. "See?" Addie asked, nudging him along, her skin prickling with gooseflesh from the energy in the air. "That was too close. Run. Run fast. Not another word."

Carl dragged his feet, cradling his branch and caressing his paper armor. Disappointment showed on his every feature, and Addie wished she hadn't had to stop his play. In a gentler tone, she said, "We'll come back. I promise. As soon as I'm sure you'll be safe."

Instead of propelling him forward, her words seemed to bog his feet down even more. Then, to her horror, he turned and ran deeper into the woods. She followed. "Carl Fieldhouse, you come back here right this minute! I said we had to go back to the school—"

Another bolt of fire speared down the sky directly overhead, cutting Addie's words off in her throat. Everything then moved at an infernally slow pace—the fire that sparked in the branches of a tree just feet away from Carl, the breeze that had earlier picked up, the beat of Addie's heart.

Everything but Carl's headlong flight into danger.

The cracking of wood resounded through the forest, kicking Addie into action. She flung herself at the boy, hugged him tight to her breast, and rolled with him over the leaf-littered ground.

With a sickening roar, the hit tree split in two and hurtled earthward, one half landing where Carl had stood only a second before. As the trunk struck the ground, Addie noticed a distinctive marking near its base.

"Dear God!" she cried. "The oak . . ."

The oak.

The only one that mattered.

In a blinding moment of understanding, Addie realized she had saved Carl's life by moving him from the path of the tree that had so radically changed hers.

Just as Robert had more than likely saved hers.

The boy had stubbornly refused to listen to reason, placing himself in the path of danger. His insistence on continued play would have done no good, as not only would the game have ended, but his life would have as well. Addie hadn't insisted he return to the school from the arrogant stance of an adult, a teacher, or from willfulness. She'd sincerely had his well-being at heart.

As Robert had had hers when he had forbidden her to return to the woods while the Morland threat remained. They had indeed tried to kill her any number of times. He had only thought of her well-being, her safety. And if she had wandered heedlessly into a Morland trap, as she could very easily have, she would have done Emmie no good.

She would have died before returning to York.

She owed her husband an apology.

But she had to get a disobedient scamp back to school first. "Young man, your father and I are going to have a very serious discussion right after school today."

A pair of scared brown eyes met hers. Carl nodded.

"Come along now. There's a bit of history I must correct."

Personal history.

Hers and that of her very own knight.

Chapter 21

ADDIE SHAW SWYNTON was about to meddle with history one more time. But this time, it was unwritten history. And she was going to change it before it came to pass.

Exhilarated from thwarting death yet again and bolstered by renewed hope, Addie sailed through the encounter with Carl's father. After the adults decided the young man needed a few pointed lessons in obedience, she left the teaching of those in the elder Fieldhouse's capable hands.

In her typical, direct fashion, she marched out of the attractive Fieldhouse stone residence and headed due east toward Sweitzer's Livery. Toward her future.

Toward Robert.

When she arrived at the gaping doorway, she faced her fears head-on. A matched pair of bays hitched to a fancy rig high-stepped through the opening, directly in her path.

She remembered Robert's words. *"Addie, love, you must get beyond your fear of horses. What happened to your parents was unfortunate, but 'twas an accident and only that."* With those words firmly in mind, she had mounted Midnight the day they first arrived in York—1885 York, of course—when everyone in town threatened Robert. She'd had to prove they had nothing to fear.

Later that night, she had gone outside and fetched hay for Midnight. Approaching the beast with caution, she had spread the feed beneath his mammoth mouth. The stallion had turned toward her, and Addie's heart had stopped, certain he would tear a vital piece out of her. Instead, gentle as a kitten, the horse had nuzzled her neck, his muzzle velvety, his breath warm and moist.

"Midnight will not hurt you . . . he's gentle, if courageous and strong . . ."

That night she had learned Robert was right about the massive warhorse she had so feared. Today she'd learned Robert had only tried to keep her from harm's way—as he had said. It hadn't been overblown pride or arrogance that led him to act as he had, and she owed him an apology.

As the reddish-brown horses went past her, Addie smiled, appreciating their strength. Accidents could happen. At any time and to anyone. Just like the one that had killed her parents. It was foolish to hold fear in her heart and a grudge against all members of the equine race—even if she continued to nurture a healthy respect for the beasts.

Entering the noisy livery, Addie looked for the ebullient Mr. Sweitzer. She didn't see him but heard his voice coming from her right. With an eye to avoiding the noxious brown pile in the center of the courtyard, she approached the stalls.

"Mr. Sweitzer!" she called.

"Ich kommen, ich kommen!"

The jowl-cheeked stable owner bustled out, pulling up short when he spotted Addie. "Fräulein Shaw! I'm surprised. Has Helmut misbehaven?"

"Oh, no," Addie hastened to say. "I've come to find . . . my husband."

"You no Fräulein no more? Who you marry?"

Addie smiled, swallowing her sudden nervousness. "Your new helper, Robert Swynton."

Hans's blue eyes narrowed. "You throw him out. He lives in *mein* stable."

She blushed. "We . . . had words. I've come to try to mend things."

A glowing grin carved a merry trough across his round face. *"Gut, gut. Es ist sehr gut!"*

With a nod and a brief smile, she peered all around and into the stalls. "I agree, but . . . where is he?"

Looking crestfallen, Hans shook his head. "Don't know. He left this *Morgen, und* he has not returned. Ve haf big storm, too, *nein?"*

"Oh, dear. Do you suppose something might have happened during the storm?" Addie asked, suddenly scared she might be too late.

Hans frowned deeper. "Don't know. He no take time off since he start work for me, but today he did. He no come back."

"Did he say where he was going?"

"*Nein.* But he took big horse."

Dread filled Addie's middle. "Did he say he was coming back?"

Hans Sweitzer's eyes widened. "He no say, I no ask. He *gut* worker, *sehr gut. Und* Midnight, fine horse. *Mein* Philomena need big horse to make big, strong babies. Robert must *kommen* back."

Addie managed a weak smile. How ironic to find herself in the same straits as Hans Sweitzer's mare!

Had Robert left for good? If so, where had he gone?

He'd been determined to find the oak. Had he done so before the storm destroyed the tree? Had he traveled back to 1485? To Swynton?

When she could no longer repeat the trip.

Misery again filled Addie's heart. "How early did he leave?"

Mr. Sweitzer shrugged. "Don't know. Not too early."

Maybe . . .

"Did he take all his belongings with him?"

Another shrug. "You want look in room?"

Nodding, Addie followed the stable owner to a plain door at the rear of his establishment. Behind it she found a spartan cubicle, its only furnishings a rope bed with a striped-tickinged mattress and a straight-backed chair. Then she spotted the armor, piled in a corner, all the dirt now removed.

He hadn't left for good! Surely not. Not without his much-loved armor.

Although . . . if he had gone to the oak, he would have known he would soon be in Swynton again, where Mortimer would gladly shower him with more helmets, breastplates, and gauntlets than any dozen men could want. And Robert had been incensed by the damage his metal shell had sustained during the trip through time. Perhaps he had simply left it, not wishing to inflict further harm to the precious stuff.

The sight of the helmet, its visor no longer dented, made Addie catch her breath. She'd never again think of anything but Robert Swynton at the sight of knightly gear, even if in pictorial form.

Tears again stung her lids, and before she made a spectacle of herself in front of Mr. Sweitzer, she turned. "I must go home," she choked out. "My bird needs to be fed. If—er, *when*—when Robert returns, please tell him I came to see him."

"Ja, ja," answered Mr. Sweitzer, sounding relieved. He patted her arm. "You no fight *mit* him again, *nein*?"

Addie gave a tight shake of her head. "I have no interest in fighting. I never did. I only want to . . . talk to him again."

"*Gut, sehr gut.* I tell him when I see him next."

Nodding, Addie rushed from the stable, blinded by the tears that refused to stay away. Despite the pile of armor in the corner, she was certain he was gone.

She'd come to see the error of her ways just a bit too late.

Robert was a man on a mission. He could do no less.

As he'd watched Addie teach her scoundrels in the woods that day, he'd come to accept a few important truths. Yes, Addie had tricked him, but he now accepted she'd only done so in order to accomplish what to her was a greater good.

She'd felt compelled to save his life, by whatever means it took.

Neither pride, duty, loyalty, nor any other lofty ideal had entered into her consideration. Her need to cherish and save lives had overridden all else. His safety had meant everything to her.

When viewed thusly, it could only mean one thing, one very important, magnificent thing.

His wife loved him.

Just as he loved her.

Addie had never meant for him to betray anyone. She had known his sense of responsibility quite well from the start. She had willingly risked losing his respect, the love she didn't know she inspired, to save his life. He had meant more to her than her own happiness.

She'd done naught that needed forgiving; he was the one in need.

There was only one thing to do. But to do it, he would have to set aside longtime family hatreds, political squabbles, loyalties, pride, and duty to king. He would have to put his wife's happiness before all else and ride into enemy territory.

With Addie's sweet face in mind, Robert rode Midnight toward Lancaster.

Every clop of the horse's hooves turned his stomach. Still and always a loyal Yorkist, Robert's distaste and mistrust of anyone and everything relating to Lancaster simmered inside him, urging him to ride the other way.

But he would not. He would do this for Addie.

He would overcome ingrained loyalties for the woman he loved. The woman who was busily working herself to a frenzy.

He doubted his wife had slept in weeks. Even from a distance, he'd noticed how pale she looked. He'd never forget her misery that night she'd cast him from her side. Addie was the sort who would grieve long and hard, and if his suspicion—his deep hope—was correct, the breach between them had only added to her anguish.

If matters worked out the way he believed they would, her grieving would soon come to an end.

As he entered the town of Lancaster, he placed a hand on his dagger's hilt. True, he would do just about anything for his lady wife, but he was no fool. He trusted no one from Henry Tudor's side.

He asked for directions and in a short while approached Herbert White's smithy.

"Howdy!" called the lanky fellow leaning against the stable's rough right wall. "How c'n I help you?"

"I've come for Herbert White. Is he available?"

The man pushed away and approached Midnight. "Hell of a horse you got there. Care to sell?"

"Not at all. About Herbert White . . .?"

"Father's with the new farrier. Go on to the rear. He won't mind. I'll take care of your horse."

Robert narrowed his gaze, deepened his voice. "Only while I speak with your father. Midnight is *not* for sale."

All ease left the young man. "I understand. I'll just water him and give him a forkful of hay."

Robert nodded and strode to the forge. The heat of the furnace slapped him when he was still ten feet away. He heard the crackling of the flames, smelled the smoke, felt the blow of the hammer on metal with each clang. As he came closer, the hammering stopped.

He picked up his pace and reached the darkened entrance. 'Twas then he saw her, alone in the cavernous room, working the bellows and chuckling at the leaping flames. Robert smiled, joy dawning in him.

There was no denying the resemblance. Aye, Emmie Shaw was much smaller and slighter of build than her older sister, and blond where Addie was not, but they shared the same stubborn chin, the same shape of eye, the same oval face.

"Emmie!" he called over the roaring fire, unable to restrain himself as sudden impatience filled him.

The girl glanced away from the flames she'd been fanning. "Yes?"

"You are Emmie Shaw, right?"

"Of course!" Emmie's eyes, a darker gray than Addie's silver, displayed the same curling lashes. "Who are you?"

He chuckled. "It might be difficult to believe, but I'm Robert Swynton, your brother-by-marriage."

Suspicion flared in her eyes. "Addie's gone. Everyone says she abandoned me." Pain broke her voice.

"Not at all," Robert countered, determined to right these wrongs. "She had . . . an accident, and was unable to return for a while. A long while. But she is back and has been told you died in a blaze. She'll be most happy to see you again."

Setting down the bellows, the dainty young woman approached. 'Twas no wonder Addie worried about Emmie. His sister-by-marriage reminded him of a flower, delicate, fragile, exquisite.

She'd squared her chin, however, in a familiar, obstinate line. "How can I know you're telling the truth? That you're not here to accuse me of setting that fire?"

Robert arched a brow. "Did you set the fire?"

Golden curls shook wildly from side to side. "I wasn't there. I'd stayed after the others left to make sure everything was ready for the display. Mr. Palotti had said he would teach me to set off the fireworks . . ."

As her voice trailed off, her expression grew dreamy, as if she saw in her head the bursts of fire she so loved.

Then she seemed to gather her thoughts. "But I left. Besides, I wouldn't have burned the building down. I'd never do anything of that sort—at least not purposely, and not then. I wanted to help set off the display. I don't know what happened. Everyone thinks I lit the fire. But I didn't. Honest!"

In Emmie's sincerity Robert found yet another similarity between the sisters. "You must come back and tell your tale. You can no longer hide. Your sister cries endlessly, thinking you dead. She'll want you home."

That stubborn Shaw chin tipped skyward, and those slate-colored eyes raked him in a pointed scrutiny. Well acquainted with the gesture, Robert nearly laughed. Nearly.

Emmie crossed her arms over her chest. "You say Addie married you? When? She never had a suitor before, yet you expect me to believe you just up and wed her?"

The Shaw sisters also shared a contrary nature. " 'Tis a fair assessment of the situation, that. But I can only say I'm relieved she did not accept anyone else's suit. It allowed me to win the prize."

Emmie gave him a crooked grin. "You can't be too dense if you noticed Addie's a prize."

He flushed. "I'll admit it took a while, but I know it now. And I'd like to be on our way back to York. Will you trust me?"

Again that piercing stare scoured him.

Then Emmie shrugged. "I'll trust you to get me home. But first I'll have to tell Mr. White I'm leaving. He's only just hired a new smith, and they're somewhere out back talking. I'll only be a minute."

As the girl went in search of her employer, Robert headed back to Midnight. He had not liked the covetous gleam on young Mr. White's face. He would wait for Emmie on his horse.

Then Robert wondered if she shared her sister's fears. For his sake, he fervently hoped not.

He found Midnight in a clean stall, with no sign of the stable owner's son. He led the horse toward the gate and mounted to wait for Emmie. Minutes later, she came forward, a small wooden box in her arms.

"I'm ready to leave for good," she said, giving Midnight an appreciative look. "Nice horse."

Robert acknowledged her compliment with a nod. "All your belongings fit there?"

"All I need," she answered, smiling and patting the box.

The smile set off warnings in Robert's head. "What have you there?"

Her eyes took on the sparkle of flames. "My pyrotechnics. I've been making fireworks in my free time. Mr. Palotti taught me a few things before the fire. I mean to start my own business very soon."

Robert groaned inwardly. He should have known. Emmie was Addie's sister after all. Nothing about those two could ever be simple or normal.

'Twas his turn to peruse with care. "You'll set no fires while you're near Midnight. I'll not be crossed on this."

"I wouldn't hurt your horse," she answered, the squaring of her shoulders most Addie-like. "Ever. I've never hurt anyone before, and I never will."

Remembering a tale of singed chickens, he answered, "We shall see." He held out a hand, and, as Emmie mounted before him, he again noted how much smaller and daintier than Addie she was. Yet they were sisters, and he was about to reunite them.

He hoped that by doing so he could somehow scale the wall Addie had built between them when she'd blamed him for Emmie's death.

He wanted his wife.

A sparrow was a poor substitute for a husband, Addie thought, as Cheepers bobbed around his cage but basically ignored her. The silence of the small house seemed greater than ever, her loneliness deeper and more pronounced.

She had tried to keep from thinking about Robert's odd departure after coming home. She had made herself prepare a meal she hadn't wanted, then forced down a handful of bites.

Now the sun was setting, and she didn't want to face her bed. She would only find tears and painful thoughts there.

"I couldn't let him die, Cheepers," she said for the millionth time, "no matter what his father did before him. I needed him."

But she hadn't wound up with him.

A tear plopped on the tabletop.

She heard voices out front and wondered who had come at this hour. Most in town still regarded her with suspicion, if not outright disdain. They believed her guilty of neglect.

Emmie had died.

As sadness twisted in her heart, Addie heard running footsteps on the porch. As she headed toward the parlor, the front door flew open and hit the wall at its side.

"Addie!"

Her heart stopped. She froze. Surely heartbreak had caused her to finally lose her mind. She could have sworn it was Emmie calling her name.

"I'm home!" cried that dear, dead voice. "Where are you?"

Addie's heart began to beat again.

"Emmie . . .?" Unwilling to face the misery of learning she had merely imagined her sister's presence, Addie took halting steps forward.

A second later, a small, warm body hurtled into her arms, blond curls tickling her nose. "I missed you so much!" cried Emmie. "Where did you go? Why didn't you take me? Why were you gone so long? And where'd you find him?"

Tears flooded Addie's cheeks. She touched, patted, rubbed, caressed, anything to verify it was indeed her young sister in her arms. Miraculously, Emmie had come back from the dead. "You're not dead . . . I'm not mad . . . you're real . . ."

Emmie chuckled raggedly, her face awash in tears as well. "I'm real, you're not mad, I'm not dead, and I'm home. I'm so glad to see you, Addie. I missed you so much. Don't go away like that again."

"I missed you, too, and I didn't leave because I wanted to. Things . . . happened." At the memories, Addie hugged her sister tighter to her. "But I'll tell you about it later. Tell me, what happened to you?"

Emmie swiped her cheeks dry. "I don't know. The building just exploded. But I knew everyone would say I did it, so I . . . left. You'd gone. I had nothing to keep me here. I found a job, a real job." Pride firmed her spine; determination set her features. "And I mean to start a business. All my own."

Addie chuckled. "Daydreaming again, are you?"

"No, not this time," Emmie answered, the maturity in her voice stunning Addie. "This time I know what I'm doing."

"And that would be . . .?"

"Pyrotechnics."

At Addie's groan, Emmie held up a hand. "No, listen to me. I learned much from Mr. Palotti and I intend to learn more. It may take me years to learn all I need to know, but I make fireworks now. Small, uncomplicated ones. I will sell them so I won't be a burden anymore."

"You weren't a burden before—"

"Of course I was. You gave up your life to care for me. But I'm a grown woman now. I can help you with expenses and I can take care of myself. I learned this while you were gone. Besides, it's time for you to think about yourself." Emmie tipped her head toward the door. "And him."

Addie's gaze flew that way, hope mingling with fear. She found Robert just inside the doorway, arms crossed over his massive chest, a tender smile on his lips.

Her heartbeat turned to a heavy thud. Breathing grew difficult, her skin grew sensitive, remembering his touch. He looked so solid, so strong, so dear. Addie couldn't tear her gaze away from his face. It had been so long since she'd last seen him, really seen him up close. All her emotions surged to the surface—love, need, desire.

He approached, wearing that devastating smile of his. That smile that so rarely brightened his face, but that had stolen her heart in a distant time.

"You're . . . back . . ." she whispered, butterflies milling in her middle, anticipation more exhilarating than a hurtling trip through time.

"Aye. 'Tis good to see the two of you together," he said.

Behind Addie, Emmie cleared her throat. "I think I'll go upstairs awhile," she said, humor in her voice.

Addie didn't respond as Robert came closer still. "She's not dead, Addie," he said as he took her hand, "and neither am I."

She nodded, unable to utter a word. The warmth of his clasp worked its way up her arm and lodged somewhere very close to her heart. "Why are you here?"

"I could not stay away, not when I realized you'd done naught that needed forgiving."

"Oh, but I do need it," she said earnestly. "I accused you of causing Emmie's death. Even before seeing her, I came to realize how wrong I'd been."

He gave her a crooked half smile. "What could change your mind without evidence?"

Addie told him of Carl's escapade. "Lightning struck the oak."

"*The* oak?"

She nodded. "It split in two. Carl would have died if I hadn't rolled him out of the way. Just as you did me the day the stone fell off Swynton's roof." She took a deep breath. "I understood then that you'd insisted on keeping me from the woods for my safety, just as you'd said. You bore no blame in Emmie's death . . . and now, she's not dead at all."

Wonder made her smile. She met Robert's gaze and blushed. "Ah . . . I've been known to be somewhat . . . difficult to persuade."

He laughed.

She smacked his shoulder. "I see no humor in my apology. I'm admitting I was wrong to accuse you of arrogance and pride. I agree that you were merely carrying out your responsibilities as I was with the children this afternoon. That you put my safety before my wants, and I made it most difficult for you. Please have the decency to keep from laughing."

He nodded, a twinkle in his eye. "I hope you recall how right I was next time we disagree, Wife."

"Wife?" she asked, hope again sparking in her heart.

"We were married, you know, and I nearly let pride put asunder what God had joined." He grew serious, his fingers tightening around hers. "I watched your history lesson this morning."

She shook her head. "Not particularly realistic, were they?"

He cocked his head. "Enough for me to see my determination to join Richard in a new light. You were right, Addie.

Death would have been the likely outcome of my efforts. I would have gained naught by fighting."

"I really didn't want you to betray—"

"Anyone," he said before she finished. "I know that now. You but thought to save me from myself." He fell silent for a moment, then sought her gaze again. "Would you tell me why it mattered so much? To you?"

Addie glanced away as her cheeks heated again. "It always matters if I can save a life. All life is precious, and I vowed at my mother's deathbed to do all I could to save—"

"Addie . . ."

She looked up and abandoned all efforts to evade the truth. "I couldn't bear to lose you, not for a useless cause. I—I love you," she said in a whisper.

"Thank God!" Dropping her hand, he swept his arms around her, bringing her close to his very warm, very alive chest. Addie nestled close, savoring his scent of wind and man and horse. "I hoped 'twould be that, I prayed 'twould be. But I was not sure."

"Why?" she asked, an imp urging her on.

He moved back far enough to study her, then raised that dark, slashing brow. "Parrying?"

She shrugged and smiled through tears, waiting.

"I love you, Addie. I couldn't bear to watch your grief. I had to tear down the wall you'd built between us, but Emmie's death formed its mortar. When I heard of a fire-loving girl at White's Smithy in Lancaster, I knew what I had to do."

"*You* went to Lancaster?"

"'Twas the least I could do for you. Since you'd braved my anger to save me, surely I could face down ancient loyalties and bring your sister home."

Addie smiled smugly. "I did more."

"Addie . . ."

"Stop it! I despise that warning tone."

He chuckled.

"Besides, I did. I went right up to that behemoth of a horse of yours and fed it."

That caught him by surprise. "When?"

"While you slept that first night."

"I slept not a wink that night."

"Hah! You even snored."

With all his considerable dignity, Robert drew himself upright. "I, lady wife, do not snore."

She chuckled. "And how would you know that?"

"I—well, I just do. I wondered, but I never heard you walk past me that night."

She shrugged. "I saw how exhausted you were and I remembered the first time I went through the oak. I knew it would take time for you to recover, and I also knew you wouldn't want Midnight to go hungry. So . . . I went to Sweitzer's Livery for hay. I fed him."

"You surprise me, Wife."

"Why? Because you'd rather I be a coward?"

"No one would call you that. I thought your memories too powerful."

"I got on Midnight once."

"And fed him once. Why?"

She placed a hand on Robert's lean cheek. "For you. I dragged you away from all you knew—all, except that horse. I knew what it was like to find myself all alone, in just that situation."

He gave a deep sigh. "I love you."

"And I love you."

As he gazed into her eyes, he lowered his head. Addie caught her breath. Oh, glory! He was going to kiss her again.

But he paused. "Say you the oak is gone?"

The kiss would have to wait. "Split right in half."

"We cannot go back?"

"I don't see how."

"Well, then, there are a few matters we must attend to."

"And those would be?"

"Those pertaining to the Swynton legacy, of course."

"Oh, no! Please, I'd much rather not discuss old issues of family pride and political loyalties—"

"Children, Addie. I meant our children, the ones I would

never have had in 1485. I'd decided never to wed again and would have gone to my death without an heir. Now I hope to leave a legacy of life, of love."

If she hadn't already done so months ago, she would have fallen in love with him then. "Oh, Robert," she said through a mist of happy tears, "I'd like that. I'd like children very much."

He tipped up her chin, dried a tear with a thumb. "I love you, Addie Shaw, my lady . . . my love . . ."

As his lips covered hers, joy flooded her heart. She would never be lonely again, not now that she'd won this man's heart. He was more than she'd ever dreamed of, all she could ever want.

He was Addie's knight.

Turn the page for a preview of
Jill Marie Landis's latest novel,

Blue Moon

Coming in July from Jove Books

Prologue

SOUTHERN ILLINOIS LATE APRIL, 1819

She would be nineteen tomorrow. If she lived. In the center of a faint deer trail on a ribbon of dry land running through a dense swamp, a young woman crouched like a cornered animal. The weak, gray light from a dull, overcast sky barely penetrated the bald-cypress forest as she wrapped her arms around herself and shivered, trying to catch her breath. She wore nothing to protect her from the elements but a tattered rough, homespun dress and an ill-fitting pair of leather shoes that had worn blisters on her heels.

The primeval path was nearly obliterated by lichen and fern that grew over deep drifts of dried twigs and leaves. Here and there the ground was littered with the larger rotting fallen limbs of trees. The fecund scent of decay clung to the air, pressed down on her, stoked her fear, and gave it life.

Breathe. Breathe.

The young woman's breath came fast and hard. She squinted through her tangled black hair, shoved it back, her fingers streaked with mud. Her hands shook. Terror born of being lost was heightened by the knowledge that night was going to fall before she found her way out of the swamp.

Not only did the encroaching darkness frighten her, but so did the murky silent water along both sides of the trail. She realized she would soon be surrounded by both night and water. Behind her, from somewhere deep amid the cypress trees wrapped in rust colored bark, came the sound of a splash as some unseen creature dropped into the watery ooze.

She rose, spun around, and scanned the surface of the swamp. Frogs and fish, venomous copperheads and turtles, big as frying pans, thrived beneath the lacy emerald carpet of duckweed that floated upon the water. As she knelt there wondering whether she should continue on in the same direction or turn back, she watched a small knot of fur float toward her over the surface of the water.

A soaking wet muskrat lost its grace as soon as it made land and lumbered up the bank in her direction. Amused, yet wary, she scrambled back a few inches. The creature froze and stared with dark beady eyes before it turned tail, hit the water, and disappeared.

Getting to her feet, the girl kept her eyes trained on the narrow footpath, gingerly stepping through piles of damp, decayed leaves. Again she paused, lifted her head, listened for the sound of a human voice and the pounding footsteps which meant someone was in pursuit of her along the trail.

When all she heard was the distant knock of a woodpecker, she let out a sigh of relief. Determined to keep moving, she trudged on, ever vigilant, hoping that the edge of the swamp lay just ahead.

Suddenly, the sharp, shrill scream of a bobcat set her heart pounding. A strangled cry escaped from her lips. With a fist pressed against her mouth, she squeezed her eyes closed and froze, afraid to move, afraid to even breathe. The cat screamed again and the cry echoed across the haunting silence of the swamp until it seemed to stir the very air around her.

She glanced up at dishwater-gray patches of weak afternoon light nearly obliterated by the cypress trees that grew so close together in some places that not even a small child could pass between them. The thought that a wildcat might be looming somewhere above her in the tangled limbs, crouched and ready to pounce, sent her running down the narrow, winding trail.

She had not gone a hundred steps when the toe of her shoe caught beneath an exposed tree root. Thrown forward, she began to fall and cried out.

As the forest floor rushed up to meet her, she put out her hands to break the fall. A shock of pain shot through her wrist an instant before her head hit a log.

And then her world went black.

One

HERON POND, ILLINOIS

Noah LeCroix walked to the edge of the wide wooden porch surrounding the one-room cabin he had built high in the sheltering arms of an ancient bald cypress tree and looked out over the swamp. Twilight gathered, thickening the shadows that shrouded the trees. The moon had already risen, a bright silver crescent riding atop a faded blue sphere. He loved the magic of the night, loved watching the moon and stars appear in the sky almost as much as he loved the swamp. The wetlands pulsed with life all night long. The darkness coupled with the still, watery landscape settled a protective blanket of solitude around him. In the dense, liquid world beneath him and the forest around his home, all manner of life coexisted in a delicate balance. He likened the swamp's dance of life and death to the way good and evil existed together in the world of men beyond its boundaries.

This shadowy place was his universe, his sanctuary. He savored its peace, was used to it after having grown up in almost complete isolation with his mother, a reclusive Cherokee woman who had left her people behind when she chose to settle in far-off Kentucky with his father, a French Canadian fur trapper named Gerard LeCroix.

Living alone served Noah's purpose now more than ever. He had no desire to dwell among "civilized men," especially now that so many white settlers were moving in droves across the Ohio into the new state of Illinois.

Noah turned away from the smooth log railing that bordered the wide, covered porch cantilevered out over the swamp. He was about to step into the cabin where a single oil lamp cast its circle of light when he heard a bobcat scream. He would not have given the sound a second thought if not for the fact that a few seconds later the sound was followed by a high-pitched shriek, one that sounded human enough to stop him in his tracks. He paused on the threshold and listened intently. A chill ran down his spine.

It had been so long since he had heard the sound of another human voice that he could not really be certain, but he thought he had just heard a woman's cry.

Noah shook off the ridiculous, unsettling notion and walked into the cabin. The walls were covered with the tanned hides of mink, bobcat, otter, beaver, fox, white-tailed deer and bear. His few other possessions—a bone-handled hunting knife with a distinctive wolf's head carved on it, various traps, some odd pieces of clothing, a few pots and a skillet, four wooden trenchers and mugs, and a rifle—were all neatly stored inside. They were all he owned and needed in the world, save the dugout canoe secured outside near the base of the tree.

Sparse but comfortable, even the sight of the familiar surroundings could not help him shake the feeling that something unsettling was about to happen, that all was not right in his world.

Pulling a crock off a high shelf, Noah poured a splash of whiskey in a cup and drank it down, his concentration intent on the deepening gloaming and the sounds of the swamp. An unnatural stillness lingered in the air after the puzzling scream, almost as if, like him, the wild inhabitants of Heron Pond were collectively waiting for something to happen. Unable to deny his curiosity any longer, Noah sighed in resignation and walked back to the door.

He lingered there for a moment, staring out at the growing shadows. Something was wrong. *Someone* was out there. He reached for the primed and loaded Hawken rifle that stood just inside the door and stepped out into the gathering dusk.

He climbed down the crude ladder of wooden strips nailed to the trunk of one of the four prehistoric cypress that supported his home, stepped into the dugout *pirogue* tied to a cypress knee that poked out of the water. Noah paddled the shallow wooden craft toward a spot where the land met the deep dark water with its camouflage net of duckweed, a natural boundary all but invisible to anyone unfamiliar with the swamp.

He reached a rise of land which supported a trail, carefully stepped out of the *pirogue* and secured it to a low-hanging tree branch. Walking through thickening shadows, Noah breathed in his surroundings, aware of every subtle nuance of change, every depression on the path that might really be a footprint on the trail, every tree and stand of switchcane.

The sound he thought he'd heard had come from the southeast. Noah headed in that direction, head down, staring at the trail although it was almost too dark to pick up any sign. A few hundred yards from where he left the *pirogue,* he paused, raised his head, sniffed the air, and listened to the silence.

Instinctively, he swung his gaze in the direction of a thicket of slender cane stalks and found himself staring across ten yards of low undergrowth into the eyes of a female bobcat on the prowl. Slowly he raised his rifle to his shoulder and waited to see what the big cat would do. The animal stared back at him, its eyes intense in the gathering gloaming. Finally, she blinked and with muscles bunching beneath her fine, shiny coat, the cat turned and padded away.

Noah lowered the rifle and shook his head. He decided the sound he heard earlier must have been the bobcat's cry and nothing more. But just as he stepped back in the direction of the *pirogue,* he caught a glimpse of ivory on the trail ahead that stood out against the dark tableau. His leather moccasins did not make even a whisper of sound on the soft earth. He closed the distance and quickly realized what he was seeing was a body lying across the path.

His heart was pounding as hard as Chickasaw drums when he knelt beside the young woman stretched out upon the ground. Laying his rifle aside he stared at the unconscious female, then looked up and glanced around in every direction. The nearest white settlement was beyond the swamp to the northeast. There was no sign of a companion or fellow traveler nearby, something he found more than curious.

Noah took a deep breath, let go a ragged sigh and looked at the girl again. She lay on her side, as peacefully as if she were napping. She was so very still that the only evidence that she was alive was the slow, steady rise and fall of her breasts. Although there was no visible sign of injury, she lay on the forest floor with her head beside a fallen log. One of her arms was outstretched, the other tucked beneath her. What he could see of her face was filthy. So were her hands; they were beautifully shaped, her fingers long and tapered. Her dress, nothing but a rag with sleeves, was hiked up to her thighs. Her shapely legs showed stark ivory against the decayed leaves and brush beneath her.

He tentatively reached out to touch her, noticed his hand shook, and balled it into a fist. He clenched it tight, then opened his hand and gently touched the tangled, black hair that hid the side of her face. She did not stir when he moved the silken skein, nor when he brushed it back and looped it over her ear.

Her face was streaked with mud. Her lashes were long and dark, her full lips tinged pink. The sight of her beauty took his breath away. Noah leaned forward and gently reached beneath her. Rolling her onto her back, he straightened her arms and noted her injuries. Her wrist appeared to be swollen. She had an angry lump on her forehead near her hairline. She moaned as he lightly probed her injured wrist; he realized he was holding his breath. Noah expected her eyelids to flutter open, but they did not.

He scanned the forest once again. With night fast closing in, he saw no alternative except to take her home with him. If he was going to get her back to the tree-house before dark, he would have to hurry. He cradled her gently in his arms, reached for his rifle, and then straightened. Even then the girl did not awaken, although she did whimper and turn her face against his buckskin jacket, burrowing against him. It felt strange carrying a woman in his arms, but he had no time to dwell on that as he quickly carried her back to the *pirogue,* set her inside, and untied the craft. He climbed in behind her, holding her upright, then gently drew her back until she leaned against his chest.

As the paddle cut silently through the water black as pitch, he tried to concentrate on guiding the dugout canoe home, but was distracted by the way the girl felt pressed against him, the way she warmed him. As his body responded to a need he had long tried to deny, he felt ashamed at his lack of control. What kind of a man was he, to become aroused by a helpless, unconscious female?

Overhead, the sky was tinted deep violet, an early canvas for the night's first stars. During the last few yards of the journey, the swamp grew so dark that he had only the yellow glow of lamplight shining from his home high above the water to guide him.

Run. Keep running.

The dream was so real that Olivia Bond could feel the leaf-littered ground beneath her feet and the faded chill of winter that lingered on the damp April air. She suffered, haunted by memories of the past year, some still so vivid they turned her dreams into nightmares. Even now, as she lay tossing in her sleep, she could feel the faint sway of the flatboat as it moved down river long ago. In her sleep the fear welled up inside her.

Her dreaming mind began to taunt her with palpable memories of new sights and scents and dangers.

Run. Run. Run, Olivia. You're almost home.

Her legs thrashed, startling her awake. She sat straight up, felt a searing pain in her right wrist and a pounding in her head that forced her to quickly lie back down. She kept her eyes closed until the stars stopped dancing behind them, then she slowly opened them and looked around.

The red glow of embers burning in a fireplace illuminated the ceiling above her. She lay staring up at even log beams that ran across a wide planked ceiling, trying to ignore the pounding in her head, fighting to stay calm and let her memory come rushing back. Slowly she realized she was no longer lost on the forest trail. She had not become a bobcat's dinner, but was indoors, in a cabin, on a bed.

She spread her fingers and pressed her hands palms down against a rough, woven sheet drawn over her. The mattress was filled with something soft that gave off a tangy scent. A pillow cradled her head.

Slowly Olivia turned her aching head, afraid of who or what she might find beside her, but when she discovered she was in bed alone, she thanked God for small favors.

Refusing to panic, she thought back to her last lucid memory: a wildcat's scream. She recalled tearing through the cypress swamp, trying to make out the trail in the dim light before she tripped. She lifted her hand to her forehead and felt swelling. After testing it gingerly, she was thankful that she had not gashed her head open and bled to death.

She tried to lift her head again but intense pain forced her to lie still. Olivia closed her eyes and sighed. A moment later, an unsettling feeling came over her. She knew by the way her skin tingled, the way her nerve ends danced, that someone was nearby. Someone was watching her. An instinctive, intuitive sensation warned her that the *someone* was a man.

At first she peered through her lashes, but all she could make out was a tall, shadowy figure standing in the open doorway across the room. Her heart began to pound so hard she was certain the sound would give her consciousness away.

The man walked into the room and she bit her lips together to hold back a cry. She watched him move about purposefully. Instead of coming directly to the bed, he walked over to a small square table. She heard him strike a piece of flint, smelled lamp oil as it flared to life.

His back was to her as he stood at the table; Olivia opened her eyes wider and watched. He was tall, taller than most men, strongly built, dressed in buckskin pants topped by a buff shirt with billowing sleeves. Despite the coolness of the evening, he wore no coat, no jacket. Indian moccasins, not shoes, covered his feet. His hair was a deep black, cut straight and worn long enough to hang just over his collar. She watched his bronzed, well-tapered hands turn up the lamp wick and set the glass chimney in place.

Olivia sensed he was about to turn and look at her. She wanted to close her eyes and pretend to be unconscious, thinking that might be safer than letting him catch her staring at him, but as he slowly turned toward the bed, she knew she had to see him. She had to know what she was up against.

Her gaze swept his body, taking in his great height, the length of his arms, the width and breadth of his shoulders before she dared even look at his face.

When she did, she gasped.

Noah stood frozen beside the table, shame and anger welling up from deep inside. He was unable to move, unable to breathe as the telling sound of the girl's shock upon seeing his face died on the air. He watched her flinch and scoot back into the corner, press close to the wall. He knew her head pained her, but obviously not enough to keep her from showing her revulsion or from trying to scramble as far away as she could.

He had the urge to walk out, to turn around and leave. Instead, he stared back and let her look all she wanted. It had been three years since he had lost an eye to a flatboat accident on the Mississippi. Three years since another woman had laughed in his face. Three years since he moved to southern Illinois to put the past behind him.

When her breathing slowed and she calmed, he held his hands up to show her that they were empty, hoping to put her a little more at ease.

"I'm sorry," he said as gently as he could. "I don't mean you any harm."

She stared up at him as if she did not understand a blessed word.

Louder this time, he spoke slowly. "Do-you-speak-English?"

The girl clutched the sheet against the filthy bodice of her dress and nodded. She licked her lips, cleared her throat. Her mouth opened and closed like a fish out of water, but no sound came out.

"Yes," she finally croaked. "Yes, I do." And then, "Who are you?"

"My name is Noah. Noah LeCroix. This is my home. Who are you?"

The lamplight gilded her skin. She looked to be all eyes, soft green eyes, long black hair, and fear. She favored her injured wrist, held it cradled against her midriff. From the way she carefully moved her head, he knew she was fighting one hell of a headache, too.

Ignoring his question, she asked one of her own. "How did I get here?" Her tone was wary. Her gaze kept flitting over to the door and then back to him.

"I heard a scream. Went out and found you in the swamp. Brought you here—"

"The wildcat?"

"Wasn't very hungry." Noah tried to put her at ease, then he shrugged, stared down at his moccasins. Could she tell how nervous he was? Could she see his awkwardness, know how strange it was for him to be alone with a woman? He had no idea what to say or do. When he looked over at her again, she was staring at the ruined side of his face.

"How long have I been asleep?" Her voice was so low that he had to strain to hear her. She looked like she expected him to leap on her and attack her any moment, as if he might be coveting her scalp.

"Around two hours. You must have hit your head really hard."

She reached up, felt the bump on her head. "I guess I did."

He decided not to get any closer, not with her acting like she was going to jump out of her skin. He backed up, pulled a stool out from under the table, and sat down.

"You going to tell me your name?" he asked.

The girl hestitated, glanced toward the door, then looked back at him. "Where am I?"

"Heron Pond."

Her attention shifted to the door once again; recollection dawned. She whispered, "The swamp." Her eyes widened as if she expected a bobcat or a cottonmouth to come slithering in.

"You're fairly safe here. I built this cabin over the water."

"Fairly?" She looked as if she was going to try to stand up again. "Did you say—"

"Built on cypress trunks. About fifteen feet above the water."

"How do I get down?"

"There are wooden planks nailed to a trunk."

"Am I anywhere near Illinois?"

"You're in it."

She appeared a bit relieved. Obviously she wasn't going to tell him her name until she was good and ready, so he did not bother to ask again. Instead he tried, "Are you hungry? I figure anybody with as little meat on her bones as you ought to be hungry."

What happened next surprised the hell out of him. It was a little thing, one that another man might not have even noticed, but he had lived alone so long he was used to concentrating on the very smallest details: the way an iridescent dragonfly looked with its wings backlit by the sun, the sound of cypress needles whispering on the wind.

Someone else might have missed the smile that hovered at the corners of her lips when he had said she had little meat on her bones, but he did not. How could he, when that slight, almost-smile damn had him holding his breath?

"I got some jerked venison and some potatoes around here someplace." He started to smile back until he felt the pull of the scar at the left corner of his mouth and stopped. He stood up, turned his back on the girl, and headed for the long wide plank tacked to the far wall where he stored his larder.

He kept his back to her while he found what he was looking for, dug some strips of dried meat from a hide bag, unwrapped a checkered rag with four potatoes inside, and set one on the plank where he did all his stand-up work. Then he took a trencher and a wooden mug off a smaller shelf high on the wall, and turned it over to knock any unwanted creatures out. He was headed for the door, intent on filling the cook pot with water from a small barrel he kept out on the porch when the sound of her voice stopped him cold.

"Perhaps an eye patch," she whispered.

"What?"

"I'm sorry. I was thinking out loud."

She looked so terrified he wanted to put her at ease. "It's all right. What were you thinking?"

Instead of looking at him when she spoke, she looked down at her hands. "I was just thinking . . ."

Noah had to strain to hear her.

"With some kind of an eye patch, you wouldn't look half bad."

His feet rooted themselves to the threshold. He stared at her for a heartbeat before he closed his good eye and shook his head. He had no idea what in the hell he looked like anymore. He had had no reason to care.

He turned his back on her and stepped out onto the porch, welcoming the darkness.